CLEAN
KILL

ALSO BY JACK COUGHLIN

Shooter: The Autobiography of the Top-Ranked Marine Sniper
(with Capt. Casey Kuhlman and Donald A. Davis)

Kill Zone (with Donald A. Davis)

Dead Shot (with Donald A. Davis)

ALSO BY DONALD A. DAVIS

Lightning Strike
The Last Man on the Moon (with Gene Cernan)
Dark Waters (with Lee Vyborny)

CLEAN KILL

A SNIPER NOVEL

GUNNERY SGT. **JACK COUGHLIN**,
USMC (RET.)

WITH **DONALD A. DAVIS**

ST. MARTIN'S PRESS 🙢 NEW YORK

This is a work of fiction. All of the characters, organizations, and events portrayed in this novel are either products of the author's imagination or are used fictitiously.

CLEAN KILL. Copyright © 2010 by Jack Coughlin with Donald A. Davis. All rights reserved. Printed in the United States of America. For information, address St. Martin's Press, 175 Fifth Avenue, New York, N.Y. 10010.

www.stmartins.com

Library of Congress Cataloging-in-Publication Data

Coughlin, Jack, 1966–
    Clean kill / Gunnery Sgt. Jack Coughlin, USMC (Ret.), with Donald A. Davis.—1st ed.
      p. cm.
    ISBN 978-0-312-55102-5
    1. International relations—Fiction.   2. Undercover operations—Fiction.
    3. Terrorists—Fiction.   I. Davis, Don, 1939–   II. Title.
    PS3603.O878C57 2010
    813'.6—dc22

                                             2009039536

First Edition: March 2010

10 9 8 7 6 5 4 3 2 1

PAKISTAN

FOR ONLY A MOMENT, less time than needed to take a breath, Gunnery Sergeant Kyle Swanson lifted his eyes from the dark path uncoiling before him and looked above the surrounding snow-covered peaks. A crescent moon rode in the cold night sky, with a shadowed edge so clean that the Marine sniper could make out the pimpled edges of individual craters with his naked eye. An early astronaut once described the lunar emptiness as magnificent desolation, and Swanson thought the same description was a good fit for the sheer and ragged mountains of western Pakistan. Up, down, or sideways, no matter where you looked, there was nothing in these badlands but more nothing. His eyes went back to the narrow trail, and he used his left hand to brush the stone face of the mountain, feeling for outcroppings of rock or tufts of weeds that could provide handholds, while he kept his boots at least six inches from edge of the trace. Beyond that was only a sheer drop of perhaps a thousand feet into a black chasm.

"I vote that next time, we just dump a bunch of cruise missiles on this place," said Staff Sergeant Joe Tipp, who was climbing right behind him. "My legs are on fire. Cupla cruise missiles would have saved us from humping these damned mountains."

The six Marines from Task Force Trident had been on the move for three consecutive nights, following a surly Afghan guide along impossible trails, up into the high elevations where the air was thin, then down into boulder-studded valleys, then up again. Before the dawns, they would take hide spots, set a guard rotation, and fall asleep exhausted, with every muscle sore and their weapons at hand. The only way through the Spin Ghars was to put one boot in front of another.

"A cruise missile wouldn't deliver the proper message, Joe. We don't want to just whip their asses; they have to know they've been beaten. This has to be up close and personal," Swanson said over his shoulder as he forced his protesting legs to make one more step, then another. Two short grenade launchers rode atop his heavy pack, while an AK-47 assault rifle was hooked on the chest harness, and encased in a special bag over his shoulder was a Russian-made SV-98 sniper rifle. Balancing the seventy-pound load was as important as the footwork.

"You really get off on sending this kind of message, don't you?"

Swanson snorted. "Bet your ass. Now shut up and climb."

This was their fourth black raid on hidden training camps across the border in the past three months. The official version of the mission stated that it was just a snoop-and-poop job by scouts from the U.S. Marine Special Operations Command, MARSOC, and the men would stay clearly inside of Afghanistan and under no circumstances venture into Pakistan. American and other NATO troops made such sweeps every day, probing for the elusive Taliban and al Qaeda terrorists.

They had ridden out from a forward operating base in three closed Humvees, went through a couple of small villages of mud huts so they would be seen by curious eyes and reported up the terrorist grapevine as heading north. Once in the wilderness, darkness fell and things changed. The Humvees turned east at a dim intersection known as the Camel Crossroads and drove without lights for an hour over a rotten road, following deep ruts up the incline toward the mountain passes. They stopped. Eight Marines and the guide dismounted, and the vehicles returned to the crossroads and continued north to another forward operating base, again intentionally attracting the notice of enemy spies who concluded it was a routine resupply run, not worth worrying about.

By the end of the first night, the commandos were deep in the mountains, at an isolated and abandoned observation position that overlooked some of the most forbidding terrain on the planet. They rested all day, and things changed again that night. Two Marines were left behind to set up a communications station that would transmit periodic false mission reports back to headquarters. The rest stepped out, wearing old clothes purchased in Afghan bazaars, carrying a variety of weapons that were not made in America and without any identification. Then they fell off the map.

Soon, not even the radio team knew where they were. No colored pins on maps at any base showed their position or their target. No unmanned Predators circled overhead for surveillance, and if things went bad, no fighter-bombers would be zooming in for air support and there would be no rescue helicopter. There was absolutely no indication that any Americans were in the Paki backyard, which meant there could be no leaks to the various tribal warlords of questionable loyalties.

Kyle climbed on, in the company of fighting men that he knew and trusted, all of them fully aware that there would be no after action reports, no medals for bravery, no mentions in the media, no memoirs later in life when they were all grandfathers and retired. Whatever happened out here, stayed here.

The only unknown was the Afghan guide, who was only about as trustworthy as any of the locals. He had worked for the Agency for five years and was given a plastic-wrapped brick of $100 bills in payment to take them into the forbidden zone. He would not be a problem. Either he did as he was told or he would be killed and left in the mountains. Such was Kyle Swanson's unforgiving world.

Climbing the rugged terrain with him now were five experienced commandos, none below the rank of sergeant or with less than seven years in the Corps. Joe Tipp was right behind him, occasionally bitching about life in general. Next was Staff Sergeant Darren Rawls, a tall African-American who was a natural athlete and hardly felt the muscle pains shared by the others on the mountain. Captain Rick Newman was in the middle of the line, technically in command of the operation but with the primary task of doing officer stuff, like talking to other officers when required, so Swanson could do his job. The fifth was red-haired Staff Sergeant Travis Stone, a grinning little killer rat. Trailing and covering the rear was the wiry and always-silent Sergeant Eliot Brenner.

Just before the mission's fourth daybreak, as the serpentine trail descended toward a broad plateau, the guide suddenly stopped, then scurried back to Swanson. The patrol froze, instantly alert as the possibility of action replaced the drudge of climbing.

"What is it?" Kyle asked.

The Afghan pointed toward a long and rocky ridge and said in fractured English, "Al Qaeda, mister. Taliban. Just there."

Swanson shed his pack and crawled forward on elbows and knees to a cluster of big rocks that allowed him to peer downward without exposing his head on the horizon. At the foot of the steep mountainside was a valley floor about five miles distant, where a crude camp of tents and small structures had been built.

Captain Newman crawled up and flopped beside Kyle and scanned the valley with his binos. "Bingo. We're here."

"Yep," Swanson confirmed. "Let's get settled."

The Tridents spread out and found individual hides for the day, caught some sleep and spent their waking hours counting enemy noses and charting range cards to the various huts and landmarks. They did not speak, just watched the base camp in which the terrorists believed they were invulnerable. The six silent men were deep in the forbidding mountains, where their enemy had been protected by a truce between the local warlords and the Pakistani army, left alone for so long they felt free do as they wished.

In the late afternoon, three civilians were brought out from one of the huts, their hands tied and their eyes covered with black strips of cloth, stumbling as guards shoved them forward. A fighter who looked like a member of the training cadre called out to the terrorist trainees and pulled a knife from his belt. Obviously giving a demonstration, he crouched at the knees and thrust quickly forward and back with the blade to show what he wanted done. A dozen of his eager students formed a circle and one of the prisoners was pushed into the middle.

The instructor then shouted out the names of individuals, and the summoned trainee would step into the circle and repeat the lunge attack, but making sure to only slice lightly into the terrified prisoner. The man had to live long enough for everyone to get a turn. When the first trainee finished, then another name was called, then the next, and the crying prisoner's garments turned crimson with blood until he finally collapsed. After a final bit of instruction from the senior fighter, one of his younger acolytes bent down and cut the victim's throat.

Another circle was formed with other trainees, and the ones who had already finished the knife exercise became spectators, cheering and catcalling to the others while the second bound civilian was slashed. The exercise ended when the third prisoner had been slain. The instructor gathered his men for a verbal review of their work, then dismissed them. The three bodies were hauled away for burial.

Swanson swallowed his rage. Emotion could not be allowed to enter his thoughts and the slaughter of those three prisoners made him focus even more. Still, he waited, chewing nuts and dates and thinking until, finally, the sky darkened. Almost time.

The moon had reached the crescent shape three nights ago and now shone like a sign to mark the start of the ninth month of the Muslim lunar calendar, the holy month of Ramadan. Thirty days of fasting. In the valley, the forty terrorists and their half-dozen instructors settled down to break their daylong fast and enjoy the first food, water, and sweet chai they had been allowed to consume since before dawn. Their voices swam up the mountainside, the giddiness of a small celebration. Afterward, they would offer the last of the five daily prayers, the *Isha*.

Swanson drank some water, wiped his hands and passed the word to prepare to move out. He called for the guide and when he approached, Kyle kicked the man's legs from beneath him and dropped him to the ground. Joe Tipp was there to wrap duct tape around the ankles and put plastic flex ties on the wrists. Another strip of tape went over the mouth.

"You have done well so far to get us here, my friend, and we do this not to harm you but just to insure your silence," Kyle told the guide. "We cannot afford to trust you. Stay still and quiet and you will be fine. I promise that we will pick you up on our way out. Attempt to warn those bastards down there and you will wish you were dead long before you actually are."

The guide stared into the set of gray-green eyes and the cold face and nodded. He understood.

*   *   *

THE SIX TRIDENT MARINES picked their way downhill, carefully planting their boots to prevent stumbling or sliding on rocks. There was no hurry. It was dark and the terrorists in the camp were still milling around, finishing their food and drink.

This was exactly when Kyle had wanted to strike. He felt no alarm at all about violating any sacred religious rites, because the men in that camp were killers, through and through. This had nothing to do with religion, and everything to do with tactical advantage, for Swanson considered the fasting and prayer times of his enemy to present extraordinary opportunities, small openings during which their guard was down, their alertness dim, and their vulnerability extreme. He knew those terrorists would do the same to him if given the chance, and believed that it was savages just like them who had flown passenger jets filled with innocent Americans into the Twin Towers.

Beneath a broad thumb of boulders about five hundred meters from the camp, the Tridents stopped so Kyle and Captain Newman could study the area one last time. Things remained normal and security was loose.

"One close sentry straight ahead and another on that ridge about five hundred yards away," said Newman.

Swanson broke out his sniper rifle and peered through the PKS-07 seven-power scope to satisfy himself that the moon was providing enough light for him to see clearly. He whispered to Newman, "Take out the close sentry and I'll drop the other one at the same time. Joe Tipp, you spot for me."

Newman passed the word to Darren Rawls, who slithered off into the darkness, his long arms and legs propelling him forward at an astonishing pace and in total silence, with only his strong fingers and toes of his boots touching the ground.

The sentry lazily walked his position, his senses dulled by the cool night temperature and the big meal of lamb and rice he had just devoured. A dot of flame flashed from a match as he lit an opium-laced cigarette until golden ashes glowed at the tip. The fasting period also meant no smoking during the day, so he hungrily inhaled, held it in his lungs, and stared up at the moon as the drug's pleasantness spread through his body.

In an instant, a shadow rose behind him, a big hand cupped over his mouth and yanked the head back, and then the heavy blade of a sharp Ka-Bar, an old-school combat knife, ripped through the exposed neck, sliced the jugular vein and dug for the brain. Darren Rawls eased the man to the rocky ground and knelt on him as he bled out. He clicked his radio transmitter once, breaking squelch to confirm his task was done.

Joe Tipp and Kyle Swanson had calculated the distance, elevation, and windage numbers for their target. Upon hearing the click in their earpieces, Tipp whispered, "Fire." Swanson applied a smooth four pounds of pressure to the trigger and the SV-98 coughed once, the flash suppressor eating up the sound of the gunshot. An instant later, a 7.62 mm bullet slapped into the broad back of the distant guard and tore out his heart and chest, dropping him without a sound.

Swanson put the sniper rifle aside and turned to Newman. "You find their commo shed?"

"Um. Yeah. It's that center building, looks like the overall headquarters. They really grouped all of those tents and buildings close together. Hooray for sloppy work."

"Shit, why not? They aren't worried about any air strikes on sovereign Pakistani soil, and the Paks sure as hell aren't coming after them. We're here to show they aren't safe, no matter where they sleep."

Tipp unstrapped a rocket propelled grenade launcher. "I still think cruise missiles would be a good idea."

"Let's go." Swanson growled and led the way down the trail, unlimbering one of his own RPG-7s. The old weapons were notoriously inaccurate and had a short range, but had been modified and updated, and in the hands of trained commandos firing down slope, they were effective and deadly. With both sentries out of the way, the group closed on the camp until they were less than a football field away, then at Kyle's signal, moved into a line, side-by-side, about ten yards apart.

They were in position within seconds, invisible in the darkness against the mountain backdrop, all with RPGs ready to fire. The terrorists were grouped together outside in the open area of the camp, kneeling in five lines on their prayer rugs and facing Mecca.

Swanson took a final range measurement, just a flicker of an invisible radar beam and spoke into the small microphone on his headset. "Set your detonators at one hundred meters. On my count of three, send the first volley into the crowd and then hit your assigned buildings with the second shot, again on my count. We want both salvos to arrive as a package. After that, we move into the camp and fire at will. There will be no survivors."

Captain Newman had assigned each commando a specific segment of the crowd of worshippers, so as to maximize the damage rather than having all of the rockets bursting in one place. The terrorists were no longer men, as far as any of the Marines were concerned: Just targets. Kyle aimed at the center of the cluster, and counted it off, "Three . . . Two . . . One!"

The six RPGs spoke with a loud, rippling bark and the rockets leaped from their shoulder-mounted tubes, whining instantly toward the gathered men below. The few who looked up saw six rocket trails etching smoke in the night sky and then the missiles exploded in a hellish roar. The odd-numbered rockets carried high-explosive warheads that ripped through unprotected skin and internal organs, while the even-numbered ones were thermobarics which erupted just above the crowd to spew a fine mist of underoxidized fuel that detonated in air bursts which sucked the air out of lungs and created massive fireballs that consumed bodies.

As the explosions ricocheted up the mountains, the Tridents were already firing the second rounds, ripping the other RPGs at the few buildings and blowing the fragile structures apart. Flames from the fuel-air explosions swept around corners and into doorways and windows and potential hiding places, vacuuming life out of every human it touched.

Kyle was moving before the roar ceased and relentlessly led the other Tridents in a mad scramble toward the shattered campsite. He estimated about 90 percent of the fifty-two man terrorist force was already dead, and was glad that no return fire was coming back toward the Marines.

"Split up!" he hollered when they reached the perimeter. The team divided into two-man units and worked rapidly through the burning ruins, firing three-round bursts at anyone who looked as if he may have somehow survived the initial attacks. There weren't many, and even the wounded drew the momentary but deadly attention of the raiders. It was not work for the weak of heart, but mercy had no place in the mountains of Pakistan on a night like this.

At the far edge of the camp, Kyle yelled, "Back!" They all turned and worked their way through the charnel houses to their starting point. Fewer shots were needed this time.

The fire was chewing everything in the camp and an ammunition dump erupted like a small volcano, but the surrounding high mountains shielded the fire and detonations from the outside world. The Tridents pulled out after leaving behind a few booby traps in case of pursuit.

They climbed the trail, picked up the guide, and disappeared like ghosts back into the unfathomable reaches of the rugged border.

SCOTLAND

THE CASTLE WAS GUARDED by everything but dragons, knights, and archers with longbows. Professional security personnel from five nations and counterterrorism teams roamed the grounds while police in small boats patrolled the black waters of the forbidding loch. Electronic and thermal detection systems webbed the woodlands and motion detectors and surveillance cameras probed every corner. Sir Geoffrey Cornwell took a sip of whisky and looked for holes in the security net as the sun set in a final blaze of bronze sky sliced by layers of purple clouds. A fine mist was on the light breeze, but he could see across the loch, which meant the weather would be fine for tonight.

It was less than a dozen miles from Edinburgh, perched on the dominating knob of a hill that sloped to the water on the east side. Patrol vehicles on the far perimeter road that led around the loch had turned on their headlights, and from the castle wall, they looked like slow-moving fireflies. Cornwell owned more than a thousand acres, from working farmland to a game-thick forest and the entire place normally would have been leased for the week to some multinational corporation for a conference of managers. Not tonight.

He had bought the fifteenth-century castle a decade ago, when it was little more than a dilapidated ruin, then had it gutted and rebuilt. The single rugged exterior wall on which he now stood was one of the few remaining parts of the original structure and still bore the scars of English cannonballs. Bathed by light blue floodlights, the broad front wall kept the castle looking medieval, ominous, and strong.

The new buildings behind the blue wall contained improvements that had never been dreamed of by the ancient stonemasons, such as electricity, flush toilets, and central heating. Corporate executives on a business retreat required ultimate comfort.

Cornwell had retired from the British Special Air Services as a colonel, then became a successful industrialist and a visionary designer of military hardware. He and his wife, Lady Patricia, lived in one private wing of the Scottish estate and left the rest to be operated as a commercial venture, for he would not allow his money to sit idle.

A WIDE LANE OF flickering torches led from the gatehouse to the area in which the limousines would arrive, and off to the left the helipad was aglow with a blinking strobe light flashing upward from the center. Security had never been tighter. Still, he felt as though he was holding a brittle piece of history in his palms, and he was worried. The slightest unexpected incident could ruin everything. He took another sip of warm Scotch and the whisky teased a burn down his throat. He placed his glass on the thick flat stone of the saw-toothed battlement and straightened his tuxedo.

"Would you please stop worrying? Let the professionals do their jobs, Jeff. Your only role tonight is to be the perfect host." Lady Patricia slid an arm around his waist and kissed his cheek. She wore a navy blue organza gown designed by Karl Lagerfeld, and diamond earrings matched the necklace, the stones glittering in the bright lights and contrasting with her tanned skin.

Sir Jeff was startled, then he wrapped a big arm around Pat and hugged her close. Gave her a smile. "You are beautiful tonight," he said.

"Yes, I am," she replied happily. "We've had many parties, Jeff, but this is at the top of the list."

Lady Pat looked around. Busy, efficient people were working hard to make the evening work perfectly. "So why are you worried?"

"Something Kyle said a few weeks ago," her husband replied.

"Oh my God, Jeff. Listen to Kyle Swanson when you need to kill somebody, not when you are seeking social advice."

There was a small laugh behind them and Sir Jeff looked over. Delara Tabrizi, their thirty-year-old personal assistant, a refugee from Iran who was now a British citizen, was standing there with a thick notebook of checklists, a personal radio-telephone in her ear, a small computer in her hands, and a big smile on her face.

He glared at her without effect. The two women in his life were not afraid of him.

"Lady Pat is right, sir. It would be a vision of hell for Kyle to figure out a seating chart, and where to place that beautiful wife of the foreign minister of Israel for maximum effect, or to plan a menu that would be memorable for Christians, Jews, and Muslims alike. That, sir, would indeed be funny."

Pat asked, "See? So what did he tell you that has gotten you so jumpy?"

Delara Tabrizi cocked her head and poked a finger in her ear to push the radio receiver deeper for better reception. She tapped her keyboard then looked up. "Excuse me, Sir Jeff, but you wanted a status report?"

He nodded. British Foreign Minister Lord Covington and the Israeli foreign minister had been overnight guests, and the others were due momentarily. The private dinner was a prelude to tomorrow's signing of a peace agreement between Israel and Saudi Arabia, a treaty that could be a huge step in bringing peace to the Middle East.

Delara replied, "The American ambassador and the U.S. secretary of state have entered the grounds. The helicopter of Prince Abdullah is in the air, with an ETA of eight minutes. The Egyptian foreign minister's plane just landed at Edinburgh, and a helo is waiting for him. Twenty minutes."

"Very well," he said, and straightened the sleeves of his midnight black tux. "Ladies, shall we go down and greet the guests?"

"Not until you tell me about Kyle." Lady Pat crossed her arms and stayed put.

"Well, I showed him all around the perimeter and described our security precautions. Where guards would be on duty in static positions and the routes of the roving patrols. The electronics. I told him that if a squirrel shat out there, we would know it."

"Jeff! Watch your language. Children are present."

"I apologize, Delara," he said. She rolled her eyes. "Anyway, I told him how all of the international teams were cooperating and how tight this net was going to be, and asked if he thought he could penetrate such a band of security and take out a target."

"Obviously he would tell you that he could," Lady Pat almost snorted. "Little bastard thinks he is Superman."

"Worse. He said it would be easy. So we extended the protective perimeter to two miles in every direction. Not only did Kyle say that still would not be enough, but insisted that protecting this place was tactically impossible. Centuries ago, it made sense to put a castle on a hill so it could dominate the region. In the twenty-first century, he says it's a security dinosaur.

"And that got you all upset. We are having this wonderful reception to mark an historic event and you let Kyle Swanson needle you. He was probably saying that just to get under your skin, and he did." She grinned. "Delara, dear, please make a note to remind me to box Kyle's ears the next time I see him."

"Yes, m'lady."

Pat linked her arm into Sir Jeff's again and got him moving toward the stone stairs that descended from the wall-walk into the castle courtyard. The first black limos were arriving. "Now smile and prepare to welcome all of these important people to our stately manor."

3

SCOTLAND

IBRAHIM **B**ILAL **WAS FIRST** out of the minivan when it pulled off a narrow farm road and into a brush-obscured driveway three miles away from the castle. A few scruffy Highland cattle grazed around him but there was no other sound. He pressed a button on his wristwatch and started the attack countdown and called for the others. "Out! Quickly now. Quickly!"

Four more men dismounted, all wearing insulated smoky branch camo overalls and strong climbing boots and with their faces smeared with NATO camouflage paint sticks. They hauled open the rear doors of the small truck, handed around backpacks and strapped them on. The loads contained only radios, water, some snacks, dry socks and shoes, and a complete change of clothing. Holstered pistols with a single spare clip apiece would be their only personal weapons. Very soon, every ounce would count.

The rest of the cargo was pulled out, then they covered the vehicle with a ten-by-twenty foot mottled mesh camouflage net and branches were used to erase the tire tracks. That done, they helped each other add the new loads, grunting with effort as they distributed several hundred pounds of additional weight among the five of them, using the backpacks to take some of the weight and better balance the loads across their shoulders. "Life isn't easy," Bilal joked. "Go now."

Moving at the head of the column, he took them through the cows toward a small hill at the far west end of the pasture. A helicopter roared high overhead and passed beyond the crest, with its bright landing lights pushing columns of white through the gloom. Bilal looked at his wristwatch as he walked. Right on time.

* * *

"I NEVER THOUGHT I'D see this day," the American secretary of state, Kenneth Waring, told Sir Jeff as the sleek helicopter touched down with barely a wiggle. The engines were shut down and the blade slowed its spinning.

"It is the inevitable outcome of the extremely difficult work by dedicated men and women of good will over many years," Cornwell replied. His hands were moist from nervousness.

"Sir Jeff, your work behind the scenes was vital in this final stage of the negotiations. I doubt that we could have done it without your assistance. You know so many influential people and they all trust you to be an honest broker. Believe me, that sort of reputation is rare today."

Jeff was uncomfortable with compliments. He felt he had just done his duty, keeping all of those hard-headed politicians and diplomats going in private meetings when they all had conflicting agendas. They had been arguing for years and Jeff had helped nudge them toward a decision. "The danger comes over the next few months, while the heads of the regional governments try to keep the fanatics under control."

"Jeff, if anybody can pull this off, it is Prince Abdullah. Either he is successful or we probably get another century of Middle East misery."

They were not the only ones having doubts.

PRINCE ABDULLAH, THE SAUDI ambassador to the United States, looked out from the window of his helicopter and saw the eager faces of his hosts and the big blue wall of the old castle. He knew that when he stepped from this aircraft, he would be changing the world and in a fleeting moment of fear, wanted to order the pilot to take off again, to rush him back to the airport so he could fly back to Washington and resume his normal and familiar routines. Let this burden fall on other shoulders.

The prince was in his early forties, tall, handsome, and athletic, and had been groomed for this role since he was a boy. Highly intelligent, multilingual, and experienced both as a soldier and a diplomat, he might never be king, for he was not the monarch's eldest son, but the family had molded

Abdullah into their version of an enlightened, modern political figure. If forced to evolve into a democracy, he would be the prince who could run for office, although that plan had also fallen into ashes in this turbulent time. His new reputation, historic as it might be, would not win him many voters. *The man who made peace with the Jews!*

Abdullah had reviewed the diplomatic cables and the latest news while on the flight across the Atlantic. There was unrest at home, which had been expected, for to have Saudi Arabia sign an official peace treaty with Israel carried huge risks. The nation where Islam's most holy cities of Mecca and Medina were located was switching sides, a monstrous development in the view of religious fundamentalists who championed a stern theocracy. Blind hatred for Israel was a bedrock belief for millions of Muslims. Violence had blossomed in dozens of places.

The royal family in Riyadh saw things differently than the imams and mullahs. Egypt had made a similar agreement with the Jewish state forty years ago, withstood the ensuing political storms, and prospered. To survive in the tumultuous twenty-first century, the Saudis also needed to make political adjustments. Controlling one-fifth of the world's known oil reserves was no guarantee of a stable long-term existence because the product was only that, a product to be sold. It was a finite resource and would either run dry or, more likely, be overtaken by other energy sources and the nation could disintegrate right back into the desert sands from which it had come, having been rich and powerful for only a few generations. Hatred of the Jews had outlived its usefulness. National survival was at stake.

Abdullah let the helicopter's spinning blades come to a complete stop before a bodyguard opened the side door. To allow the powerful rotor wash to whip his regal robes like laundry on a line was unacceptable. The British foreign minister, the American secretary of state and Sir Geoffrey Cornwell welcomed him and they all left the gleaming helipad for a reception area in which Israeli Foreign Minister Nathan Simhon stood waiting. *The moment of truth*, thought Abdullah. *Inshallah.*

Then Simhon, with a genuine smile, unexpectedly broke protocol and stepped forward to shake hands with the prince and a private photographer recorded the historic moment.

"Mr. Foreign Minister, we shall be great friends!" declared the prince.

"We all look forward to that," responded Simhon. "I am honored to be signing the letter of intent with you tomorrow."

LADY PAT WAS INTRODUCED to the prince as the evening's hostess, and stepped between the two men to lead the group into the huge banquet hall, a corridor of stone and tapestries and ancient weapons that maintained the castle theme. A massive oak table ran almost the entire length of the room. Sir Jeff escorted the wife of the Israeli ambassador, a gorgeous brunette who had once been an actress.

Delara Tabrizi took her notebook and her PDA and retreated to her basement office, which was serving double duty as a storage area for spare parts for the event's beefed-up communication center. A bank of color television screens was aligned along the wall and she could watch things unfold while directing the cooks, waiters, and various staff members. Delara allowed herself a smile of sheer joy. It felt like only yesterday that she had barely escaped from Iran with her life and she knew this historic moment would not please the mullahs. However, it pleased her greatly.

The reception was running smoothly and everything was on schedule, so she touched up her makeup before heading back upstairs to retrieve Sir Jeff and get him out to the helipad to greet the Egyptian foreign minister, whose helicopter was making its final approach.

She noticed a member of the prince's entourage whisper to Sir Jeff, who pointed to a side door, and the man immediately relayed the comment to the prince. Delara suppressed a laugh. All of this hullabaloo, peace treaties and history coming together, and the main guy had to go to the bathroom.

SCOTLAND

AS HE TRUDGED UP the stony hill, Ibrahim Bilal remembered going on hikes as a child with his father when the family lived in High Wycombe in England. He had become an engineer, but a bored young man with no enthusiasm for life until he found Islam. Along with discovering inner change and comfort, he became aware that a smart and brave young believer could earn a good living as a fighter and a maker of explosives. After his conversion, less than a year ago, he had abandoned the family name for a new identity, then departed from the family itself, for they were infidels and impure.

This climb had been rigorous, but not really hard, other than carrying the extra weight. Within ten minutes, Bilal reached the crest and could see the glow from the big house, a bubble of blue and white light in the gathering darkness. "Now!" he commanded to those who followed him. "Set it up!"

While the men dumped their burdens and packs, Ibrahim examined the perimeter road as a slow-moving vehicle passed by and a small spotlight illuminated clumps of bushes along both sides. When the car moved on, he removed a laser rangefinder from his pack and measured the distance between the hilltop on which he was crouched and the castle across the water. The digital readout told him they were 3,800 meters away from the big wall, and 600 meters outside of the two-mile security perimeter.

By the time he checked his team, the tripod had been pulled from its container and the legs were unfolded, fanned out and locked in place. The men were forcing the stabilizing prongs into the hard ground. Then they heaved the fifty-two pound launch system into position and locked it atop the tripod.

Bilal heard the low hum of another vehicle engine and snapped his attention back to the road where headlights and another spotlight gleamed, but were pointed down toward the edges of the road and not up the hill. Another patrol, only two minutes behind the first one. The loch road was a busy place.

The team unhooked the day-night sight package from one of the backpacks and affixed it to the angular device they had already built, plugged in the connections and activated it. Another narrow cylinder was opened and a long object was withdrawn and was smoothly slid into the thick tube atop of the weapon. The tube-launched, optically-tracked, wire-guided missile, known worldwide as a TOW, was ready to work.

This one had been removed from a U.S. Army Humvee in Iraq the previous year after an ambush, smuggled into England, and stored away to await a suitable target. Ibrahim looked at his stopwatch: More minutes had flown away and the big hand kept sweeping over the numbers. He was still on time and he crouched beside the TOW, a loader standing by with another missile, and the others taking overwatch positions to keep track of the patrols.

Bilal adjusted the thermal optic sight until the crosshairs rested on the bright, glowing castle wall. He took a deep breath and pressed the firing mechanism. The missile, more than four feet in length, tore out of its tube with a deafening, thumping roar and a flash of fire which violently jarred them all, but Ibrahim had expected it, recovered and brought the crosshairs back onto the target. The roar was replaced by the hissing whisper of a thin wire unreeling behind the TOW that would relay the built-in computer commands to adjust the small fins on the flying missile. Ibrahim Bilal was sweating, counting off the twenty seconds until impact and holding the thermal sight steady on his target.

The loader was readying the second rocket. The team would do both shots in less than a minute, and then be gone.

SOLDIERS ON THE ROVING patrols—in vehicles, on foot, and on the lake—heard the distinctive, muffled *pop-boom* of the TOW launch and came to a slight halt as their brains began issuing threat signals. Eight seconds had elapsed before any of them spotted the brilliant red streak tearing through the night sky, and three seconds more ticked off before the first man could understand what was going on. He hit the TRANSMIT button on his throat mike and yelled, "INCOMING MISSILE!"

An anti-missile team stationed in the woods had no chance. The TOW had come and gone before they realized it was even there, and relentlessly plunged over the top of its slight arc and sped toward the castle.

The security apparatus was big, but had miles to cover, which made it comparatively slow. It was hampered in the struggle to adapt to the instant threat because the multiple nations represented in the dining hall used different radio frequencies.

In her office, Delara Tabrizi heard the panicked warning being broadcast in several languages as guards tried to cut through the established procedure and reach their own people. She stood rooted in place, unable to mentally process the information. *An attack? Here?*

The bodyguard stationed near each dignitary also had to mentally process the alert call that was shouted in their earpieces and a few managed to lurch forward to protect their people, but were out of time.

The powerful TOW, pushed by its tight tail of fire, slammed into the castle wall with a 12.4-kilogram warhead that was capable of blowing through the armor of a tank. It obliterated the ancient fortification with an explosion that sent chunks of concrete scything through the air, followed by bolts of flame and waves of debris.

FROM THE HILL ACROSS the loch, Ibrahim Balil watched a giant fireball rise above his target but did not remove his eye from the sighting scope. Sweat poured down his face and he could feel the vibrations through the reusable launcher as the loader fed the second missile into place. Forcing himself to remain steady, Balil pressed the trigger mechanism again and the new TOW thundered away.

Thirty seconds after the first missile strike, the follow-up shot plunged down and the old stone wall was no longer there to impede its progress. The missile hit the conference building with another spectacular explosion.

THE CONCUSSION BLAST OF the first missile threw Delara Tabrizi over her desk and all the way across her office, and cracked her head against the cement wall. She crumpled to the floor, stunned, and then the second missile tore the place apart. Walls began to sag and fall.

She dreamed she was struggling against a riptide current as she swam back to reality and found herself in a corner beneath the heavy weight of her desk. Her head felt as if was breaking, breath came hard into her aching ribcage and her ears rang. She shook her head. *What just happened?* One moment she had been watching the security cameras, getting ready to go back upstairs, and then the world had ended with the thunder of doom, and . . . ? That was all. A horrendous crash, flying through the air, and bright flashes of red and orange. Oh, and something about a missile.

The castle's emergency generators kicked on and the remaining light fixtures bloomed, dropping pools of dim illumination through the darkness and piercing swirling clouds of settling dust. Her digital wristwatch lit up when she pressed a button: ten minutes after eight o'clock. They had entered the great hall only six minutes ago, so she had been immobile for too long, but she was covered with debris and junk. Although the office was destroyed, the scattered material provided some inanimate reassurance, for it was familiar and she could recognize individual items. The small desk tilted against her had become a protective shield that diverted much of the blast force. The bottom half of the chair was still on its wheels nearby but the back had been snapped off by a large chunk of falling concrete. She wanted to get up and run, but remembered Kyle's motto for times of danger: *Slow is smooth, smooth is fast.* Delara took several breaths, counted her hands and feet, stretching her fingers and toes and determined that no serious damage had been done. The air was so thick with dust that breathing made her cough, and jabbed sharp pains through her side, where perhaps a rib had been cracked. When she raised a hand to her scalp, there was a patch of wet blood, but no gaping wound. Her legs worked. She could move.

Using the desk as a prop, she rose, and then pulled open a drawer in which she kept her jogging gear, found the gray sweatshirt and pressed it against the soggy head cut. The fancy dress shoes were gone, so she rummaged around to find her Nikes. More familiarity, more personal comfort, the dawning realization that she must go find Lady Pat and Sir Jeff. Moving across the room was like navigating a maze, her path hampered by fallen chunks of wood and nails and shards of brick and glass. She worked toward the stone stairs.

A large wooden beam leaned at a diagonal across the doorway to the main floor, but the big door was gone. Sliding beneath the beam, Delara found herself in a wonderland of destruction, and stumbled into what had once been the grand dining hall. Not another soul was standing, and she rushed into the dark ruins, shouting as loudly as she could: "Pat! Jeff! Where are you?" To her left, several small fires gnawed at the rubble.

Moans and cries of pain were coming from various points of the big room, and in moments, security men from outside were charging into the area, the beams of their strong flashlights crossing like sabers. Someone shouted orders to put the fire out before it spread. Her hearing was returning.

Delara recalled the seating chart. Sir Jeff was to have been at the head of the table, but no one had yet taken their seats for the dinner, so he and Lady Pat were both likely still at the far end of the room. She headed that way. "Pat! Jeff! It's Delara! I'm coming!!" Her foot slipped and she fell hard onto a body in a tuxedo. It did not have a head. She gagged in horror and someone grabbed her arm and lifted her up: a uniformed soldier with a flashlight. He saw her head wound and said, "You're bleeding, luv. Let's get you outside for some medical treatment."

She shook him away. Pointed to a doorway on the left. "I'm all right, so tend to the others," she said, her voice surprisingly strong, regaining the tone of certainty that she used to run this massive place. She pointed to a side door. "Go look in there. Prince Abdullah had just gone to the loo when the bomb hit. I am Sir Geoffrey Cornwell's assistant and I need a torch."

The soldier handed her his own flashlight and ran to the bathroom, calling for others to help.

Delara worked her way over to the far wall and probed the shining point of the flashlight across piles of debris. The entire wall along the right edge of the room had collapsed, which brought down most of the ceiling with it. She recognized the dark brown tapestry that had depicted a royal hunting scene and had hung on the far wall. It had been thrown down like a blanket. She lifted an edge and shined the light beneath. The legs of a woman and the bottom of a torn navy blue organza gown were visible.

"Pat!" she screamed and turned back to the soldiers. "I need help here! I've found somebody!" Several men jumped through the rubble and knelt beside her, then peeled away the heavy tapestry and the debris holding it in place. With their bare hands, they dug deeper into the wreckage. Pat Cornwell was on her side and Sir Jeff lay diagonally across her midsection, having used the split-second of warning before the first explosion to throw them both beneath the edge of the heavy table and between two sturdy chairs. The soldiers rolled him onto his back and finished clearing the heavy load that pinned his wife. A medical officer wiped away the dirt and blood from their faces and felt for vital signs. "Two live ones here," he called. "Bring some stretchers!"

Delara used her cotton sweatshirt to gently wipe Sir Jeff's face, her fingers gingerly dislodging clumps of dirt from his mouth and nose. He began to cough, and his eyes flew open and he managed a panicked whisper: "Pat . . ."

Delara Tabrizi felt a jolt of happiness. He was coming back! She grabbed his hand and placed its palm on the arm of his wife, and let it rest there. "She's right here beside us, sir, and the doctor says she's still alive, too. Getting beneath the table saved both of you. You're going to be okay."

His eyes fluttered and he was about to fall unconscious again. "Delara?" he asked softly, and she leaned closer, tears in her eyes. "Delara," he repeated, the voice just a bit stronger. He had to say something.

"Yes, sir. I'm right here. Don't worry. I shall stay with you and Lady Pat." She took his other hand in both of hers.

Geoffrey Cornwell shook his head, and looked into her eyes, then whispered, "Delara. Get Kyle. I need Kyle."

6

WASHINGTON, D.C.

IT WAS THREE O'CLOCK in the afternoon. Sybelle Summers had been at work for half of her shift and had not yet come up with a new excuse to get out of her job. She was running out of reasons, and had been turned down by every boss she had, even the guy in the Oval Office. The president of the United States, Mark Tracy, was so tired of listening to her bitch that he had recently snapped that she had better get used to being his military assistant because she was going to be in the position for a while, so just shut the hell up. It was the most boring job she had ever had.

So she sat in an uncomfortable chair at a little desk just outside the Oval Office and stared at the black leather Halliburton suitcase beside her. The hefty Glock pistol dug into her hip, so she shifted it. The White House Military Office had wanted her to carry a prissy little Beretta, because it was easily hidden and therefore not as obvious when she was in public with the president. The Secret Service would take care of any real threats, she was told. Sybelle liked the Secret Service agents, but no guard detail was ever perfect, and if she ever had to shoot, she intended to blow a hole in any bastard stupid enough to try to steal the Nuclear Football.

Major Summers, of the U.S. Marine Corps, was one of five military officers, a single representative from each branch of the armed services, who worked in shifts to lug the Football around so that it was always available to the commander in chief. No one knew much about her beyond that she was beautiful and obviously competent. Her life had been studied in detail during the ultra-top-level Yankee White background investigation before she assumed the new job, but it seemed that everything in her personnel folder was stamped

"Classified" or "Top Secret" or "Need To Know." Top marks at the U.S. Naval Academy, the only woman ever to graduate from Marine Recon, and a bunch of decorations on her uniform that signified valor in combat, although the citations gave no clue as to when, what, where, and why.

Summers had a reputation as an up-and-comer and had come to the White House after being the operations officer of a black ops team known as Task Force Trident. The only time her personality emerged while she was on duty at the White House was when a senior officer from within the elite Spec Operations community came to see the president. Those really hard men always took time to say hello to Summers and joke about the fancy loop of braid on her right shoulder, teasing her about becoming a staff weenie and getting a death glare from the dark blue eyes in return.

"Can't cut it in the field anymore, eh, Major?" one lieutenant general had quipped.

"Your pants are unzipped again, sir. Another senior moment?" she replied in her distinctive, quiet voice that was polite but carried a sense of menace, like the purr of a puma feasting happily on an elk.

The three-star automatically looked down at his pants. They both laughed. It was the kind of rude exchange that passed for respect among such warriors.

The weight of history and grandeur of the White House had weighed upon her on that first trip through the uniformed Secret Service cordon at the gates and then on the walk up the long driveway to the main entrance. After that, it became just another job. The suitcase stayed within arm's reach because it contained everything the president needed to launch a nuclear strike, whether it might be a small tactical weapon or the final, full-blown, tear-the-roof-off attack. Summers was the unanimous choice if somebody had to be on call to help the president launch Armageddon. She would probably just lean over his shoulder, a gentle aura of perfume surrounding her, and casually coach him through the authentication codes and leaf through the pages in the folder that listed the deserving targets, printed in red. She would not flinch from such an awesome responsibility and since everybody was probably about to die anyway, she might throw in a few suggestions of her own and anybody on her personal shit list would be catching a nuke on the head.

Sybelle got along fine with the other staff members whose duties also put them in close proximity to the Oval Office, and a couple of agents of the Secret Service protective detail had even asked her out for a date. She always declined and the agents grumbled about the wasted personal life of such a beautiful woman. She stood five six, weighed no more than 125 and, since she was currently based in Washington, Sybelle's black hair was trimmed at an upscale shop, short but flaring just a bit at the collar. She was frequently called upon by the White House Social Secretary to escort a single man at an evening event, but those relationships never left the grounds. Sybelle was fierce about protecting her personal life.

She looked at the Football again. It hadn't moved. Still there, with one end of a steel chain attached to the handle, the other end dangling free, a handcuff ready to be snapped onto her wrist.

Things had been routine around the Oval Office, with a steady stream of visitors coming and going. Then a little after three, the President's chief of staff threw open the door of his adjoining office and bolted across the narrow hallway, barking at the two Secret Service agents flanking the door. "Code Red! Lock it down," yelled Steve Hanson. "Evacuate him to the shelter!"

The agents spun and followed him through the door, talking into their wrist microphones as they went. The entire atmosphere of the White House changed in an instant. From calm backwater to hurricane in the blink of an eye. Sybelle unbuttoned her jacket and pulled out the Glock, knelt beside the Football and clicked the steel handcuff onto her left wrist. Then she stood again, with the pistol in her right hand, pointing it toward the floor as her eyes quartered the area.

Two more agents ran up and one dashed straight into the office while the second assumed post at the main door, holding a small machine gun. He and Sybelle exchanged the briefest of glances, and he was startled about how cool she appeared to be in this emergency. The White House was plunging into total lockdown, nobody allowed in or out, the threat unknown and security accelerating to a maximum. Snipers removed their rifles from their cases on the roof, the antiaircraft missile system was activated, and uniformed agents scrambled into defensive positions. The big gates were locked.

Summers stood there unconsciously humming a little tune, her eyes glittering like polished stones. The pistol did not twitch, although it was held in only one hand. It was almost as if she *wanted* somebody to attack.

There was a flurry of activity inside the Oval Office, since the president had been in the middle of a meeting about the upcoming elections in Iraq. He was whisked out, each arm held by a Secret Service agent. One spoke into his sleeve microphone to alert the agents' command post: "Buckskin is moving." The code name had been assigned to the president by the U.S. Army Signal Corps because the president was from Tennessee and had constantly used Davy Crockett symbolism during his campaigns.

As the group cleared the doorway, the president looked over at Sybelle, gave her a slight grin, and said, "Major Summers, maybe you had better come along. Bring our suitcase."

"Yes, sir," she said. Sybelle holstered her weapon, hefted the forty-five-pound case and wrapped both arms around it as a Secret Service agent pushed her into the fast-moving group heading to the secure shelter beneath the second basement. *Finally,* she thought as she trotted down the stairs, toting the country's secret nuclear codes, *something interesting.*

THE WEARY TRIDENT TEAM called for a ride home as soon as they were safely back inside Afghanistan and a Dark Horse MH-47 helicopter from the 160th Special Operations Aerial Regiment soon arrived overhead to extract them from a long and barren plateau. Once aboard, the two thundering rotor blades of the SOAR bird prevented any attempt at conversation, so they loosened their gear and got comfortable for the long haul back to a forward operating base.

When they reached a safe altitude, the crew chief flashed a white greaseboard on which he had scrawled a one-word question: SWANSON?

Kyle pointed to his own chest and the crew chief struggled over, stepping around the other guys' boots. "I'm Swanson," he yelled when the crew chief approached. "What's up?"

"Wait one," the sergeant called out, handing over a flight helmet containing a radio.

Kyle pulled the little microphone arm into a speaking position and adjusted the cushioned ear pieces into place. The crew chief flipped a switch, turned a knob, and gave him a thumbs-up.

"Gunny Swanson?" the pilot's voice was clear, despite the racket, and almost casual in tone. For the SOAR crew, this quick mission was a total milk run and they were all relaxed. No one had shot at them.

"That's me," said Kyle.

"We won't be taking you to the FOB. After your team was on the map again, the brass changed our flight plan. We're to deliver you straight to Bagram."

Swanson exhaled in disappointment. Military regulations were looser at a forward operating base, while the huge Bagram facility meant rules and regulations, even though they would be sticking close to the special operations compound. "Any idea why?"

"Nope. Just that a lot of people have been asking about you guys during the past couple of days and were getting pretty antsy. Lots of shit happened while you were out of pocket, partner. When your radio didn't respond, a VIP flew and really started kicking ass."

"Batteries got wet. Radio didn't work."

The unseen pilot laughed. "Yeah. That does seem happen on these recon missions. What about your emergency radio?"

"Radios don't work well up in those mountains."

The pilot laughed again. "Well, you can explain all about it in person to the head cheese in just a little while."

"Who's the VIP?" He had visions of some Pentagon staff puke running around with papers that had Kyle's name on them.

"One of your own Trident people. Major Sybelle Summers, her own pretty little rotten self," the SOAR pilot said. "I'd like to tell you more about what's happening, but she ordered me to keep my mouth shut and I'd rather remarry my second ex-wife again than disobey Major Summers. So we are just dropping you off and getting gone."

"Roger. Don't blame you a bit. Out." Kyle peeled off the flight helmet and tossed it back to the crew chief. *Sybelle? She's supposed to be at the White House. What the hell?*

THERE WAS A PALPABLE sense of tension when the bird entered the air space around Bagram. Not a shot had been fired, but pre-battle nerves stretched taut as the Marines picked up on the strange and familiar feeling that something was going on. The Dark Horse helicopter leaned into a circling pattern. Special ops helicopters were never put on hold during a landing; they always go straight in, touch down in their private habitat, and hurry out of sight. Now the MH-47 was in a stack, for the skies were thick with allied aircraft. Fighters, bombers, tankers, passenger planes, and other helicopters howled about, both inbound and outbound. During the time that the Trident guys had been out of contact, the world apparently had changed beneath their boots.

Finally, the huge helicopter's number was called and the SOAR pilot took them in, flared and touched the tarmac. The ramp lowered and the Trident Marines stepped off, grimacing in the bright desert sun. The runway was crowded, the sky busy. In the distance they could see troops marching.

Joe Tipp shaded his eyes for a better look. "Jeez. It's the day after 9/11 all over again."

Travis Stone, who had slept on the flight, yawned, stretched. "Look at all that shit. Makes a man feel kind of small."

"That's because you *are* small." Tipp gave him a friendly shove.

Sybelle Summers threw open the door of a nearby Humvee and got out, adjusting her narrow sunglasses. She wore a plain dark blue baseball cap, tan BDUs and desert boots, and looked like just another soldier or Marine except there were no name strips on her tunic or her butt. She walked to the team and nobody saluted. Task Force Trident was an odd organization. Rank was only acknowledged in public places. Otherwise, it was the equality and respect of first names.

"Hey, guys," she said. No smile. "Glad you're all back okay."

"Jest a regular ole recon," said Joe Tipp. "Nothin' special."

"You can cut the crap, Joe. General Middleton briefed me, and I'm back in the loop as Trident ops officer again. Anyway, your raid is so—well, *yesterday*—that it has become about the lowest item on the totem pole." As the helo powered back up and the rotor downdraft created cycles of sand and wind, she led them all over to the Humvee to wait until the bird lifted away.

In the idle interval, Sybelle eyed them all. Tired but still ready to rock. Each man had been handpicked, but she would immediately get rid of anyone she did not think was up to a job. Trident was not for sissies.

In the early days of the war on terror, certain powerful people in Washington recognized an opportunity when the various federal security agencies were being shuffled to better deal with the new challenge facing the United States. After a series of private meetings with President Tracy at Camp David, a small organization was created to aggressively carry the fight to the enemy through unorthodox methods, and it was named Task Force Trident. It was a hybrid; not strictly military, although its offices were in the Pentagon; nor was it civilian, although it could draw whatever resources were needed, from analysts to hardware, from any branch of the government. It did not have a budget.

On official organizational flow charts, Trident was given a little box somewhere under the broad black umbrella of MARSOC, lost in the secret labyrinth of special operations, down among such common things as beans and bullets. On a final Sunday of discussion at Camp David, President Tracy authorized the unit with a presidential finding. Because the potential was great that such a team might be misused for political gain, he implemented strict caveats: Only he would give the orders. By necessity, Steve Hanson, his chief of staff, knew about Trident, as did the chairman of the Joint Chiefs of Staff and the director of the Central Intelligence Agency. No one else. The secretary of state was not in the loop, so that office would have deniability if some Trident mission went sideways. Congressional leaders were not included because their staff members leaked like wet noodles.

The idea for the bold new organization had come to President Tracy as he studied the exploits of a relentless warrior named Kyle Swanson, who had overcome incredible odds to brazenly rescue a kidnapped Marine general in Syria. Valuable and very expendable, Swanson would be the point man, a lightly controlled renegade running operations that were far off the books, and hunting terrorists in distant pastures.

Major General Bradley Middleton, the officer whom Swanson had pulled out of Syria, was put in command of Task Force Trident and answered directly to the president of the United States. If Swanson needed something, he just hollered up the stovepipe, and he would get it.

Middleton intentionally kept the task force as small as possible to avoid attention. He brought in the tough, beautiful, and uniquely talented Sybelle Summers as operations officer. A Recon legend, Master Gunnery Sergeant O.O. Dawkins was drafted to handle general administration. And reaching beyond the Corps, Middleton snared Lieutenant Commander Benton Freedman of the Navy, a technical genius. Freedman was called the Wizard at the Naval Academy, a nickname that his Marine co-workers quickly changed to "Lizard." The team would plus-up as needed with specialists picked for exact missions.

Everyone in Trident knew their real job was to support Kyle Swanson and help him inflict maximum pain and damage on the enemies of the United States. Almost from the moment it was activated, Kyle and Trident had stayed busy with targets who thought they were untouchable, and even taking down the demented terrorist named Juba, who detonated high-casualty biochemical bombs in London and San Francisco.

There was never any lack of work, and as the sound of the rotors faded at Bagram, there was going to be even more.

"I'VE GOT BAD NEWS, gang," Summers said. "The Israeli-Saudi peace process has been literally blown all to hell." She removed her glasses and stared at Kyle. "Terrorists hit the private reception for the main players two nights ago with a couple of TOW missiles. Seventeen dead, including Secretary of State Waring and his wife, and the foreign ministers of Israel and Great Britain. More wounded, including Prince Abdullah."

"Holy shit!" exclaimed Darren Rawls. "Did they get the bastards who did it?" He turned suddenly, in time to see Kyle drop his backpack and collapse on it, staring up at Sybelle with a look of fright on his face. Rawls had never seen such a change in the man's iron character.

"Yeah. It was a four-man suicide squad. It gets worse. The attack apparently was the trigger for a coup attempt in Saudi Arabia. Low-grade fighting is going on throughout the country."

Kyle had his face in his hands. *The party!* He had warned Jeff about the impossible security situation up on that hill! "Fuck all that. What about Pat and Jeff?"

She took a knee beside him and lowered her voice. "Both injured, but alive. Pat is going to be okay because Jeff managed to throw her under a table and covered her with his own body. He's hurt bad."

The other five members of the Trident team looked at each other for a moment, then down at their two leaders, and back into the sky full of planes . . . it all began to make sense. It wasn't just another 9/11: It might be the start of World War III. Rawls asked, "So what are we supposed to do, Sybelle? And why aren't you still at the White House?"

"I hated the job, so the president and Middleton decided to put me back on temporary duty with Trident. We might balloon up to a full-sized platoon of dirty fighters like you people and be ready to do whatever Middleton is assigned."

"So are we going to rotate back to the States?"

She handed Rawls a thick manila envelope filled with orders and vouchers. "No. You guys will be the nuggets around which we all will build the new strike team. You have a few hours to get cleaned up, grab some chow, and sleep before your plane leaves for Kuwait. Someone will meet you on the other end and take you to a special ops camp where we will be putting this thing together. I'll follow soon."

Swanson stood, and so did she. "I'm going to see Pat and Jeff before I go back anywhere else," he said. It was not a request.

"I know," she said. "Me, too."

SYBELLE SPED THE HUMVEE out of the Special Ops area and along the perimeter road to the complex of big hangars alongside Bagram's 10,000-foot runway. Waiting inside one, out of sight, was a Cessna Citation X, with its two Rolls Royce jet engines already idling at a soft whistle. The swept-wing aircraft with the high tail wore the markings of Excalibur Enterprises, Ltd., entirely white but for two slim dark blue stripes along the sides and the gold corporate symbol. It was another of Sir Jeff's toys, a luxury mid-sized business executive jet being flown today by a pair of pilots from the commando arm of Britain's Royal Air Force.

They dumped the Humvee and jogged up the stairs into the lap of luxury, each grabbing a cold beer from the galley before plopping into cream-colored seats across the standup aisle. A crewmember looked back to check that they were buckled in, and the plane rolled. The protective shade of the hangar gave way to the bright sun and the aircraft took its place at the end of the taxiway, third in line for takeoff behind an AC-130 Spectre gunship and a giant C-141B Starlifter transport. Moments later, the engines whined louder, the brakes were released, and the Citation X slipped away from the ground.

Kyle and Sybelle drank their beers but said little while the plane climbed to 37,000 feet, banked to the west, accelerated to a comfortable pace of Mach .92, about 600 miles per hour, and began chewing up the time zones. Kyle went into the curtained dressing area in the rear of the cabin, got out of his Afghan outfit, did a towel wash in the basin and changed into fresh clothes that had been placed there for him. Sybelle took her turn changing while Kyle opened fresh beers. Both now wore tan slacks, white running shoes and socks, and white polo shirts that were embroidered with the Excalibur gold emblem on the right chest. A casual observer would see just two more workers from somewhere within Sir Jeff's multinational corporation. They were a couple of spooks hiding in plain sight.

An entertainment center at the front of the cabin doubled as a secure communications console, and Sybelle closed the door to the flight cabin and called the Trident headquarters office at the Pentagon. The face of Benton Freedman, his black hair rumpled, appeared on the big flat screen. On his own screen, he could see Summers and Swanson. "Hello, Kyle. Welcome back," Freedman said.

"Hey, Lizard," Kyle responded.

"Is General Middleton around?" Sybelle asked.

"No. He's been dashing all over Washington from the White House to Foggy Bottom to the Hill. I'll tell him that you checked in. I assume you are on your way to London, and not coming directly back here?"

"You assume right," Kyle said.

The Lizard picked up some papers, glanced at them, put them aside, found a tablet, and read the notes. "I've been in touch with Delara Tabrizi over there and she is arranging transport so you can drive straight to the clinic. A package will be waiting with everything you need, including FBI creds. Kyle, there has been no change in the conditions of the Cornwells. Sir Jeff is scheduled for surgery tomorrow morning for a head wound and to pick out chunks of shrapnel that peppered his lower spinal area. Both legs are broken."

"How's Delara?" Kyle asked. It was not a well-kept secret that he and the strikingly beautiful Iranian woman were lovers.

"She got through the attack with some minor scrapes and I don't think she has slept since then. She's worn out, but refuses to leave them."

Kyle nodded. "I'll make her get some rest. She's the one person we cannot have keeling over from exhaustion. Can you give us a SitRep on Saudi Arabia?"

"Not over this clear channel. Just tune in Sky News and the BBC, and as usual, al Jazeera is getting cameras into places that others cannot. The Saudi government insists that everything is under control. It is obviously getting messy." The Lizard stared at the pinhole camera on the edge of his computer screen. "Sybelle, your former boss is very unhappy with what is happening over there."

He let the oblique reference dangle in empty air.

"Yeah. I'm sure he is," she said. "Tell the general the rest of the team is heading back to the base as planned. We'll contact you again right after we see the Cornwells."

"Right. Give them my best." Freedman clicked off the transoceanic call.

Kyle bit his lip in thought. "I think the Lizard was saying that the president may be planning some sort of military response. He can't stand by and let the Saudi government fall."

Sybelle typed on a small computer built into the narrow polished wood shelf that ran along the fuselage beside her seat, and Googled up SAUDI ARABIA OIL. Too many items to read, so she turned it off. "Losing that country would be ten times worse than losing Iraq. It would unhinge the entire global economy."

Swanson yawned, stretched his legs. "And the Russkies aren't going to politely stand aside if we make a grab for the oil patch, and everybody in the Middle East already hates the Russians. The Chinese will be watching, and every country in NATO. Toss in the Indians, for good measure, which also would mean Pakistan."

"So who's the enemy?" Sybelle kicked off her shoes and tucked her feet beneath her.

"Everybody." Kyle said. He closed his eyes, turned off his mind, and went to sleep.

MOSCOW

A **LOW, STEELY GRAY** Ferrari F430 Spyder with the top down ripped crossed the cobblestones of Red Square and dashed through a gate in the tall brick wall of the Kremlin. In a metropolis where ransom kidnappings of rich men were commonplace, this driver moved freely.

His safety was born from the union of respect and fear and security forces, and Russian President Andrei Vasiliyvich Ivanov was untouchable. As the best criminal dynasties always do, his family had a history of adapting to the times, no matter whether a ruthless Stalin or a reformer like Gorbachev ran the state. With the collapse of communism thirty years earlier, they became the cutting edge of the violent and bloody *mafiya*, then anticipated the oncoming typhoon of capitalism and embraced it. His father took that same sense of unrelenting toughness into the emerging private oil business, one uncle became a media magnate, and another was a venture capitalist who helped start fledgling businesses only to later take them over. It was a powerful combination.

Young Andrei was sent into politics with a purpose, plenty of money, the backing of important allies, and an overreaching hubris. Assuming the role of a populist, he was generous and kind and was adored by common Russians. Bad things happened to anyone who challenged him.

He was not a foolish man, however, and although he drove alone, a large SUV brimming with bodyguards and automatic weapons trailed sluggishly at a respectful distance in the Spyder's wake. Andrei packed a holstered Makarov pistol and a submachine gun was beneath the seat of his car. Forty-four years old, single, muscular, and healthy, he seemed to possess limitless energy and could work for hours on end. He had been at it until after midnight and now it was just after lunchtime. The clocks seemed to always cheat him.

As if fate had written his name in big letters, Ivanov had found the right place at the right time. Only a year earlier, Prime Minister Vladimir Putin had surprised everyone by appointing young Ivanov to be president of the Russian Republic, expecting to have a useful puppet. Then the old man was unexpectedly forced to the sidelines by a mild stroke. Instead of being just a political figurehead, Alexei was thrust into the job of actually running the country and he responded with vigor and determination. While Putin struggled to regain his ability to walk and still had some problems speaking, Alexei Ivanov set about making him irrelevant. The young leader's personality won over many international critics who had grown wary of Putin's harsh attempts to re-create a Russia in which little was possible. By racing through the streets in his private automobile and making personal, surprise gestures to help individual citizens, Ivanov cemented his popularity with the masses.

The common touch was leavened by his family's belief that Russia needed a new *tsar*, and Andrei had more than a bit of imperial arrogance. He intended to not only make a name for himself, but to make history.

Once through the old crimson walls, Ivanov braked to stop against a curb where two people were waiting; his chief of staff, wearing a neat dark suit, and an efficient-looking, beautiful woman in a conservative dress, who was his personal secretary. He switched off the ignition and got out, taking off the black Prada sunglasses that shielded his startlingly light green eyes and flashing the blazing smile that was so familiar to television viewers.

He trotted up the broad granite stairs that had been laid down hundreds of years ago by craftsmen working for Peter the Great. The aides followed. In contrast to their careful choice of wardrobe, Alexei wore a parka of soft black leather, a dark blue turtleneck sweater, black trousers and hiking boots.

"Is the old gentleman in today?" He would have been surprised if Putin had shown up, but it was best never to underestimate the old KGB chief.

"No, sir. Not today," replied Veronika Petrova. His secretary, known as Niki, had once been a professional fashion model and was frequently Andrei's escort to evening functions. With both the personal and professional links, she also had become one of his few confidants.

"Well, Niki, please send him my warmest regards and ask if we can have lunch or dinner together soon." He winked at her. *I want to know if the old fart is dying yet.*

"Yes, Mr. President." She made a note on her pad.

All three went through a broad door into his office, Andrei threw his parka onto a sofa and settled into the soft chair behind the big desk. His assistant, Sergei Petrov, placed a leather folder before him. "The initial operation in Scotland was a success, as you know, sir. Now the unrest is taking shape within Saudi Arabia. This information before you is fresh as of thirty minutes ago."

"How did Prince Abdullah survive? I don't understand how he got away unscathed."

"Luck. He actually was well protected in a bathroom when the attack hit. The prince has been taken to a private clinic, and the SVR already has a follow-up strike underway. We'll get him." The SVR, Russia's Foreign Intelligence Service, had succeeded the old KGB and was firmly in Ivanov's pocket.

Ivanov flipped through the pages. "Good, then. It's a good start. Now get Dieter Nesch on a secure call for me. I want his personal read on how things are going."

"Very good. Would you like some lunch?"

"Not yet. Any important appointments this afternoon?"

"Nothing immediate, sir. I thought it best that you have today free. Another SVR briefing is scheduled in two hours."

Niki and Petrov left Andrei Vasiliyvich Ivanov alone in his big office, with a news channel chattering away on a TV set. Andrei poured a tumbler of vodka from the carafe on his desk, took a deep drink, and settled back to watch the news. He smiled and put his boots on the desk. By the time his plan was accomplished, Andrei would have brought Saudi Arabia to heel in a masterful coup accomplished without the use of a single Russian airplane, soldier, or tank. Once that was done, Ivanov could proceed to toppling some other Middle East regimes with the ultimate goal of wringing the oil out of those places—every last drop—and bringing the riches home to Mother Russia.

THE PLANE SMOOTHED IN for a faultless landing at a private air terminal in northern England and Kyle and Sybelle had no trouble spotting their next ride. A young man dressed just like them, in a white polo shirt and tan slacks, met them at planeside and reluctantly handed Kyle a set of keys. "Ms. Tabrizi insisted on sending her personal car for your use."

Sybelle snatched the key ring. "I'm driving. You're too tired."

"No way. She sent the car for me. You're just a passenger." He reached for the keys.

She playfully dangled them just out of his reach. "Stop whining, gunnery sergeant. You don't even know how to drive on the wrong side of the road."

The young man did not know these two people, but couldn't blame them for arguing over who was going to drive the lynx yellow Saab 9-3 Bio-Power convertible, a car that looked as if it were grinning. "Ms. Tabrizi has nice taste in motorcars," he said. "This has a top speed over 150 miles per hour. I just wish I had been able to try it over on an autobahn with no speed limit. Instead, my instructions were to deliver it to you, then go home."

"Jeff must be paying her pretty good. What was the price tag on this thing?" Kyle asked.

"This one, with all of the extras, goes for about £40,000."

"Awright, *girlfriend!*" Sybelle laughed. "That's about $80,000 in real money." She was already in the comfortable leather driver's compartment. The five-speed stick shift on her left console would control the 2.8V6 engine. She arched an eyebrow at the young man. "Now, if we only knew where we were going."

He pointed to the compact flat display screen in the dashboard. "I've programmed the voice control navigation system. A map will show on the touch-screen monitor when the ignition comes on, and Linda will guide you from here to there, every turn of the way as soon as you clear the airport. It will take a little more than an hour if you do the speed limit."

"Linda?"

"That's what Ms. Tabrizi calls the female voice imbedded in the avionics of the car. Linda gets quite peeved if you do not mind her."

Sybelle turned the key and the big engine thrummed. "So do I," she said. She had no intention of doing the speed limit, no matter how peeved the Linda machine might get.

Kyle adjusted the passenger seat and belted in, and the young man handed him a plain cardboard box. "I am also to give you this, and here's my business card in case you need anything else," he said, stepping away.

In five minutes, they were out of the airport and the soft, polite voice of Linda instructed Sybelle to turn left. A colorful map on the screen pinpointed their exact position. Kyle opened the box and found a pair of black leather identification holders with Federal Bureau of Investigation shields and identity cards and a Glock 17 for Sybelle. He took the heavy Colt .45 semiautomatic for himself. After checking out the weapons, he returned them to the box and wedged it between his feet.

"Please, do not exceed the speed limit," Linda reminded in a pleasant tone. The top was down, the day was pleasant, and the wind whipped over their heads. Sybelle adjusted her dark glasses and punched the accelerator.

KYLE SOON TIRED OF watching the countryside. He would see Jeff soon, but what would he say? The man was more of a father to him than his real father, whom Kyle never knew. The fact that Jeff was badly wounded filled Swanson with worry. And what of Pat? She had seen Kyle at all of his many extremes and somehow kept bringing him back to believing that life was worth living.

Now there was Delara, she of the hot car. Kyle had led a raid on an Iranian bioweapons laboratory and saved her life, then she helped on another raid that brought down an even bigger lab. The former schoolteacher was beautiful and brave and was branded as an outlaw in her home country. She never wanted to return to the nation that had slaughtered her family and where she and all women were second-class citizens. He figured that this fast yellow sports car was most likely a gift from Jeff, an in-your-face insult to the religious zealots who controlled Iran.

Kyle knew he was falling in love with Delara, but would not admit it. He could hardly wait to hold her again, and knew she felt the same. The idea that the three people he cared for the most having been in jeopardy filled him with a seething rage. Sir Jeff had tried to bring some old enemies together to see if a new peace could be forged, and had been repaid with disaster.

Loud rock music brought him out of his reverie. "I'm trying to drown out Linda's constant bitching," Sybelle explained. "Make yourself useful and see what else is on that CD player."

He worked the buttons on the console, the map replaced by the names of available albums of music. When he leaned forward to hunt for the CD controls, he heard a sudden sharp curse by Sybelle and was thrown violently against the seatbelt straps. He looked up and saw the checkerboard dark and light green side of a boxy East of England ambulance flash across his spinning vision. It had pulled onto the road right in front of them, and Sybelle was doing about 90 miles per hour. She hit the brakes and swerved sharply to the right, cutting the front tires back into a controlled skid. Sliding rubber screamed against the road.

Kyle grabbed the dash for support as the belt held him tight against the centrifugal force that threatened to fling him from the open car.

Sybelle worked the gears, accelerator, and the emergency brake, pulling the Saab through a complete 360-degree turn before it steadied and stalled out. "Motherfucker!" she said, exhaling hard and her hands gripping the wheel so tightly that the knuckles were white. "He damned near T-boned us. Missed us by inches." She got the Saab running again and spun the steering wheel. "I'm going to catch that fucker and kick his ass!"

"Wait!" Kyle said, reaching a hand to the steering wheel to stop her. Something had caught his eye. "Hold on for a minute." He switched the computer screen back to the voice navigation system. "Linda, how far are we from the hospital clinic?"

"You are now exactly ten and one-half kilometers from our destination," said the warm voice. "Have you had an accident? I can notify the proper authorities."

"No. We are fine. Do not do anything."

"Please slow down," Linda said.

"Shut up," Sybelle responded. "What's going on, Kyle?"

"Up there. Straight ahead about a half-mile. Check out that jumble of junk off the edge of this side road. Some metal gleaming in the sun? Let's take a look. Something weird is going on."

As they drove forward, Kyle saw the dark blue, square rear-end of a minivan disappearing in the distance, speeding away from them, raising a layer of dust. *Why?* He picked up his Colt .45 and tucked the Glock beneath Sybelle's thigh as she coasted to a halt. Kyle stepped from the car, and Sybelle moved out to his right and a little to the rear, both of their guns ready. He stepped over a shallow roadside ditch and into the thick bushes and she followed.

The polished rails of an ambulance gurney were reflecting the flare of the sun. A dead woman, small and old, and frail, was strapped to the mobile stretcher, with an oxygen mask still on her face. Uniformed ambulance attendants lay on each side of her. All had been shot twice in their heads. Kyle and Sybelle hastily checked for vital signs. All of them were dead.

Without exchanging a word, they ran back to the Saab. Sybelle did a three-point turn on the narrow road and gunned the big engine. By the time they regained the main road, there was no sign of the green ambulance.

"Get him, Sybelle." Ten and a half klicks to the clinic, only about six miles, and the ambulance had a good head start and was probably hauling ass. Kyle studied the console map and Linda continued to complain until he turned down the audio voice. "It's a straight road all the way and there will be signs for the hospital. Damn, we can't call this in because we don't even know who to call."

The speedometer needle climbed to one hundred miles per hour without any engine strain, then higher as the Saab flashed around a delivery truck and a few cars. Kyle turned the audio back on. "Distance to destination!"

"Three kilometers. Please slow down and drive safely!" Insistent. Strident. Kyle turned it down again.

"I see him!" Sybelle called, and Kyle picked up the tight square edges of the ambulance. The driver was unsteady behind the wheel, whereas a real ambulance driver would have been smooth at even a high rate of speed. When the vehicle slowed for the hospital turnoff, the driver for the first time turned on the flashing lights and the shrill *beep-burp* of the siren. By the time he was coming out of the turn, Sybelle was screaming into it, neatly flattening the skid and gaining ground. The brick clinic and its rows of shiny windows loomed on the right. "See any guards?"

"A couple of civilian cops out front, and one is waving the ambulance into that entrance to the underground parking. Get me up beside him, Sybelle!"

The yellow Saab lunged for the final distance like a big leopard and blew by the startled policeman. Kyle unbuckled the belt and took a knee in the soft seat to gain some height, gripped the edge of the convertible's front windshield with his left hand and brought up his Colt with his right. Sybelle swerved and drew alongside the beefy green ambulance, which had to slow to get beneath the low roof of the parking garage.

They went into darkness. Swanson pointed the weapon at the head of the surprised driver, squeezed the trigger and the big pistol roared in the cavernous basement. Three bullets pulverized the driver's head, and the ambulance swerved into the Saab, the collision ripping Kyle's hand from its brace on the windscreen and flinging him over Sybelle, who stomped the brakes. The vehicles slid along the concrete ramp in a tangle until the ambulance rammed a concrete column and tore free.

Swanson was moving as soon as he regained his balance, levering himself up as Sybelle pushed him from behind and below, trying to free herself. He leaped from the wreckage, ran to the far side of the ambulance, jerked open the door and emptied the rest of the Colt's clip into the dead driver, just to make sure.

Police guards were running toward them, yelling, their bright yellow-green warning vests almost glowing in the gloom.

Sybelle held up the badge. "FBI!" she called. "We're both FBI! Americans. Kyle, drop the gun!"

Swanson tossed the empty weapon over his shoulder but scrambled into the cab and grabbed the hand of the dead driver to keep it away from a red-button pressure switch attached to a bulky vest of explosives around the waist. He fished out a knife and started hacking at wires. Sybelle yanked open the doors in the back. Cylinders of gas and boxes of TNT had been thrown about by the collision and lay scattered at cockeyed angles.

One policeman grabbed his radio from his belt, ready to transmit a message but Sybelle screamed for him to stop, that using the radio might set off the weapon. He ran back up the ramp to find a landline telephone as she climbed into the back of the ambulance and began pulling out wires and detonators.

For two full minutes, Kyle and Sybelle worked feverishly to disarm the makeshift suicide bomb. "Clear back here!" she finally called.

"Clear up here," he replied, and backed slowly out of the cab. They stood together, taking deep breaths and looking at the Saab, which had been smashed and torn by the bigger truck.

"Delara is going to be pissed," Kyle said.

"Linda, too," Sybelle answered.

"Let's get inside. This may not be over," he said, and bent down to retrieve his pistol.

JEDDAH, SAUDI ARABIA

GERMAN FINANCIER **D**IETER **N**ESCH hung up his telephone to end the call from Moscow, shook his head slightly, then shrugged away the call. His client, Andrei Ivanov, was checking in still again. The young man's normally confident voice betrayed a sense of nervousness. Nesch considered it to be just a normal reaction for anyone who backed such schemes, which were very expensive to fund and risky to pursue. Nesch had seen it before, when other men with other dreams suddenly found themselves in an unsteady boat with their fates in the hands of others. The tendency to micromanage the situation was overwhelming.

His pale blue eyes moved to the calming scene beyond the window of his villa beside the Red Sea. Tall and skinny palm trees and broad manicured grounds spread toward the nearby beach, and small pleasure boats and sailing craft danced about on the water. Nesch was not nervous at all, and had counseled Ivanov to remain calm. Everything was going fine. The peace process had been utterly destroyed by the attack in Scotland, and that was only the lighting of the fuse. There was much more to come before Saudi Arabia plunged into the abyss.

Dieter Nesch was a most unlikely terrorist, and actually did not view himself that way. It was just another form of business, because somebody had to specialize in handling the money in these situations. He decided to have a bite to eat, and summoned his chef to fix a small plate that would tide him over until dinner. Nesch, in his forties, was only about five foot six and was slightly overweight because of his love for good food and wine. He was always neat and always calm.

That serene ability to remain unflappable usually worked to his advantage. Novices in the game, like the Russian president, usually bordered on panic. Part of his job was to keep them calm. Trust the plan. Trust the man. Nesch had hired the best of the best to handle this coup. They had worked together on numerous occasions in Europe. For now, he must stand back and allow this mad genius to work. From where Nesch stood looking out at the Red Sea, things seemed perfect. The storm was coming soon enough.

INDONESIA

The person whom Dieter had hired to run the show wore only a blue printed batik sarong that reached from his hips to his ankles as he stood barefoot on an immaculate floor of dark teak wood. He used the remote control to surf television news channels: American, Canadian, British, French, and Arab. Things were simmering nicely.

The old castle in Scotland lay in rubble, the historic peace agreement between Saudi Arabia and Israel scuttled, and a number of diplomats dead. The first step was complete. Without sitting, he used the remote and replaced the chattering news people with the web site of a private Swiss financial institution that served only very wealthy customers. The agreed sum of a million euros had been deposited to his private account.

He had never met his benefactor, who had argued for a quick and final strike against the Saudi ruling family, wanting to get it all done in a single day. They were fools. With Dieter Nesch acting as intermediary, he had told them that to achieve permanent changes on such a scale, they had to give up any idea of a temporary upheaval or one day of headlines.

Small scale protests were underway already in several locations. As scheduled, the religious leader Mohammed Abu Ebara was emerging as a spokesman, cloaking his fiery words in the mysteries of Islam. The correspondents were getting interviews, and were putting the bearded face and burning eyes before an international audience of viewers. He turned off the television set and decided to take a nap.

The wide windows in his bedroom of his mountain mansion were open to the sea, with the heat of the afternoon broken by the shade of large trees and a nice breeze that stirred through the big house, heralding an evening rain. He dropped the sarong and climbed naked between light sheets of cool cotton.

No one on the island knew his background. There was speculation, but no one ever asked about the webs of white scars that were lined starkly on the tanned skin of his face, neck, and left shoulder. He had the use of only his right eye and wore a patch over the other. The mouth was always down-turned on that side of his face, as if the muscles were awkwardly locked. The left ear was only a shriveled piece of skin. There were no mirrors in his home and the locals felt an unusual presence of sorcery about him, for how could anyone who had endured so much exterior damage possibly still possess a spirit that had not been equally crippled?

The islands of the Pacific were magnets for such broken men. Throughout the years, soldiers and sailors, writers, adventurers, criminals on the run, businessmen, and others who tired of their old lives, wives, looks, and luck drifted to such havens in Asia and stayed. Many would become bent into commas from spending too many hours leaning on bars and drinking away their dreams. Life could be quite pleasant, but those with get-rich-quick schemes always learned the hard way that the poet Kipling did not lie in warning Occidentals of the fate that befell those "who tried to hustle the East."

Most of them were merely part of the human flotsam and jetsam on the Pacific trade routes, pushed about by the tides of centuries until they eventually were washed away. Nevertheless, generations of *gaijin* in Tokyo, the *farang* in Bangkok, the *gwai-lo* in Beijing, the *tipua* among the Maoris and generations of expats from everywhere had come to Asia to scrub off their homelands and make a new try at life. The Australians said such men had "gone troppo." However hard they tried, they would always remain the big-nosed foreigner, a large person who usually had filthy manners, a loud voice and strange customs and would be welcomed and tolerated, but never truly accepted, even by a new bride's family. There were rare exceptions and the disfigured man on the mountain was one of them.

He knew all about the negatives of living in Asia and did not care. After all, he had to live somewhere and there were not many choices left; certainly none as pleasant as being in this rambling house that overlooked the ocean on one of Indonesia's more than 13,000 islands. Maybe he had gone troppo himself.

HERE ON THE ISLAND, the scarred man was known as Hendrik van Es, a reclusive Dutch entrepreneur, and seemed to be a rather mild person. He stood just under six feet tall, weighed a lean 150 pounds and his full head of hair had turned completely white, although he was still relatively young. His intelligence, generosity, and quiet kindness had won over the inhabitants of the nearby village. Girls who came occasionally to spend the nights would confide to their friends the next day that the lonely man was a good lover, once they closed their eyes, pretending sexual ecstasy but in reality avoiding looking at the awful scars.

He existed in near seclusion, with a Javanese staff running his house and technicians handling his various enterprises out of an attached office complex. He hired only Muslims, although he had long ago rejected the tenets of any religious faith.

The perception of gentleness was inaccurate. He had another name, Juba, and he was once the most wanted terrorist in the world for killing thousands of men, women, and children with biochemical attacks in both London and San Francisco.

Juba lay in his comfortable bed, knowing that sleep would not come. It never did without the aid of narcotics or alcohol. The dreams arrived, however, the pages always turning backward to memories of the man who had turned him into a hideous hermit who lurked on this Indonesian mountain. The thoughts flooded back, unbidden and unwanted.

As a young man, Juba had been a master sniper in the British army, decorated for bravery and promoted up the ranks to color sergeant ahead of his peers. He had worked hard and believed no one was better, a belief that came to a bitter end when he met Kyle Swanson, the best scout-sniper in the U.S. Marines. Worse, Swanson did it more than once, always one step faster, one thought ahead. What had begun as a once-friendly rivalry eventually became fierce combat duels with many lives at stake.

After the biochems, Swanson had hunted him down and left him for dead beneath a destroyed house in Iraq. Juba, a legend among Muslim fighters, had been dug out by villagers, barely alive. At that point in the voyage of dreams, Juba could allow himself a smile. He had endured the pain and re-created himself, almost as if he had risen from the dead. Eventually, some day, somewhere, he would repay Kyle Swanson in full.

The time would come. He would make certain of that. Meanwhile, the burning desire for revenge had become secondary to his resurrected career. Once he had regained his health, Juba organized a private network with a global reach and fielded teams that would provide specialist services for terrorist groups and nations. London and San Francisco had been his high points; now he could reach even higher. It was good to be back in the game.

HE CLOSED HIS ONE good eye and breathed deeply, sliding into meditation. There was no hurry. He would take the next step later, maybe even waiting until after a nice dinner before pushing a button on his computer in Indonesia and making something happen in Riyadh.

The e-mail would hurry through a meet-your-true-love Web site to an address in that troubled country, a warm and flirty message that would raise no curiosity. On the other end was supposedly a woman in Medina, but she did not exist. The true recipient was a soldier who had created the account with a false résumé, complete with the comely photograph of a young woman that he had pirated out of Photobucket.

Who guards the guards? Juba had pondered. More specifically: *Who guards the guards who guard the King?*

KYLE SPRINTED FOR THE front entrance of the clinic, with Sybelle on his heels. A large police sergeant stood in the doorway, arms outstretched and three stripes on each sleeve. "Here now!" he bellowed. "Stop right there! You cannot go inside!"

Swanson raised the FBI credentials.

The cop stood his ground, barely glancing at the wallet. "Sir, I must point out that I don't take orders from you. Would you step back, please?"

Kyle brought the big Colt .45 up and leveled it at the policeman's nose, the smell of burnt cordite still oozing from the barrel. "Get out of my fucking way," he said.

The man still was not budging, despite the pistol. Kyle lowered the weapon. A rugby player, with muscles that bred confidence, he thought, and used the hard metal barrel of the gun to punch him in the solar plexus, folding the sergeant up like a shopping bag. Another guard moved to help, and Sybelle raised her Glock and said, "No." The second policeman stopped.

Kyle put away his Colt and rolled the guard on his side as the man gasped for breath. "We don't have time for this, sergeant. The clinic was just attacked by a suicide bomber. Have your men block every road with their cars and then call for support. Get your SWAT teams, Scotland Yard, or the military, and the sooner the better. I don't think this attack is over. More terrorists may be on the way."

The husky sergeant stared blurry-eyed at the two Americans, then grunted that he understood.

Kyle nodded in sympathy and helped the man to a sitting position. "I'm sorry about hitting you. We are going upstairs to Sir Geoffrey Cornwell's room and set up some interior security. Really, friend. Please. Take this seriously. You absolutely must get some armed security in place, and do not let any unarmed policemen come rushing inside if they hear gunfire. We will handle it."

The second guard protested. "We have two dozen officers protecting this site!"

"This is a war, officer, not some traffic disagreement on a roundabout. That ambulance went right through your police cordon and almost blew this place to hell. My friend and I are standing here holding weapons and you can't do a damned thing about it. How much more proof do you need that your security is for shit? Call now and get some help, for God's sake. Get help!" Swanson and Sybelle left them and barged through the heavy glass doors.

The sergeant sucked air to fill his lungs, then picked up his radio. "Lad seems a bit touchy," he observed to the other officer.

In the distance, they heard the faraway buzzing drone of an approaching small plane.

"WHERE ARE SIR GEOFFREY and Lady Pat Cornwell?" Sybelle had stuffed her weapon into her belt and flashed the FBI credentials as she spoke with a courteous lady at the reception desk at the main entrance. She had moved to the front because she didn't want Kyle blowing away some snotty orderly.

The middle-aged receptionist wore a starched white uniform, buttoned to the neck, with silver hair pulled back in a tight bun. She was polite, but frosty. She had seen what had happened just beyond the glass door and rubbed her hands together in worry. Violence was quite unnecessary, in her opinion. "I cannot reveal any information about our guests, but I have already summoned the clinic administrator. You may speak with him."

Sybelle looked as though she had swallowed a trout. A suicide truck and a possibly imminent terror attack being countered by unarmed cops and a proper stiff-upper-lip Englishwoman at the front desk. "We can't wait," she said, and reached across the desk and snatched several clipboards filled with papers. "Look, ma'am, we have quite an emergency going on right now, and we need to move in a hurry. Some terrorists may be on the way to murder your . . . *guests.* If and when your supervisor arrives, tell him to put the staff into rooms with any other patients, lock the doors and stay put. Help is on the way."

The reception lady protested, "You are not authorized to see those documents. The police are right outside! I shall have them remove you both from the building."

"Whatever." Sybelle had chatted long enough. She knew the woman was not really being contrary, she was just in shock, and would be all right in a few minutes.

Kyle was waiting at the shiny metal doors of the elevator, and Sybelle flipped through the clipboards as she joined him. "Jeff is on the top floor, at the east end of the building. Pat is right next door." The portal opened with a quiet hiss and they stepped inside. The elevator was wide enough to ferry patients on gurneys and smelled antiseptic but with a whiff of lavender. She pressed the button and it lit. "Why do you think more bad guys are on the way?"

As the elevator lifted, Kyle switched magazines in his Colt. "I don't know for sure, but that minivan that we saw pulling away from the ambulance obviously contained at least one more man, the driver, probably more. He might have just been hauling ass away from the area, but the reverse may also be true. These terrorist assholes have evolved in their tactics. Like in Iraq, they are using the old Irish Republican Army trick of staging one attack to draw a crowd and then hitting again."

"A follow-up attack." She continued to check the clipboard.

"Possibly. Maybe a second suicide bomb. Maybe they were planning a ground assault once the bomb went off. Better not to take a chance." The little button lights flashed on the elevator panel when they rose past other floors. "Are there any other high value targets in this place?"

"Are you inquiring if there are other important people amongst our guests?" She mimicked the proper reception desk lady.

"Yeah. Guests who already have had their shit blown away once and are receiving the best medical care money can buy, but nowhere near the best protection."

"There is a Saudi prince who happens to be their ambassador to the

United States occupying the suite at the west end of the corridor on the top floor. Must have been at the castle." Her mind whirred with computations and possibilities. Two of them against who knows how many terrorists, using who knew what kind of weaponry, with no armed and trained counterterrorist force around. Not so much as a kid with a peashooter. Sybelle, however, was confident that the odds were not insurmountable. She was pretty damned good at this game and Kyle was focused and steady. He already had that cold sniper look in his eyes, the curtain had lowered over his emotions and he was easily the most efficient killing machine she had ever met. He caught her glance and winked. She tossed the clipboards aside and made a quick check on her Glock. *Hell, we'll just kill them all by ourselves.*

The elevator stopped and they stepped out with their pistols sweeping the area, Sybelle going right and Kyle heading left. Not a guard beside any door, emphasizing the quietness of a private hospital for the very wealthy. It was a genteel place, more used to providing services to drugged-out entertainers and cosmetic surgery to ladies of a certain age. People on the National Health Service didn't come here, and, to the staff, protection meant keeping away nosy photographers. It was not designed to stop terrorists.

Two nurses behind a central counter looked up, startled. One was young and the other middle-aged, both wearing hospital scrubs with pastel flower tops. Sybelle put a finger to her lips for them to remain silent.

"I'll get to Jeff and Pat," Kyle said. "You take one of these nurses and bring the prince down into Jeff's room. We can set up a barricade in the hallway."

The older nurse instantly sized up what was happening and had no questions. She marched around the counter and told Sybelle she would escort her to the prince's room.

"Kyle!" A shout came from the east end of the hall.

He turned and saw Delara Tabrizi running toward him. With his Colt still in his right hand, Kyle swept her off the floor in a big hug, followed by a kiss that was not much more than a peck. He could not afford to let anything, even happiness, slow him down until they were all safe. Kyle pushed her back gently, bent over, and pulled the .22 caliber pistol from his ankle holster. "Great to see you, honey, but we have to take care of some business before we can celebrate properly. We just nailed a suicide bomber down-stairs and there may be another assault. Your car got scratched. Here. You know how to shoot, and we may need the extra firepower."

"You have the strangest way of saying hello," said Delara, examining the little pistol with the practiced eye of someone used to handling weapons. "Come on. I'll take you to them. What happened to my car?"

"Sir! Mister!" the young nurse called to him. "I have a policeman on the line who says it is urgent that he speak with you." She handed him the tele-phone.

"Are you the FBI bloke what just punched me in the gut?" It was the big cop.

"Yeah. What is it?"

"One of me lads with binoculars says three skydivers have jumped from a little plane about a kilometer away and are using those dark, elliptical airfoils that can be steered. All three are angling this way, coming in fast and hard toward the roof of the clinic. And, mate? They seem to be strapped up with automatic rifles."

SYBELLE! **T**HREE MORE TANGOS parachuting in!" Kyle dropped the telephone receiver and his voice rang loudly in the spacious hallway. "We need to get up there." He looked at the young nurse. "Where is a service door that leads to the roof?"

She was a pale blonde, whose sky blue eyes were huge in confusion and fright. Frozen. Glanced down. "I don't know. Never go up there, do I?"

The senior nurse looked at her, rimless glasses low on her nose. "It's the helicopter landing area, Pauline. Where we bring in guests with serious conditions."

"Oh," said the girl. "I just thought . . ." The rest of the sentence was lost.

"Never mind, dear." The older nurse had been through more than enough emergencies to keep her going straight through a crisis. She pointed to a small door next to the elevator. "Right behind you there, that green door beside the lift," she said. "One flight of stairs up to another green door. It opens outward beneath a sheltered overhang. There is another entrance two floors below, going to a lower roof on the adjacent wing."

"What about the Saudi prince?" Sybelle asked.

"Never concern yourself. I'll get the guests together in the room with Sir Geoffrey," said the nurse. "You two, up the stairs!"

Kyle flashed a smile. "Yes, ma'am. You heard her, Sybelle. Let's go."

They slammed through the door and into a wide, brightly lit stairwell with yellow and white stripes painted diagonally along the edges of the steps. The walls were blue, with neat white trim, and the antiseptic smell trapped in the windowless shaft was almost overwhelming.

"They're going to be armed and might be wired to blow," Kyle said as they took the stairs two at a time. "So we have to kill them before they can land and take control."

"Shit," Sybelle exclaimed. "If these guys are good enough to parasail onto a roof, they'll be well trained."

"Fucking Alamo time. No retreat from here." Kyle held up his hand, in a fist, when he reached the top landing and Sybelle pressed back against the opposite wall. "Probably rigged their harnesses so they will be able to fire while still in the air. As soon as we open the door and step outside, they will try to lay down some suppressive fire."

"Yeah, but they can't work the toggles of their chutes and aim at the same time. Their first job is to get down, and then to use the superior fire-power in the attack. Until then, we have an edge."

"Ready?"

"Do it."

Swanson pushed hard on the exterior door and when it flew open, he followed it around. Sybelle came out in a crouch, running the other way.

Three parachutists were coasting in a line of rectangular chutes, with the lowest one just about to touch down and eyeing the target zone rising beneath his feet.

"You take number one. I got the second guy," Kyle yelled.

Sybelle ran toward the first man, closing the distance fast so that her pistol would have a chance. Beyond twenty-five meters she was toast. The guy was sailing fast and right toward her, helping resolve the distance equa-tion, and did not see her until one of his comrades yelled a warning. By then, Sybelle was in a combat stance with her Glock sighted center-mass on the descending parachutist. She followed his drop for a few feet, then blasted almost a full magazine into him before breaking her stance and div-ing back into the protection of the stairwell as a burst of machine gun fire from the uppermost skydiver stitched the rooftop and the door behind her.

Kyle ran at an angle that kept the air-filled dark parachute of the body that Sybelle was shooting between himself and the next man in the set of paratroop assassins. Only a thin, silk wall of concealment, but better than nothing. Sybelle's target collapsed when it touched down and the canopy lost its air, falling over the body like an instant shroud. Kyle saw that his target had drifted off to the right and was frantically working the toggles of his parachute to control the landing while simultaneously attempting to bring up an automatic rifle into a firing position. It was almost impossible to do both at the same time.

Swanson scrambled behind a small air-conditioning unit to get a little bit of cover as higher up and some thirty meters back, the final skydiver popped off a long burst of fire that chewed around Kyle, then stopped to control his own parachute, working the nine elliptical panels of his canopy to alter the final glide path away from unexpected danger below.

Swanson now could plainly see his target and sighted in with his Colt. Had the man been just a little farther away, the chances of hitting the falling, moving target with a pistol would have been only a fantasy, shooting on a wing and a prayer, but with the reduced distance, Kyle had him cold. The man wore a black full-face helmet and a black jumpsuit and a chest vest packed with extra magazines. Various grenades hung on his web harness. He was only ten meters away, looking across his right shoulder toward Kyle and trying to swing his rifle around but watching the big pistol tracking him, looking to be about the size of a cannon, and then Kyle opened fire.

He squeezed the trigger and ignored a return burst of machine-gun fire, the ricocheting, *zzzzzing* sound of the bullets passing close and chipping concrete in order to match the movement of the skydiver who was descending about 45 degrees to his right. He got a hit in the man's right thigh, then kept the bucking pistol tight on target and let the torso of his man fall through the target picture. The large .45 caliber bullets marched up to the head, the final shot smashing through the helmet. Kyle spun to look for the third skydiver. Not there.

THE SPACIOUS SUITE IN which Sir Geoffrey Cornwell lay immobile on a bed occupied the entire east end of the hall on the top floor of the clinic. It included the patient's room and an adjoining private bathroom. The sterile look of the medical area ended at the doorway, for a comfortable sitting room separated the patient's room from a second bedroom, giving the suite a hybrid look of being both a physician's paradise and an elegant hotel. Everything had been considered during the design process except that the room might some day be the site of a last stand during a terrorist assault.

Jeff was a former colonel in the British SAS, but his normally sharp gray eyes were unfocused due to the light sedation and he could only see what was happening as if he were watching it underwater. Both legs were in casts and a thick bandage was wrapped around his head, a rubber tube leading from beneath the covering to drain fluid from the head injury. He had already undergone emergency surgery for internal bleeding caused by tiny fragments of stone.

Lady Pat, her own left arm in a sling, and both eyes circled by purple-green bruises, was seated beside the bed, gently stroking her husband's cheek and whispering to keep him calm.

Delara Tabrizi stood just inside the open door, keeping the small pistol pointed at the floor. There was no option of moving Jeff to a more secure location, but the nurses pushed the bed out of the direct line of the doorway, and were busy adjusting the IVs and monitors.

Prince Abdullah, a tall, slender, handsome man wearing freshly pressed black trousers and a loose blue shirt instead of Arab robes, hobbled down the hallway toward the room, leaning on a cane with one hand and with the other upon the arm of his fifteen-year-old son, a younger version of himself. He smiled at her.

"Miss Tabrizi. Fully armed and dangerous," he joked when he saw the small pistol.

"Mr. Ambassador. Please excuse me for having a weapon in your presence." She gave a slight bow of her head in respect.

"Nonsense, Delara. That shooting we are hearing up on the roof means that your weapon is most welcome in our current situation." He looked over the situation, shifted his attitude and took command.

"Let me have the pistol, Delara. I'm an old soldier. I will stand guard while you and my son and the nurses shift all the furniture you can just outside the doorway here to create an obstacle. Make sure the legs are pointed outward, toward any attacker. Lock the adjoining doors to the sitting room."

The prince looked over at Sir Jeff. Lady Patricia could not smile back, and ever so slightly shook her head in dismay. Abdullah walked over and squeezed Jeff's hand, then went back to the door, checked the pistol and knew it was really no protection at all against a military-style assault. The only open question was whether the man and woman who had gone charging up the stairwell were really capable of fighting trained terrorists. He shrugged and settled a shoulder against the doorframe. *Allah's will.*

KYLE SWANSON HUSTLED TO the small parapet that lined the edge of the roof, keeping his head low but still having to duck when a crisp three-shot burst of fire slashed into the concrete and sent big chips flying. He fired blindly twice over the edge, then carefully looking over it, he saw only a thick and spreading cloud of gray smoke. "He popped a smoke grenade! Probably going inside two floors down."

Sybelle was rummaging through the equipment on the two dead terrorists, tearing off the H&K MP5 submachine guns and pulling spare magazines from the chest pouches. She gave one of the weapons to Kyle as he ran past and followed him back into the stairwell.

The intruder was disoriented. The firefight had forced him to land on the roof of the third floor of the clinic and his target was on the top floor. Under the smoke cloud, he kicked his way through the door of the adjacent building and found himself on the floor of a wide landing that led to the ascending staircase. With the MP5 tight against his shoulder, he moved slowly up the steps.

SWANSON HALTED BEFORE GOING beyond the landing on the fifth floor and whispered to Sybelle, "Don't use the MP5s yet. We have to draw him out, so stay with the pistols. Make him think that's all we have." He cracked two rounds from his Colt .45 down the stairwell, the sound amplified by the enclosed, area, and the bullets gouged out chunks of the wall and whined away in wild ricochets.

The attacker below paused on his step, but did not see anyone, which meant the defenders had no clear line of sight and the firing was meant only to slow him down. A pistol, not an automatic. Move. He ascended two more steps and stopped at the middle landing, where the stairs zig-zagged higher. A blue door with a white number 4 painted on it was to his right. He leaned out and fired a short burst through the door to clear it, then another burst upward in retaliation for the few shots that had come down. Keep their heads down.

Kyle shifted back into the main corridor on the fifth floor and tucked into the slight recess of the elevator entrance, which provided partial concealment and a minimum of cover along the length of his body. On his call, Sybelle dashed out, closing the door behind her and then rolled over the flat counter of the vacant nurses' station.

At the east end of the building, the doorway to Jeff's room looked like a porcupine, with the legs of chairs and small tables pointing outward in a jumble of furniture that had been stacked to block entry. Kyle saw a few heads of people watching, and waved for them to get their heads down and take cover.

Almost as he signaled, the door to the fifth floor hallway was blown inward by a small amount of C-4 that the terrorist had applied to the hinges. A terrific roar jarred the entire floor and debris needled straight out into the hallway opposite the destroyed door. The man was moving fast, knowing he had to complete his mission before assistance could arrive for the opposition.

Kyle had counted on that. He turned away from the blast, then spun back and triggered the Colt twice at the empty portal. The metal door was gone. Sybelle added two more rounds into the whirling smoke.

"I'm dry," Kyle called in a panicky voice, dropping the .45 and bringing up the H&K submachine gun.

"I have a few rounds left," Sybelle responded, making her voice also sound shaky. She also laid aside her pistol, charged the MP5 and rested it on the countertop.

The terrorist on the landing was listening and deciding his next move. He had counted two opponents on the roof, but they were armed only with pistols and almost out of ammunition. If he kept the pressure on with a spray-and-pray assault he could overwhelm them, and then deal with the Saudi prince he had been sent to kill. He pulled a grenade from his belt and removed the pin.

The cylindrical device came bouncing out of the doorway and Kyle yelled, "Flash-bang!" He stepped away from his hiding place and gave the explosive device a perfect kick that sent it spinning down the west end of the hall. Then he dove face-first back into the elevator alcove and Sybelle ducked her head and covered her eyes.

Designed to stun opponents long enough for a soldier or a policeman to breach into a room, the little grenade erupted with a blinding blaze that bathed the corridor with light that seemed brighter than the sun as a simultaneous cracking peal of thunder made the walls vibrate.

The intruder stormed through the door, trigger held back, firing on automatic. His eyes were protected by goggles, but his overall vision was obscured by the curling smoke. He let the MP5 chatter constantly as he ranged it from side to side and managed to take three running strides before Kyle and Sybelle both opened up and caught him in a crossfire at point-blank range. The bullets chewed at him mercilessly, jerking the body upright, and then pounding him backward and finally down.

When the shooting stopped, Kyle stepped over to the fallen terrorist. There was something strange about the face. He was not a man from the Middle East. White skin, no beard, and light brown hair. The terrorist appeared more Slavic, like someone from one of the Eastern European nations, and had performed as if he had been steeped in professional training. No matter. Swanson pressed the muzzle of the H&K to the man's temple, and squeezed off a final shot. The head cracked like a melon.

"Clear!" Swanson called.

RIYADH, SAUDI ARABIA

THE **BRITISH!" PRINCE GENERAL** Mamoud Ali al-Fahd, the commander of the Saudi Royal Guard Regiment, had been raging since the first reports of the terrorist attack on the castle in Scotland. "They refused to believe that something like this could happen! They pledged their honor!"

The general's job was to protect the king, which he did with a beefed-up elite force of three light infantry battalions and an armored battalion. Putting a similar shield around Prince Abdullah should have been someone else's problem, and was impossible to accomplish from Riyadh, because the prince was the Saudi ambassador to the United States and spent most of his time in Washington. But His Majesty had declared that Abdullah was too important to be left with just ordinary diplomatic protection and al-Fahd had been personally instructed that in addition to his regular duties, the general also would coordinate the prince's security and see that no harm befell him. Geography alone forced al-Fahd to delegate others to carry out that royal edict, and that weakness had been its defeat. The general could not be everywhere at once and if the others failed, it would still be Prince General Mamoud al-Fahd who would be blamed.

Vice Sergeant Mas'ud Mohammed al-Kazaz, the soldier who had been his valet for seven years, quietly placed a polished silver tray with hot tea and small cakes on a table beside his general. "Please have something to eat, sir. You must keep up your strength, for the good of the kingdom," the valet said.

"I am not hungry." The general waved at the tray. "Take it away."

"Not until you eat, sir." The valet stubbornly left the tray. He was one of the few men who could talk back to the general, although he did so with a polite and reverent tone. "Please sit down so I can pull off your boots."

Al-Fahd propped one boot on the sergeant's broad behind and raised the other leg between the knees of his aide. The vice-sergeant grasped the heel and gave it a hearty pull. He flipped it to the side, the general changed feet, and the second boot was pulled off. The general gave into the moment and had a drink of tea and bit into a sweet cake. Delicious. Another bite and another sip before the anger returned.

Al-Fahd got back up and paced the private suite of rooms that comprised the living space at his private headquarters. He had just returned from another tour of his forces in the field, heightening their alert status due to the incident in Scotland and the rash of confidential reports about civil unrest that were coming in from around the country. The general felt that the narrow line of light that held back the darkness of chaos was cracking, and smacked a fist into a palm in frustration.

"They assured me that our ambassador would be supremely well-protected and that nothing could possibly happen to him because so many security people were involved at an isolated location." Al-Fahd rubbed his red-rimmed eyes. "Did they think this was some *Lawrence of Arabia* film and a British hero would ride in on a white camel to set things straight? We were allowed to have only three . . . *three* . . . of our own security men with him. Outrageous. The Brits were arrogant and insolent and wrong!"

Vice Sergeant al-Kazaz was used to hearing his general grumble while they were alone, when the man could express the intense thoughts he would never utter to a staff officer or outsider. "Yes, sir, they were. But may I remind my general that the ambassador survived, and that our king is safe and the guard lines are strong. That is your primary duty, and you have performed it well." The valet unbuckled the brass round hasp of the pistol belt and laid the holstered weapon on a table, then helped the tired man remove his sweat-stained tunic and also laid it aside to be cleaned.

The prince gave him a tired smile. Al-Kazaz was always there, a comfortable shadow and as much of a friend as any common soldier could ever be to a prince of the House of Saud. The hard-working son of a small business owner from an allied tribe had compiled a good military record and after a thorough background check, won appointment to the Royal Guard. Intelligent, quick, quiet and competent, he was an ideal aide, hardly ever noticed but always around, usually carrying whatever was needed before the general had to ask.

"Yes. Prince Abdullah was saved by the hand of the Prophet and his wounds were not serious. He is now in a private clinic, and the British have promised even more that he is safe." Al-Fahd paused. "How can this be believed? I have scheduled a plane to take him back to Washington as soon as possible."

"They cannot be believed, sir. The plane is the correct response," answered his valet, agreeing with anything his general said in order to push him along. "Your trousers, please, sir, and then into the shower. You look like a camel herder. Smell like one, too."

Prince General al-Fahd had to laugh. "You dare order me around like I'm a private. I should have you whipped!" He went to a safe imbedded in the thick concrete wall, turned the dial, and opened it. The general removed a thin chain from around his neck that contained not only his military dog tags but also a small key, and placed it in the safe. From his wallet, he withdrew a small red plastic card embossed with black numbers and also put it inside, atop a small book lanced with the red stripe of Top Secret material, then closed and locked the little door. When those two items were not on his person, they were always in the safe. Allah forbid them falling into the wrong hands.

He stripped off his remaining clothes and went into the bathroom and entered the enclosure where the valet already had a steaming shower running. The flood of cool water washed away worry as well as dirt. When he stepped out, al-Kazaz handed him a warm, huge blue towel.

"I have your family on the telephone, sir," he said.

The general sat on his bunk and had a brief conversation with his wife and both of their children. All was well at home, Allah be thanked. "A fresh uniform, if you please, vice-sergeant."

"Sir, this would be a good time for you to get a few hours of sleep. You must rest if the country is to survive this crisis. A fatigued man makes mental mistakes," insisted the mild, polite voice. He handed over a set of pressed pajamas.

"There is no time to sleep, Mas'ud," the general replied, although the soft bed seemed to tug at him. He yawned. "There is just so much to do."

"I will awaken you if there is a real emergency. The appropriate forces are dealing with this rebellion of dogs in the slums, sir, and it will all be over soon. We protect the king and I must not let your attention be diverted from that holy cause. I'll fetch the chief of staff in four hours to brief you."

"All of these developments . . . so awfully bad." The general stretched out.

"There is nothing more you can do about it for the time being, sir. I am sure that Prince Abdullah is now probably the most protected man on earth. I will finish my chores here and then take a chair right beside your door."

Prince General al-Fahd felt his muscles agree to what his mind was fighting, and he relaxed. "Very well, vice-sergeant. You're the boss."

"Rest then, soldier. It is lights out for you." He had dimmed the two big fixtures and only a soft 75-watt bulb of a lamp beside the bed remained on, not enough to tempt him to read more reports. The valet turned off the final switch and the room went pitch dark.

Soldier? The tension was broken by the small impertinence. The general turned on his left side and stretched and began to doze immediately although sounds still came to him. There was the low buzz of the central air-conditioning, and Mas'ud was busying himself gathering the dirty laundry, the boots, the pistol and the belt, and the tea tray. The full uniform would be cleaned, brass bright and leather polished, by the time the prince general awoke. He listened to the familiar sliding of oiled metal and clicks of his 9 mm Heckler & Koch pistol. Just Mas'ud unloading the magazine and clearing the chamber to be sure the weapon was safe before taking it away for cleaning.

His soldier's mind registered something odd. The procedure, which he had heard thousands of times, didn't sound right. Something was out of sequence. He snapped awake in the darkness and managed to partially turn onto his back but was out of time, and could neither see, fight, nor shout.

Mas'ud had wrapped the dirty uniform around the pistol, aimed the muzzle close to the face, and was already pulling the trigger. The head of Prince General al-Fahd was punched open by the big bullets. Blood, brains, and bone fragments from the commander of the Royal Guard Regiment spewed onto the cot and slapped onto the wall in a fan-shaped pattern. The folded clothes had silenced the gunshots.

The valet snapped the table lamp on again and carefully checked his own uniform and body for blood spots. There were none. He threw the clothes onto the dead man and reloaded. The turncoat assassin hurried over to the safe and unlocked it. He had watched the general do it so many times that he had long ago memorized the combination and even practiced opening the little vault when he was alone in the room. Grabbing the key, the red card, and a small booklet, Mas'ud stuck them in his pocket, turned out the light and left, locking the door behind him. Leaving the building, he passed along the order to the chief of staff that the general did not wish to be disturbed until 0600 the next morning.

The vice sergeant slid behind the wheel of the shining black staff Mercedes and drove away unmolested, heading for a nearby mosque to deliver the key and the red card to his imam, and then onto the fashionable home of the prince general to murder the general's family. Only one more task would remain after that: He would turn the weapon on himself and become a martyr, trading his life for the good of the jihad and a promised payment of money to his impoverished family. He had received a love note by e-mail.

THE WHITE HOUSE

WHAT DO WE HAVE on this soldier who pulled the trigger on his own general?" President Mark Tracy was interrogating his team of close advisers in the Oval Office.

Steve Hanson, his chief of staff, sighed and leaned back against one of the small couches on the edge of the huge circular rug that bore the eagle symbol of the United States. A bright sun streamed in through the bullet-proof glass windows but the air-conditioning kept the inside comfortable. Hanson worked in rolled-up shirtsleeves and had assembled the various dossiers compiled by the CIA, the U.S. embassy in Riyadh, and the Defense Department. "Sir, the guy was a product of the Islamic religious schools, a *madrassa*, where the Koran is their primary text. Saudi intel says one of his teachers long ago was a hate-based radical who preached the need for a religious government in Saudi Arabia. By the time the preacher died in prison about nine years ago, he had churned out some pretty violent followers. There's no way that he actually could have steered this soldier for this exact operation, not so many years in advance, but he certainly planted the seed."

Bartlett Geneen, the director of the CIA, was on the other couch. Wisps of white hair curled around his balding head and deep worry lines etched his face, tracks of having been around the spook business for a long time. "It has all the looks of a one-man terrorist cell. The soldier bided his time, followed his instincts, and waited for the right moment. Those are almost impossible to detect or stop."

The president sat still and considered that, taking a sip from a cup of coffee, then returning the sturdy Navy mug to a little table beside him. The

Saudis had helped bring this crisis down on themselves in so many ways. How far had the rot penetrated the supporting structure? A Muslim kid going to a village school twenty years ago had learned the wrong lessons and now his problems had become the world's problem. "So he acted alone? Killed the general and the general's family? People who apparently treated him kindly and considered him a friend, and then he commits suicide? It makes no sense."

"No, Mr. President, it doesn't. Such things happen, so we can't rule it out. But I agree with you. This one smells. It happened right on the heels of the Scotland attack, and that is too much of a coincidence for me to accept. We can't prove it yet, but I think he was acting on someone's specific order to hit that specific target."

"Then there's the other odd piece of that puzzle that hasn't been put in place yet," said Hanson. "The safe was found open in the general's room and the aide's fingerprints were on the dial, but it doesn't look like anything is missing. There was cash in there and some secret military plans that might have been given to the radicals. They were untouched."

"So what was he after? A lone wolf murderer doesn't murder an important officer then stick around to open a safe just to exercise his fingers."

"That we don't know yet, sir," answered Geneen. "The Saudis say they are working on it."

President Tracy shook his head. "Keep me posted, but let's move on to the central question: The rebellion is growing, but will it succeed?" His eyes darted back to the CIA director.

"Too early to tell, Mr. President. So far, the military seems to be holding it all together, but crowds are making things tricky in the cities and the religious police are really ramping up the shouting, hollering about how the royals betrayed Islam and have to be eliminated."

"Eliminated?"

"Killed or driven out of the country." Director Geneen snapped shut the buff folder that was propped on his knees. "The murder of Prince General al-Fahd will shake the confidence of the ruling family. If the commander of the Saudi Royal Guard Regiment can be assassinated by his valet, then who among them is truly safe? We're picking up backchannel traffic that some of the minor princes are inquiring about possible emergency flights to other countries."

Hanson studied his notes. "It's the domino effect. If some leave, they all could start pulling out with the idea of living on their fortunes in investments abroad. The princes head for Monaco, Paris, and New York while the House of Saud falls to the clerics and the mobs."

"We can't let that happen," said the president.

"We can't stop it," responded the CIA official.

"So the question is going to boil down to military intervention to support our friends. Do we have forces available to help?"

General Hank Turner, the chairman of the Joint Chiefs of Staff, picked up the conversation. "Yes, sir. We have one carrier battle group in the area and another can be on station in a week. For ground forces, we can retask divisions out of Iraq and shift armor in there fast. Plenty of air power available throughout in the region."

"Jesus," said Steve Hanson. "We jump from one war to another over there. No offense, general, but I don't know if that's going to be the answer this time."

"I never said it was, Steve. The president asked to know his options," said Turner, unruffled by the oblique challenge. Part of the game.

"What's on your mind, Steve?" The president and Hanson had come into political office from the business world, where they had headed one of the biggest electronics corporations in the nation. Hanson was never shy about sharing his opinions.

"We need another full-fledged war like a dog needs a scooter. The bottom line is the Saudi oil, which is the only reason the king and his court are important at all."

"The United States gets more oil from Canada than it does from the Saudis, and almost as much from Mexico," the CIA director pointed out. "We could actually get along without them for a while, particularly if Iraq develops its full potential."

Hanson agreed, with a serious look at the president. "It will disrupt the flow, and I don't think Americans are going to like to deal with oil that could cost hundreds of dollars per barrel. Nevertheless, the kingdom is the world's gas station. It has one-fifth of the entire global reserves and we're not the only ones watching what is going on over there. Those reserves need to be protected and traded legitimately on the world market."

"I don't like where your scenario is heading, Steve," said the president. "We will not throw our friends in Riyadh under the bus, let their government fall and then just move in ourselves to take over the Saudi oil operations, even as an honest broker."

"Sir, the hardest decision the Saudi government might have to face in this crisis would be deciding whether to allow thousands of American troops to enter the country if their own military proves insufficient or riddled with disloyalty. Just because we are willing to commit forces in there does not mean they will allow us to intervene."

The president crossed his arms and chewed at his thumbnail in silence for a few moments. Thoughts rushed through his mind. *So much to do. A new secretary of state must be appointed right away and there will be a state funeral at Arlington tomorrow for my old friend Ken Waring. Saudi Arabia is coming to a fast boil. Perhaps a UN force to stabilize the oil fields? All that and a half-dozen other crisis points on completely different issues that have nothing to do with foreign relations.* He rubbed his eyes.

"Is the Saudi ambassador back yet?" President Tracy stood. The meeting was over.

"He's on the way. Our last word was that he was planning to leave the clinic in England today. Prince Abdullah will be a good guy for us to have around right now."

"Please let him know that I want to see him as soon as he gets in," said the president. "There must be some way out of this problem."

Hanson looked at the others and gave a silent nod and they began to leave the room. "We're on it, sir," he said. "Look at it this way. Things could not be much worse."

"Steve, the one thing that I've learned in this job is that things can always get worse."

ENGLAND

WITH THE FIREFIGHT DONE, the British police again took control of the clinic. No medical personnel rushed to assist the downed gunmen. The assassins were no longer objects to be feared, just garbage to be carried away. Kyle handed his H&K MP5 to the first cop he saw, a burly youngster who came through the destroyed stairwell door and stopped abruptly at the sight of the dead man in the hallway.

Swanson walked fast toward the makeshift barrier that blocked the doorway to Sir Jeff's suite and helped tear it down. He brushed past Prince Abdullah with hardly a glance to get to Lady Pat, who threw her good arm around his neck and hugged him tightly. He bent over and kissed her on the check.

"That took you long enough," she said with a mocking smile.

Delara Tabrizi also gave him another hug, and stood to the side, knowing that her own true welcome would be better delivered in private. She wanted more than a polite hospital room embrace.

Kyle turned to the bed and fought to keep his face neutral. Jeff's normally round and florid face was almost narrow and the hearty body seemed deflated. Tubes and the bandages and leg casts left no doubt of his grave injuries. The only thing unchanged were the bright gray eyes under the heavy brows, gray eyes that were focused on Kyle. He put his hand lightly on Jeff's arm. "Hey, buddy. How about you get dressed so we can go have a few pints, chase women, and smoke cigars?" Almost nothing there. He took Jeff's hand and held it.

Jeff nodded recognition, fighting the sedation. "Not today, lad. Pat won't allow it," he whispered. The voice was hoarse from having a breathing tube down his throat for two days. "Glad you're here."

The man's eyes shifted momentarily. "Sybelle?"

"Yes. I'm here, too." She kissed him on the forehead.

"I thought I heard gunfire. Just a dream?"

"Nothing to worry about," Sybelle said in a soothing tone. "Kyle and I sorted it out."

Kyle changed from the serious. "So what the hell happened to you?" Kyle slid a hip onto the bed, his tone remaining gentle.

"You were right. The castle was vulnerable."

"No shit? Hard way to prove the point. How do you feel, old man?"

"I've been worse. Cannot feel my legs and the rest of my body is not much better. Got some kind of hole in my head. Been beaten up harder than this in a rugby scrum." The frail smile returned.

"Sure you have. I understand they are gonna open your skull tomorrow morning and poke around inside. God knows what they might find. Bats, maybe."

There was a slow nod. "No choice. The neurosurgeon says I may sail right through the operation without a problem. He also says I may die on the table or become a vegetable. After that, they will play with my spine."

"You can't believe doctors. We'll be lucky if he doesn't sew a glove up inside you."

Jeff chuckled and laid his head back further onto the soft pillow. Winced. "Yes. Quite. I'll make it fine, to be sure."

Lady Pat put her finger to her lips, signaling Kyle to back down. She recognized that the joy of the reunion was sapping up Jeff's strength. "We need to discuss something with you, Kyle," she said.

He raised an eyebrow as Jeff and Pat exchanged looks, and she proceeded. "We have been talking about the future."

Jeff put pressure on his hand. "You must take care of Pat if I don't make it."

"Of course I will take care of her. Always." Their relationship had begun years ago when Kyle had been loaned by the Marines to Cornwell as a technical advisor. The initial casual relationship had grown into a strong friendship and then beyond that, until it had almost reached a family situation.

Lady Pat said. "We believe the time has come to bring you directly into Excalibur Enterprises."

"What? You know I can't do that!" Swanson protested, feeling as if a bucket of water had just been poured over him. "Damn, you saved this bombshell for a hospital bed? I'm cornered like a rat here. You know I don't want to leave the Marines, and I can't have a conflict of interests by working for you at the same time."

"Clever, aren't we," Jeff grunted.

Pat looked at Kyle with cool eyes. "Oh, do not panic. Jeff is going to be fine, but this incident has demanded that we firm up some planning. When you finally leave the Marines, which you must do some day whether you like it or not, we want to add you to the board of directors. It is not hard work: You would attend meetings in London twice a year."

"Look, guys. We have gone through your job offers before and my answer has never changed. I love you both, but I'm a gunnery sergeant in the Corps, not a businessman. I don't have a college degree and, anyway, I'm American, not British."

Pat batted away the protests with a flip of her fingers. "Kyle, the university degree is meaningless compared to your life experience and your loyalty. Our lawyers tell us the nationality makes no difference, because we are an international company."

Swanson wanted to shout that he was a killer, not an accountant, but they both already knew that. He had spent a long military career weighing battlefield options in emergency situations, believing there was always hope, always a way out, always something that he could do to tilt a situation in his favor. This time, there was nothing at all he could do except rely upon the skills of the surgeons to bring Jeff through safely. Rejecting the offer outright might demoralize this man who meant so much to him.

Jeff managed another hand squeeze. "For now, you stay in the Marines and remain our best friend. When the time comes, that position will be waiting for you. Generals and admirals go to work for defense contractors all the time, Kyle, and most of them work out their deals unofficially before they retire from the military. So why can't a gunnery sergeant do the same?"

Pat fussed over her husband for a minute until she was certain that he was not exerting himself too much. All of the monitors read normal numbers and lines. She continued the discussion. "Excalibur posted a 34.1 percent growth last year with more than $300 million in sales, and we have a work force of about 500 people. To keep growing, we need to bring in capital for expansion. We will offer ten million shares at ten dollars a share. The under-writers think it will rise to at least forty a share after the initial price offering and will double that in five years."

Lady Pat winked. "You didn't think this old girl knew about all of this business stuff, did you? Your compensation on being appointed would be a hundred thousand shares of Excalibur stock, enough to make certain that the two of us maintain the controlling interest on the board. You're going to be a rich man, Kyle."

Swanson was stunned. *Damn, those were a lot of zeroes.* He wanted to run from the room and get away from this hobbling sense of obligation. He chose to temporize. If he agreed, it would take a big worry off Jeff's mind as he prepared for the delicate head surgery. If the worst happened, Kyle did not have to join Excalibur until he retired from the Marines, and by then he might figure out something or Pat might let him out of the deal.

Something could be worked out and Pat would come out of it all fabu-lously wealthy. It could all be fixed. He just could not go negative now and let an argument tear at Jeff's strength.

He gave a reassuring smile. "Okay. If that's what you want, I will give it my best. I mean, how bad can it be to be filthy rich?" He hated himself for lying.

"A THOUSAND PARDONS," said a deep voice behind them. "Lady Patricia, Sir Geoffrey, I am so pleased that you did not suffer further harm on my ac-count. These attacks! They never seem to stop!" Prince Abdullah was stand-ing nearby, in total control of himself. He extended his hand to Kyle.

"My thanks to you, sir. I have seldom witnessed such courage as shown by you and Major Summers. You saved us all."

Lady Pat made the introduction. "Mister Ambassador, let me present Gunnery Sergeant Kyle Swanson of the U.S. Marines. Kyle, this is Prince Abdullah of Saudi Arabia, the kingdom's ambassador in Washington."

Kyle stood and shook the offered hand, surprised to find a muscular grip that was not the sign of a gym rat. "I'm glad we were able to be in the right place at the right time," he said.

"I understand that you two also dealt with a suicide bomber in a truck downstairs."

Kyle shrugged. Something was there behind those dark eyes.

"My country is in your debt, Gunny Swanson, and you have my gratitude. If ever I can be of assistance, please call on me."

"Thank you, sir." Swanson remained polite. The prince had used the term "Gunny" without hesitation. A civilian would not automatically make that slang connection. So was this dandy also a soldier?

Abdullah turned to the others. "Now, I have interrupted your reunion long enough. I am preparing to fly back to Washington immediately. The kingdom has been thrown into great turmoil and I need to be at my post. Sir Geoffrey, we are all wishing you well tomorrow, and I am confident that you will be recovering quickly. It will take more than a bash on the head to slow down such a warrior as you. Your efforts to broker peace eventually will be successful. We are determined to make it happen. Lady Pat, you put on the most unusual parties." He took her hand and kissed it, then shook hands with Delara. When he walked away, trailed by his son, his stride was one of confidence. The ruling family of Saudi Arabia would not give way easily to terrorists and plotters.

"Interesting guy," Kyle said. "He does that diplomatic tap-dance pretty well."

"He is sort of a mystery to most of us," Pat said. "He has a hard core in there somewhere. Like when he took the little pistol to be our final guard. He did it without hesitation and I have no doubt he would have faced death without flinching."

Kyle felt Jeff touch his hand again. The eyes were closing because a nurse had increased the sedation flowing through the tubes. He was about to go back to sleep, but wanted to say something first. Kyle leaned close. "What is it?"

"Don't trust him . . ." Jeff managed to say, the words fading. The hand squeezed weakly, urgently. The next words could barely be heard. "They . . . have . . . nukes!"

DELARA TABRIZI CAME AWAKE in the big, soft bed with the covers pulled to her chin as if someone had tucked her in. *Kyle. Where is he?*

It was after midnight and they had been together since leaving the clinic some six hours earlier. Delara stretched, letting her fingers touch the wooden headboard as she relished their urgent, hungry rush to sex, their clothes flying off almost by the time the door was closed. They had not seen each other for weeks and the extreme emotional situation that had brought them back together only heightened their needs. The first time wasn't making love, it was just a confirmation that they were both still alive and in each other's arms. The second time took a lot longer. She had fallen asleep wrapped in his arms, her dark hair spread on his chest.

She pushed away the covers and wrapped herself in the dark blue terry-cloth bathrobe furnished by the hotel. A nightlight in the small kitchen of the hotel suite glowed a dull orange and she moved toward it soundlessly, her bare feet on deep, plush carpet and then onto chilly tile. Nobody there. She went into the darkened living room and found him standing before the big windows, staring out into the thick fog. His face was a grim mask, his eyes fixed out on the water, the chest rising and falling with heavy breaths and his fists clenched at his side. The muscles of his naked body were as taut as cables.

Delara stopped and pulled the robe tight around her body, realizing that her lover was dreaming, almost fighting, and still sound asleep.

KYLE **S**WANSON STOOD BESIDE *a broad, swift-flowing river wearing full combat gear, from boots to helmet, and cradling his custom-made Excalibur sniper rifle in*

his arms. The Colt .45 rested in a holster at his waist and a large Ka-Bar combat knife with a razor's edge and some grenades hung from his vest. His feet
were apart but only as wide as his shoulders, giving him perfect balance. He
watched with an intense alertness as the small boat approached, emerging
from a rough cloud of dark ash that swirled over the water's surface.

"You can't have him," Swanson announced. It was a declaration. No nego-
tiation.

The Boatman giggled, and the shrill tone warbled on the night air. A filthy
black robe hung loosely about him, with a tail of rotten cloth drooping over
the side of the boat and into the water. With a last hard shove on the long
stern oar, the bony figure nudged the boat forward. "Of course I can have
him. I can take anyone I want."

"Not Jeff. Not now."

The Boatman cackled again. "Now, look at you standing there with all of
those weapons. Surely you do not believe that you can stop me with them?"

"I just wanted to show how serious I am. These weapons have provided you
with a lot of passengers over the years. You owe me."

The boat swung broadside, facing into the current and a small wave of
foam divided around the bow. The Boatman steadied it. "Yes. I am here to
clean up from your work yesterday. Four more souls." He raised a thin arm and
pointed. "Here they come. Right on time."

Swanson detected movement and turned. Four shadowy figures with dead
eyes, gory wounds in their phantom bodies, stumbled along in a single line,
stepped onto the surface of the water without causing a ripple and then into
the craft, taking seats, facing forward. Kyle recognized them as the terrorists
he and Sybelle had killed at the clinic, but felt no pity. They had chosen their
fates.

"To hell with these guys," he said. "What about Jeff?"

"To hell with them, indeed." The Boatman lowered his voice to a menac-
ing hiss. "And with the many others who will be coming over soon. Watch how
my garden grows." A scrawny arm in a flapping sleeve swung around and
pointed to a far horizon. The ash falling on the water changed to black rain.
An incandescent white and orange light flashed, seeming to push a moment of
absolute stillness ahead of it and a cyclone of wind swept over the water and a
volcanic explosion vibrated the world. Five mushroom clouds blossomed in se-

quence, clawing and rolling in the sky, pushing the acrid smell of burning sulfur across the vastness.

"Nuclear winter is coming," said the apparition.

"Not if I can help it."

The specter gave a dismissive, coughing laugh. "Ah. You cannot."

"What about Jeff?"

"He is not yet dead, not for several more hours," said the Boatman. "I will take these passengers and collect him on my next trip. I always have plenty of time. An eternity."

Swanson carefully laid down the sniper rifle and removed the Colt .45 from the holster, raising the muzzle until it touched his right temple. "Let me take his place. I'll pull this trigger right now and get in your fuckin' boat."

The Boatman leaned on his long oar again, preparing to shove off. "I already have you. We both know that. Right now, you remain my faithful assistant, a mass murderer who provides a remarkable stream of corpses for me. I decline your dramatic offer because you are a tool of destiny."

"If I blow my fucking head off, you get no more passengers from me."

The Boatman held out his skeletal palm inches from Kyle's face. "Wait, then. You are irrational, but that is an interesting point. So, hmmm, I will agree to a bargain. I do not want to remove you from this plain of misery yet because I still need you here. Put down the pistol. I won't take your friend, for he really makes no difference to me, but you must continue killing."

There was silence. Kyle put away the pistol and picked up the Excalibur rifle. "Deal," he said, his gaze going beyond the little boat to stare at the big explosions rocking the imaginary horizon. The end of the world.

The boat was in motion when he looked at it again, and the Boatman was rowing away with a slow rhythm. Swanson brought Excalibur to his shoulder, locked into a standing position to shoot. He centered the scope on the head of the Boatman and pulled the trigger, sending out a heavy .50 caliber bullet that delivered a powerful kick to his shoulder. The cloth covering the Boatman's head flicked as the bullet passed through.

A bark of laughter came back loud and clear and strong. "Yes! We have a fair bargain. You get half and I get half. You may keep your friend, but you may not like what you get!" The boat and its dreadful captain vanished. Black rain dripped from Kyle's helmet and raw ash flew in his face. He sneezed.

* * *

KYLE TOPPLED TO THE carpeted floor of the hotel room when his legs collapsed. Delara rushed forward and wrapped her arms around him. His muscles shivered in iron-tight spasms and his eyes opened and rolled back momentarily, then the lids closed again. Over the years, he had developed a habit of finding a quiet time after significant battles to let his mind process the carnage he had wrought, and the Boatman often paddled in for a talk during those moments.

The shaking eased away and his breathing steadied. The Boatman accused him of being a mass murderer and Swanson had yelled back in the silence of their private world, shouting that it was bullshit. He was no psychotic maniac, no serial killer with a placid exterior, for he took no pleasure in killing. Somebody had to do what was necessary in these times of desperation and Kyle Swanson happened to be talented in that unique line of work.

"I am no murderer," he said, just loud enough for Delara to hear him, and then he slept.

He finally awoke two hours later when the first rays of the new day came through the window. The fog was gone and there was no Boatman, no mushroom clouds, but it had been more than a dream.

He was warm beneath the down blanket with Delara asleep beside him on the carpet, her arm thrown protectively across his chest, her soft breasts against his side and her legs resting against his. Her breath was warm on his neck. Kyle Swanson kissed her lightly on the top of her head, closed his eyes again, and decided not to move.

Another ten minutes and then they had to get back to the clinic before Jeff was prepped for surgery. Just ten minutes. Was that too much to ask? Yes. It was too much, for now there was something else. He was still putting things together, the real world and the fantasy, the nuclear weapons of the Saudis and the Boatman's mushroom clouds. Even in his sleep he had been thinking about the new and dangerous situation that was brewing in the ever volatile Middle East.

Sir Jeff had floated in and out of consciousness and the effects of the medication and fought to stay coherent in order to fill out the story for him. The accountants and analysts of Excalibur Enterprises, which had expanded to include an intelligence-gathering branch for major corporations, had found strange discrepancies among engineering contracts in Saudi Arabia. Jeff decided to follow the trail and had bribed and threatened enough sources to put it all together. The Saudis had spent years and millions of dollars to secretly purchase the components necessary to build a small nuclear arsenal, avoiding any sign of launching a production program that would have drawn international scrutiny. The huge expenditures and assignments had been easily masked within the massive construction and infrastructure projects that were constantly underway throughout the kingdom.

Against impossible odds, they had five special missiles that were now operational. Jeff told him that he was sure of the location of only one of the weapons, at a small Saudi army base in the oil patch city of al-Khobz on the Arabian Gulf. Khobz and its giant port was a natural invasion point for any enemy military force, as had been proven when Iraqi dictator Saddam Hussein sent his troops over from Kuwait during Gulf War One. A defensive nuke missile system could plug that hole nicely, but Kyle realized that it could just as easily become an offensive weapon that could maim an entire American naval battle group.

The information had staggered Kyle: A country facing possible revolution had a secret arsenal of nuclear weapons. As Jeff faded back into a sedated sleep, Swanson found Sybelle Summers and brought her up to speed on the revelation.

Using her FBI creds, Sybelle got a ride aboard a police helicopter all the way to the landing pad at the U.S. Embassy in London. Once in a secure room, she drafted a FLASH message to the Lizard back at Trident headquarters in Washington. General Middleton, she thought while writing the explosive memo, was going to have a cow when he read this. He would take it immediately to General Turner and President Tracy.

NINE MORE MINUTES OF rest, with Delara in his arms. Swanson thought of the immense potential for catastrophe that would soon be exposed, forcing untold actions and reactions. Ten minutes might be all that he had left. It might be all any of them had left.

AL-KHOBZ, SAUDI ARABIA

RISHA AL-HARBI AND HER best friends, Hanaa and Taja, were rocking at the mall. The three teenagers wore identical flowing black abayas that covered them from their shoulders to their feet. It was above the shoulders where their conservative nation's customs could be bent a bit, and the girls had colorful scarves over their heads and had spent hours applying makeup to their eyes while shaping and polishing their nails, the only parts of their bodies that were visible. They were total social rebels.

Risha was the worst offender. Beneath her cumbersome and tent-like abaya, she even wore pink sneakers, pink socks, a T-shirt, and a short denim skirt. Her crimson nails flashed with flecks of gold.

"He is *so* cute!" Hanaa checked out the picture of a boy on Risha's cell phone, a strong and smiling youngster with a thick mop of black hair and piercing eyes. She passed it to Taja.

"I cannot believe that you really called him," said Taja. "Why do you do these things, Risha? We get numbered all the time, but I would never actually call a boy. My family would freak."

"I have never actually spoken to him. We just text," Risha argued. "What's the harm? It's not like we're mingling or anything." A tune from the latest boy band pounded through the iPod ear buds beneath her pink scarf and she nodded with the rhythm. The slang language of the West came easily to them because of their access to cell phones and satellite television. They were even more technologically advanced than the earlier Saudi girls of the Oprah generation. They were connected!

"That picture is a lot more than just being texted," Taja warned. She lifted her full niqab veil, sipped some mocha frappachino, and wiped foam from her lips. Even the Starbucks at the Khobz Mall could be a dangerous place for girls. "Erase that picture. Please. I don't want you to get into trouble."

"What's his name?" asked Hanaa.

"Gabir," replied Risha as she theatrically hugged the portable cell phone to her body.

"Please tell me that you did not give him your real name!" Hanaa's eyes were wide. The risk that her friend was taking was incredible.

"Yes. Of course. He *loves* me!"

Both of her shocked friends laughed nervously. Hanaa said, "This boy, your dreamy Gabir, did not even know you existed until two days ago! He and his friends spotted you coming out of this mall and when we got into your father's Mercedes limo, they followed us. I remember them blaring their horns and cutting around in their cars and holding out cardboard signs with their telephone numbers. You actually checked them out while I was screaming in terror."

Risha looked again at the picture. "Remember how Gabir actually opened the door of the car he was in and stepped out while it was still moving at fifty kilometers an hour, sliding along the pavement on his leather slippers like he was a surfer? So brave. I just had to contact him. He is my beautiful lion!"

"Your lion wants to drive you out to the desert and rape you," scoffed Taja. "Then it would only be a question of who would kill you first: your father, your brothers, or the Committee on Virtue."

Risha looked hard at her friends. "I won't be raped. Ever." She opened her fashionable shoulder bag wide enough for them to see the slim knife that she always carried, a little four-inch switchblade with a smooth ivory handle that she had taken from her father's collection. She defiantly shifted the contents of her purse some more to also show them a narrow can of pepper spray, then she snapped the purse shut. "I will kill anyone who tries to attack me or kill myself before it can happen."

"Nothing good can come of this. Think about what you're doing."

"That's exactly what I've been doing," Risha argued. "We're all sixteen years old now and are stuck in this awful, oily place. I'm a faithful girl and follow the teachings of the Prophet, praise be unto him, but I reject being controlled by men and stupid laws that are not in the Koran. They just make up this stuff! Women can't ride horses. Women can't vote. Women can't be seen in public with unrelated males, so we cannot go on innocent dates. There is not a movie theater for us to go see in the entire country and the censors clip out the good pictures in magazines before we can see them. I'm really, really tired of all of it." She paused and took a deep breath. "I want out."

Hanaa pushed back in her chair. "You have been watching too much MTV, Risha. You will be soon wearing a bikini top and bootie shorts in public. Calm down and face reality. You will stay here, just like us, and we will all be married off to some distant cousins or friends of our fathers. A dull but pleasant life with a rich man who pampers us, just like our mothers and our grandmothers."

"You want to leave, too," Risha shot back. "I know you do. Remember that Victoria's Secret catalogue that we found? What's the point in wearing that sexy stuff if you cannot show it off?"

Taja was not as brave. She loved Risha and Hanaa but both of them pushed the bounds of propriety. "Be quiet, Risha. People can hear."

"So let them listen. I don't care." She went back to her cell phone when it buzzed in her palm, and passed it over to Hanaa. "Gabir wants me to send him a picture."

"Don't you dare!" Taja was horrified.

"Oh, I won't." Then the dark eyes flashed beneath the long bangs of dark hair that swept across her forehead. She spun the cell phone around, held it at arm's length and snapped a picture of herself, holding up the cardboard coffee cup with the company's green logo in plain view. She attached it to a text message and hit the SEND button.

"You fool!" Taja hissed. "Don't you understand what you just did? He already knew your name and now he knows exactly where we are because this is the only Starbucks in Khobz. What will we do if he comes here with his friends? He can blackmail you into doing anything he wants just by threatening to show your picture to your family, or even to the *muttaween.* He owns you now, Risha. He owns you! We must leave."

"Well, you didn't do anything at all, Taja," said Risha. "Anyway, Gabir would never betray me, so nothing is going to happen. The Religious Police cannot monitor cell phone traffic and Wi-Fi. So we can go, but let's do some shopping first. I feel like buying a bright new scarf with daddy's money. And wouldn't it be just terrible if Gabir actually decided to come down to the mall for a café au lait?"

RISHA WAS THE FIRST one grabbed when the girls emerged from the upscale clothing boutique on the second floor, then rough hands snatched Hanaa and Taja and pinned them both against the glass display window.

"You little whore!" roared a deep voice as a man with a shaggy beard and in the robes of the *muttaween*, the feared Religious Police, hurled Risha to the floor. As she fell backward, the abaya rode up past her ankles, and then was snatched upward further along with the edge of her denim skirt to expose her knees and thighs. The first stroke of the camel-hide whip was instant and hard, and laid a bloody stripe across her right shin.

Risha screamed, more from surprise than pain. She had hit the floor so hard that she bounced and slid a few feet, and clawed for balance. The second whip stroke slashed her right knee and brought another yelp, this time in pain. Two *muttaween* were wielding the whips, one on each side of her, the signature loose red clothes circling their heads and with their eyes lustfully on her naked legs. She heard Taja and Hanaa scream and saw them being held against the storefront by other *muttaween*.

"Stop! Don't hurt me! I have done nothing wrong," she yelled as loud as possible.

Another whip stroke came down, but she rolled away from it, only to go into the path of the whip of the second man. It sliced her thigh with a deep sting and blood flowed from the wound. A crowd was gathering and some young men were laughing, one of them recording the beating on his video camera. In the front row, cheering on the whip handlers, was Gabir.

A dark sense of betrayal and outrage seized Risha's soul. He was a police informant and had used the Web to track her down! They intended to make an example of her to instill fear in other girls. Hot tears came to her eyes.

Another whip stroke fell across her legs, but this one didn't seem to hurt as much, hardly at all as the pain was soaked up by her rage. Risha knew she had only a few moments before they took her away and she grabbed for her shoulder bag and fumbled it open. The *muttaween* were still yelling. She could not understand what they were saying and did not care. Gabir! The bastard!

Her palm found the canister of pepper spray, she yanked it out and pointed the nozzle at one of the whip men and pressed down. The surprise was total. A mere girl was fighting back! Her attacker stumbled backward, dropping his whip and rubbing his eyes with a yowl of pain, causing the second one to pause briefly before coming at her even harder. He dodged in close until he was standing directly over her, then knocked the can from her grip. It bounced away into the crowd.

His lashes were being aimed at her upper body and her face, in pure vengeance. Although she felt the whip crack her cheeks, Risha was not going to give up. She reached into the bag again and her fingers closed on the bone handle of the knife. The little button! Her thumb found it and she pressed hard, and the blade flipped out and locked. She would kill Gabir for betraying her!

Using her left hand trying to protect her eyes from the whip, Risha jabbed directly upward with the knife and the sharp point slid smoothly into the groin of the attacking man standing over her. She pulled back and jabbed again, and again, as hard as she could. He screamed and dropped his whip and she slashed even more, the blade ripping into the femoral artery deep in his inner thigh. Blood spurted out in a purple rope.

The crowd went silent. This petite girl had blinded one *muttawa* and stabbed another one in the balls! Both had fallen. Impossible!

Risha still had the stained knife in her hand and her own blood oozed from the long whip marks. She ignored the pain and rolled to her knees. The scarf and the abaya had been torn from her head and her long black hair hung before her face in disarray, giving her the look of a rising evil spirit. Her eyes locked on Gabir and she moved toward him. He dropped his coffee cup and backed away.

The two *muttawas* who had been holding her friends had released them and now crashed into her, knocking Risha back onto the slippery, bloody tiles, screaming and punching her. The thick butt ends of their whips became bludgeons that rose and fell against her head. Risha managed to deeply slash the hand of one before the knife was knocked away and the two heavy policemen beat her savagely. She was already unconscious by the time one of them grabbed a handful of her raven-black hair and repeatedly slammed her face onto the hard stone until she was dead.

THE WHITE HOUSE

PRINCE **A**BDULLAH **NORMALLY WOULD** be wearing a well-tailored business suit when he visited the Oval Office. His driver would slip quietly through the back gate on East Exec and stop beside a green-canopied walkway used by special guests to enter the White House with some protection from the media cameras. This time was different: The prince was driven up the long, curving driveway in full view of the press corps, which had been alerted to his visit and was waiting in a pack as he arrived at the front entrance of the West Wing.

The immaculate ebony limousine halted beneath the colonnaded entrance and a Marine guard in dress blues opened the car door. The prince stepped out, wearing elegant white robes that flowed like a wind-smoothed sail and an Arab *kaffiyeh*, a square of pristine white cloth folded into a triangle and held to his head by cords of spun gold threads.

He paused to smile and wave for the cameras and then turned to his left to do the same for the startled tourists gathered across the green lawn, beyond the big fence. Reporters shouted out questions, but he only continued to smile and wave, and then he stepped inside. Neither the president nor any senior member of the administration had been sent out to greet him.

It was an intentional piece of media theater, a show carefully crafted for maximum effect. Before even setting foot inside the White House, Prince Abdullah had sent an open visual message, that despite the dire news coming from Saudi Arabia, the House of Saud was still in control. This was a time to display strength and confidence, and not whimper. He had received reports that some of the weaker princes were thinking of fleeing the country during this crisis. Where was their pride? To do so was to deny their heritage and their names. Shameful. Abdullah had determined that whoever left now would be called to a severe accounting for their actions later.

Chief of Staff Steve Hanson was waiting just beyond the entrance portal and formally welcomed Abdullah, then escorted him directly to the Oval Office. President Mark Tracy was waiting, ready with a diplomatic smile that masked the bitterness he felt inside. This was not going to be pleasant.

The prince showed an equally formal smile as he shook the hand of Tracy, who was an old friend, exchanged polite greetings with others, and bowed slightly toward former Senator Catherine Hart, the new U.S. secretary of state. "Congratulations on your appointment, Madame Secretary, although it is terrible that you have been called into the position due to the tragic death of Secretary Waring. Your experience in foreign affairs will serve us all well in this troubled time."

"Thank you, Mr. Ambassador. We are all happy that you were not seriously injured in that same, horrible terrorist attack." Hart had been chairwoman of the Senate Foreign Relations Committee and when Waring was killed, President Tracy demanded an experienced hand at the reins over at Foggy Bottom. Hart would not miss a step in transferring her political power to the State Department, where career diplomats knew that her bite was worse than her bark. She was a stylish woman with short red hair and light blue eyes that expressed nothing she did not want them to show.

When everyone was seated, President Tracy began the conversation. "We have been monitoring the news reports, Mr. Ambassador. Perhaps you could advise us as to what is actually happening in your country. It appears quite serious."

Abdullah knew that question would be asked and had chosen his response carefully. "There was already some unrest in a few places because of the proposed treaty with Israel. That was expected and being watched. The unexpected terrorist strike unleashed more disruption, but only in scattered areas. For the present, our security forces believe that the trouble is limited and that they have it under control. A handful of rogue conservative extremists stirring up trouble."

"That seems quite contrary to many of the public reports," said Secretary Hart. "The pictures on television show a situation that could only be described as rioting in some urban areas."

"Television," Abdullah said with a smooth smile. "The cameras will rush to a house fire and portray it as an entire city in flames. The TV people are using that broad brush approach because we have strict rules on censorship. Madame Secretary, Mr. President, I assure you both that we have it under control."

"What about security in the oil fields?" President Tracy decided to get to the point.

"Nothing untoward is happening, thankfully. It seems quiet in those important places. We have forces stationed at all of the production facilities and they are on the highest alert."

The president pushed casually back on the small sofa and let Secretary Hart roll out the next point. "And what is your conclusion on the assassination of the commander of the king's private guard, and his family? Is there a loyalty problem within the Saudi military, Mr. Ambassador?"

Abdullah still remained unruffled. No questions that he had not anticipated. "The work of a solitary lunatic. Just as your intelligence people occasionally find a single spy in their own ranks, this zealot was swept up in the excitement. I can assure you that our troops remain committed to His Majesty and to the protection of the kingdom and its people."

President Tracy looked across and met those powerful eyes. "Prince Abdullah, please be totally honest with us. We only want to help. Just ask for our support and we are here for you," he said. "Whatever you want in supplies or materiel or manpower will be provided. Your government must not be overthrown. My planners tell me we could have boots on the ground in a matter of hours. I have spoken with other world leaders who are also willing to form an international coalition to protect those fields while your forces quell the uprising."

Abdullah knew this was a turning point. "No. The kingdom appreciates your support, Mr. President, but a foreign military presence is the last thing we want or need. We are aware of your carrier battle group that has entered the Arabian Gulf and must insist that you keep your distance. This is an internal problem for our country. We are under assault by a gang of terrorists and we will deal with them appropriately. U.S. combat troops would only exacerbate the situation, not help resolve it."

Cathy Hart spoke again, her voice firm. "Those oil fields need to be tightly guarded, Mr. Ambassador, and we cannot stand idly by if the fanatics somehow do gain the upper hand. Establishment of another theological government that is violently anti-American and anti-Western cannot be tolerated in the region."

"Madame Secretary, you must learn to veil your threats better." Abdullah laughed softly. "What you describe is a nightmare scenario that simply will not take place. Impossible. Your troops are not wanted. Do not make the mistake that was made in Iraq, when Muslims of various sects united in common cause against you as a foreign invader."

There was a moment of silence as the development soaked into everyone present. The United States was thinking of committing forces. Saudi Arabia might deploy against the U.S. to increase its popular support. By changing the face of the enemy, the internal rebellion might be quelled.

"It may not be that easy any longer, Mr. Ambassador," said President Tracy.

The president paused, then walked to his big desk and sat down to give one final read to the extraordinary document that was the main topic of the meeting, and one of which Abdullah was not aware.

"We have uncovered a very serious issue: your country possesses nuclear weapons, Mr. Ambassador." The president removed some satellite photos of specific bases. Once the CIA and the other intelligence agencies knew what they were looking for, the locations were identified. "We demand that you get rid of them."

Abdullah fought to keep a straight face and not appear stunned by this development. *How did they find out?* "We have no nuclear bombs," he said, his eyebrows rising in protest. "How could you have gotten such an idea, Mr. President?"

"Do not bother to deny that they exist, my friend." He tapped the satellite photographs. "And I did not say 'bombs.' I said 'weapons.' There are five nuclear-tipped missiles stashed around the country and they must be dismantled forthwith. The risk of a nuclear device falling under the control of the terrorists who are trying to take over your country is simply unacceptable to the international community. Those madmen would not hesitate to fire one and ignite a global holocaust."

Abdullah fought to maintain his composure. "I will certainly have to

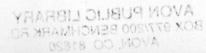

consult with my government in Riyadh on this matter, Mr. President. The weapons were secretly emplaced only as defense weapons for the utmost emergency, one on each border."

"Please convey to His Majesty that this administration, a long-time ally of your country, considers this a matter of paramount importance, Prince Abdullah. When I learned of it, I felt personally betrayed. So in the interest of world peace, I must spell out a terrible consequence. Dismantle those nuclear missiles and show us proof, or the United States will go to the United Nations to seek a resolution to both demand their removal and to have the oil fields placed under the protection of an international security force. After that, it won't really matter who is in charge in Riyadh."

"Mr. President! You cannot be talking about a possible war between our two countries?"

"No, sir. Not at all. It is not our wish to take any action against your country. But I am talking about reality. Your government is drifting toward the rocks and the fanatics may pick up some nuclear missiles as part of the coup. That would place Israel and the oil shipping routes under a nuclear threat. We cannot let that happen." The president stood, signaling an end to the meeting.

"Very well. I understand your position," said the prince as he also stood. "Sadly, I am sure I speak for my government in stating that we will not allow any outsiders to meddle in what we consider to be internal Saudi affairs. But I thank you for your time and guidance, sir."

President Tracy said, "Please express our warmest regards and friendship to His Majesty." The president grasped the hand of the ambassador and placed his other hand on the man's elbow and looked him in the eyes to be sure he had his attention. "Now, off the record, you guys have gotten yourselves, and us, into a hell of a mess and you have to figure a way out in a hurry. Don't let things get out of hand."

SCRETARY HART RETURNED TO the State Department immediately after the meeting to start picking up the reins of her new job. Once she had cleared the White House grounds, President Tracy went down to the Situation Room, which was as secure as electronics could make it. CIA Director Bartlett

Geneen and General Hank Turner, chairman of the Joint Chiefs of Staff, stood when he entered the room, and he shook their hands. Steve Hanson sat to one side of the room, leaving only the three men at the big table.

"It didn't go well," Tracy said. "I think the ground is shaking beneath their feet over there, and the information about the nukes blindsided him. He even indicated the Saudis would fight us if we tried to militarily intervene."

General Turner picked absently at a loose thread on his tunic. "It's not our best option. It would take months to really do it right, and we don't have the time. If we have to go in, it could get messy."

"Nevertheless, the United States must not allow another government in the Middle East to be taken over by religious fanatics. Particularly Saudi Arabia. What about the guy who is leading the rebellion, Bart?"

Bart Geneen had been around the spook business for a long time. Wisps of white hair curled around his balding head and deep worry lines etched his face. He opened a folder, then worked a keyboard and a grainy picture of a tall, bearded man wearing a red headdress flashed onto a wall screen. He had deep, dark, mad eyes that seemed to reach through the lens of the camera. Geneen had spent a career looking at ruthless men like this one. "He is Mohammed Abu Ebara, the top dog in the Committee for the Propogation of Virtue and the Prevention of Vice, better known as the *muttaween,* or the Religious Police. Officially, the Grand Mufti is in charge of religious matters in Saudi Arabia, but Ebara already has become the face of the coup. He and his cops are absolutely vicious."

"If the king falls, would Ebara replace him?" asked the president.

"More likely is that they would do away with the throne entirely. The government would become something along the line of the Iranian model, sir. Some goofy front men would be set up with a titular head, but Ebara would be the man behind the scenes, with his religious police forming the backbone of the enforcers. The Grand Mufti would be isolated."

"Well, gentlemen, I simply am not going to allow that to go forward much further. This emergency is to be placed beneath the Al Qaeda Network Executive Order. Bart, do I have to increase the ExOrd authority in order to do that?"

"No, sir. Al Qaeda could very well be involved. The ExOrd was designed to combat terrorists on many levels. This certainly qualifies."

Under the secret ruling issued shortly after 9/11, the United States was allowed to employ its military assets beyond official war zones. The members of the Principals Group that performed oversight were all in that one room of the White House at the moment. Secretary of State Waring had also been part of it, and his successor would be brought aboard only after she had settled into her new job.

"General, I want you to put Task Force Trident on this Mohammed Abu Ebara. If the rebellion spins much further out of control, he will be dealt with. Bart, your Agency will assist in every way possible."

"Are we talking about an assassination, sir?" asked Geneen.

Tracy dodged the question. "At this time, I just want to bring Task Force Trident and Kyle Swanson into the game. In fact, Swanson can pull double duty for us by going into Saudi Arabia to help check on the nuclear weapons at the same time that he checks on Ebara."

"A precise and low-visibility solution, Mr. President," said Geneen. "Swanson is effective and reliable, and after all, he was the one who brought us this development about the nuclear weapons in the first place. And the actions of any one man will be lost in the chaos of a national rebellion."

General Turner laughed. "Gunny Swanson is not just any one man, Bart. He's a dangerous weapon himself and has to be carefully deployed. Things happen when Swanson gets involved. What kind of authority do we give him, Mr. President?"

Steven Hanson moved to the table and laid a leather folder before each man. Inside the folders were orders that gave Trident a Green Light Package, pre-authorized permission to do whatever was necessary.

20

ENGLAND

SYBELLE SUMMERS ENTERED THE clinic dressed for success: blue silk blouse beneath a cream jacket, a single gold locket and matching earrings, black high heels, and her long legs striding beneath a black skirt cut several inches above her knees. Her eyes were startlingly clear. Her hair had been freshly trimmed, with a few touches of gold offsetting the black sheen. Light makeup. Men turned for another look as she went through the hospital doors, unaware that a large caliber pistol rested near her manicured fingernails in the leather purse over her shoulder. She pulled a small black suitcase behind her. A Green Light Package had come in from Washington, so she would not be returning to the hotel.

The repair and cleanup of the damage from the terrorist attack was well underway, the smell of fresh paint lingered on the hallway walls and the destroyed door had been replaced. As Sybelle entered Sir Jeff's room, she took in a scene that reminded her of old, melancholy Dutch paintings. Muted sunlight reluctantly illuminated three tired people seated in chairs near the bed, where Jeff lay thoroughly still, sedated, and sound asleep. His head was swathed in bandages and an array of medical devices monitored his condition, constantly reporting electronic readings. A clear plastic oxygen mask was on his face, but no breathing tube was down the throat.

"Hey, everybody," she said quietly and took a knee between Lady Pat and Delara Tabrizi, kissing both on their cheeks and taking their hands. "How's our boy?"

"Hey," Kyle said. "What's with the fashion show?"

"None of your business."

"You went out on a date, didn't you?" His head was cocked to one side as he took in the outfit, head to toe, and mischief played in his eyes. He was used to seeing her in casual jeans or battle dress camo, but he thought that Sybelle could make a burlap sack look good.

"There was no date, so drop it, Kyle." Her voice was soft but with a hard edge. "We have some urgent business to discuss."

Lady Pat shushed them both. She had long grown used to special ops warriors exiting suddenly and reappearing just as quickly, never offering an explanation for anything. If Sybelle had not been around, there was a good reason. "Jeff made it," Pat said. "He's going to be okay."

"Thank God for that."

"Yes." Pat glanced at Kyle, then gave Sybelle a tired smile. "Just ignore Kyle. You look lovely today."

Sybelle padded over to the bed, slid a hip onto the mattress, then reached out and stroked Jeff's mussed hair. Leaned close and kissed him on the forehead, then closer and whispered for a time, so quietly that the others could not hear a word. She smoothed the sheet around his shoulders and went back to Lady Pat, stood behind her and massaged her shoulders.

Delara got up and walked toward the door, motioning Sybelle to follow, and the two women went silently down the hallway, past the nurses' station, to gain some distance from the room.

"What's the prognosis, Delara?"

"Sir Jeff has a long recovery ahead. The spinal injury will confine him to a wheelchair during physical therapy, but should heal enough that he eventually might walk again." She exhaled and her shoulders slumped, as if she was carrying a heavy weight. "The concern is that his brain sustained some damage and the neurosurgeon says that only time will tell whether Sir Jeff will ever come back 100 percent. We've seen it already. His thoughts can be totally normal one moment, then just fade out like a bad radio signal. The doctor says some of that is the sedation at work, but that the brain is so complicated that he cannot predict the future with certainty."

"Oh, my God! How is Pat taking that?"

"She's just happy that he's still alive. Oh, Sybelle, what a tragic thing to happen to such a nice man."

The two of them embraced, then Sybelle held her at arm's length and looked squarely in her eyes. "I'm going to need your help now, Delara. I have to take Kyle away, and he won't want to go. You and Pat have to help to push him out the door. Believe me, Delara; it is a true emergency."

Delara composed herself. "I know. That trouble in Saudi Arabia is drawing you two like a magnet pulling a paper clip," she said, crossing her arms. "There's really nothing else Kyle can do right now to help Jeff, and I will make sure that Pat does not slide into depression. She hasn't fully come to grips with what the future may hold for them."

She looked at Sybelle, at the warrior steel behind the pretty face. "Promise that you will send Kyle back to me safe and sound? I hate that he has to be gone so often."

"You know I can't make that promise, Delara. These are dangerous times and his focus has to be total. He is going to be in a quiet rage when we make him leave here, then when he gets on the scene, he will become scarily unemotional and normal on the surface. Once into the fight, he will be burning. My job is to point that fury in the right direction."

Delara nodded in understanding and they walked back to the room. "So why *are* you so dressed up? It's a terrific outfit. Are you in a relationship of some sort?"

"I just like to get out of my work clothes from time to time. Remind myself that I'm still an attractive woman who likes bubble baths and candlelight."

"He must be a special guy."

"It's nothing serious. I just have to keep him separate from my professional life. He thinks I work for a real estate trust."

Delara gave a small laugh. "Real estate trust, huh? Married?"

Sybelle changed the subject. "How are things with you and Kyle?"

"We're getting there. Sometimes I feel like a lion tamer in a circus. He's so strong and determined, but with a very tender side that he keeps under wraps most of the time. Terrible memories haunt his subconscious."

Sybelle said, "He's a very complex individual who operates on several different levels at one time, like he is playing three games of chess simultaneously. His mental computer is always humming, especially in combat.

Since he cannot talk about what we do, he deals with his actions only after the fact, when the dust has settled."

"How do you deal with it?"

"I'm smart enough to take some time off and go back to my fictional job in commercial real estate for a while. Go places and do fun things and hang out with normal people. Don't read newspapers or watch the news. Oh, by the way. I'm sorry about wrecking your pretty car," Sybelle said, with a gentle hint of sarcasm.

Delara kept her voice low. "Jeff bought it for me. I would have preferred a little sedan, but he insisted on that big beast. I couldn't handle it and even programmed the talking map thingie on the dashboard to remind me if I exceeded the speed limit."

"Ah. Our friend Linda. That's why she got so bitchy when I was speeding."

"Linda has issues."

"Not any more."

NOTHING HAD CHANGED IN the room, where tension hung like a curtain because Kyle knew what was coming. A potential war was brewing out in the real world and he would have to play a part. The decision on whether he would have to get involved in Excalibur Enterprises had been lifted with the prospect that Jeff would recover. Postponed, not decided.

Sybelle took an envelope from her purse and handed it to him. "Read it," she said.

Kyle only held the folded sheet. Did not open it. Tried to give it back. "Doesn't matter. I'm not moving. I've got plenty of built-up leave time."

"Read the damned thing, Kyle."

He looked over at Pat, who gave a slight nod, and he reluctantly unfolded a single sheet of paper. The jaw muscles tightened.

"A Green Light Package, Kyle. We have to go now."

Pat put her elbows on her knees and bent forward until her eyes were shaded by her hands. Her back shook in sobs and Delara slid a comforting arm around her.

"I can't leave," Swanson said.

Pat snapped her head back up. "Yes, you can . . . You must go, Kyle! I do not want Jeff waking up to discover that you are disobeying a direct order. That would upset him even more, particularly because of why he is here in the first place."

"But, Pat . . ."

She shook her head sharply. "No. Don't say anything else."

He twisted the paper into smaller folds, creasing it with his fingernails. "Things have changed. The Excalibur business, this situation with Jeff now . . ."

Pat shook away Delara's arm and stood, defiant. "All of that can be re-solved when you return. Forget whatever is on the paper. Here is an order to you straight from me, Lady Patricia Cornwell to Kyle Swanson: Go out there and find the terrible people who did this to my husband. The suicide squad is dead, but whoever ordered the attack is still on the loose. You find them and then you kill them. Understand me, Kyle? Am I making this clear enough? I want their damned heads on pikes and their guts served to me on silver plates!"

Swanson slowly rose, and wrapped Pat in a big embrace that picked her off her feet for a moment. Then he put her gently down and said, "Yes, ma'am. I can do that."

"When do we leave?" he asked Sybelle.

"As soon as I change clothes," she replied. "Say your good-byes and we're out of here."

SAUDI ARABIA

FLYING IN THE OPEN skies over the desert countryside had been life's greatest pleasure for Captain Nawaf bin Awadh of the Saudi Royal Air Force. In the cockpit of his F-15C Eagle, he never ceased being awed by the amazing power at his fingertips. All of the flight data was on a heads-up display and each of the two Pratt & Whitney turbofan engines produced more than 23,000 pounds of thrust. Thousands of gallons of fuel in the internal and external tanks, an M-61A1 six-barrel 20 mm cannon in the nose and wing rack slung with Sidewinder and Sparrow missiles.

He keyed his microphone as he blazed over the trackless brown countryside, with the pure sky above. "Palm Leader to Palm 2. How are you on fuel?"

"Palm 1. It is odd sir, but since we just took off, the gauges are in the green. The ground crew did not forget to fill it up." First Lieutenant Fayez al-Khilewi smiled beneath his oxygen mask. His flight leader was a man of few words but was in a good mood today, as determined as always to put in a flawless mission. His words had been almost pleasant.

They were flying combat air patrol over a long stretch of air space that was off limits to all other aircraft and was centered on a remote royal palace in which the king was spending a few days. Fayez could easily see the place, a bright spot of green trees and water in the middle of an otherwise empty landscape.

A new voice came up on the circuit, the flight controller in an E-3A AWACS, fifty miles away, the radar-studded bird that directed all traffic in and around the area. The controller quickly guided them into the protective circle and allowed the two fighters that had been on station for several hours to return to base. They were all part of the most sophisticated air force in the region, but the C4I—the command, control, computer, and intelligence—system had never been foolproof. It was a vital weak spot, because without capable communication in a combat crisis, things could get dangerous very quickly. They had the tools, but not the experience born of years of practice.

Ten minutes later, the captain went to the private, internal radio circuit and spoke a single word to his wingman, "Execute."

Fayez wheeled his F-15 in a sharp turn, kicked in his afterburners to increase speed and was dashing toward the AWACS almost before the controller recognized the course change. The lieutenant turned off his radio and activated his weapons display to paint the lumbering, defenseless control plane with a radar beam. In a matter of seconds, he was within range and fired a pair of AIM-9H Sparrow air-to-air missiles. The weapons slid off the rails with a jolt and Fayez felt as if the fighter jet had hit a speed bump as a thousand pounds of dead weight flew from the wings. The twelve-foot-long missiles spewed white vapor trails from their solid-propellant motors as they burned straight for the AWACS and smashed the 88-pound high-explosive warheads into the target. Fayez nosed straight through the fireball and heard bits of flying debris from the destroyed plane click against his fuselage. He curved up and around to join the captain, who was already attacking the palace.

When their ordnance was expended, both of the fuel-loaded planes crashed into the smoking wreckage of the building.

BEIJING, CHINA

LOOK OUT THERE. **T**ELL me what you see," said Jiang Julong with a sweep of his arm toward a broad window.

General Zhu Chi obeyed. "Not much, Mister Chairman. The pollution is very bad today. I had to wear a mask coming over here."

The chairman of the Central Military Commission of the Chinese Communist Party smiled blandly and resumed his theme. "I will tell you what we both see, comrade general. Progress. We see large avenues filled with automobiles. Where once there were only bicycles, the Beijing area alone now has a thousand new cars on its roads every day. China leads the world in buying new Rolls Royces. We see women who used to wear peasant clothing now adorned with boutique makeup and buying designer label dresses. We see factories turning out products that are snapped up in foreign lands: Eighty percent of all toys and seventy-two percent of all shoes bought in America are made in China. Millions of Chinese workers are making money to spend at our own stores, which are stocked with consumer goods. We see a nine percent growth rate per year. Despite economic bounces, we see a new and strong and proud China."

He paused. Enough statistics. He reached to a nearby shelf and carefully picked up a round-bellied 1000 milliliter Pyrex laboratory flask that was about half-full of a viscous liquid. Oil. A printed label identified it: Saudi Sweet. He handed it to the general. "Here is what will sustain our future growth."

General Zhu had expected the private meeting to be a discussion about the deteriorating situation in Saudi Arabia, but wanted the chairman to broach the subject. It was unwise for a soldier to say too much to a politician. So he carefully returned the flask to its metal stand, put his hands behind his back and rocked on his heels, remaining silent.

Both were well aware that China's main oil fields in Manchuria, the South China Sea, and the Bohai Gulf had not been keeping up with increased domestic demand since 1993. Those once-deep domestic fields were being rapidly emptied of the precious resource. Drilling in the Tarim Basin was difficult if not impossible. China was now the second largest oil importing country in the world and in a few years it probably would surpass the gluttonous United States.

"Half of our imported oil comes from the Middle East, comrade general." The voice was silky, confident. "I have been asked to assess how the events in Saudi Arabia might impact our economy. At first, I believed it not to be our concern, because we do not need to meddle in the internal politics of other countries from which we purchase oil, as long as the oil flows."

The chairman began to pace in measured steps as he read from a piece of paper. He stopped and dropped it on his desk. "Things have changed. The deaths of the king and his heir apparent have created a political power vacuum and now we have these intelligence reports that the Saudis possess some nuclear weapons. Suddenly it is an unstable and very serious situation for China. The delicate balance has been upset."

"I agree, comrade chairman."

"This information on the nuclear missiles is reliable?"

"Absolutely. It is not just street gossip, but was confirmed by well-paid sources inside the Saudi military itself and is also being discussed in Washington."

"Nuclear weapons! If one of those weapons falls into the hands of those religious extremists it might be detonated in the gulf, ruining production for decades."

The general wasted no time commenting on foreign and economic policies. That wasn't his job. "Should we plan a military intervention?"

"Something might be needed," Chairman Jiang said, returning to his window to gaze at the gray sky. "Of course, it is too far away and not enough time. What is your opinion of making such a movement?"

The general joined him at the window. Direct eye contact was to be avoided when speaking in such general terms, so they stared at the big, blank buildings. The ornate and distinctive Chinese architecture of ancient times had given way to monstrous, bland concrete boxes.

"Looking at it from a normal military perspective, it is virtually impossible. Xinjiang Province in our northwest shares borders with Afghanistan and Pakistan, but we cannot consider marching through either place. The Americans would stop us in Afghanistan and the Pakistanis would never agree. It would result in costly fighting and not get us much closer to the Saudi oil."

The chairman noted that the window that had been cleaned last night was already sandpapered again by specks of soot and dirt. "No, that would not be the answer. Perhaps there is something smaller that could protect our interests?"

"The logical move would be to go through the United Nations and perhaps join, or even lead, an international coalition to protect one of the world's major oil supply networks? We could also move units of the People's Liberation Army to Africa, closer to Saudi Arabia, while the diplomats are debating."

The chairman agreed. "We may, however, have to move without UN approval, by claiming that the imminent danger forced us to act. Once we are in, we would offer to help establish an international force."

General Zhu Chi stiffened. "To be clear, comrade. We should consider actually capturing the Saudi oil fields?"

"Just consider all options, comrade general. The UN could be a useful ploy to delay a countermove by Washington. It should not ultimately determine our decision."

"Then I shall leave you now, comrade, and order the planning staff to start working on possibilities."

They bowed slightly to each other, and the general headed back to the elevator. As it descended, he found his handkerchief and mopped his brow. General Zhu had 2.3 million men under arms in the PLA, a total military head count of seven million people, and could get uncounted millions more if needed. He had a generous budget and could also get more money, if needed. Somewhere in the matrix had to be an answer that might stop short of World War III. The first need was to put some new eyes on the ground.

JEDDAH, SAUDI ARABIA

A_LLAHU AKBAR!_ **GOD IS** _Great!_ Mohammed Abu Ebara allowed the small metal chain to trickle through his fingers like a child's toy, and then lifted it to eye level and examined its only ornament, a long-bladed key.

It was part of the contents of an envelope that was hand-delivered to him by an excited imam who had personally sped down from Riyadh to explain the magnificent gift from God.

"The material was entrusted to me by Vice Sergeant Mas'ud Mohammed al-Kazaz, our martyr who eliminated the heretic who commanded the Saudi Royal Guard Regiment." The imam was nervous and afraid in the presence of the powerful leader of the Religious Police. He fished in an envelope and handed over a scarlet red card of thick plastic, stamped with a string of black letters and numbers.

The imam bowed his head in reverence. "The vice-sergeant confided that the items now in your hands are the codes and key needed to launch a missile carrying a nuclear warhead. The missile is at the base."

Ebara wanted to shout in glee, but reined his emotions in tightly to show no weakness to the lesser religious figure. Inside his chest, his heart was beginning to soar. A nuclear weapon!

"Anything more?"

"Yes. This book." It was a slim volume with a red stripe across the cover and the seal of the House of Saud. "It contains top secret military documents and I took the liberty of reading it on the trip down here, in order to spare you valuable time."

"What does it say?" Ebara let the book rest on a small table and did not touch it. To even extend a hand might display his eagerness and the imam might think him weak.

"Although I am not a military expert, my reading of the material indicates that it contains the locations of five nuclear missiles within the kingdom, and instructions for computers, such as pre-set latitude and longitude positions of possible targets."

"Humnh," Ebara grunted, then sucked in a deep breath. "You have done well, my brother. Leave this with me and return immediately to Riyadh. Tell no one of what we have been given. Your loyalty and alertness will be amply rewarded when the rebellion is concluded."

The imam stood and bowed. *"Allahu akbar!"*

"The peace of the Prophet, praise be unto him, remain with you," Ebara replied.

WHEN THE OTHER MAN left, Ebara remained alone in the dimness of a large room in his mosque and let his thoughts weigh what was before him. Nuclear weaponry. This changes everything!

He was a tall and gaunt man, whose robes hung loose around his bony frame. Thick black eyebrows met atop a long nose. The mouth seldom smiled behind the long beard. He had risen swiftly through the ranks of the Religious Police with his unforgiving view of the world as an evil place and his patchwork philosophy of violence that he could trace to specific parts of the Koran.

Through years of behind-the-scenes maneuvering, he had taken control of the Committee for the Propagation of Virtue and the Prevention of Vice, and wore the trademark red headpiece with great pride. Ambition, hard work, and a single-minded dedication to power had paid off. Now he was at a peak of power, a place in which he could do no wrong simply because he was the one doing it.

When the mysterious outsiders had come quietly shopping for an accomplice who might be installed to head a new government for Saudi Arabia, Ebara had been a natural choice. He was, by careful stages, outraged at the idea at first, then reluctant, and eventually, a full participant. In exchange, he had become extremely rich.

The goals of the plotters had been mutual. A coup to displace the House of Saud with a stringent, theology-based government and a shift in the control of the petroleum production facilities. Ebara would become even more feared and ever more powerful.

His only direct contact with the outside was with a German banker, Dieter Nesch. Through him, a message could be relayed to the president of Russia, who was funding the overthrow of the king. Ebara played with the key and the card and the book, thinking about the situation. The balance of power had tilted as suddenly as shifting sand in a storm, and Ebara, after all, was still a Saudi. Bargaining was part of his blood. The new weapons meant new negotiations. He could remain the visible head of the rebellion and ratchet up the pressure and the rhetoric, as outlined in the original plan, but more money could now be demanded, and more control must come to him in the eventual takeover of the oil business.

The Russian should pay dearly for a workable cache of nuclear weapons already in place in Saudi Arabia.

Still, Ebara knew nothing about nuclear bombs and such. He had not been recruiting scientists, since they were part of the intelligentsia that he had been targeting and persecuting for being in league with the current regime. The military still was unreliable, so those officers could not be trusted. Might some foreign scientists be hired to make these things work? No, it would take too long and tempt foreign rivals to enter the fray.

Dieter Nesch was the one who funneled the money from Moscow that was making things happen, and it was Nesch who had personally found the terrorist known as Juba to run the tactical portions of the rebellion. So far, Juba had done a brilliant job. That was the answer. Juba would know how to use the missiles.

Ebara shouted, and a young servant appeared. The boy was instructed to go immediately to the seaside villa of the European businessman and escort him back to the mosque for a private meeting. No topic was given. Just tell him to hurry.

To impose a savage control on this new situation, Ebara would order Dieter Nesch to immediately get the terrorist genius to emerge from hiding, fly into Saudi Arabia, and take direct control of the nuclear arsenal. He would work directly for Ebara. No one else.

KHOBZ, SAUDI ARABIA

KYLE SWANSON INVADED SAUDI Arabia all by himself, scrunched in a window seat on an ancient King Air 90 twin-engine turboprop that was grinding its way south down the coast of the Arabian Gulf over the one hundred kilometers from Kuwait to the oil patch semiautonomous city of al-Khobz. His documents identified him as a specialist in fiber optic sensor security systems and stated that he was on contract with a company within the massive al-Khobz Joint Operations petroleum complex.

The cream-colored plane was flying just out over the shoreline and Kyle watched as oil rigs, boats, piers and pipelines, storage tanks, and support facilities passed below the wing. There was a long, curving beach at the eastern edge of a cluttered city. At the western edge, bleached raw desert extended all the way to the horizon. Somewhere in between those borders, a nuclear-tipped missile was hidden. Kyle's job was to find and destroy it.

The border town at the tip of Saudi Arabia was a neutral zone shared by Saudi Arabia and Kuwait, and foreigners were plentiful, for the worldwide oil business created its own polyglot culture wherever it drilled, built, and manned the rigs and support facilities.

Behind Kyle was a talkative Belgian engineer whose gabbing about his work on the offshore control system modifications filled the otherwise peaceful cabin. He was a geyser of meaningless statistics and acronyms and discussed at boring length how his company's numeric instruments would work so much better in linking the digital measurements with onshore equipment so they could phase out the old tie-worm system. It was good cover. Swanson didn't want to at talk all.

Kyle tuned him out and took in the passing panorama, trying to remember the background briefing about Khobz that had been sent to him a few hours earlier by the Lizard, Trident's brainy intel officer back in Washington.

The city did not exist until a few decades ago. Back in those rough days, there was only a collection of a few huts near the beach, where traders did business with roving Bedouin tribes. Then the British discovered a huge reservoir of oil just offshore and money roared in. "Khobz" was the Arabic word for "bread" and was an appropriate name for the new settlement that had been created to farm the oil, which was on its own a guarantee of life-giving sustenance. Glittering new construction replaced the trader huts and the place grew daily. About two hundred thousand people now lived and worked there, with most of the foreigners residing in a special compound that was separated from the Arabs by a big fence, armed guards, and strict religious and cultural differences with their Saudi hosts.

He liked what he saw, for cities were his sanctuary. Since he was a child roaming the narrow streets of South Boston, Kyle Swanson had been accustomed to the deep, subtle rhythms of metropolitan areas, learning the advantages and dangers of shadows and corners, rooftops and doorways. Nothing focused the attention on the streets like being a short six-year-old Irish kid running one step ahead of a gang of older Italian boys. The Marines and special ops training and experience had intensified that knowledge. Although the names, languages, and skin colors of the people might change, all cities shared things in common and those things were etched in his memory.

Out in the open desert, a solitary man stands out in a landscape of nothing. Here, he could blend into the population as just another person. Swanson knew how to work cities and considered al-Khobz to be just another stop on the sniper bus, a new place in which he could be an urban predator. Something was going to happen here. He could smell it.

THE PLANE WAS OPERATED by the Boykin Group, one of the many small foreign contract companies that supported the oil operations, and it routinely made the hops between Khobz and Kuwait City, Qatar, Dubai, Bahrain, and the other nearby countries. It carried six passengers today: Kyle, the talkative Belgian, a Kenyan engineer working on the submarine fuel pipeline from a gas lift platform, two Malaysian rig rats, and a pleasant Chinese accountant from Hong Kong who was heading down for an audit.

Kyle had mentally examined them all and decided it would be worthwhile to exchange greetings with the Chinese guy seated directly across the narrow aisle. The man introduced himself as Henry Tsang, immediately producing a pale business card with dark embossed Chinese symbols on one side and the English translation on the other: Henry Tsang, an accountant from a Shanghai auditing company. He wore blue jeans, a maroon golf shirt, and a blue baseball cap with a faded Beijing 2008 Olympics logo. The English was fluent, with a British accent that indicated an education in Hong Kong, and his handshake was strong. The skin had been hardened by exposure to the weather and a thin scar ran just above his right eyebrow, like a healed wound. Accountant, hell. This guy was no pencil pusher. The Chinese were sniffing around the oil patch. "Call me sometime. Perhaps we could have a lunch or dinner together," Tsang said. "Do you have a card?"

"Nope, but I do have a number." Kyle scrawled his name and an 800 number on a slip of paper torn from the edge of a magazine and handed it over. They had opened a back channel: Muscle to muscle, spook to spook.

Everyone on board wore a necklace of plastic credentials. They were just men coming to work, part of the ongoing, ever-changing force required to keep the wells pumping out three hundred thousand barrels of oil every day. Routine jobs, routine flight, routine day. The twin-engine aircraft slowed, lowered its wheels and joined the landing pattern that came in straight over the bustling city.

A BULLET SMACKED INTO the right engine with a loud, tearing thud and the Belgian screamed, "They are shooting at us!" The King Air plane jolted sharply to its right as the engine began to smoke and a spinning prop stuttered. Several more rounds popped through the right wing, boring holes in the thin metal but not striking any fuel or electrical circuits. The window beside the Chinese accountant sang as a bullet glanced off of it with a loud *smack*, webbing the thick Plexiglas with fracture lines. Henry Tsang did not flinch.

The pilot fought the aircraft under control and brought it level as a fire suppressant sprayed the smoking engine. Less than a minute after the shots were fired, the plane touched down on the long runway and began its roll to the terminal. The copilot leaned out of his seat and looked back down the aisle. "Emergency over. Anybody hurt back there?" he called.

The pilot shut down the steaming engine and steered off the main runway toward the fire engines racing out to meet them.

"You okay?" Swanson asked the Chinese man, who had seemed quite unperturbed that a bullet had just missed him.

"Yes," he replied. "That was exciting. Now I have a story to tell my children back home. Accountants like me don't have many exciting stories."

Swanson just smiled. A normal accountant would have been pissing his pants.

The small door opened and a man with a tanned, sweaty face stuck his head in. Obviously American. "End of the line, folks. Everybody out. Right now, and follow me to the minivan." The six passengers hurried toward the hatch. Outside, fire crews had doused the wrecked engine with foam and a mechanic was opening panels to review the damage.

The minivan had the same color scheme as the plane and magnetic signs stuck to the sides identified it as another vehicle of the Boykin Group. When everyone was aboard, the man who had met the plane slid into the front passenger seat. He had an old-style crew-cut with flecks of gray, was of middle age but still muscular, and wore wrinkled khaki trousers and a red-and-white plaid shirt with short sleeves. He adjusted his big body so that he could partially face the passengers. As the minivan moved toward the terminal, he dealt business cards to everyone and spoke with a pleasant voice that reflected Oklahoma roots.

"I'm Homer Boykin, the head honcho of the Boykin Group, which is made up of me and my driver here, Jamal Muheisen. You might call us fixers. We arrange things. Any of y'all need anything while you are in Khobz, just give us a call."

Swanson pegged him as an old-time oil roughneck who had worked his way off the platforms and into an office job.

"You're the third flight today that has been hit by random fire from the rooftops," Boykin continued. "Only one person has been slightly wounded, but bet your asses that the landing patterns are going to change so we can circle in from the water. The powers that be don't like air traffic other than helicopters flying over the rigs. Well, fuck them. We don't like being slow targets." The voice was steady and matter-of-fact, as if he was reciting dry data.

The nervous Belgian spoke. He had lost all interest in telling everyone about his important job. "What is happening? The Saudis announced just this morning that everything was calm throughout the kingdom. Are we in danger?"

The beefy American laughed and punched the shoulder of the driver, Jamal, who glanced at him with a touch of humor in his own eyes. "The Big Lie, boys. Things are still pretty quiet because of all of the security protecting the oil fields, but little ole Khobz is no bed of roses. I will personally escort y'all through customs, which is tougher than usual but still not a problem if you have the right papers and some *baksheesh*, bribes. You *do* have your IDs, right? I'm supposed to tell all of you that everyone is confined to the protected zone, absolutely no going beyond downtown, and that a nine o'clock curfew starts tonight."

Kyle asked, "So since the king is dead, who's really in charge?"

"The government is still in control, very truly so, but no successor has been chosen. Without the king to keep them in line, the Religious Police are getting pretty harsh and that's building resentment among the locals. Some gangs are running around claiming to be enforcing their *sharia* law, through the quasi-governmental outfit called the Committee on Virtue."

"So the extreme clerics are grabbing power," Swanson observed. "That's a pretty familiar song."

"Looks that way. They ain't the Taliban yet, but some of the fanatics want to see how far they can push. That squeezes the government, which has been allied with the guys in the mosques from the very start of modern Saudi Arabia."

"Are we talking about civil war?" asked Henry Tsang.

"Not quite to that point, buddy. Not even with the assassination of the king. The princes are still in charge, so they will pick a successor pretty quickly, but the trouble is growing. Take right here in Khobz. A teenaged girl was murdered a few days ago at the biggest mall in town by the religious cops for talking with a boy on a cell phone. She pulled a knife and carved up one of them so badly that the bastard died, good for her, and she hit a second one with pepper spray. Normally, the Saudis would blame the girl for causing the trouble, but the *muttaween* went too far and dozens of witnesses saw her beaten to death by those mean bastards."

"Are we safe?" The Belgian was almost frantic.

Homer Boykin waved a big hand and smiled. "Oh, yeah. Y'all just be careful and keep yourselves informed through your company security teams and international news channels; don't expect any straight answers from the government. Information has never been available on almost anything in Saudi Arabia; they block Internet sites and they don't like reporters. The truth is getting hard to come by, but you boys are oil dudes. They aren't about to start killing off the guys who bring in the gold."

"They shot at us!" The Belgian protested.

Boykin just chuckled, and the minivan coasted to an easy stop. He led them into the customs area. The large room was patrolled by uniformed soldiers with machine guns, and all new arrivals stood in line to be thoroughly searched and have their papers carefully examined.

Kyle went through the process with disinterest, having anticipated the heightened arrival security procedures. His first task had just been to get into Saudi Arabia, which he was doing. Somehow, between Sybelle and the Lizard in Washington and some spec ops magic, weapons and assistance were to be provided.

He used the time in line to watch what was happening in the terminal beyond the customs area, where a crowd of civilians milled about. Worried men were talking with airline representatives and women tended crying children. Couples were embracing as if they would never see each other again, and the tension was almost electric. *Civilians getting their families out*, he thought. *Little private planes drawing fire. Not good. There has been no warning by either the American or the Saudi governments for noncombatants to leave the area, but the foreigners who live here obviously feel trouble is on the way and are heading for safety.*

Their group finally cleared customs and the Belgian engineer and the Chinese accountant drifted away to find their companies. Kyle went to the airport's small restaurant, bought a sandwich and a soda, then moved to a table near a big window to continue his surveillance. Women, kids, and a few men were loading onto small charter planes that were lined up in a row, awaiting their turns at the two departure gates. Baggage carts were stacked to overflowing. Lot of folks getting out of Dodge, not many coming in, and nobody seemed to be enjoying their day. He bit into a soggy egg salad croissant with lettuce and tomato sliding out of the middle and sipped the warm Coke.

Boykin, the big American with the crew-cut hair approached his table with a Pepsi in his hand and sat down uninvited. "Welcome to a brewing shitstorm, brother." Boykin fished an ice cube from his glass and used it to write *XUSMC* by tracing water on the smooth blue plastic tabletop. Then he wiped it away with his palm, found a fresh cube and drew a crude symbol that looked like a pitchfork: *TRIDENT.* Boykin wiped that off, too, and broke into a friendly grin. "I've been in contact with my boss and Sybelle Summers, so let's get you gunned up and take a ride around town."

THE **BOYKIN GROUP WAS** headquartered in a nondescript building in an industrial district cluttered with small warehouses, stacks of steel shipping containers, and pyramids of pipe and other oil line gear. The company sign was painted on a weathered wooden door behind a little screened entranceway that kept out the flies. Jamal, a short and muscular man who moved with smooth efficiency, went into the screen enclosure, unlocked the wooden door and pulled it outward. Behind it stood a strong steel door with two heavy locks that threw bolts into the surrounding steel frame.

The office was nothing much. A floor of bland greenish linoleum with some of the tiles torn, and plaster walls covered with many coats of cheap white paint. Two second-hand desks faced each other. Thick shades covered the windows on each wall to keep out the sun, but if he chose to look outside, Boykin had an almost 360-degree view of the surrounding area. Bulletin boards were peppered with pinpoint holes, some hanging notes and a few old clipboards hanging on nails, their jaws chomping wads of paper. Overhead fluorescent lights hummed and flickered. The place looked as common as the dirt.

"This joint was built years back when construction was booming around the new port and nobody raised an eyebrow," Homer explained. "Lots of weird construction was going on back then and our contractors and laborers were flown in along with the necessary specialized equipment, did their jobs, then left. No locals were involved. Did it all in less than thirty days."

Kyle Swanson recognized it for what it was as he stood in front of an air-conditioning vent and let it blast the sweat on his back. "CIA safe house," he said. The intelligence-gathering outpost was created because the Agency wanted trained eyes and ears in one of the world's most important oil instal-lations.

"Come on downstairs," Boykin said, pushing a panel button. A section of the wall folded back, revealing a staircase. "The builders had a hell of a time drilling and pouring support columns for the basement. They kept striking oil. Damn stuff just oozed out of the sand and would fill the holes overnight if they didn't pump it out."

The basement was larger than the house above it and was cooler by being below ground level. Fans kept filtered air moving around the communica-tions suite along one wall where secure computers, printers, speakers, and security camera feeds were in place. Cupboards containing emergency ra-tions and boxes of bottled water were built along another wall and a chemi-cal toilet and a small shower were curtained off in a corner. Folding cots leaned against one cabinet. At the far end, a steel ladder ascended one corner up to a hatch that exited into a rusting shipping container anchored on a concrete pad that was separated by a small driveway from the headquarters. It was maintained to appear to be a storage shed for tools. Emergency exit.

Another section of the basement was sectioned off with a locked cage of steel wire and contained the armory. Boykin twirled the combination lock and swung open the gate. "I understand you've done some work for us be-fore," he said. "We probably have anything in here that you will need, but let's keep it to a sidearm until we finish the recon drive."

Kyle found another Colt .45 and took a quick and approving look around the armory. It was spotless and the weapons were perfectly maintained. Crates of ammo were neatly stacked and explosives were sealed in plastic. The city of Khobz had been under construction for more than four decades. Swanson figured the Boykin Group and its predecessors in this little CIA operation had been modernizing and accumulating gear throughout that entire time.

Another result of that long tenure was that the intelligence specialists based here over the years had created a cartographic masterpiece that was secured to a nearby table. "Impressive," Kyle said.

"We keep it current," Homer responded, looking at it with undisguised pride. "Jamal and I pace off the distances while we hustle small contracts around the town and we photograph potential obstacles. Even the best satellite photo can still miss vital points that an operator on the ground would need to know."

"You got that right," said Swanson.

Boykin pulled up a chair and sat down and Jamal poured a cup of coffee for himself. "Major Summers told me this was a one-trick mission and that you would pass along the instructions. Langley approved. So here we are. What's up?"

"No offense, but I assume Jamal has been vetted?"

The Jordanian laughed, showing white teeth and a sense of humor. He dropped the façade of being a semi-ragged Middle Eastern hired hand. "My family comes from Jordan, but I'm first-generation American, born in Tennessee," he said. "The Agency recruited me eleven years ago straight out of law school at Mister Jefferson's University in Virginia because of my languages. Obviously my cover works. What are we supposed to be doing with you?"

"There's a missile with a nuclear warhead hidden around here somewhere. My job is to destroy it," Kyle said. His statement sucked the air out of the basement room.

"Be damned." Homer Boykin shot a look at Jamal. "We've been telling Langley for months that something was strange with that Saudi anti-missile battery just outside of town. Our reports have been totally ignored." He shook his head in disgust. "Those second-guessing fuckers thousands of miles away drive me nuts."

Jamal agreed. "That's a good place for a nuke missile. Hide it among a bunch of other missiles that are allegedly protecting the oil fields." He placed his finger on a map location about three miles south of the city center. "It's got to be right there, alongside the living quarters for about a few hundred soldiers who guard the production facilities."

THE BITE HAD GONE out of the scorching sun when they set out to drive around the city, Jamal at the wheel and Kyle in the passenger seat. Homer Boykin was on the long seat in the middle row of the van, leaning forward between them to talk in a normal voice.

"This place has always had a bit of nastiness to it. Used to be a rest stop for the foreign fighters going into Iraq. By the time one group was trucked off, a new batch of those hard-eyed sumbitches would be gathering," said Boykin.

"Any of them still here?" Kyle adjusted the pistol tucked in his belt.

Boykin pointed. "You bet, and Jamal hears that some of those outlaw militia types from over in Basra have come in *from* Iraq for a change. Let's go over near the mosque, Jamal."

The minivan went around a corner and edged through the narrow street of an outdoor covered bazaar. The food stalls were doing the most business, swirls of anxious shoppers and women carrying plastic sacks that bulged with goods. "More people out this evening than normal," Jamal commented.

"Like last-minute shopping before a hurricane," said Kyle. "Everybody stocking up."

Boykin's trained eyes saw more. "Despite the increase in business, the shopkeepers are shutting down early. Not as many tents in the streets and the doors and shutters on a couple of stores are already closed."

Jamal reached the broad road that was the main axis through the urban area. Boykin pointed. "There's the main mosque up ahead at twelve o'clock. It's the headquarters of the Committee on Virtue and that's where the fighters stay."

Oil money and political favoritism had been lavished on the mosque, which had a classical Arab architecture of graceful arches and long, straight lines. Men streamed in and out of the three entrances that were open behind the stone columns, and tall towers rose from the sides, where the *muezzin* could call the faithful to prayer. The towers also provided sentries with high perches from which they could see everything around the mosque. The building marked the separation point between the commercial district and the residential area. *Nobody up in the towers. Only one guard at the entrance*, Kyle thought. *They're overconfident.*

"Go around," said Boykin, and Jamal swung through traffic. An irregular ring road circled the big mosque and as they approached the back, they found a line of pickups and flatbed trucks, some minivans and small cars. "Convoy," he said.

"Trouble, Boss," said Jamal. "Police roadblock."

"Turn through the alley," said Boykin. "We've seen enough here. Those are cops, not soldiers, obviously there to stop people from being too curious about those trucks."

Jamal waved to the few uniformed men at the roadblock as he made the turn and accelerated away. "You guys stay low. We don't want to be showing white faces around here," Jamal said. "I'll take a shortcut back to the foreign compound. Then we can head south to the missile base."

The first rock sailed up from behind them and clattered on the metal roof of the van, followed by a flurry of stones and bricks from the sides. "Gangs of kids are coming from all around. Get us out of here," Boykin called.

Rocks and soda cans and debris of every sort rained from the rooftops, doorways, and the mouths of alleys as the minivan passed. No adults were out, just kids, their eyes wide in excitement, bombing Satan.

"What the fuck? Are we in Somalia?" yelled Kyle, covering his head with one hand and grabbing the pistol with the other. A rock the size of a softball smashed through the back window. People whistled and yelled.

"We ride out here all the time and never have trouble. These people know us," Jamal responded, spinning the steering wheel. They flew around another corner and the crowd disappeared, evaporating as if nothing had happened. "The kids are the early warning system to keep outsiders away from the mosque," he said. "Something's coming down."

A FEW MINUTES LATER, Jamal drove through the gate to the foreign compound, nodded to the single soldier on guard, and entered a different world. It was a neat layout with straight roads and cookie-cutter, Western-style homes, cars in the driveways and TV satellite dishes bolted on the rooftops, a complete opposite of the nearby communities of square mud huts interspersed with a few grand homes of the local residents. The people of the desert lived out beyond the wire.

"Mostly only guys are still living here," Boykin explained. "Khobz is not pleasant for Western women, and absolutely no place to try to raise a kid because the *muttaween* religious cops rule outside the fence and really in-fluence what can go on inside this perimeter, too. This is not a diplomatic quarter with any sort of immunity, so Saudi law rules. Families are better off in nearby countries where Daddy can go see them on a long weekend and spend the big oil paychecks."

Many of the houses seemed empty and forlorn with no lights on, al-though darkness was beginning to fall. Kyle mentioned the exodus at the airport and Boykin said that unofficial withdrawal had been going on for several days. "Anybody with a brain and a choice is leaving," Homer said.

The supermarket in the mall was still open, but the bowling alley was closed, as were the public swimming pools and the clubhouses, as if the lit-tle community was holding its breath.

"We need to pick up anything from our house, Homer?" Jamal asked, pausing at the driveway of a two-bedroom home that was identical to its neighbors in every way.

"No. We're good. Let's get on out to the military pad before the light gives out."

Kyle shook his head. "Let's not. Judging by what we just saw, they won't let us anywhere near the place and we don't want to seem to be overly curi-ous. I can go out tonight for a look."

Homer said, "Okay, if that's what you want. You up for some pizza?" he asked. "Got a place down by the beach run by a Chinese family. They oper-ate 24/7 because the oil business never shuts down. Make more money sell-ing thick crust slices than they would sweating out on the rigs. We'll pick some up and go back to the shop." He took out his cell phone and hit a speed dial number for Dragon Pizza. "Hope you ain't a vegetarian."

They returned to the safe house with two large pizzas stacked with meat and redolent with onions and peppers, went through the steel door and down to the basement. Boykin grabbed a slice as he booted up his com-puter, typed in his password and checked the e-mails. Nothing.

Jamal was telling a joke about camels when his cell phone rang with a Stones tune. He looked at the caller ID, raised his eyebrows and answered, "The Boykin Group." He listened, closed the connection without respond-ing and tossed the phone on a counter.

"The convoy is leaving the mosque," he said, stuffing one more bite of pizza into his mouth and opening the armory cage. The first salvo of explosions could be heard dully stomping around the foreign compound.

Jamal and Homer actually watched Kyle Swanson change before their eyes, as if some motion picture special effect stunt was turning an ordinary man into an icy machine. A steadiness settled over him like a cloak and his eyes sparkled, the mind racing. He was instantly amped and ready, went into the armory cage for an MP5 submachine gun and a couple of spare magazines. He also picked up a set of bolt-cutters and a combat knife. Jamal handed him a headset radio.

"I'm going to use the noise and distraction as cover to check out the missiles." Swanson was up the stairs and gone.

Homer finished the pizza while helping Jamal load up the van.

RIYADH

A **FEW HOURS AFTER** dark on the day the king was murdered, small processions of expensive automobiles began to arrive at a restaurant on the outskirts of Riyadh. As usual, the chairs around small tables on the sidewalk out front were occupied by men drinking sludgy *gahwa* Arabian coffee from tiny cups and sharing the pipes of hookahs filled with rose-water. The men were the outer cordon of guards for the meeting that was about to take place on the second floor of the plain-looking building.

Personal representatives for six of the most powerful men in the kingdom of Saudi Arabia arrived separately, with their own bodyguards, and moved through the tables, beneath an archway and through a double-door that opened into a bland dining area lit only by strings of naked 100-watt bulbs that dangled from loose cords. Other guards, these openly carrying weapons, were in the corners. The restaurant owner welcomed the men in turn, and passed them through the downstairs area to a staircase that ascended to the second floor. Their retinues and personal bodyguards were left downstairs. Only six men were allowed up.

The principals did not attend because even with the safeguards that were in place, it was the kind of tense evening when long knives might flash. The half-dozen men who went up the dusty stairs represented the royal family, religion, the military, major nonpetroleum business interests, the tribes, and oil.

There was an immense difference between this room and the rest of the building. It was brightly lit, neat and clean. In one corner was a fully stocked bar that included exclusive brands of alcoholic beverages. A large round table occupied the middle of the room, with six chairs spaced evenly around it, the places marked by sealed bottles of water. A feast of food was spread in the middle: plates of fresh pita bread, bowls of spices, falafel, rice, hot peppers, and mutton and other meats that had been vertically roasted on spits.

The group was gathering for the most urgent of reasons, to decide who would be their next king, but Arab tradition required a certain informality that showed friendship, respect, and honor. Only when the men had helped themselves to the food and drink and exchanged small talk about their families could they get down to business. No one was technically in charge.

The talk did not get around to the business of the night for almost an hour, until Prince Aziz, a minor member of the royal family, tore off a final bit of pita, rolled it around a chunk of rice and lamb, dipped it into a spicy mixture and shoved it into his mouth. He chewed, swallowed, licked his fingers, and gave a loud burp. His demonstrated appreciation of the fine meal marked the end of the first phase of the meeting and a termination of the uneasy politeness. The belch was a starting signal to launch the serious discussion.

"The line of direct succession has been severed," said one voice and everyone looked at Aziz, who was representing the sprawling royal family. "The king had appointed his eldest son to be the heir, but the simultaneous death of the crown prince has left the position open. We must choose a new leader and announce him as soon as possible."

"Agreed. The question is, 'How?'" said a colonel who was the military envoy to the meeting tonight. He was not in uniform. "The successor must come from among the king's sons or grandsons. I cannot see either of His Majesty's full brothers ascending."

The construction magnate from an influential family, chosen as the spokesman for the nonpetroleum businesses, agreed. "Both of the brothers are too far along in years to assume day-to-day responsibility during this crisis. His Majesty had three sons in direct lineage. With the crown prince also dead, only two of the true sons remain as candidates. The sons by other wives do not qualify."

"The eldest is a corrupt playboy and is unacceptable to the tribes," snorted the sheikh who was a Bedouin chief from the south. "The youngest has not proven himself as a man, for he is a father of daughters—no sons at all. He is also unacceptable to us."

The conversation lapsed into silence for a few moments. Not only royal succession, but competing commercial pressures were in play at the table. Fortunes were on the line.

The executive from the rich oil industry coughed to get attention. "Let us not forget that there is a rebellion going on outside these doors, my friends." He cast a stony glance across at the imam who was the religious faction's man at the table. "Our king was murdered by zealots who are out of control."

The imam retorted, "The rebellion was caused by a corrupt government that strayed from the will of Allah and the words of the Prophet, praise be unto him. The Grand Mufti is not involved in any way in this matter."

The eyes of the oil man swept around the table. "You are wrong. The overall population is not in rebellion. They are still sitting it out, huddling in their homes, just like our exalted Grand Mufti. His silence has allowed that vile dog Ebara and his *muttaween* to seize leadership of the rebels. Ebara is a disgrace to our faith."

Prince Aziz steepled his fingers before speaking. "Our religion and our politics are threads in the same fabric. The House of Saud ruled with the support of the Wahhabis, and the monarchy in turn allowed them to spread and enforce the tenets of our beliefs." He turned to face the imam. "It appears that the religious leaders are no longer satisfied with that longstanding arrangement."

There was a rumble of private discussions around the table for a minute before the oil representative again spoke. "All of us are worried about the future," he said. "Saudi Arabia is not Iran. The citizens will not accept a totalitarian theocracy, nor rule by the *muttaween*. We must show our people that our new king has unanimous support, so he can assume the throne immediately."

The imam was sweating beneath his robes. "There are proper groups already in place to make this decision. Why should just the six of us tell the rest of the nation what to do?"

The colonel slapped the table. "Yes! We have the Consultative Council and the *ulema* and the *Majlis* and the *Shura* and the *muktars* and twenty million other bargaining Saudis. They would never even agree that a circle is round, much less come together on a decision of this magnitude."

Prince Aziz sighed: "I have thousands of cousins in the royal family and all of them would like to ascend. Even me. But we can haggle later. Right now our people need a king and our military needs a leader in order to quell this rebellion. If you are all satisfied with the House of Saud, please, just pick somebody!"

The powerful executive from the oil industry concurred. "This tawdry rebellion threatens to swallow us all. We need to stabilize this situation fast or risk having some outside force come in to seize our production facilities. If that happens, our very lifeblood will be under the thumb of international supervision for many years to come. Our most precious resource will be beyond our control."

The imam had his own instructions from the leaders waiting in the mosques. "There is much more to consider than the oil and money," he stated with a cold glare. "If it is the Will of Allah, praise be unto him, that a new kind of government is rising to save our nation, then we are all bound to obey."

The tribal sheikh stared at him. "You would let a foolish thug like Ebara take over? I will tell you here and now that the *Bedu* will never stand for it."

"Then let us choose," someone said. "Who among the grandsons? I put forth the name of Prince Abdullah, who is easily the most qualified among those in the true bloodline."

The imam became stiff in outrage. "The ambassador to the United States? That disgraceful man was about to sign a peace treaty with the Jews!"

"He was following the decision of our government," the colonel reminded him. "Our country has never fought Israel and let's hope we never do. Many in our generation are tired of hearing sermons about how the Jews are to blame for everything that goes wrong. The military has no objection to Abdullah. Does anyone else have a nomination?"

"Prince Abdullah has the diplomatic and military experience to take over. We can live with him." The man from the oil sector settled back into his chair. The tribal sheikh agreed.

"That is our decision, then," said Prince Aziz. "It is unanimous, is it not?"

"I shall inform the Grand Mufti of your suggestion," the imam said. "His decision will be rendered after appropriate thought."

That was too much for the sheikh, a man known for his fiery temper. He rose from his chair, his eyes darkening and the muscles of his jaw quivering with barely suppressed fury. He was a man of the desert, a Wahhabi Bedouin, a tribe that never hesitated to purify the wishes of the Prophet with the blood of enemies. Violence was part of his heritage and he brooked no respect for preachers. He pulled back his robe and a jeweled dagger glittered in his belt. "That is not good enough. You are stalling. You will take this to the Grand Mufti as the choice that he must endorse immediately! Or, perhaps you may not go back at all. Perhaps I should cut off your ears and give you a better reason for not hearing what we have all decided? We can always send another messenger."

The colonel rose. "I believe the sheikh and the imam have a few private matters to discuss. I would be honored if the rest of you would join me downstairs for some coffee." They all walked out, closing the door behind them.

Five minutes later, the imam came stumbling down the stairs and went through the group without a word, his face pale and his fingertips shaking. The sheikh followed, a sneering smile on his dark face. "It is now unanimous. Tomorrow we announce a new king."

INDONESIA

JUBA WATCHED THE TELEVISION news on the 42-inch flat plasma screen, mentally keeping track of the score. The bodies were piling up and he was winning easily. The House of Saud had been decapitated, the country was temporarily leaderless and that sanctimonious weird preacher, Mohammed Ebara, was busily stirring the religious pot. Everything going as planned.

Using the remote control, he replaced the chattering news people with the Web site of a private Swiss financial institution that served only very wealthy customers. The money was piling up in his private account, and more than enough was available to pay the people he had hired to continue the pressure. Slowly, slowly, he would stoke the fire with unexpected strikes throughout Saudi Arabia. The fighters were already in place, just waiting for him to release them. It was a tight schedule that eventually would build to a crescendo of violence.

The complicated scheme did not provide him with the same instant thrill as in the old days, when he pulled the trigger on his sniper rifle and could watch a bullet strike home and a target die in his scope, but he had moved beyond such things as routine assassinations. The stakes today were so much higher, and the overall effects of his work were so much more important!

The achievements so far called for a bit of private celebration and he opened the seals of red wax on a new square bottle of Jewel of Russia vodka, a new brand distilled from wheat and rye. He poured and raised the glass in an imaginary toast to the old philosopher-scientist Isaac Newton, who had figured it all out many years ago with his first law of motion: Every object in a state of uniform motion tends to remain in that state of motion unless an external force is applied to it.

The royal family of Saudi Arabia had been paddling comfortably on their underground sea of oil. Juba pictured himself as the external force needed to change that.

He had done a lot of homework before putting the final plan together. In the tumultuous inner circles of the Saudi royal family, there had always been plots and counterplots about which prince of the House of Saud should be the actual ruler. In 1975, the sitting monarch was shot to death by his nephew. For Juba, a simple assassination would not have been good enough. He wanted something spectacular, a showy attack that would paralyze the confidence of the people and open the door for a government takeover by Muslim extremists. By the time he was through, the whole country would be moving backward in time. The vodka was tracing a pleasant burn down to his stomach when a maidservant softly announced, "Your guest has arrived, sir."

An Indonesian man stepped through the wide entranceway to the mountain mansion. He was of middle age, with black hair retreating on the high forehead and a belly that pushed hard against the buttons of his shirt. With narrow shoulders, Muhammed Bambang Sukarnoputri was shaped like a pear.

"Governor. It is good to see you again." Juba shook hands with the smaller man and led him to a comfortable area with overstuffed chairs. They made small talk until the maid returned with a tray of fruit and juice for the pious provincial governor, who did not drink alcohol. Juba had only a glass of chilled water.

Officially, the Indonesian government kept religion out of its politics, although the country was 88 percent Muslim and Juba had found it simple to cultivate powerful allies. On the far side of the mountain on which he lived was a government weather research facility that secretly fed him all of the electrical power and telecommunications and scientific support that he could possibly use. With his own computer network feeding from those secure grids, Juba was guiding the upheaval in Saudi Arabia, half a world away, and the TV reports were flashing across the big screen.

"This television coverage reminds me of the make-believe carnage in American movies about the end of the world," said Sukarnoputri. "Your work has been astounding."

Juba gave a small nod. "International reporters are surging into Saudi Arabia in invasion-level numbers, and with the death of the king and the crown prince, the street demonstrations will grow more violent. The military will have to respond with force, and that will only create more demonstrators." Juba handed the provincial governor several computer printouts held together at the left-hand corner by a spring clip.

"Some army units already are hesitating to perform their duties if it means killing civilians. When the cameras show children and old people being bloodied and killed, it will appear that a popular uprising is trying to overthrow a ruthless and immoral royal family."

"Very good. However, I bring a private and important message from our mutual friend," the governor said. "Is there somewhere we can speak that is beyond the hearing of any servants?"

"Certainly," Juba said. This was curious. There was a hint of strain in the voice, a touch of alarm. Sukarnoputri was not the jittery sort. Not only was he the governor of the local province, he was also the brother of the powerful Mobile Brigade of the Indonesian National Police Force. Since both had political and military protection and government-protected communications security, he frequently acted as a cutout between Juba and Dieter Nesch.

They walked outside into the cool and gentle wind and along a stone path that led through a garden ablaze with flowers. A rugged rock wall, about waist high, bordered the edge of the outcropping, beyond which was a sharp slope all the way down to the sea. From this vantage point, they could see for miles.

"I am afraid that something has arisen that will require some changes in your plans, my friend," said the governor.

Juba fixed the man with an unsettling one-eyed stare. With so much at stake, with the game successfully underway, a late operational change was wanted? Nesch knew better than that. "Go on."

"This will sound quite unbelievable, but our mutual acquaintance has sent word that Mohammed Abu Ebara has somehow come into possession of five nuclear missiles, including their launch codes. I was instructed to tell you that Ebara demands your presence on the ground in Saudi Arabia, as quickly as possible, to handle them."

Juba leaned on the stone wall and listened to the sea while he thought. *Leave here? He "demands" that I spend many hours in an airplane and run all the way to the Middle East at his command?* He took a deep breath. "That was not part of our original arrangement," he said. "It does not matter whether he has found some nuclear weapons or slingshots in the sand, we cannot stop the current operation in its tracks."

"I know that and so does Dieter. But Ebara is adamant. He apparently is having visions from paradise, voices that are guiding him."

"Damn. What does the Russian want?"

"Apparently, our friend in Moscow is letting Ebara have his way."

"So I am supposed to just close down shop, abandon months of careful planning and the spending of millions of dollars to get things ready, just to go hold the hand of Ebara?" Juba walked slowly around the area, tasting the breeze. "Without me here to control things, the overthrow of the government may not work. Everything depends on the timing of the coming attacks. This is a huge risk."

Governor Sukarnoputri spread his palms in a helpless gesture. What can we do?

Juba's thoughts were reeling, trying to find some way to make it all work. The coup had been his primary goal. What could be gained with nuclear weapons? They could not be used within Saudi Arabia during this uprising.

Perhaps afterward? A potential new reward began to surface in his mind. Consider them as a separate matter and not part of the current strife. With nuclear weapons in his possession, he could be recorded in history as one of the most dangerous men who had ever lived! He could destroy Israel! Europe might be within reach. England? His thoughts began to race. Would it be possible to smuggle one to the U.S.? A smile twisted on his deformed lips. A few hours of discomfort in an airplane in exchange for an eternity of notorious fame.

"It will cost more."

The governor said that he had already taken care of the renegotiation, and Dieter Nesch was promising another million euros for Juba just to make the trip, assess the possibilities, and soothe the growing mania of Ebara. The governor and his brother would both rake off a commission.

28

AL-KHOBZ

GOLDEN-RED FLASHES OF EXPLOSIONS flickered in the night sky, painting the buildings in sharp silhouette. The rattle of small-arms fire echoed through the streets while shadows hurried past him, civilians running for their lives. The rebel attack was centered at the main gate to the foreign compound and Swanson veered away to the south. For a change, he was not looking for a fight.

He jogged steadily for about five minutes, listening to the sporadic crack of gunshots. Personal weapons were forbidden in al-Khobz, but almost every house had at least one. Even so, resistance would be isolated and ineffective unless some organization was brought to bear, and that was where the experience and better weaponry of Homer and Jamal would help. Swanson could not provide that tonight. For him, the shooting was a distraction to help him slip away.

He loped along for another six minutes, following the main road south and keeping to the dark areas as the congested urban center gave way to more open space on the right side of the broad avenue, while the waterfront and the rigs glowed like groups of holiday lanterns to his left. He jumped the drainage ditch and darted into a small alleyway partially blocked by plastic bags filled with trash.

Settling low, he could see a bright necklace of floodlights that threw white circles along the fence of the army base about two kilometers away. An alert siren was groaning. Kyle slipped his radio headset into place and keyed it. "You guys there?"

"Yeah," Boykin replied, his voice already heavy with exertion.

"How's it look?"

"The rebels are streaming in through the main security entrance like a bunch of cockroaches. The guard is sprawled out, apparently dead, alongside a second body. Western civilian. A pack of SUVs, pickup trucks, and cars are parked outside the gate and men are hiding behind them to fire into the compound. The shitty part? A pair of blue and white police cars are out there, too. Uniformed cops are working with those assholes."

"Any organized resistance yet?"

"Bits and pieces. We're working on it. I sent two guys to round up everybody they can find and Jamal and I have set up a cross-fire from a couple of buildings overlooking the main breach area. That should stop the ground assault. One surprise is that quiet Chinese dude who came in on the plane with you: He knows how to shoot."

"Not surprised at all. I'll let you know if I spot any rescue force rolling your way."

"Are you sure about where you're going?" asked Boykin.

"I can see the Saudi army base from here. It's all lit up, and there is a lot of movement. Out." He made a final check around his hiding place and saw two shadows doing a fast creep toward the military camp. He flipped down the Cyclops night vision goggles for a better look and found they were an ambush team carrying rocket propelled grenades. Swanson darted from his hide and swung in behind them.

FATEHI AWWAD, A FORMER Egyptian soldier and drug smuggler, hugged the ditch as he stalked toward the site he had picked for a blocking position. A film of sweat and dirt covered his face. He was nervous. Salid, the young fighter carrying an AK-47, was trailing behind. The boy was supposed to be protecting them but had been caught up by excitement. He was anxious to become a martyr, and Awwad was constantly reminding him that their job was to stay alive and stop any attempt by the Saudi soldiers to rescue the foreigners who were under attack in Khobz. The young Salid disregarded the lectures and was falling far off the pace.

"Keep up!" Awwad demanded. "Forget the other fight!"

"I should be back there, helping our brothers slay the infidels."

"Be quiet, boy. Carry out your assignment!"

The 40 mm rocket launcher rested easily on Awwad's right shoulder as he moved toward the illuminated missile base. He had scouted the area and found a large concrete culvert that ran beneath the road to connect the drainage canals. He dropped into the crossing ditch and slithered into the culvert. "Now we wait," he said.

There was no response, no hurrying footsteps. Awwad took a deep breath, listened, then cursed. Salid had given into the craving for action, the lust for blood and glory that could override good sense. Son of a pig!

Awwad adjusted. Children should not be trusted with important assignments. He would have to carry out the ambush on his own and would fire his RPG when the first vehicle, most likely a Humvee or a small truck, came out of the base camp. That would block the road, idle the rest of the rescue convoy, and force a delay while officers assessed the danger. While they were doing that, Awwad would disappear, for there could be no follow-up shot. Salid had taken the only other RPG round with him.

SWANSON WATCHED THE MAN in the rear hesitate, then stop instead of following the leader who carried the RPG. For some reason, this one was not advancing, but just standing there with an AK hanging around his shoulders. A wolfish grin spread over Swanson's face.

He moved with a quiet grace, soft and low to the ground, invisible to the hesitating fighter who was blind to the darkness. Swanson found a crumpled depression in the side of the ditch, slipped into it, and lay on his belly in the dry sand. The night vision goggles clearly painted the fighter who was only five steps away and standing, undecided.

The fighter looked back toward the RPG man, who hissed, "*Keep up! Forget the other fight!*"

The loud whisper of a younger voice responded: "*I should be back there, helping our brothers slay the infidels.*"

"*Be quiet, Salid. Carry out your assignment!*" Then the RPG carrier continued forward.

The rifleman was concentrating his attention back the way he had come, looking past the prone Swanson, attracted by the sounds and flashes of distant gunfire. He took one more step forward to follow his leader, then decided to go back to the guns. He started running back down the ditch, out of breath, panting with anticipation.

KYLE ROSE LIKE A specter as the young man passed, and threw an anaconda on him. Swanson's right forearm wrapped around the front of the neck to crush the windpipe, while his left hand grabbed his right to increase the leverage. Immediately, all air was cut off to the boy's brain and Swanson snatched him from his feet with the rear naked choke hold. Swanson knelt down, taking his opponent with him, then lay on his back and flattened out, clamping both legs around the victim for a full body lock, steadily squeezing harder the entire time. Salid was out cold within fifteen seconds without having uttered a sound.

When the body went limp, Kyle rolled out, stood, slung the prisoner across his shoulder and returned to his secluded hide behind the garbage bags.

In seconds, he had the kid blindfolded and gagged, with his arms tied behind him, but the legs left free. Swanson looped the sling of the AK-47 around the young fighter's throat, twisted it once and let the weapon dangle down the back. If the prisoner tried to run, Kyle could just yank on the AK and choke him back into submission.

Swanson roughly awakened the youngster, jerked him to his feet and gave him a push. Sticking to the darker patches, Kyle soon found the service road that looped around the edge of the city to a side gate of the base. He slowed, moving cautiously until he closed to within a kilometer of the mesh steel fence that was topped with concertina wire. Despite being able to hear the gunfire back at the foreign compound and knowing an ambush was waiting at the front gate, Swanson did not hurry, adhering firmly to his own prime rule: Slow is smooth, smooth is fast. He shoved the prisoner to the ground, sat on the young man's back and took time to study the target through the Cyclops. Careful surveillance was seldom time wasted.

On its surface, the base had the primary purpose of supplying a guard force of several hundred men to protect the oil production, storage and shipment apparatus in the area. As part of that assignment, it supposedly maintained a contingent of antiaircraft missiles that could spread the protective umbrella out beyond the rigs. It was reasonable to assume that it was all part of the same package, but Swanson tried never to assume anything.

Remembering the map in the Boykin Group basement, he knew the base was sliced into four equal parts. A perimeter road followed all the way around inside the fence line. A north-south road ran from the main gate to the far side of the camp, dead-ending at the fence. It was bisected in the middle by an east-west route which emptied onto the supply road where Swanson waited. The headquarters building was in the middle: a standard military layout, there was genius in its simplicity. Everyone could get any-where smoothly.

Soldiers and vehicles were surging toward the front of the compound, with troops running from the living quarters located in the uppermost left hand corner. Several Humvees tore out of the motor pool and equipment area in the lower left quadrant and gunners were already standing in the vehicles behind machine guns. Officers coming from smaller buildings in the upper right hand quarter were marrying up the troops and vehicles, putting together a rescue mission for the besieged foreigners. Swanson heard the orders being shouted and the motors revving.

So if this was an AA base, where were the antiaircraft missile sites? It would have been logical to have them in protected hard stands with open fields of fire all around, probably near the corners to eliminate obstructions. Instead, he found the missiles nestled near a long, narrow building in the area closest to him. A group of three Humvees sat in a line, the lead one decked out with aerials, which denoted the command and operations ve-hicle. The next two Humvees had bulky pedestals on the rear deck, where gunners would sit between reloadable pods of heat-seeking Stinger missiles. The group presented a genuine threat against any marauding helicopters or low-flying planes. They remained idle tonight because they were not needed in the coming urban fight.

Swanson thought for a moment, then spoke in Arabic to his prisoner. "Junior, here's a free scout-sniper lesson for your future military career: More important than just seeing something is to know what you're looking at. The only reason for having those missiles on wheels is to move them somewhere. Let's go look inside that building."

NO BULLETS WERE COMING his way, so Fatehi Awwad knew he had not been seen crouching beside the culvert. He sighted his RPG launcher on the main road coming out of the base and patiently waited for his enemies to play their part. The crossbar arm at the guard shack was being raised and four Humvees were ready to move out in column, their big engines rumbling and the huge tires crunching on the road. As the first one came out, Awwad sighted on it and pressed the trigger.

An igniter exploded a ball of gas inside the RPG launcher and flung the pointed antipersonnel grenade from the front end of the tube while the enormous back-blast from the rear disappeared in the ditch behind him. The rocket covered the first eleven meters of flight in a tenth of a second, then automatically armed itself. Stabilizer fins popped out. A fuse kicked in the propulsion system, and the Russian-made grenade increased to 294 meters per second, with a clockwise spin. Designed to penetrate armor, it easily bored into the Humvee and exploded with full fury inside.

The explosion tore the lead vehicle apart and killed four soldiers. The wrecked and burning Humvee plugged the gateway, stopping the convoy before it started. Soldiers opened fire, shooting blindly beyond the edge of the lights, but hitting nothing. The Egyptian terrorist threw down the empty launcher tube and ran.

THE ARMY BASE HAD not been designed to repel any real attack, so the surprise was total. Years of routine patrol duty had dulled a low sense of military readiness and the soldiers, with no combat discipline, were stressing out, fixated on whatever was in front of them and running toward the burning Humvee. The antiaircraft missiles were left unguarded.

Swanson knew that if he did not stop the RPG attack, Saudi soldiers would be killed and the relief column would be delayed in reaching the besieged foreign compound to battle the rebels in the city. Still, it was a sound tactical decision, for this was not about who got hurt, but the sacrifice of a few to be measured against the greater good. The presence of a tactical nuclear missile easily trumped the lives of a few individuals. He would take that opportunity first and worry about the decision process some other time. To overthink the situation would only muddle what needed to be done. He went forward, dragging his prisoner along.

To MAKE OPERATIONS ON the military base simple, a pattern had matured over the years. Everything from supplies to people alike was funneled through the primary entrance and exit. The secondary gate had fallen into disuse and was secured by nothing more than a big padlock on a chain. Swanson found no fresh tire tracks to indicate recent use.

He shoved Salid to the ground about six feet from the unused gate, beside some scrub brush next to the fence. Using a set of Homer Boykin's bolt-cutters, Kyle chose a link about three inches above the ground and snipped it, then did the next link and kept going until he had opened a gap about eighteen inches square, held in place by the links at the top. He pushed Junior through the open flap in the wire, crawled through himself and folded the fence back into place. The opening would not be noticed by a casual observer. Any guard would know that the secondary gate was supposed to be chained and locked, and would see exactly that, since the chain and lock were right where they were supposed to be. The nearby fence would not even be inspected.

Swanson led the captured man like a puppy on a leash and went to the side of the long, low building, stopping in the deep shadow of the wall. He wrapped some duct tape around his prisoner's legs to immobilize him. "Stay, Junior," he said in Arabic, pointing a finger at him. The young man nodded. He had no idea who this man was, but they were in the middle of an enemy military camp, so there was no escape anyway. Any noise would serve only to alert Saudi soldiers who would kill him.

The front of the building had two large doors in sections that would roll up and out of the way at the touch of a button. A regular door stood between them. The big doors were down but the smaller was open and a long, thin bar of startlingly bright light spilled outside. Kyle hugged the wall as he moved in from the left. When he reached the portal, he leaned forward and listened for any sound that would indicate someone was moving inside. Swanson slid an eye around the edge. No movement. Safe.

At the front gate, soldiers were reorganizing and pushing the wrecked Humvee out of the way to resume their mission into Khobz to save the embattled foreign workers. Kyle cut the tape from Junior's legs, grabbed him and shoved him through the doorway. They stood exposed in the bright lights of the large building.

Two boxy, flat-tracked vehicles squatted in the middle of the building, side by side, each pointed toward one of the rollup doors. Swanson recognized them as variants of the familiar old M-113 armored personnel carriers that the U.S. Army had introduced a half-century earlier, during the Vietnam era. The basic design had been steadily modified and updated to meet different needs and the versatile APC became a standard armored vehicle for many jobs in many armies.

He climbed aboard the nearest one and peeled away a sand-colored tarpaulin that stretched the length of the vehicle. Below it, a pudgy missile was nested in the cargo bay above a web of pipes that made up the hydraulic launch system. Kyle grunted in satisfaction. From his days of hunting mobile SCUD missile launchers in the deserts, he was familiar with this system.

When ready for action, the rear deck of the APC would be lowered to create extra space, then the missile would be raised into position and it could be fired by remote control from the second APC, the command vehicle. This pair matched up with the modern Humvees parked outside. The entire operation was not for air defense at all. It was a shoot-and-scoot missile launching system. They could drive it almost anywhere and target almost anything.

The missile was blunt on its nose, which told Swanson what was in the cargo hold of the other APC. He climbed down from the first, tied Junior to a protruding metal strut, then jumped aboard the second one. A large weatherproof container was secured in the cargo hold and it was stamped with yellow and black circular radiation warnings: a tactical nuclear warhead.

In his mind's eye, he could envision the little convoy rushing to a mapped firing position, the removal of the warhead from its box, and how it could be married to the missile body and launched in a matter of minutes. Whether the target was an invading Iraqi army or an Israeli city or an American naval battle group, this was a dangerous puppy. Kyle estimated it was relatively low yield, since it was for battlefield use, but still more powerful by itself than the bombs that were dropped on Japan.

Time was sliding away. Once the military relief column from the base reached the foreign compound, the fighting would end quickly and guards would resume their standard duties, including checking the base. The warehouse building would not stay empty forever. He called Homer on his sat phone and told the CIA agent what he needed.

THE ROUND ARMORED HATCH cover above the driver's position was folded back and Kyle dropped easily into the compartment on the front left of the M-113 that contained the nuke. Again, he was on familiar ground because he had driven these boxes before. To break the monotony of long hours of down time in Afghanistan, he had occasionally joined some other guys in taking a few old APCs into the empty desert for some totally unauthorized off-road racing.

He adjusted the seat on its post so that he could see through the viewport and also use the infrared periscope. Swanson was not planning to shoot anybody, but did not want to have his head sticking out of the hatch as an easy target. His right foot rested on the large accelerator pedal. He checked the hand brake and the hydraulic service brake pedal. The only major change he could see was that a sort of steering wheel on a yoke had replaced the twin tiller handles to make driving easier. It had an automatic transmission. Sweet.

There was no key, just a switch to turn it on. Kyle clicked it and the big 350-horsepower diesel coughed and grumbled to life. The dials flickered and showed a full tank of diesel, which would give him a range of more than a hundred miles.

Swanson hoisted himself back through the hatch and went over to his prisoner, stripped away the AK-47, and tossed the weapon into the other APC. The young terrorist's eyes grew wide in fear. "Relax, Junior. You're free to go," Kyle said. He removed all of the tape and stuffed it in his pocket so as to leave no sign that the man might be there against his will. "Good luck."

The prisoner stood perfectly still for a moment, rubbing his wrists as his captor disappeared back inside the big armored vehicle. The hatch slammed and locked. When the engine roared, Junior broke from his trance and ran to retrieve his rifle. He had been left behind as bait.

Swanson slipped the transmission into gear, pressed down hard on the accelerator and the powerful engine roared as the 23,000-pound vehicle lurched into motion. Its rolled aluminum armor made quick work of the closed, thin door and he plunged through, straight out onto the concrete apron. He turned the steering wheel to the left without touching the brakes, as easily as he would have turned a pickup truck. Lining up with the secondary gate, he stomped the accelerator and the APC chewed across the open area. The improved tracks and suspension kept the ride steady and the big machine smashed through the locked gate.

Off to his right, tips of fire still pierced the dark sky as buildings blazed in the foreign compound and Kyle took a side road that led far around the fighting. Within five minutes, the broad tracks of the APC were off the concrete and onto desert sand as he headed into the deep nowhere.

THE WHITE HOUSE

HE DID *WHAT?*" **STEVE** Hanson, the chief of staff for President Mark Tracy, pushed away from his desk in surprise. After a career in the turbulent world of high-tech start-ups, bitter political campaigns, and a long stint in Washington, Hanson believed he was immune to shock. "Are you bullshitting me, General?"

"Not at all. You heard me right." Major General Bradley Middleton, the commander of Task Force Trident, was seated in a brown leather chair in front of Hanson's desk. A small fire burned in the fireplace, giving off a faint, pleasant tinge of smoke. "Gunny Swanson stole a nuke last night."

"Good Lord. The man never does things by half measures, does he? Just outright stole it?"

"Like a thief in the night, Steve. He broke into the Khobz military facility, found the tactical nuclear warhead mounted in its very own APC beside the missile launcher and drove off with it. With CIA help, a heavy-lift CH-43 helicopter made a rendezvous with him in the desert about twenty klicks outside of town and Swanson took the APC straight on board. The TNW is secure in the weapons bay of the USS *Enterprise* even as we speak. The armored personnel carrier was dumped overboard."

"Incredible. The Saudis have no clue?"

Middleton shook his head and ran a hand over his close-cut hair. A big smile spread over the square jaw. "No. That's the real beauty of it. Swanson also snatched up some terrorist beforehand and abandoned him inside the missile storage building, where he was killed during a shootout with the Saudis. They look at the corpse as proof that the terrorist was part of the group that had also attacked the Khobz oil workers' compound. He actually was to be part of a rebel RPG team that ambushed a convoy rushing out of the military base. So the obvious conclusion was that his terrorist buddies took the TNW. Is that confusing enough?"

"And Swanson is okay?"

"Yep. The chopper dropped him off on a stretch of beach north of Khobz and he walked back to the CIA safe house. He radioed a report to Major Summers in Kuwait and she forwarded it to me."

Hanson stood up, holding the yellow legal pad on which he had made notes. "This might be a game-changer, Brad. We know something the Saudis don't, about their own nuclear weapon." The chief of staff lapsed into a terrible Hispanic accent for a quirky Ricky Ricardo imitation from *I Love Lucy*: "The new king has got some 'splainin' to do."

"Right." Middleton laid a folder on Hanson's desk. "Steve, you keep that copy so you can brief the boss and I'll privately feed you any more details as they come up. The CIA and the Pentagon obviously already know about what happened, but I told them to keep the secret compartmentalized since it was a black Trident operation. I told them that President Tracy would land on them hard if there were any leaks. So, you need anything else?"

Hanson placed the folder atop his tablet and headed for the Oval Office. "Yeah. Tell Kyle to find another one."

KHOBZ, SAUDI ARABIA

NO LOOSE ENDS. **KYLE** Swanson remained absolutely still, concentrating to-tally on the final stages of the fighting that had unrolled at the mosque only 400 meters from his hide. The window on the far side of the shadowed room was open and his emotions were replaced by purpose.

Since the Saudi authorities did not know what had happened to the nuclear warhead, other than that it had disappeared, he intended to keep the mystery tight and intact. To do so meant he was going to have to kill some people. That did not bother him, because in his judgment, they were enemy combatants. Swanson's personal habit was that when presenting a gift to an enemy, one should wrap it very carefully so as to keep their atten-tion on the unimportant things, like the shape of the box or the crinkly yellow paper wrapping, and not the bomb inside. The trick was as old as the wooden horse at Troy and usually worked. Today, he would add a final flourish of distraction on his theft at the base by tying a big bloody red bow.

Kyle had returned to the safe house just before daylight and found both Homer and Jamal busy closing up shop, arranging det cord and explosives in a pre-arranged pattern that would not only destroy the structure but make it cave in upon itself.

"The Boykin Group is out of business," Homer declared. "It won't be long before the Saudis start wondering about how a handful of foreign workers just happened to have enough automatic weapons, ammo, and gre-nades to whip a pretty big onslaught of rebel bad guys. Come dark, we will be gone." He rubbed his eyes, and then looked fondly around the well-stocked basement that had been maintained over the years. "Shame to lose all this, but we've got no choice. Our cover is blown."

"Probably," Kyle agreed. He got a cup of coffee and sat on a foldout cot. "How'd it go out there?"

Jamal was planting C4 bricks beneath the communications console, and his voice had a dim echo. "The soldiers in the Saudi relief column were pretty pissed off that they had been ambushed back at their own front gate. Came barging in on the left flank of the rebels with lots of firepower and pretty good maneuvering. The terrorists were pushed back into the urban area."

Homer was puttering with a timing device. "That's when we gathered up our toys and came back here. A while later, when they got the word that their nuke was gone, the Saudis went big league mean and are still bringing in more troops and armor and attack helicopters. It has degenerated into house-to-house fighting."

Kyle finished his coffee. "I assume that all of the action is pointing toward the mosque?"

"Yep," replied Homer. "That's their problem. Despite the king being assassinated and the nuke being gone, the commanders are hesitating. They are squared off against the Religious Police and the Committee on Virtue as well as the rented terrorists, which means a Muslim-on-Muslim showdown."

Swanson walked over to the sand-table model of the city and studied the area. "Will they attack the mosque?"

Jamal came out from beneath the counter and got busy with a screwdriver and pliers to pull out hard drives and memory boards on phones and computers. "No doubt," he said. "They have to capture the mosque in order to get some prisoners to question about the nuke."

Homer agreed. "I wouldn't want to be in the same room when the prisoners are being asked to assist with the investigation. Gonna be messy."

"Torture," Jamal agreed.

"Big time. They know that anybody will crack under torture, sooner or later." Homer's eyes suddenly came up and met the steady gazes of Kyle and Jamal. "You think the prisoners might actually convince the Saudis that they really *don't* know anything about the missing weapon?"

Swanson walked into the armory cage. "We won't take that chance."

* * *

SNAVPERSKAYA **V**INTOYKA **D**RAGUNOVA. **N**OT his first choice of a sniper rifle, which would have been his custom-made Excalibur, or even his second choice, the familiar U.S. Marine M40A3, or even a Barrett, or an Armalite. But this wasn't a gun show. He needed a good sniper rifle with no American finger-prints on it, and Homer Boykin had both the SVD Dragunov and a Chinese-made NDM-86. Swanson took the Dragunov. In his opinion, the rough NDM was only a small step up from an AK-47 and had the look of being stamped out in an old Commie tractor factory. Not what he wanted for prime-time combat.

Jamal helped Swanson find a deserted third-floor apartment in a build-ing that provided an unobstructed view of the mosque. The sun was almost directly overhead, so the room was darkened by shadows while he crawled around to set up his hide. He wiped grime from the floor and rubbed it onto his face and neck to camouflage the white skin. Jamal helped push the sparse furniture around to further break up his silhouette and also to create a firm rest for the long rifle. Kyle braced the Dragunov in a comfortable posi-tion and took his time adjusting the PSO scope with its red reticle in the illuminated range finder. It read exactly 347 meters to the front plaza of the mosque. Smoke from the sporadic shooting outside the building hung thick in the air before drifting away on a light breeze from the north and he fine-tuned the scope for a minimal wind. It would probably be no factor because he was so close to the target zone.

Jamal left him alone and went down to their car. Kyle needed a getaway driver more than he needed a spotter.

The eerie sense of once again entering a slow-motion film flowed over him. Noise faded and his vision sharpened, but he did not sweat, even though the mid-day temperature was hot. In a combat situation, it was nor-mal for his senses to heighten, for the mental thought to give way to the physical muscle memory of years of scout-sniper training. His body already knew how this movie would end.

ONCE THEY RECEIVED AUTHORITY through their own chain of command, the Saudi soldiers had moved in with admirable violence of action. They assaulted the mosque by savaging the building with helicopter gunships and raking it with .50 caliber machine guns and mortars, pounding the exterior into rubble. As soon as the heavy fire lifted, infantry assaulters went in to finish the job.

After about twenty minutes of searching, and with sporadic fire, they had yanked out three survivors and brought them into the plaza of smooth stone. A badly wounded man lay sprawled and moaning, bleeding from the gut and in obvious pain. To the right stood a sullen fighter wearing the red headgear of the Religious Police, wiping dirt from his eyes. In the middle was a stout, middle-aged man in a turban, the imam of the mosque. He was moon-faced and arrogant.

Swanson watched dispassionately through the scope of the Dragunov. He had nothing personal against the three men, even though two were obviously terrorists while the imam was the instigator of the attacks. Kyle didn't care, for his own secret was much bigger than any of theirs. He rested his finger lightly on the trigger, looking over the heads of the Saudi force that had relaxed after capturing their objective. No one looked his way, up and behind them. It had been assumed to be empty and secure. He wanted to shout: *Where is your fucking rear security?*

His hand was comfortable on the grip and he held steady on his first target, the religious cop. Although the man's wrists were tied, he would be the most likely to make a quick move upon realizing the threat. His tunic was torn and the beard was caked with mud. Kyle had him center-mass and squeezed straight back on the trigger until the Dragunov roared and bucked against his shoulder. The shot ripped across the small distance and into the man's throat. The bullet tore out the neck and spinal cord before exiting lower through the back. Firing a little high, Kyle thought.

The semiautomatic rifle cycled another round into the chamber as the target flipped over, the bolt moving with such smoothness that he silently thanked Homer and Jamal for keeping the weapons so clean. The Saudi guards stood frozen for a decisive moment, never having considered an outside attack on their prisoners. Beads of sweat were starting to worm through Kyle's scalp as he firmed up the sight picture on the imam, who had been allowed to remain standing untethered.

The man had his arms crossed, his hands hidden within sleeves, and was haughty even in captivity, certain that no harm would befall him. From his height of piety, he had sent many men to kill many infidels with his heated, distorted versions of hate from the Koran. The imam was part of the religious food chain in Saudi Arabia and answered to the leaders of the entire religious establishment in his country. They would protect him. Reality was dawning on him as he stared at the blood and gore that had splattered his robes.

Swanson paused his breath, waited for the instant between heartbeats, never wavered the crosshairs and with a liquid smoothness, squeezed the trigger for the second time. The bullet struck solid in the center of the imam's body, taking out the lungs, with splinters angling down to chop the kidneys. The moon face was seized in shock as the target jolted back, somehow remaining on his feet for a moment before slumping to his knees and keeling over forward.

Kyle was out of time. *Three shots and move!* The Saudis were stirring, horrified that their prize quarry had been murdered before their eyes, and so fast that they could not react immediately. After all, nobody was shooting at them! Swanson brought his scope on the wounded man on the plaza. He was dying anyway, but why take the chance that some medical miracle might save the bastard's life. The final bullet gouged into his heart, the force making the body bounce on the stone.

Swanson left the rifle, dodged out of the door, and pounded downstairs to the waiting car.

Nobody would be questioning those three prisoners, with or without torture. No loose ends.

INDONESIA

JUBA POPPED A **V**ALIUM and slugged back a stiff Cragganmore single-malt Scotch, hating himself for being weak. It was not really a weakness of the ravaged body, but an invisible curse: He was claustrophobic.

In his home on the mountain, the windows were always open to usher in steady breezes, even on the hottest days. Overhead fans and plenty of shade trees kept the place cool. Long, overhanging eaves blocked the rain out except during typhoon blows. Air-conditioning was allowed only in the servants' quarters and the hot kitchen, because maintaining a chilled temperature meant closing doors and windows. Wide doorways led into spacious rooms and onto the open verandah. The light and airiness kept him calm. In the house, he could work and exercise and eat proper food and feel good.

So there was an unusual tightness in his throat and chest as he climbed into the small executive helicopter for the journey to Jakarta. When the hatch closed, Juba felt chained, and as the bird lifted away from the ground, the feeling grew into one of total imprisonment. He broke into a sweat and released his knuckles from the grips of the seat only long enough to take another Valium. It did little good. He was glad to be alone in the passenger compartment so no one would hear him groan as the panic pecked at him.

In the British Army, he had learned to control his nerves, and by the time he became a terrorist, his heart had grown too hard to accept emotion. That singular ability had abandoned him in his new life. He looked out the window of the helicopter, through the rolls of clouds and down to the verdant green of the islands and the sun-stroked waters, wishing there was some way out of the buzzing bubble that confined him in the sky. He no longer held any belief at all in any Higher Power of any name, so there would be no spiritual comfort. He felt truly alone.

On the mountain, Juba did not even own an automobile. To squeeze into one made him feel like he was climbing into his own coffin. Now he was faced with a monstrous endurance test, flying 4,500 miles from Indonesia to Saudi Arabia, trapped inside a tight little cocoon of an airplane for hours on end. Juba bit his lip.

His manner was already curt when the helicopter reached the private terminal in Jakarta and he was immediately shuffled aboard a luxurious Bombardier Challenger 604 twin jet. It was larger than he thought and he was surrounded by comfort and treated with respect by the three crew members. Still, Juba could think of nothing but the ordeal that lay ahead and he seized up, feeling old and crippled.

When the slim hostess pulled the door closed and the tube shut around him, it was as if he was being held in a fist. There was no space, no room to move, no ocean vista, no air, no way out, and no real air to breathe.

"Get me a drink," he snarled. "Not any of that piss in a bottle in your bar. Some good gin out of my valise. Ice and a slice."

The uniformed young woman found the bottle, made a double martini with a slice of fresh lemon and gave it to him. The passenger had a mane of totally white hair, was horribly scarred, and wore a white patch over his left eye. He shot her a defiant glare.

"Why are you staring, you ugly cow? Go away!" Juba took a deep swallow and fished around in his shirt pocket for the green plastic bottle of medicines. He hurt, dammit! The mental fear was changing into sharp physical manifestations. *The tunnel! Oh, it hurts. Somebody help me!* He gobbled two Percocet and drank some more of the strong martini as the engines whined. His stomach churned as the plane lifted into the air.

The nervous hostess called the flight cabin and a tall, neat man in dark trousers and a starched white shirt bearing golden wings above his left chest pocket came down the aisle and sat across from the lone passenger. The flier had a look of concern on his face. The one-eyed man looked like hell and for a moment, the copilot thought they might have to return to the terminal and get him to a hospital. "Are you all right, sir?"

"No, I am not all right!" The single eye rolled wildly. "Get me another damned drink, bitch."

"Sir, please. Calm yourself." The copilot reached out his left hand to touch the man's shoulder in sympathy. Juba grabbed the wrist in a lightning-quick move and twisted over hard, pulling the flier out of the seat and throwing him into the aisle.

"Try to touch me again and I'll kill you. I'm stuck up here with you fools and you will do only what I tell you. You get your ass back into that flight cabin and I want to hear the door lock behind you. Then fly the fucking plane and if I want you, I'll call." He twisted harder on the wrist and jammed his thumbnail into a pressure point.

The copilot screamed in agony.

Juba laughed and stomped the ribs before releasing the arm. "Get out of here. And you. Get my drink!"

IT WAS NOT A straight line trip, for the aircraft had been forced to take a more circuitous route to stay out of harm's way and avoid discovery. Hour after hour droned past in the sky and there were three refueling stops at strategic points along the way. At each one, the crew crept silently out onto the tarmac to take a breather from the plane which seemed to crackle with a horrible menace from the passenger that had grown obnoxious under the influence of booze and narcotics. They watched in silent disgust through a cabin camera as he drank himself into oblivion, with a detour into roaring anger, until he passed out somewhere over Pakistan.

JUBA WAS IN THE tunnel, his body and face torn by a sniper's big bullet and the tight hideaway collapsing beneath the thundering explosion of a huge bomb. Blinded and unable to breathe, the weight of the falling dirt crushing the final sparks of life from him, lost in blood and pain and darkness, badly wounded and trapped underground with dirt in his mouth and eyes. *Oh, it hurts.*

He had lived several lives and despaired that this was the way it would all end, dying slowly in an underground tomb.

The plane hit an air pocket, dropped momentarily, and the sudden jolt caused the passenger to moan loudly and shift in his seat until the aircraft steadied and droned on. His mind spun with a mixture of hallucinations and true memories as the drugs and booze played him—letting the British army train him to be a terrorist, fighting for al Qaeda in Afghanistan and Iraq before going out on his own with deadly biochemical weapons that he used to strike both London and San Francisco. Those acts had made him the most dangerous man in the world, a terrorist with a price on his head, a fortune in the bank, and a secret weapon that commanded respect and support from political and religious fanatics.

Then everything had been taken away in an instant. Juba still tried to convince himself that it had been only a fluke shot, an unfortunate accident, just bad luck, one of life's more unfair moments, for no other man possessed his rare skill with a rifle. He changed positions in his seat again. Could not get comfortable. Heard noises. Even felt the wrinkles in his trousers, hard as rocks.

He remembered it all—the duel of single sniper bullets, the explosion, being buried alive in the suffocating tunnel, and, after giving up all hope, pinpoints of light breaking through the dirt. Frantic Iraqi villagers digging with their hands freed him from the grave. That bastard Kyle Swanson somehow got off that lucky shot. Tears leaked from his right eye and creased his face.

Two strong men came aboard the plane when it landed in Saudi Arabia and propped the limp, sniffling passenger between them, got him down the short staircase and into the rear of a waiting limousine. The copilot followed with the valise and threw it into the vehicle's trunk, slammed it closed, and stalked away, glad to be done with him.

A young man in a dark suit and a white shirt open at the neck was also in the rear of the stretch limo as it drove away toward downtown Jeddah. He studied the figure plopped across from him. The man was disheveled, stinking and grunting like a filthy animal. *This is the hero to whom we have paid so much? This lump is the mastermind?* He extended his index finger and pushed a button to open the window beside him. It was still humid and hot, but he needed to flush out the foul odor.

33

KUWAIT

CRAAACK! THE BIG SNIPER rifle kicked back hard against Kyle Swanson's shoulder and 800 meters away the .50 caliber bullet gouged out a hole in the paper target. The three other Marines with him also were running rounds downrange into the great nowhere in a mad fusillade designed to keep their muscle memory sharp.

The four of them had taken a Humvee from the special ops camp, loaded it with ammo and an assortment of weapons, from light machine guns to pistols, and ventured into the heat wearing full body armor. They would spend some time making sure every tool they had, including themselves, was in top working order. Training never stopped, no matter how good you were.

Staff Sergeant Darren Rawls, a tall African-American from Alabama, ripped through a thirty-round magazine with an M249 Squad Automatic Weapon, the faithful 5.56 mm air-cooled, belt-fed, gas-operated SAW. Sergeant Travis Stone, a sweaty bandana covering his stubble of red hair, chunked away with an XM203 40 mm grenade launcher, blowing up fountains of dirt. Staff Sergeant Joe Tipp was testing a small-grip SIG SAUER P250 combat pistol that he had liberated from a Navy SEAL in a poker game. It sounded like a small war.

After an hour, they took a break and retreated to a rectangle of shade provided by the Humvee, where they shucked the heavy helmets and body armor, drank bottles of water, and sat on the dirt. The land all around was flat and hot and brown, nothing to see all the way to the horizon.

Rawls studied it, squinting into the bright sun, then raised his eyes to the crystalline blue sky. "Space ain't the final frontier. This is."

Joe Tipp raised his nose and sniffed the air. "Anybody else smell another Rawls scam?"

"Fuck you. Just listen. Space tourism! Rich assholes are paying millions of dollars to go into space and even want to go to the moon. Now what's up on the moon?" He pointed to the bleak horizon of Kuwait. "Same shit as out there."

Kyle Swanson finished his second bottle of water, feeling the cool wetness all the way down to his toes. "Brilliant analysis. You got a point?"

"We've got all those freako tourists who show up at the edges of a war, thrill-seeking motherfuckers who think combat is some kind of paint-ball game. So how about we form a little company, sell escorted trips out here. Get the muthas all armored up, ride around in civilian Humvees, let 'em pop off some rounds like we've been doing. Like a safari in Africa."

Travis Stone stopped eating a pouch of peaches and tossed the sticky plastic spoon at his buddy. "Again with the money schemes. Remember the reality TV series for Elvis impersonators? The golden treasure of the Spanish kings in Memphis? Drill an oil well in Harlem? At least the soft porn movie idea had naked women involved."

"Those movie people lied to me! I wrote a damned good script!" Rawls shrugged away the criticism.

"And lost your investment. Again."

"You never want to expand your mind, try nothin' new. When I put in my twenty years with the Corps and get that retirement paycheck, I'm gonna invest, man. We gotta think ahead if we want to be rich in our old age."

If they only knew, thought Kyle. *These guys will never have to worry about a job if I go into Excalibur.*

Joe Tipp spoke. "You keep on thinking, Darren. I kind of liked the porn idea. Just watching some of the interviews with the actresses was worth my thousand bucks."

Darren Rawls started cleaning his SAW, fighting the ever-present talcum of desert dust that could foul a barrel or jam a magazine. "So I'll do another script. This time, the four of us will do the whole thing. How difficult can it be? Joe does the camera, Trav does the sound, Kyle directs, and I'll be the star! You white rabbits don't have the qualifications that I do for a good sex show. Sell it on cable or on the Internet."

Travis looked over. "What about the combat safaris?"

Rawls gently stroked the automatic weapon with a soft, oily cloth. "No hurry. That can come next, after the movie. The Middle East ain't goin' nowhere. And writin' is hard, so I can't even think about it now. Anyway, got something else on my mind."

"What?" Joe Tipp asked.

Rawls smiled broadly. "Killin' terrorists."

WHEN THE BANTER AND insults quieted and they were reluctant to leave the square of shade, Kyle spoke: "Okay, guys, listen up. I hauled your asses out here for more than just some shooting. Needed to get away from curious ears back at the base."

The other three locked their eyes on Swanson. He had been back for less than two days and had been withdrawn and curt with everyone except Major Summers.

"I need to bring you up to speed on the situation next door, over in Saudi Arabia," he said. "Top secret."

"We see it on TV every night and it's all over the Internet," said Joe Tipp. "What else is there, really?"

"A lot. It's pretty complicated," Swanson said, stretching out his legs and closing his eyes, reciting what Sybelle had briefed him on last night. "You probably know that the president and the new Saudi king are friends, but they really had it out during a meeting in the Oval Office a few days ago, when Abdullah was still the ambassador in Washington. He told President Tracy that any American movement to protect the oil fields would be considered an unwarranted military intervention by a foreign power and would be resisted."

Travis Stone doodled in the dirt with an empty brass cartridge case. "You think there's a chance that our good buddies might actually fight us?"

Swanson's eyes blinked open and he stared at them, each in turn. "That was the implied threat, but nobody wants it to go that far. Then things happened fast and, bingo, next thing we know, Ambassador Abdullah becomes King Abdullah."

Darren Rawls stood, brushed off his pants, and stretched his six-foot-two frame. Loose and lanky with a shrewd mind, Rawls had been a star high school basketball player and a better student in Alabama. When his brother was killed in Iraq, Rawls walked away from the college scholarships and joined the Marines. He was tough, an excellent sniper, and a voracious reader who carefully sheltered his intelligence beneath a homeboy speech pattern. "That was kinda weird. The crown normally would go to another old relative. It's a family thing."

"Way our intel people piece it together, installing Abdullah in the position represented an internal, bloodless coup. With both the king and the crown prince dead, there was no clear line of succession. The country was, and still is, on the verge of falling apart. So the real movers and shakers in Saudi Arabia apparently got together, flexed their muscles, and chose the toughest, smartest member of the bloodline to take the reins. Abdullah was jumped over a whole generation but the monarchy remains absolute."

Swanson paused to drink some water, then continued, "Let me get to the point. I met this Abdullah dude in England."

"You know the new king?" Stone was surprised.

Swanson nodded. "He was wounded during the terrorist attack in Scotland and was a patient at the clinic where Sybelle and I took out those tangos."

"Sweet," said Travis Stone.

Swanson's eyes blinked open and he stared at them, each in turn. "Not so fast, Trav. Just as the rebellion cooked off, we found out that the Saudis had five nuclear missiles. Only bargain basement nukes, but the threat is huge."

Rawls said, "Ghetto nukes? Civil war. Oil. Terrorism. Can this get any better?"

Swanson peered up at him. "Sure. One of their missiles has gone missing."

Rawls groaned. "You're shitting me."

Swanson smiled. "When King Abdullah learned about that, he did a flip-flop on refusing all American help. He wants to turn the remaining four missiles over to the United States and asked the White House specifically to name me as the U.S. liaison during the handover. Like I say, he knows me."

"So what's our mission?" Travis Hughes asked.

"I leave for Riyadh tonight to meet with King Abdullah and finish setting up the transfers. You guys will be in charge of removing the four missiles that are still scattered around the country. You each will command a plane that will fly in to do the pickups, personally take charge of the warheads, and stay with them until they can be safely stored on a ship. A platoon of MEUSOC Marines will provide overall security. Your only concern will be the nukes. Sybelle will oversee things from here. You report only to her. This is a Trident show all the way."

Tipp asked, "Uh, what about that fifth one?"

Kyle Swanson gave them his special, meaningless smile. "Not to worry about that one. I snatched it while I was visiting over in Khobz and it's already aboard a navy carrier."

JEDDAH, SAUDI ARABIA

JUBA STRUGGLED BACK TO consciousness on a comfortable bed in a private villa. His stomach remained queasy, but not as bad as the first two times he had been awake, when he had vomited. His mind was emerging from the cobwebs and lethargy caused by the strong alcohol and narcotics. Someone had placed a bottle of spring water on the bedside table and he drank deeply from it.

He did not know exactly where he was, but trusted that the damned airplane had delivered him to the right place, Jeddah, the second largest city in Saudi Arabia. The room was spacious and when he forced himself from the bed and over to the window, he was pleased to see bright sunlight glinting harshly on a vast body of water, the Red Sea. He pushed the windows open wide and inhaled the hot air.

A clean bathroom with intricate tiles and polished fixtures lured him through the open door. He turned the shower water until it was hot before stepping into the enclosure. Strong waves of steam played over his face and body and he put his head directly beneath the big showerhead. He leaned forward with his hands against the wall to let the water slosh away the remains of the horrible trip. After soaping up and using the shampoo, he adjusted the water slowly to a cold setting. He was feeling almost awake as he finished, stepped out, and grabbed two towels from the warming rack.

His own shaving gear had been placed on a white towel beside the sunken basin and he quickly lathered his face and scraped off the rough whiskers. Juba smirked at his own reflection. *You are a mess.* He brushed his teeth. Someone had hung his clothes and neatly put away the shirts and underwear, leaving the valise in the closet. Juba decided on lightweight grey slacks and a starched maroon shirt with long sleeves, dark socks, and shined black loafers. Hendrik van Es from Indonesia, who padded around his own home in sandals and a sarong, was no longer present. Juba slid easily into his old skin. He opened the door of the bedroom.

The young man who had picked Juba up at the airport was settled in a large chair, with his long legs crossed. He had a long face framed by a well-trimmed beard and his hair was naturally curly. Juba estimated he was not yet thirty years old, probably stood about six foot two, and had a body that was slim and showed some work, although the manicure indicated that the muscles were the result of gym workouts and not from labor or soldiering.

"Get me something to eat," Juba softly said.

"My name is Amin," the man said. He had a strong edge in his tone as he stood, wanting to establish immediate authority. "I am not your servant."

"I don't care who you are and that was not a request." Juba adjusted the eye patch to a more comfortable position. "I had to stop my work and fly halfway around the world to return to this shitty country. If some food is not out here in ten minutes, I'm leaving and your revolution is fucked. I want fresh fruit, croissants, and scrambled eggs. Strong tea. Then go get Dieter."

Amin was stunned by the extraordinary change. This did not seem like the same person! Not only had the passenger washed away that awful smell, but his commanding manner was that of someone used to having his orders obeyed. Juba walked to the large television set standing blank in the corner, turned it on, and started surfing channels in search of news. He had to catch up.

"Very well. I shall inform the kitchen staff and summon my employer." Amin did so by picking up a telephone and using an internal system. With that done, he hung up and intentionally moved to stand behind Juba, a tactic that he employed routinely so that his size would intimidate visitors. Maybe this stranger was no fool, but the white hair, the single eye, and other deformities left an overall unimpressive image. "Your food is on the way."

Juba ignored him and was frustrated by the television broadcasts. Almost everything was being blocked and or heavily censored. "Unbelievable," he muttered.

Amin said, "I cannot believe that you are the magic one who has been orchestrating the overthrow of the royal family."

Juba snapped off the TV and dropped the remote, moving silently to the dining table in the next room and taking a chair in a place that had been set for him. A dark blue plate with gold trim matched the rest of the setting and a maid placed a pot of tea beside it. He poured and sipped.

Amin followed, growing more irritated at the treatment he was receiving, as if he were an underling. He pulled out a chair for himself, angled it and sat, unbuttoning his coat, leaning back and crossing his legs again. A pistol was visible in a shoulder holster. A tight smile came to his lips. He felt that his pressure was working as he reasserted his authority.

"*Juba!*" he said with a mocking tone. "I have heard so much about the famous fighter and jihadist, the maestro of death." Amin shook his head. "And I finally have the opportunity to meet this hero, only to discover that he is just a frail old man."

Juba put down the tea, unrolled the folded blue cloth napkin and arranged the dull knife, a spoon and fork, still without saying anything. He emptied a spoonful of sugar into the tea and then added a bit of cream. It tasted good. Food would settle his stomach.

"No wonder you hide in a place where no one can see you," said Amin, accusingly pointing his left index finger. "I will no longer tell children that they must behave or that the scary Juba will come in the dark and snatch them from their beds. You may have some people fooled, old man, even Dieter Nesch, but I see you plainly for what you are."

Moving with the speed and force of a bullet, Juba stood in a single move, grabbed Amin's hair in his left hand and pulled him forward. The table knife was in his right hand and he extended his arm parallel to the floor, with his thumb on the bottom of the blade, and swept it across the bigger man's left shoulder to plunge it into the soft throat.

Amin gagged as the short, stubby blade went in and was immediately jerked free again. His eyes flew wide in shock and he grabbed at the iron fingers holding his hair, then the knife flashed in again. This time, Juba buried it up to the handle, dug for the larynx before pulling it free, then stabbed in hard for a final time, digging in the soft internal tissue and feeling the blade grind against the spinal column. He left the makeshift weapon sticking from Amir's neck. A final push sent the dying man toppling backward from his chair and onto the floor, choking with a cackling sound and flailing helplessly as blood gushed from the multiple ragged wounds, panic and fear written on his face.

AN HOUR LATER, GERMAN financier Dieter Nesch stepped into his modern villa and the confident smile fell from the face when he saw that his aide, Amir, was sprawled dead on the floor of the dining room. His housekeeper and the chef were trussed up and gagged and scrunched into a corner. The pale blue eyes moved over to where Juba sat at a window overlooking the harbor. Nesch shrugged. "I see you still have your skill at this sort of thing."

"Good to see you again, Dieter. The boy was disrespectful," said Juba, rising to shake the hand of the money man handling the entire operation. They had worked together on numerous occasions in Europe and Juba considered Nesch to be one of the few men who could be trusted in the dark world of terrorism.

"And I am happy to see you, Juba. Thank you for not killing the other two. They are good people and will not say anything." Nesch moved over to the maid and untied her, then freed the chef and had a quiet moment with them. They vigorously pledged that they understood that any loose talk about what happened to Amir would result in their own deaths, too, for the special visitor was obviously unpredictable and violent. The financier threw a rug over the corpse. "Too bad about Amir. He was a promising young fellow with a real knack for numbers. I warned him many times about that arrogance. Now I have to find a new assistant."

Nesch opened a rosewood cabinet, found a bottle of dark cognac and poured two glasses, giving one to Juba. "Cheers, old friend. Thank you for coming. I am delighted that you have recovered so well from your terrible wounds."

Juba accepted the stiff drink and raised a silent toast. "Thank you. I did not expect to see you again until this was all over. Tell me about the nuclear missiles."

Nesch took Juba gently by the elbow and guided him to the window. Tall and skinny palm trees and broad manicured grounds spread toward the nearby beach. Small pleasure boats dashed about on the water. "I really do not know very much and frankly advised that it was unwise to start changing plans at this late date. Your arrangements were doing very well, but this fellow Ebara got excited when he learned that nuclear missiles were in the country. I tried to convince him that it was just a pleasant coincidence: The assassination of the general and the murder of his family had been the point of that particular mission and it was successful. But Ebara sees it as the hand of Allah at work and ordered me to call you to supervise the targeting and the launch."

"And the Russian agreed?"

"Ah. Another young man in a hurry, with more money than brains. This started out just as an oil grab, but now he also sees a nuclear destiny in the Middle East. Ivanov decided to let Ebara reach for a new, higher star."

Juba nibbled on his lower lip. "Dieter, just what is it that Ebara has?"

"Well, I can only tell you what I have—a package in a safe deposit box at my local banking facility. Within the envelope are the launch codes for one missile, the key to work it and a booklet about the overall program which discusses the locations of the other missiles. The key and codes are for a missile that is parked within that huge military base at al-Kharj, outside of Riyadh."

Juba slowly put his empty glass on a table. "That's all? Ebara's people do not actually control the weapons? Goddamn it! Those codes for that nuke will have already been changed! Useless, like a trinket sold in the souk! Perhaps I can find something useful in the book. Maybe the key is a master key for them all. Maybe not."

His anger was climbing and his mouth twitched in exasperation. "We have momentum building in this uprising. Pulling me away from the control point risks wrecking everything. I thought I was coming here to oversee the firing of a missile, only to find that the rebel priest does not even really have one, much less five."

Nesch spread his hands wide. "Ebara is not a sophisticated man, Juba. A bright student from the slums, the first boy in his class to memorize the

Koran some twenty-five years ago. That got on him on the fast track with the imams and his ambition carried him to the leadership of the Religious Police. You know how everything around Saudi Arabia is wrapped in religion. He is a charismatic and harsh leader, which makes him the perfect front man for the coup. He enjoys being on television."

"With an uneducated zealot in control of the government, the Russian could loot the place," Juba responded. "We anticipated that. By then we will have been paid in full and gone from this dreadful place. Let them do with it as they will. I don't care."

Dieter smiled at that last thought. "Yes, we are professionals. Ebara is an amateur. When you provided initial successes and brought down the king, Ebara began believing that it was almost over and that the people were going to rise up and follow him. You will see for yourself. Maybe you can talk some sense into him. I have to tread lightly because these people have incredible amounts of money to spend."

"When do we meet him?"

Nesch laughed quietly, his shoulders shaking with his own humor. "Since you just killed my chauffeur, I'll have to personally drive you over to the mosque. Amir's body will be gone by the time we return."

"Can we have Ebara come here instead? I don't like walking into his nest of snakes." Juba was thinking tactically. Handling a kid like Amir was not the same as taking on the bunch of jihad bodyguards who would be protecting the leader of the Religious Police.

"I am afraid that would be impossible. Don't you understand it yet, Juba? Mohammed Abu Ebara no longer considers himself just the leader of the Committee for the Propagation of Virtue and the Prevention of Vice. He craves recognition and has, in his opinion, graciously granted us an audience to instruct you about how to conduct your business to best expand his horizons. Somewhat of an imperialistic drama for a man who detests a monarchy, in my opinion. Ebara already envisions himself as a glorious warrior-prophet riding a white camel adorned with golden trappings in from the desert to lead a revolution that stands on the edge of triumph. The fool believes he has already won!"

RIYADH, SAUDI ARABIA

KYLE SWANSON WAS UNCOMFORTABLE wearing a suit, but the occasion demanded decorum. Last year in London, Lady Pat had hauled him to a tailor who made one that would be appropriate for almost everything, from a wedding to a business meeting. The fabric was of lightweight dark blue wool, with quieter threads woven in to offset the single shade. He wore a cream-hued shirt, a solid powder-blue tie, and shined shoes of soft Italian leather. He would rather have been in jeans, but a royal court expects better. Worst of all, he was not allowed to carry a weapon, which left him feeling somewhat naked in a nation that was in the middle of a coup.

The well-fitted suit provided the needed cover, for Swanson wanted to be as far as possible from the image of some common tough-guy American mercenary with pointy sunglasses, a bald head, and a drooping mustache. This visit demanded dignity and diplomacy.

An executive jet had flown him into Riyadh, where three ink-black SUVs waited on the tarmac. A few soldiers with semiautomatic weapons stood guard and a polite diplomat who spoke fluent English met him at planeside. He was hustled into the middle SUV. No customs inspection, no delay, and no American Embassy types. A person could get used to this VIP stuff, Swanson thought as he settled into the spacious seat. With the gunboat up front wailing its siren and flashing its lights to expedite the trip, the three vehicles arrowed out of the airport and hit the highway. Armored troop-carriers were parked near most intersections and military patrols walked the sidewalks as the curfew time of nine o'clock neared.

Kyle was surprised at the quietness of the downtown streets, for he had anticipated seeing clashes between the authorities and rioters. Instead, everyone seemed to be heading home, not toward some confrontation. *Never jump to conclusions.* It was natural that security would be extremely tight in any area leading to the royal palace. Mobs would have been broken up before having a chance to coalesce.

A man's view of a battlefield never extends beyond what he can see. The vision of a private does not stretch far beyond the brim of his helmet, while a headquarters general with only a map usually has no personal idea of the ground over which his troops are fighting. Both are effectively blind to things beyond their immediate area of responsibility. And riding in a tightly secured convoy would give Kyle no indication about what was really happening throughout the broad country of Saudi Arabia. Still, he mentally noted that he was not seeing chaos and fires, nor hearing gunshots, nor having to crash through street barricades in Riyadh.

The SUVs rushed out of the city center and soon swept through a huge stone gate that marked the entrance to the palace grounds, the heavily guarded private preserve of the royal family. When Swanson stepped from his vehicle, he felt transported into some Arabian fairy tale. It was not really a palace at all, not a single sprawling building, but a small city unto itself, a labyrinth of streets and structures so vast that the palace staff drove battery-powered golf carts to reach from one end to the other. He was escorted down a long and wide corridor bordered by tall columns, through another high and beautifully ornate gate, then across a courtyard of inlaid marble that was veined with green and black streaks. A spouting fountain broke the quiet of the place and they stepped into a vestibule, beyond which was a large, high-ceilinged room with thick carpets on the floor. A row of men in uniforms, regal robes, and business suits stood along one side. At the end of the room, standing next to a long sofa of gold brocade, was King Abdullah of Saudi Arabia.

"Kyle Swanson! Welcome!" he called, raising his hand in greeting.

Kyle felt the eyes of everyone in the room on his back as he walked closer to Abdullah. "Good evening, Your Majesty. It's good to see you again."

Abdullah put a hand on each of Swanson's shoulders and looked into his eyes. "And under much different circumstances, eh?"

"Yes, sir. Quite."

The monarch motioned toward the other men in the room. "These are my closest councilors, family members, and friends, all of whom you will meet later. And, gentlemen, you have heard me speak of Gunnery Sergeant Swanson's bravery during the terrorist attack at the hospital in England. I emphasize again that I trust this man. If he wanted me dead, he would have already killed me. You will all do your best to make his mission here a success. He has my total support and confidence. I trust that my wishes on this are clear."

There was a murmur of agreement among the diplomats, government officials, and military officers. King Abdullah nodded. "Now, Gunny Swanson, please come with me for a few minutes of private time before you set to work."

Kyle followed the king into an adjoining private chamber, across a floor patterned in blue and white tiles. "Close the door and have a chair," he said. Swanson did so, remaining silent until the king might indicate a response would be welcomed.

"First, I have some excellent news for you from England. The physicians say that our friend Sir Jeff is recovering well. A long road of recovery lies ahead of him, but he is on the mend. I know how close you are."

"That's good to hear, sir," Kyle replied. "I was very worried about him."

Abdullah picked up a rectangular box made of shining wood. "I want to formally express my thanks to you and Major Summers for saving my life at the hospital. I won't forget that." He handed Swanson the container. Resting inside on a cushion of maroon velvet was a double-edged Arabian dagger, a *jambiya*, with a blade that curved up from a bone handle decorated in bright stones held tight in a web of silver.

"Your Majesty, I cannot accept this. I was just doing my job. We're not allowed to receive private gifts." Swanson was stumbling for words. *Are those rocks real?*

"Ah, but you must!" The king smiled at Kyle's discomfort. "I obtained the explicit permission of President Tracy. You and the major are to donate it to the National U.S. Marine Corps Museum in Quantico as a symbol of our friendship. You are quite a pair, and this is the least that I can do."

"Well, sir, thank you." He slid the blade from the scabbard. Razor-sharp and as old as sand. "I appreciate it, sir. Major Summers may pry out one of those stones to make a ring."

The king laughed and took a seat behind a broad desk. "Now let me tell you the main reason that I was speaking with President Tracy: the presence of nuclear weapons in my country. In retrospect, I understand the reason for getting them, back in the days when Saddam Hussein in Iraq and the Taliban in Afghanistan were growing menaces. Now, however, they are a destabilizing influence. I want to get rid of them as soon as possible, for I have no intention of starting nuclear war. Trusted people will facilitate our end of the handover, but if a dangerous situation develops, I give you my permission to handle it. I will back you up. Just help us get rid of those things."

"Thank you, sir. It's the right decision."

The king shifted his position. "I suppose that you were briefed that one of the missiles may have fallen into the possession of the terrorists?"

"Yes, sir. I am confident that your military will recover it. We should process the remaining four as quickly as possible."

"Exactly. We have a large force now searching for the missing device. Only the warhead was taken, not the delivery system, so it is not just something that any common soldier can operate. Too many built-in technical and redundant safeguards for that."

"To consider my role properly, sir, may I ask your opinion of the overall situation in the kingdom at present? Obviously, I have already been sworn to secrecy."

Abdullah pulled gently at his goatee and defiance flared in his dark eyes. "I think we have great challenges ahead, but there are positive signs, too. The most telling point is that the overall population does not seem to be deeply involved. Our citizens are devout and conservative, but will not throw away everything we have earned and learned in the past century. Without the people, the plotters cannot succeed."

Kyle had one more question. "And have your intelligence people figured out who is behind all of this? Who do the rebels want to take your place?"

"There seem to be several major players. To answer your main question, no one is going to take my place because they want to replace the monarchy entirely. A religious regime would be established instead, and the prime candidate to become its leader is Mohammed Abu Ebara, the head of the Religious Police. Ebara is a dirty piece of work and somewhat mentally unstable. For instance, it was his decision a few years ago to let that school in Makkah burn down with fifteen girls trapped inside. His police would not allow the students to escape from the building because they would be unescorted by male relatives. Similarly, the firemen, as unrelated males, were prevented from going inside. It was medieval stupidity."

"Does this Ebara have the support of the entire religious community?"

"That remains to be seen. As usual, the Grand Mufti has not been heard from, which hinders Ebara covering his uprising with that needed permission. We believe that Ebara's campaign is being financed from outside of Saudi Arabia. We have picked up reports of foreign financial supporters. Russia and China are likely suspects."

Kyle leaned forward, elbows on his knees, lost in thought for a moment. "I can understand how this Ebara guy might be the one whipping up the support for a rebellion by going on television and shouting his sermons. But I assume most of the Saudi military is still loyal to the House of Saud, despite the horrendous attack by a couple of rebel pilots. Am I right?"

"Yes," replied Abdullah. "It appears that this spirit of rebellion is a momentary thing within most of the units. Overall, the soldiers are still obeying their orders."

"So that leaves a good question, sir. If the officer corps is still loyal to the throne, who is running the tactical side of the coup?"

The king paused. "We don't know."

"Whoever it is, is a professional. He knows what he is doing," said Kyle. "Let's get all our intel people here and in Washington working to identify him. Chop off the head, the rest of the snake dies."

The king rose. The private audience was over. "I will give such instructions," he said. "Meanwhile, collect those nuclear weapons as fast as you can."

JEDDAH, SAUDI ARABIA

MOHAMMED **A**BU **E**BARA **TOOK** a long look at the bright cover of the entertainment magazine. It featured a beautiful young woman in a bikini walking hand-in-hand on a sparkling beach with a muscular male who also was in a tight and skimpy bathing costume. Ebara found the public display of nudity and affection to be both disgusting and offensive. A headline over the color photograph read:

STEFI AND BARNS:
CARIBBEAN HONEYMOON?

Stephanie Haddad of Lebanon was among the most popular singers in the Middle East, a product of the MTV generation, known as "Stefi" by her millions of fans. Only twenty years old, she was mysteriously sexy with black hair that had been lightened with color until it was a tawny waterfall that reached past her shoulders. She had a reputation for being wild, was rich, dressed provocatively, drove a red Porsche convertible, and openly dated British football star Barnaby Weathers. They were a stunning couple whose unblemished faces and perfect bodies were often displayed in magazines, and her hard rock songs and sultry dances were among the most downloaded items among the young people of Saudi Arabia.

Ebara flung the disgusting magazine into the trash. It was a lie. The harlot was not in any holiday resort in the Caribbean with her infidel boyfriend. Right now, she was cooped up in one of Ebara's barren jail cells, alone and wearing nothing but a dingy gray scoop-neck prison shift that buttoned along the back.

*   *   *

IN ADDITION TO BEING a celebrity, Stephanie Haddad was also a Muslim and had decided to fulfill a requirement of her religion by making a *haj*, the pilgrimage to the holy city of Mecca in Saudi Arabia. She was much too well-known to appear during the proscribed time for the real festival, but she felt safe in making an *umrah*, an off-season visit that would still be spiritually satisfying. When she was older and no longer in the spotlight, perhaps she could perform the true ritual visit. This time at least she could make the walk seven times around the black cube of the *Kaaba* and stone the devil.

Her trip was planned in secret and her publicist announced in Lebanon that she and Barnaby were taking an extended holiday at a villa on a Caribbean island. The photo of Stefi and her boyfriend had been staged on a secluded beach in Spain and leaked to the media. Then, with the color washed from her trademark mane of hair, the makeup removed, and the Victoria's Secret lingerie left behind, Stefi entered Saudi Arabia under an assumed name. She was covered and pious, a proper young woman traveling with her brother, naïvely believing that her fame could be left behind.

ONLY TWO HOURS AFTER she crossed the border, Mohammed Abu Ebara knew she was in the country. What better way to demonstrate his authority than by publicly degrading and whipping this particularly insulting harlot who pranced naked before the face of God? Before Stefi even had a chance to leave Jeddah, the gateway to the holy shrines, he struck.

A political riot was arranged while she was out shopping and Religious Police swept her up to slam her into the dirty cell. Ebara announced the arrest on television and charged the slim singer with public blasphemy. His judges came to a quick decision, because the defendant was not entitled to an attorney, a jury, or even allowed to hear the evidence against her. There would be no embassy contacts, no telephone calls, not even a prior notification to the Shura Council, which might oppose his intentions.

The three judges sentenced her to fifty lashes with the cane. Ebara balked: not enough! A thousand lashes, he demanded, and the cowed jurists, fearful of making a powerful enemy and perhaps ending up in jail themselves, agreed.

ABOUT NOON THE FOLLOWING day, two female guards entered her cell, clamped handcuffs on her wrists and took her out. She thought for a moment that she was being released, but found herself being hoisted into a dank, covered truck that contained four male Religious Police guards who leered at her as she sat on a side bench. A wooden chair also was in the truck.

At the downtown marketplace in which she had been arrested, she was still handcuffed in the truck, while Ebara's men spread the word that a special event was about to occur in the square. Foreigners and journalists were particularly encouraged to attend. A crowd gathered, thinking that there might be a brutal beheading and there were some noises of disappointment when the chair from the truck was placed in the middle of the open area: just a flogging.

Stefi began to lose some fear as she waited, replacing it with a growing sense of defiance. *I'm Stephanie Haddad! They can't get away with this!* She would offer bribes, or ransom, or whatever it was called down here.

EBARA WAS SATISFIED AT the way the event was unfolding. Like the rebellion, it was another public demonstration of his soaring power. Straying Muslims around the world would quake, then rally to his cause.

Ebara had postponed the flogging until Dieter Nesch and the terrorist Juba arrived, so he could judge their reactions when he meted out this remarkable punishment. They also needed to understand his determination and strength to do whatever was necessary as a true leader. Guards shoved aside the crowd to make room for the two special visitors. Nesch, the short, pudgy banker, was in a buttoned suit. Juba was casual in a dark shirt and gray slacks, his face shaded by a wide-brimmed straw hat that disguised the eye patch. Neither seemed particularly interested. Ebara intended to change that attitude of indifference by showing them sharia law at work!

"Bring her," he told the guards. He gave the long and flexible bamboo cane a good shake. The tip swished back and forth through the air, like the pendulum of an evil clock.

Despite her increased resolve, a tear rolled down Stefi's cheek when the guards came. They laughed and said they were not interested in a bribe from a whore.

The guards took her out of the truck and into the bright sunlight to parade her slowly around the edge of the crowd. Gasps of recognition trailed them. That looks like Stefi! It is her! Men began to jeer and spit, and women could not stop staring. Word spread rapidly and the crowd started to build. Stefi was to be flogged! The television crews could not believe their good fortune.

Ebara adjusted the sleeve of his robe and brushed back the edge of his red *kaffiyeh* while the guards made the little whore ready. The shift covering her backside was unbuttoned to the waist and she was thrust forward hard across the chair, with her buttocks and thighs and those famous legs totally exposed. The crowd of men cheered as the guards clamped tightly onto her wrists to hold her in place.

"Please! Don't do this! Please!" Stefi screamed, twisting her partially nude body in fear. The cameras would prove to the world that Mohammed Abu Ebara was unafraid to carry out his divine duty. By beating this guilty woman, he would give pause to anyone who opposed him during these troubled times. They, too, might face his stern vengeance.

Ebara walked around his victim, loudly reciting *surahs* from the Koran to endorse the punishment, while swishing the long bamboo cane aloft. Cheers from the gawkers increased. Only the initial fifty lashes would come today, and he would personally administer the first five. Then the girl would be sent back to her cell to recover. When she was healthy again, fifty more lashes would be administered. It would take a very long time to reach a thousand and this devil child would never perform her debauchery again.

The sacred female parts that he would now desecrate in the name of Allah were exposed. Ebara brought the cane high overhead and crashed it down with all his might across her thighs, bringing a loud, piercing scream from the young woman as the pain ripped through her. The scream and the new scar on her naked flesh infused Ebara with a strange, personal, sexual excitement, and he laid the next stroke on even harder, but with great care, crossing it over the first. Then he furiously flailed away to finish his few lashes. Long red welts and trails of blood oozed from ruptured flesh as his reward. The scars would last a lifetime.

He handed the cane to the big guard who would conclude the day's punishment. As he turned away, his gaze moved to the two Europeans. The crowd was berserk in excitement, but the banker was looking down, working his BlackBerry, a strange hand-held electronic device, with rapt attention. Juba, with his arms crossed, yawned.

EBARA MET THEM IN a cool room in a nearby mosque, beads of sweat still dappling his shaggy hair and beard but the hard dark eyes reflecting a sense of triumph. They remained silent while a servant brought a tray of tea, figs, and goat cheese, then withdrew to leave the three alone.

Juba had removed his hat. He took a sip of tea and then checked the large watch on his wrist before staring with his single eye at the renegade Saudi cleric. "Exactly four minutes ago, a series of explosive devices began blowing up in Dammam, an important city and the center of commerce in the entire Eastern Province. As you know, Dammam is right on the Persian Gulf and is an important oil, gas, and transportation center. Only an hour's drive on the causeway out of Dammam, and you can be in Bahrain, so the detonations will indicate to everyone that this rebellion in Saudi Arabia is threatening to spill over to other countries."

Ebara tried to interrupt, but Juba held up his palm, flat, to stop any response. He coolly continued, "That attack was part of my overall plan, a very careful scheme that has been two years in the making. Now that plan might not work, because I am not directly controlling it from my headquarters. You, Mohammed Abu Ebara, are not the only important person involved in this, but you are the only one who is screwing it up."

Ebara was watching Juba as a predator wolf stares down a lamb. Who was this infidel to speak to him in such an insulting manner? The guards were right outside and he could have Juba arrested and taken to prison and executed in private. A seething anger was building inside him, but he kept his voice soft. "We now have nuclear weapons that must be considered."

Then Dieter Nesch spoke for the first time, in a normal tone, telling Ebara, "Our sponsor is nervous about this disruption of the schedule and is concerned that you have taken your eyes from the goal of toppling the monarchy," he said. Nesch held up both his cell phone and BlackBerry for the cleric to see. "I sent a message and pictures of your performance today to the Russian. He is not happy, not at all. He instructed me to say that if you are this unsteady and confuse what is really important with a minor situation, perhaps you may not be the man for the massive task that lies ahead."

That jolted Ebara. The only sign to betray his sudden nervousness was a quickened bobbing of the Adam's apple in his gaunt neck.

Juba said, "You ordered me to drop everything and come here to meet with you personally! So I had to put many attacks on hold, because the fighters will remain idle until they receive my personal authorization codes to carry out their assignments. Since I am not there to issue those orders, the attacks will not happen. So I am here in your presence, as you wished, but I hope that you understand that by choosing to emphasize the nuclear weapons, you may have stopped the revolution in its tracks. Not the royal family, not the army . . . you!"

Mohammed Abu Ebara would not tolerate being spoken to in such an insulting manner, but Juba leapt to his feet, flushed with fury. "I flew halfway around the globe to see about these nukes, weapons that could instigate a holocaust, only to be kept waiting in the sun while you whipped a helpless child! Your priorities are strange, preacher. The whipping was stupid, totally unneeded, a work of lust by a perverted old preacher who has probably never fucked a willing woman. We are trying to win over Muslim support in other countries and you decide to publicly humiliate and flog the most famous pop music star in the Arab world. Your actions today will cost us the support of an untold number of young people. Maybe millions."

Ebara shot a glance back, but did nothing. His confidence was cracking under Juba's onslaught. This man had once been the deadly tool of some of the greatest men of the age, including Osama bin Laden. There was no pity, generosity, or politeness about him. Nothing there at all but a pure killer.

The banker was equally uninterested in Muslim protocol. Neither offered him a dram of respect. Ebara felt a jab of fear. "The girl is a disease and must be eradicated," he said, feeling that he must say something in his own defense. "We must teach women to stay in their place."

"You will release her immediately," Dieter Nesch said quietly, grimly resting his pale blue eyes on Ebara. "That is not a suggestion, Haj Moham-med. You will appear gracious by suspending the rest of the sentence and kicking her out of the country. The damage this has done to our cause has been incredible and now your personal show of brutality will be spread all over the Internet. You will appear as a madman and a fool to the rest of the world. I cannot believe you were so stupid."

Ebara stared back. "I could kill you both for talking to me like that."

"No. You couldn't," Juba snarled. "Try. I will snap your neck right now and we will get some other stooge to finish this rebellion."

Nesch sucked in some breath, making a tut-tut sound. "Now, I know I will sound like a banker, but can we please complete our real business? I must send a report."

"Yeah. Let's do that." Juba said, putting his hands on his hips and lean-ing forward toward Ebara. He screamed, "WHERE ARE MY FUCKING NUCLEAR MISSILES?"

AL'S GARAGE, SAUDI ARABIA

EVEN WITH HIS DARK sunglasses and the tinted windows of the Land Rover, Kyle could barely look into the morning sun, which was still a dull orange balloon rising over the amazingly flat airfield. A dot coming out of the glare grew larger, a plane that was headed straight into the base.

"Here we go," said Prince Colonel Mishaal bin Khalid, son of the minister of defense and a nephew of the king. He opened the door and hot air poured into the SUV to immediately overwhelm the air conditioner. His hustling, no nonsense aide, Captain Omar al-Muallami, followed his boss.

Swanson winced as he stepped into the early morning heat. It was going to be one of those searing days with a steady wind blowing sand that streaked like gritty, little bullets across the open miles of the Prince Sultan Air Base, about sixty miles south of Riyadh. Mirages were already shimmering off the tarmac. Everyone wanted to get this over with as soon as possible, before the place began to bake. The temperature was already knocking near a hundred degrees.

The huge military installation had risen from nothing during the Iraqi wars, with millions and millions of American and Saudi dollars creating something from nothing not far from the town of al-Kharj. The thousands of American troops who had been stationed there or transited through called it "Al's Garage." The U.S. troops were satisfied in 2003 to turn it back over to the Saudis, the camel spiders, and the carpet snakes.

Most American military personnel left, but a training cadre and several hundred private U.S. civilian contractors remained behind to help the Saudis keep things running. Kyle, wearing his old jeans, a loose blue shirt, and a tan web vest with lots of pockets, looked like one of those ubiquitous, faceless American civilians. The floppy shirt easily covered the Marine Special Ops .45 ACP pistol that rested in a holster on his belt.

The dot in the sky was bigger now, riding down on four huge engines in a smooth landing approach.

"Prepare the loading area," Mishaal bin Khalid told his aide, and Captain al-Muallami snapped the order with authority. A company of forty armed troops fanned out in a wide cordon around a parking area at the end of a fifteen-thousand-foot-long runway. Humvees mounted with machine guns roamed beyond the soldiers. No one was around who was not supposed to be there.

Swanson stood beside the APC that contained the tactical nuclear warhead. He reached out and patted the steel armor, making sure that the heavy vehicle had not somehow disappeared. This was the first warhead to be officially transferred from Saudi to American custody.

He was the point man for the U.S. transfer team. Prince Mishaal, who might one day become a senior prince in the royal family, was his counterpart. The king had personally paired them up to maximize authority and expedite the process.

Mishaal roamed the protective cordon like a stalking panther. He was six feet tall, a weightlifter whose sculpted body was a strong 200 pounds. Whether in uniform or in white robes, he possessed the natural command presence of someone born to lead. At thirty-five years of age, the prince was a handsome man with sharply planed cheeks and a strong chin that was covered with a perfect goatee.

Right behind him was his stern aide, whose busy eyes and agile brain tried to anticipate everything. Mishaal personally examined each soldier in turn, not necessarily trusting any of them. The assassinations had thrown a net of suspicion over everyone in the military services and Captain al-Muallami had combed the dossiers to select the guards prior to the prince authorizing their presence at the site.

Nevertheless, Kyle would not be content until the security platoon of U.S. Marines aboard the incoming plane was on the ground to "assist" in the final stage of the handover. Trained and trusted guns would extract the worry from the process.

A C-130-J HERCULES, THE most reliable transport warhorse in the U.S. airlift stable, touched down and its big tires and the blast from the six-bladed props on the four Rolls Royce engines churned a hurricane of dust in its wake. It slowed and turned onto a taxiway, then followed a Humvee into the circle of waiting Saudi troops.

The big ramp lowered in back and the Marines poured out to form a tight inner position within the Saudi cordon. A tall, black officer strolled confidently down the ramp and walked to Prince Mishaal. He saluted and the Saudi colonel returned it.

"Colonel, I am Major David Lassiter from the Marine Expeditionary Unit, Special Operations Force, and I am ready to receive the item as stated on this manifest." He presented a clipboard containing several sheets of authorization papers.

"Very well, major. Ordinarily, I would offer our traditional hospitality to you and your men. Due to the urgency of the situation, I feel it would be best to forego that."

"Yes, sir. I agree. Perhaps next time," Lassiter said. "Gunny Swanson, it's good to see you again. Perhaps you would like to check the hold of the Hercules while the colonel and I finish the paperwork."

"Aye, aye, sir. Good idea. I want a word with the loadmaster." Kyle walked away from the two officers, through the Marine cordon, and up the ramp. Darren Rawls was playing a major today, for the show was all Trident.

The cavernous cargo hold was big enough to carry an armored vehicle or even a helicopter with blades folded. The Herc could shuttle thousands of pounds over hundreds of miles and it had been fitted out specifically for this mission, to receive the APC waiting on the tarmac. Kyle waved to the loadmaster, who had brought along two assistants, and moved toward the darkened front of the plane. The lights had been turned off. Someone waited in the shadows.

"Hey," he said.

"Hey," replied Sybelle Summers. With her black hair, and wearing black jeans and a black sweater, she was almost invisible. "You know what pisses me off?"

"Far as I know, just about everything. What?"

"This friggin' country! Here I am helping to save them from catastrophe and I can't set foot outside of this damned plane for fear of upsetting their frail little sensibilities. Rawls has to pretend to be a major while I, the real deal, have to stand around doing nothing. Whole nation of men traumatized by tits and ass."

"I'm very sorry you feel that way, Major Summers, but I don't really care at the moment. Did you bring my stuff?"

Sybelle laughed. "I have to express my outrage at their sexist behavior. Yeah, I got it." She nudged a booted foot against a titanium alloy gun case and a smaller secure briefcase. "You sure you want to do this?"

"Absolutely. I've got a get-out-of-jail-free card from the king, and I'm partnered up with his nephew. No worries."

She peered out beyond the distant rear of the aircraft. Men were pulling the tarps off of the APC and the loadmasters were laying markings to guide the machine aboard. A Marine sergeant climbed into the APC to replace the Saudi driver while Major Lassiter and Prince Mishaal bin Khalid worked through the papers.

"That prince is a good-looking guy, but how good is he in a fight?" Sybelle asked. "I don't like not being here to cover your back."

"Nice enough dude and seems capable. Bright guy, educated in Great Britain, went through our Army Ranger School and has become the troubleshooter for the royal family. The princes only trust each other these days and I don't trust anybody. Just in case, I want you to run a thorough background check on my new best buddy, Prince Colonel Mishaal bin Khalid, and his kick-ass aide, Captain Omar al-Muallami."

"Understandable," said Sybelle. "Meanwhile, General Middleton wants to know if the Saudis have figured out what happened to the missing nuke over at Khobz."

"No," said Kyle. "They are still blaming it on the terrorists. Tell the general that since King Abdullah is now on the same page with us, I recommend telling him that we have it in our possession. Take some worry off his shoulders. Now do I still have the Green Light for this, uh, other job?"

"Middleton approved it. He is not passing it on to the White House. Pull it off without getting caught and we're all home free. If you screw up, Middleton will cover it under a bunch of top-secret excuses."

"Don't worry. Am I going to get this kid Jamal from the CIA as a backup? He's good."

"Done. His contact number is in here." She handed him a sealed manila envelope.

"And the Lizard is tracking my target?"

"You kidding? Freedman is having a ball with it and the NSA big ears are all over this dude. He's operating on open frequencies and you could probably just follow him by watching television. His schedule for the next few days is in the package. Un-fucking-believably arrogant and stupid."

"Finest kind," Swanson said. "I can let his ego work for us. Have the Liz keep Jamal up to speed on the guy until we get together."

They both turned as the APC moved to the bottom of the ramp, the engine was gunned and the armored vehicle growled aboard so the loadmasters could secure it with hooks and chains. Darren Rawls saluted the Saudi prince again and marched back up the ramp. "Y'all done here?" he asked.

"Yeah," Kyle said. "I'm gone. Take this big bird away and secure that TNW. It's the second of the five." He stuffed the envelope into a vest pocket and picked up the gun case. "We should have the next warhead ready for pickup soon, but you may have to work a lot faster, so stay ready. See you then."

Sybelle had a look of concern. "Kyle, be careful. You're alone out here, like a fisherman on a big ocean with a whale pulling on the hook."

"I got it. Really," he said. He walked back out through the cargo bay, past the APC and down the ramp into the heat. The long gun case bumped against his thigh. His personal sniper rifle, Excalibur, was in it and that was a difference-maker as far as he was concerned. A smaller case contained a good map of Saudi Arabia, a battery-powered satellite telephone and a backup cell phone, a GPS tracking device, and a goody bag of things that might come in handy.

At a shout from Darren Rawls, the lieutenant handling the security pla-toon saluted his own Saudi counterpart and the Marines hustled back aboard the plane.

Kyle loaded his cases into the Land Rover as the Herc revved its engines, which had never shut down throughout the brief operation. It turned around and moved out to the vacant runway, already cleared for takeoff while the Saudi soldiers were dismissed and got aboard trucks.

Mishaal returned to the SUV and started it, clocking the air-conditioning up to high. The chill breeze was delicious.

"One down, Gunny. Three to go. One still missing. What's in the fancy new luggage?"

He turned to look at the prince. "A secure telephone and some personal shit. Brought along my own weapon because it is custom-made and I might find a use for it. Hope you don't mind."

Mishaal smiled. "Not at all. I've heard my uncle bragging about you, so I would love to see if you're up to Ranger standards."

Swanson grinned as the cool air made life worthwhile again. "I'll try not to disappoint you."

An off-key chirp of little bells sounded in the back seat, from the cell phone on the belt of Captain al-Muallami. He flipped it open, identified himself, and grimaced as he listened. Then he closed it, dropped it on the seat, wrote something on a small notepad, folded the page in half, and handed it up to the prince. "From headquarters, sir," he said.

Mishaal read it. "I may get to see you work sooner than expected, Gunny. All hell has broken loose down in Ash Mutayr, a divisional head-quarters on the southern border near Yemen. The troops have mutinied and heavy fighting is underway. They seized some armor."

Swanson let his head slump forward. "Ash Mutayr? That was going to be our final nuke pickup site," he said.

"It just moved up the list to be our next stop. It's more than four hundred miles from here, beyond the biggest desert on earth." The prince popped the Land Rover into gear and accelerated toward the flight control building. Captain al-Muallami was already on his radio, ordering up a private jet with a fighter escort.

Kyle was silently changing his own plans. He had hoped to go directly over to Jeddah, meet up with Jamal, and go take a look at the guy heading the Religious Police, who was the other half of his Green Light Package. Swanson had to make a decision on whether the man was a true danger, or just a dupe; to kill him or let him live. That trip had just flopped right in the shitter with the uprising at the southern base. Jeddah would have to wait.

THE PENTAGON, WASHINGTON, D.C.

LIEUTENANT **C**OMMANDER **B**ENTON **F**REEDMAN, the Task Force Trident electronics expert known as the Lizard, chewed on the smooth plastic of a blue U.S. Navy ballpoint pen as he read the Bloomberg business Web site. Small importers in America were howling about the disruption of shipping from China.

Kara Henderson in Santa Barbara, California, was experiencing the same problem that was bugging Charles Tyson in Seattle and Eileen Mc-Namara in Chicago. Their ship had not come in. That wasn't normal and the Lizard was always itchy when "one and one" did not add up to "two." He checked the source story from the Associated Press, which had gathered specific incidents of the curious small-business crisis from its bureaus across the nation.

The compiled report stated that Kara ran an upscale clothing boutique, Eileen sold leather purses to department stores, and Tyson was a toy distributor. Each had made their annual trips to Japan and China earlier in the year, met with manufacturers, studied the catalogues, attended trade shows, and placed thousands of dollars worth of orders. Christmas would be coming in a few months and time was required to fill those orders, pack the containers, and ship the goods. In the U.S., Henderson, McNamara, and Tyson were already taking advance orders from their own customers. Reliability was important.

Then all three had received startling e-mails from the Chinese shipping agent, a bland, so-sorry announcement that the giant cargo ship *Peh Shan* was no longer available. Reasons unexplained. Efforts were being made to reassign their cargoes to a South Korean carrier, but a delay of at least thirty to sixty days could be expected.

"Sixty days from now, I may be out of business," Eileen McNamara complained to the reporter. "If the big stores don't get those purses that I promised, they will cancel my order and buy from somewhere else." Tyson had bet the farm on a full container load of the latest surprise toy that was going to sweep the nation during the Christmas season. "What am I going to do with a half-million Marko Giggle Birdies in January?" he asked. Kara's situation was equally dire: Her boutique would fall behind the fashion curve if those new rags did not arrive on time.

Their protests went unheeded and the three business owners, among many others just like them across America, watched helplessly as their Christmas marketing plans fell disastrously behind schedule.

Freedman knew that it was not at all like the Chinese business world to falter on something this important, but nevertheless the *Peh Shan* had been unexpectedly removed from commercial service. It was the sixth Chinese container ship in a week to be sidelined without explanation. None were in shipyards for repair. They were just sitting at anchor near the coast, apparently empty.

He called up the specs on the vessel. It was a monster, stretching almost a quarter-mile in length and wide as a football field. The Lizard cocked his head as he stared at a picture of the monster ship and its massive deck. "I wonder . . . What if . . ." he whispered to himself, gnawing harder on the plastic.

He logged onto an internal Pentagon network to read the Navy's study on its own Maritime Pre-Positioning Force. Alarm grew as he felt the pieces of the puzzle click into place, and he dug deeper into the current status of the Chinese Navy. U.S. satellites had fresh images of two new Jin-class nuclear submarines on the surface, one in the Arabian Sea while the other almost leisurely sunned itself in the Indian Ocean. A dozen JL-1 SLBM missiles and plenty of torpedoes were aboard each. A pair of Type 052C Luyang-II class destroyers were churning at high speed into the area, with no effort to maintain radio silence. Almost as if those carrier-killers wanted to be seen, he thought.

The cargo ships kept forcing their way back into his thinking. Cargo ships by definition carried things. The big beasts could hold thousands of troops in their vast holds. As his mind grappled with the possibilities, his computer brought up recent satellite imagery that clearly showed a Z-10E attack helicopter, the newest powerful war bird in the Chinese inventory, parked on the deck of the *Peh Shan*, with sailors folding the blades and lashing it down. When he saw it, he bit all the way through the plastic and he had to stop to spit the remains from his mouth.

"Stop playing with your food, Liz." The booming voice of Master Gunnery Sergeant O.O. Dawkins came from over his shoulder. Dawkins was a large presence in any room, and he shared this office with Freedman. One of the few men in the Marine Corps to hold the highest enlisted rank, "Double-Oh" was Trident's chief administrator. He had watched Freedman chew the pen to pieces, a habit that surfaced only when the Lizard was onto something quite unusual. Dawkins walked over to Freedman's desk and looked over his shoulder at the rapidly flashing computer screen. His dark gray eyes could not keep up with the images that flipped across the computer screen as the Lizard darted about in his electronic world. "Have you gotten something new on Swanson's mission?"

"Unh-unh. That target hasn't moved in hours and the CIA has humint eyes on it."

"Okay," Dawkins replied. Human intelligence was the best kind of recon. "Having some dude on the ground watching the target is a good thing."

"I'm keeping Gunny Swanson updated."

"Then why are you flying at warp speed?"

"Something is going on that doesn't make sense. So I'm putting together a briefing for General Middleton. He's going to think I'm crazy," Freedman said absently as his printer spun out more paper.

"We all think you're crazy. What have you got?"

"Take a look." The Lizard scooped up a stack of pages from the printer tray and verbally sketched the information he had downloaded so far.

Dawkins listened to the Lizard's excited recitation of data without comment as he thumbed through some of the sheets, patiently waiting for Freedman to get to the point. Usually, that took a while. Freedman barely took his eyes from the screen. Click, change sites and databases, click, point, click, drag, print, again and again. The stack grew.

When the Lizard finally ran out of breath, Dawkins said, "I understand where you're going with this, Liz, but China doesn't have a blue-water navy. They only have one aircraft carrier, which is still at its home port. They are not going to try to force a path through the Strait of Hormuz with just a couple of submarines and destroyers when we have a carrier battle group plugging that gap. And loading thousands of Chinese troops in those cargo ships? Even if they tried, it would take them forever to get to Saudi Arabia: That's more than four thousand miles! Sorry, commander, but in my opinion, you're way off base on this one."

"I'm not quite finished, Master Gunny. Look at these land and air traffic patterns of some of China's key military units. Planes are surging toward forward bases. There is significant activity around both large and medium landing ships along the coast."

"Liz. Listen to me. They may be making a lot of noise, but they aren't about to take their fleet on a long trip over to invade Saudi Arabia."

Freedman hit the keyboard one last time and stood up. "No, no, no. Yes, you're right, of course. Four thousand miles. Ridiculous. It would not be Saudi Arabia! Could not be that." He walked to a map of the world that dominated the far wall and put a finger on the coast of China. "But look at this port, Fuzhow, only 155 miles from Taipei. While our attention is riveted on the crisis in the Middle East, the Chinese are making exactly the preparations they would need to jump across the Strait in a lightning move and invade Taiwan!"

Dawkins looked at the map, dumbfounded. "So those Chinese subs and destroyers are prowling around in the Middle East waters to keep us busy watching them instead of getting ready to fight for Taiwan?"

"Yes. Absolutely," replied the Lizard. "It's the only logical answer. And unless we commit to fight for Taiwan, Beijing will put a couple of hundred thousand troops on that island pretty darned quick. Taiwan won't stand a chance alone."

Slowly, Dawkins reached into the shirt pocket of his uniform and withdrew a plastic ballpoint pen bearing the eagle, globe, and anchor symbol of the Marines. He gave it to Freedman. "Here. Eat," he said. "Then pull this World War Three shit into coherent shape while I go find the general."

The Lizard grabbed Master Gunnery Sergeant Dawkins by the elbow, almost jerking the large man off balance. He stared at him through the big glasses for a moment, released him, got up and began to pace, talking to himself. Counting off items on his fingers and clenching his fists.

"What the fuck now, Liz?" Dawkins was impatient to get this information to the man who needed it most.

"I'm a naval officer. You other people in Trident are not."

"Correct. You're a squid and we are spec ops."

"Yes, of course. Squid. Giant squid, from the family *Architeuthidae*. Largest eyes of any creature. Sorry." He flapped his arms. "One thing I have learned from you, Double Oh, and from Sybelle and Kyle and the general, is how highly you value deception, to make the enemy look the other way while you execute your tasks."

Dawkins said, "That's exactly what the Chinese are doing. We look left and they go right. I've got it, Liz. Our forces in the Pacific have a lot of work to do in a hurry."

"Yes." The skinny lieutenant commander hurried over to the closed door and stood before it, blocking Dawkins's path as if he might actually impede the master gunny's progress if he tried to pass. "No."

"What in the hell are you trying to say, man! Say it!"

Freedman held his hands at about chin level, palms parallel and shaking. "I'm wrong, master gunny. Stupid, stupid. *The Taiwan thing is the deception!* What better way to launch a special operation than to hide it within a massive buildup and a shifting of all of your forces? Our intelligence sources are wonderful, but we can't track everything, and they are throwing all of this into motion at once. It's a beautiful ploy to overwhelm our capabilities. Or, that's what I think they are thinking that they want us to think."

Dawkins gently placed a large paw on each of Freedman's shoulders and moved him gently to one side of the door. "Calm down, Commander Freedman. Don't crack up on me now. Anything else?"

"No. That's all." He licked his lips and looked at his wristwatch. He took a deep breath. "Okay. My assessment is that the Chinese are going to drop a bunch of paratroopers on the Saudi oil fields in about seventy-two hours."

ASH MUTAYR, SAUDI ARABIA

THE AR RUB'AL KHALI Desert is a quarter-million square miles of sand, with dunes as high as a thousand feet, fearsome hot mountains that move with the winds. From a small plane sailing high above the Empty Quarter, the marching dunes reminded Kyle of a restless ocean. A man could drown in either one. There was nothing worthwhile down there in those waterless, blistering hot sands along the Tropic of Cancer; nothing other than some of the biggest oil fields in the world. Villages and dry tracks were built to help suck the oil from the sands. Just thinking about living under such harsh conditions was enough to make one sweat.

"It might as well be the end of the world," he said to Prince Colonel Mishaal bin Khalid.

"Not to us," Mishaal replied, taking a sip of fruit juice. "Our history is down there. Bedouins are in every walk of Saudi life today, but thousands of them still live in the great desert. That lure of the sands is magical and never leaves us. Even in cities, it is not unusual to see the owner of a home have a tent in his garden."

"Have you ever even ridden a camel?" Swanson asked with a grin.

"Of course. Once. For a holiday photo." The prince tapped the soft cushion of his seat. "I also do not sleep on a goat's hide, nor do I use an abacus to count. We embrace modernity and technology but have leapt from camels to pickup trucks in an incredibly short time."

"Oil," Kyle commented.

"Yes, oil," Mishaal agreed, and changed the subject. "Are you ready to get to work?"

"I am ready to help," Swanson replied. He was more than ready. The prospect of action was surging through his mind and body.

"I have a feeling we will need every gun we can get." The prince looked at his watch and picked up a telephone handset on the nearby bulkhead to call his aide, who had been up front at the communications console tracking the developing situation. The prince told him to come back to the main cabin and give them a briefing. They would be landing in about twenty minutes.

BLACK SMOKE RISING IN columns folded into a single dark cloud over the military base that dominated the flat landscape at Ash Mutayr. A small village by that name lay on the west side of the military facility, between the base and National Route 15. Smoke also spouted from inside the town. The mutiny had spilled beyond the fence.

The long, paved airport runway was considered unsafe by the local commander, so their plane swooped in for a fast landing on a hard dirt strip on the far side of the main highway and taxied to a halt. The aide popped the door open and they hurried down the stairs and ran toward an old Bradley M2A1 fighting vehicle that was trundling forward to collect them.

Bright streaks of recent bullet strikes shone against its armor and it paused only long enough to spin on one track and lower the hydraulic rear ramp enough so they could scramble inside. It smelled of spent gunpowder, and all of the cradles that normally held TOW anti-tank missiles were empty. This Brad had been working hard.

The track commander was a lieutenant in a dirty, stained uniform who was also acting as the turret gunner. He yelled an order for the driver to get moving and opened up with his 25 mm chain gun toward a pair of armored M113 APCs that were charging toward them out of the base and down the main runway.

The chain gun slammed away like a jackhammer and incoming rounds whonked against the Bradley's armor. As the brawny vehicle lunged ahead, the lieutenant screamed in pain and toppled from his seat, a chunk of meat missing from his right shoulder. The prince and Captain al-Muallami jumped to aid the wounded officer while Swanson climbed into the turret and took the handles of the big automatic weapon.

Swinging it around, he opened fire on the nearest APC and saw that the second armored vehicle was attacking the plane that had just landed. The aircraft attempted to escape but it was too slow and as it rolled forward, the rebel APC easily kept pace and tore it to shreds with machine-gun fire. The aircraft exploded on the sand and the APC raked the wreckage to be certain there were no survivors. The second rebel APC broke off its pursuit of the Bradley, and Kyle stopped shooting.

BRIGADIER GENERAL MOHAMED HASHIM could not even salute when the prince ducked into the command post. The base commander's right arm was broken and rested awkwardly in a sling. Dots of blood were on his shirt from small shrapnel wounds. He was working the radio with his left hand. Hashim had been a soldier all of his life, starting as a common National Guard private. He eventually graduated from the King Khalid Military College and was a veteran, but the fire was gone from within him and his eyes were dull with fatigue.

"What happened?" asked Prince Mishaal, taking the radio handset and giving it to a nearby officer. He guided Hashim to a chair. "Stay seated, my friend, and tell me what is going on."

Hashim grimaced. When he was not busy, he could feel the pain. "I am happy to see you, Mishaal. I just wish you were leading ten thousand soldiers in here to crush this rebellion.

"The local imam had turned his mosque in town into an antigovernment platform. Yesterday, during the evening prayers, he called for an uprising and convinced several hundred soldiers that they had a holy duty to kill their officers and take over the base. When I learned of that, I had the imam arrested."

Mishaal nodded, his eyes probing those of the general. He saw pain and shame. "That was the correct thing to do. You posted additional security?"

The general said that he did. "About midnight, an armed squad of soldiers decided to rescue the imam and a firefight started. That was all it took, colonel. Just a few shots and everything, all of the simmering tensions of the past few days, blew up. The soldiers started choosing sides and with access to weapons, the mutiny grew larger by the hour."

Kyle Swanson saw a map hanging on a wall of the two-story home that was serving as a command post. He did not like the defeatist tone in the general's voice. The American listened with one ear as he studied the map. The base was laid out in a huge rectangle that began on the edge of the town and stretched several miles to the east. A military runway that was ten thousand feet long underlined the base on the south like a black streak, with a parallel and narrower taxiway. A two-story control tower was at the center point and big hangars were at the eastern end. Swanson guessed, based on his experience in Khobz, that the missile and warhead were down there in the hangars. Various buildings were clustered along internal roads, and a fence lined the perimeter. To the west lay the town, the long runway marked the southern edge, but to the north and east was only desert, as far as the map extended.

"Where is the rebel command post?" he asked an officer, who hesitated before responding.

"Tell him everything," came a sharp voice from behind, and Captain al-Muallami appeared at his side, his tunic stained with the blood of the wounded Bradley track commander.

"They are using the control tower beside the runway." The officer put his finger on the map.

Swanson moved to a window. The square, whitewashed multistory structure topped with aerials stood out in sharp contrast to its surroundings.

"Do they have any air assets?"

"There are seven helicopters in the hangars, but apparently none of the fliers defected, or the choppers were disabled. The armor has been our biggest problem."

Kyle heard a groan of pain and looked over to where the commander was falling from his chair. A doctor had ripped off the shirt and found a wound pumping blood from beneath the right arm. When he tried to remove the broken limb from the sling, the colonel passed out.

Prince Mashaal stood aside to let the doctor work. He would have taken charge of the base defenders anyway, but with the general being put out of action, the transfer of command became easier. "Everyone! Give me your attention!" Activity in the room stopped and the officers and soldiers looked to the new, hard men who had arrived. "I am Prince Colonel Mishaal bin Khalid, and by order of His Majesty the King, I hereby assume command of this base. My American friend here is to be given every consideration, also by order of His Majesty. My aide, Captain al-Muallami, speaks with my authority, so listen to him, no matter what your own rank may be. Return to your duties now and someone bring me up to date on the current situation."

THE SHOOTING OUTSIDE HAD not increased in volume, nor in proximity, which allowed Mishaal to establish a sense of calm in the tight confines of the headquarters, simply by his confident demeanor. Kyle listened in on the update.

There were about 4,000 men on base at the time the rebellion began, and about 2,500 were estimated to be in revolt. They had used the captured armor and exploited the sudden breakdown of command to push the loyal units entirely off the base itself and into the town, where house-to-house fighting was underway.

Kyle asked, "Prince Mishaal, would you please have him draw a line around our estimated position?" When the briefer did so with a red grease pencil on the map's plastic overlay, it was clear that the command strongpoint was at the southwestern edge of the city, about 500 yards from the end of the runway and 200 yards from the big highway, near where their plane had been destroyed. Beyond that, smaller red circles denoted other random strong points.

"Since we are outnumbered, we have to consolidate our force," the prince said, folding his arms as he stared at the map. "We protect Highway 15 so a relief column can drive in. Maybe we can get an air drop of supplies or some airborne units."

Kyle said to him in a soft voice no one else could overhear, "Prince Mishaal, most of your air force is grounded for a good reason. Remember what happened the last time some of those planes went up. Best keep it that way."

"You have a suggestion, Gunny Swanson?"

"Yes, sir. I'm going outside to look around and make a call on my sat phone back to Kuwait to get a C-130 launched to come pick up the nuke. That's really our goal. You handle the defense of the base. This will be over soon."

Mishaal turned to face Kyle and the two men again spoke in whispers. "In case you did not notice, Gunny, we're outnumbered and outgunned."

"Just hold the fort, sir. Pull all of the friendlies back into a strong position around this block of buildings."

"Is that all?" The prince was almost sarcastic. It was not his nature to let the other side keep a combat advantage.

Kyle slung his satellite phone over his shoulder, picked up a couple of grenades and a spare M-16. He slapped in a fresh magazine and stuffed more into his pockets. "No. There is one other thing I need. Where is the prisoner?"

Mishaal repeated the question to the captain, who pointed to a white-washed house next door. "Still under arrest, sir."

Kyle winked at his Saudi partner. "We will need to let him go."

ASH MUTAYR, SAUDI ARABIA

SWANSON DASHED ACROSS AN open area to a line of storage buildings on the rebel flank without drawing a shot, searched for danger among the street's rooftops, windows, and doors, and then picked a huge, sturdy structure for an observation post. It was about the length of five normal houses and slightly taller than the neighboring buildings, which would give him some elevation to oversee the area.

The place looked vacant, as if the workers had closed shop when the shooting started and retreated elsewhere for safety. The door was locked. Kyle paused until there was a burst of some gunfire about a block away to cover the sound of him kicking it open. Finding no opposition, he closed it again. With the M-16 at his shoulder, he carefully cleared room after room as he made his way to the roof. At the top of the stairwell, Swanson gently pushed open the topmost door and when there were no shots, squirmed through, closing that door behind him, too.

He was not surprised to find the roof unoccupied and quickly made the place his own. *First things first: Cover your six, baby.* He was alone, and without a partner for cover, he had to be certain that no enemy would show up unannounced. Swanson placed a claymore mine in position to face the doorway, then stretched the tripwire taut and tied it to the knob. Anyone pushing the door outward would trigger the booby trap and some 700 small steel balls would scour the area with a single horrendous blast.

Next, he needed to construct a hide that would not draw attention from the street or another building. There were four square, vented air-conditioning system ducts available, and he considered tearing the back off of one of them and squeezing inside next to the machinery to peer out through the vents. But there was a lot of junk spread around, which provided a better option. He decided to arrange some empty crates and boxes and other debris just to the left and slightly behind one of the boxy air-conditioning ducts, with cracks and openings to give a good view of the surrounding area. Anyone who chanced to look up would just see the boxes which masked his silhouette. He moved in, sat down, laid his rifle beside him, and took out his binos.

He was soaked in sweat by the time he looked out to see what the rebels were doing. Damn, there were some easy pickings down there. It was hard for Kyle Swanson to suppress his sniper instincts in such a target-rich environment. For the moment, the satellite phone and his binos were much more important than the rifle.

Having captured the buildings along the edge of the town next to the military base, the rebels were shifting into positions to press their attack. Their probes were finding points in the defense that were intentionally being left uncovered by Prince Khalid, and rebel patrols were moving to occupy them.

The rampaging soldiers were trained on flat desert with heavy tracked vehicles and were interested only in an armored slugfest. In the town, the battle was rolling fast, surging between buildings and down streets, with the emphasis on brute force. After taking a building, the rebels would immediately leave it before doing a thorough search and move on, screaming about victory and Allah and ceremoniously firing their AK-47s into the air. Kyle had seen that false euphoria before. It was a comfortingly normal event to him.

Things were ragged down below, which was also something he had expected. Many officers had been executed in the first hours of the uprising, and other sergeants and soldiers had escaped from the insurgent force. Without leaders, unit cohesion had disappeared and the reins of the fight were in the hands of a bunch of ill-trained morons, Kyle thought. Prince Colonel Mishaal bin Khalid should be more than able to handle this bunch. *Keep coming, boys, keep coming.*

＊　＊　＊

THE SAT PHONE, ONLY about the size of a police walkie-talkie, had a folded aerial that popped into place when Swanson pulled it from a pocket of his gear vest. The electronics hummed to life when he switched it on and a built-in global positioning system provided his exact coordinates.

His first call went to Kuwait. "Trident Base, Trident Base, this is Bounty Hunter. Over."

There was only a momentary hiss of static, then a familiar voice came back: "Bounty Hunter. This is Trident. Send your traffic. Over." Joe Tipp was on the horn.

"Roger that, Trident. Another package is ready for pickup," Swanson said. He wanted the Hercules and the Marines on the way over as soon as possible and it would take the big, slow bird a lot of time to cover that distance. He read out the grid coordinates for Ash Mutayr.

"Uh . . . Bounty Hunter. Intel advises that area is hot." Tipp obviously was surrounded by staff members.

"Roger that. Just pick up the package, Trident. I will not attend the meeting. Work with my counterpart."

The staff people wanted to know what Swanson had in mind, but Tipp cut them short and gave the confirmation. He trusted Swanson's judgment. "Solid copy. Trident out."

KYLE MADE ANOTHER SECURITY check around his perimeter and noticed that the gunfire had become sporadic. Mishaal was breaking contact and pulling back to gain space between the attacking rebels and his defending units. Settling back into the hide, Swanson raised the binos again and scanned the airfield and then looked deep into the base. The rebels were mistaking the sudden lull in the shooting for a preliminary sign of coming victory, taking it as an opportunity to regroup for a final push.

Armored vehicles were rolling back to a rendezvous point to refuel and rearm, falling into lines at the pumps and ammo sheds. Teams of soldiers were also coming back out of the city and settling beside the perimeter road of the base for a rest and to get some food and water while the armor was replenished. When everything was ready, they could launch the assault.

He checked his watch. Time to call Mishaal. "Crown, Crown, this is Bounty Hunter."

"Bounty Hunter. This is Crown. Go," the prince responded.

"In exactly thirty mikes, be prepared to release the imam. Tell him that you wish to negotiate a cease-fire and surrender your remaining forces, but only after he has a guarantee that the rebel leaders will spare the lives of your soldiers. Have a vehicle deliver the imam to within a hundred meters of the control tower at the airfield, then cut him free."

"I don't like this," said the Saudi officer, with some strain in his voice.

"You will," promised Swanson. He briefed the prince about the current rebel activity, then did a time check and ended the call.

THE NEXT CALL WAS going to be more difficult and would cause a ripple that would reach all the way back to the White House. Precision was necessary, so he paused to do some careful math homework before making it. A battered green sniper's logbook and a ballpoint pen came from the vest so he could make notes.

The GPS in the sat phone had provided his precise position, and using a pocket compass, he determined the exact directions from his location through azimuth readings to the control tower, to the fuel and ammo dump zone, and to the broad area where the tired rebel troops were gathering to rest. The third part of the equation was solved with his laser range finder, and he measured the distance between himself and the targets.

Now for the tricky part. He dialed up a new frequency and called, "Frequent Flyer, Frequent Flyer, this is Bounty Hunter."

A U.S. Air Force captain at the communications console aboard an AWACS plane flying in high circles over the Arabian Sea answered with a stone calm voice: "Bounty Hunter, this is Frequent Flyer Seven-Oh. Send your traffic."

"Roger, Frequent Flyer Seven-Oh. I have a Black Flag mission. Stand by to copy."

"Send your traffic."

"Roger. I have targets at grids six niner seven four, five niner six four."

"I copy. Six niner seven four, five niner six four. Is this correct? Over."

"That is a solid copy."

There was a slight pause as the captain punched the numbers into her computer and it flashed a bright red warning. "Bounty Hunter, that is a no go. Those coordinates are in a friendly country and we have no authorization for that."

The moment of truth. "Frequent Flyer Seven-Oh. Bounty Hunter. Stand by to copy authorization codes."

"Roger that. Send your traffic." The captain's fingers were poised over the keyboard on the electronics warfare plane and her total concentration was on the voice coming over her headset. She did not want to miss a syllable.

"I send: Zulu Delta, One Niner Seven, Whiskey X-Ray."

"I copy: Zulu Delta, One Niner Seven, Whiskey X-Ray."

"Roger that."

"Bounty Hunter. Stand by one." *This is above my pay grade, thank goodness*, the captain thought, touching a switch to alert the colonel who was overseeing the day's flight at the far northern edge of the carrier battle group. "Colonel, we have received a Black Flag request with a presidential-level approval code from inside the kingdom of Saudi Arabia. Call sign Bounty Hunter. Switching to you."

Swanson had expected initial disbelief and then eventual capitulation by everyone who handled the call. From his rooftop hide, he was summoning a strike by U.S. warplanes on a precise target within an allied country. He would provide timing and other directions to the individual pilots once they were in the area. The AWACS colonel read the traffic, acknowledged receipt and sped the request up the chain of command to the battle fleet commander.

Aboard the carrier, the admiral's chief of staff was a cautious man and advised his boss that they probably should check the request first through Washington. The admiral snapped, "No, goddammit! I don't know who or what this Bounty Hunter is, but he has all of the proper codes and has verified authentication. A Black Flag means that he wants us to get in there and help, not to waste time climbing the cover-our-asses telephone tree. Tell him that we're on the way. If I'm wrong, I'll retire early."

* * *

SWANSON LET TEN MINUTES pass, drank some water and talked to the pilots. The tired rebels had spent their initial burst of energy and excitement and had settled into lethargy, as if the outcome of their mutiny was now certain. They had won and had plenty of time to clean up the remnants of the old regime.

"Crown, this is Bounty Hunter."

"Go ahead, Bounty Hunter."

"Turn him loose. When he reaches the control tower, I'm going to pop smoke."

"Then what?"

"You guys hold your line and keep your heads down. Do not venture out beyond your positions."

KYLE WAS CAREFUL IN sorting out the calls of aircraft arriving on station, finding out what weapons they had and stacking the planes in packages, flying in circles starting at fifteen thousand feet and fifty miles away. He heard the grumble of the APC heading up the runway and put his binos on it. A white flag was tied to the machine gun in the turret, flapping as the vehicle slowly ventured onto the black tarmac. Picking up the sat phone, Swanson gave a command and a single aircraft peeled away from the stack and headed in toward Ash Mutayr.

The armored personnel carrier came to a cautious, rattling stop and then the track commander lowered the ramp. The imam, a short and bearded man wearing dirty robes, stepped out and walked with calm confidence toward the rebel command post in the tower. He would deliver the surrender message of Prince Colonel Mishaal bin Khalid, but order the rebels to ignore it. Kill all of the heretics and spit on their bodies! The APC buttoned up its hatches and sped back to its position, fleeing sporadic fire from men to whom the flag of truce meant nothing.

Within three minutes, the imam's voice was heard warbling over the loudspeaker system throughout the base, announcing his miraculous escape through the hand of Allah, and exhorting the troops to finish their glorious battle.

* * *

FORTY THOUSAND FEET OVERHEAD, a U.S. Air Force B-2A bomber made a slightly descending approach. Illuminated dials and computerized figures were projected on the heads-up display, but the pilot wanted to get his eyes on these targets. The radio in his headset crackled.

"Nighthawk, Nighthawk, this is Bounty Hunter."

"Go ahead, Bounty Hunter."

"Roger. My position is as follows: Six niner, seven four, five niner, six four. Your target is an ammo dump and refueling depot that is 1,150 meters from me at 38 azimuth. I will identify my position with red smoke."

"I copy, Bounty Hunter. Target is a gas station 1,150 meters from you at azimuth 38. Over."

"That's a solid copy."

The data was locked in the stealth bomber's computer, which passed the settings to the smart bombs. "Roger that, Bounty Hunter. I can see them now. Quite a crowd."

"I'm popping smoke." Kyle snapped the pin on the smoke grenade and threw the oblong device into the street alongside the building, where it cracked open and spewed out a ballooning column that was thick and crimson, starkly visible against the brown landscape.

The B-2A bomber pilot now knew exactly where to deliver the load, and where not to bomb. "Roger, I see red smoke." As the computer made its final calculations, he opened the big doors in the belly of his plane and confirmed, "Starting my bombing run." In moments, eighty GBU-39 small diameter bombs, each weighing about 300 pounds, spun away from the internal rotary bomb racks and the pilot hauled the stealth plane, the *Spirit of Georgia*, into a gentle turn and whooshed quietly away.

THE CLAYMORE MINE THAT guarded the door to his rooftop perch exploded with a flash and such sudden violence that it shook the building. Kyle jumped at the surprise blast and heard a man scream. Some rebel nosing around the building had tripped the booby trap and was blown out of his boots. Automatic weapons began stuttering, with the bullets zipping harmlessly through the smoke of the destroyed doorway. Kyle shifted the phone to his left hand and grabbed his M-16 with his right. *If a woman can steer a* *car, apply makeup, text-message, and drink coffee at the same time, I can do this.*

FROM THE CONTROL TOWER, the imam's shrill words were still goading his former captors, and bringing shouts of delight from the cheering rebels when the first smart bombs from the B-2A crashed into the lines of armored vehicles at the fuel farm and ammunition depot. A jackhammer staccato of violent explosions crushed the columns with a thorough carpet-bombing, and the storage areas of petrol and ammunition erupted. The ground underfoot shook as the typhoon of destruction consumed the entire area in a firestorm. Blazing battle tanks flipped about like ruined tin cans.

Before the roar of the first attack ceased, Kyle had a pair of Marine F/A-18 Hornets barreling in low. They had been flying a mission in Kuwait when the Black Flag was unfurled and arrived as the first package in the circle. Swanson read them the location and azimuth of the wide field that was jammed with rebel soldiers, all of whom were watching the disaster at the tank pens.

THROUGH A CRACK IN his hide, he saw an enemy soldier creeping slowly along the roof. Kyle held his fire because the man was not specifically hunting him. All the soldier really knew was that a claymore had blocked the doorway and caused casualties. Swanson judged the enemy strength was most likely just a few guys, a squad at most, and the claymore already had sheared off a few. The soldier probed around an air-conditioning duct and found nothing, then turned and saw the hide. The rebel's eyes grew wide in alarm as Swanson took him down with a careful three-round burst.

THE FAST F/A-18 HORNETS sailed in on a south-north run and laid a trail of bombs and rockets through the massed infantrymen in the open area. Shrapnel chewed through them like broad razors and their shredded bodies fell in bloody heaps.

Kyle figured one more strike would be needed and he assigned the target of the control tower to two Navy F-35 Joint Strike Fighters just as another pair of rebel infantrymen darted from the wrecked rooftop doorway, charging toward him with their rifles on full automatic. Swanson kept the radio tight to his ear and put his M-16 over his head, pointed it at open space, and pulled the trigger to let it rock and roll on full auto. The bad guys would either have to take cover or hit the deck. There was another scream and he gave the final instructions to the planes.

The JSFs came in low and hard to lay a long, fiery string of napalm that wrapped the control tower in broiling flame and smoke.

The entire attack required less than ninety seconds and had left the rebel force broken and its leaders dead. The aircraft were gone almost before any of the rebels even had a chance to look up.

"Frequent Flyer. Bounty Hunter. End mission. One hundred percent success. No more help is needed from the planes waiting in the stack. We owe you all a drink."

"Roger that, Bounty Hunter." The captain was on the line again and was sounding upbeat and flirty. "Stay safe."

THE FLIMSY WALL OF the hide crashed down in a tangle of debris as the final rebel soldier slammed into it at a hard run, his thought process unhinged from reality by the ferocity of the fight. The man had lost all sense of reality and was gripped by a temporary insanity: He just wanted to kill the unseen tormentor, face-to-face.

The attack knocked Swanson down and the M-16 was trapped beneath a board. The furious soldier was on top of him, trying to untangle his own rifle from the wreckage. Kyle slapped him hard in the face with the sat phone receiver in his left hand, a move that broke the bridge of the nose and caused the eyes to water. The head snapped to the left, but the momentum was still propelling the man forward. Kyle released the M-16, lunged forward, and buried his own chin against the enemy's right cheek. Wrapping his arms around the man and clasping his hands together to complete the body lock, he used remaining momentum to complete a judo throw back over his shoulder. The soldier's feet left the ground and he sailed overhead.

The rebel was still holding his AK-47 and the middle part of the weapon smacked Kyle hard in the forehead, cutting the skin and making him see stars momentarily. He held on. When the roll was completed, Kyle was kneeling on top of the soldier in a full mount. He folded his right arm and drove the sharp elbow straight down into the left temple of his opponent, dropped the sat phone so he could yank the Ka-Bar knife from his harness with his left hand. He stuck it hard into the neck, twisting it. He did not have to examine the soldier to know he was dead, so he moved away from the corpse and grabbed the M-16 again, then visually scanned the rooftop while he caught his breath. It was quiet. That was the last one.

SWANSON RETRIEVED THE PHONE and changed frequencies one more time. Blood was dripping from his forehead into his right eye and he wiped it away.

"Crown, Bounty Hunter."

"Bounty Hunter, this is Crown. That was a bit of a surprise."

"Yes, sir. The Saudi Royal Air Force is a splendid unit and deserves commendations for its action here today."

"Roger, Bounty Hunter. Care to join us in the attack to finish off the stragglers?"

"No thanks. Best that this remain an all-Saudi fight. I'll see you in a little while. Good hunting."

TRUE REST WAS HARD to come by; sleep, virtually impossible. Three of the nuclear missiles had been scooped up. Kyle Swanson felt an unreasoning pressure to finish the task and get the remaining two. It was as if an unseen clock was ticking and he did not want to lose the impetus he had going. Keep pushing over the dominoes. Keep stirring the pot.

The end of the fighting at Ash Mutayr came with a whimper, and a sight that was peculiarly tribal. To a Western military observer such as Swanson, it was incomprehensible. He had seen the phenomena before and still didn't understand it.

While the smoke from the air strike was still rising, the remaining rebels began to surrender, walking away from their positions, with their hands up. Some still held weapons, but were smiling. Prince Maashal's main task turned from fighting to orchestrating the surrender of hundreds of rebel soldiers who only minutes earlier had been trying to slaughter those loyal to the crown. Instead of acting like prisoners of a defeated army, they acted like they were attending some weird high school reunion. They immediately started mingling with their captors, who were content for now just to round everybody up and take away the weapons. The hair-raising violence and threats evaporated like a mirage. Friends again. Comrades once more. Muslims together. Return to the barracks and the mess halls and pray and get ready for tomorrow's big cleanup, as if nothing ever happened. It would take some time to sort out appropriate punishment.

He had caught an hour's worth of relaxation in an air-conditioned office while the prince's troops went to the hangars at the far end of the airstrip and hauled out the nuclear warhead and the missile launch system, both of which were still intact because Swanson had made sure the U.S. bombers and fighters had not torn up any air facilities except for the control tower. Some helicopters were also safe inside and he had Mishaal appropriate one for his use and have it checked out and fueled.

"I want to get up to Jeddah right away and prepare to pick up the next nuke at al-Taif," Kyle said.

The prince was at a desk, alternating his attention between maps and radio and telephone handsets. "I cannot leave yet, Gunny. A new commander for this base will arrive from Riyadh early tomorrow. We are temporarily assigning the job to a major general, who will bring along his own staff and some fresh troops so we don't have to go through this loyalty issue again. At least not here."

"So how about if I start the arrangements and we can finish off the transfer when you come in tomorrow?"

The prince nodded agreement. "Do you want one of my staff members to go with you?"

Kyle shook his head negatively. "No. There's not much to do and I have the authorization to set up my part of the deal. By the time I get up there and contact my people to set up the next flight, I will be ready for some sack time."

"You've earned it, Gunny."

"So have you."

Swanson walked alone to the waiting helicopter. In minutes, he was in the air and gone. He closed his eyes and was immediately asleep. He awoke when the blades changed their sound and the helicopter headed into Jeddah. He saw the friendly face of Jamal smiling at him from a waiting automobile and they went straight to the CIA safe house to get to work.

It was after midnight before Swanson took a shower and went to bed. The red digital readout of a bedside clock again reminded him that time was rolling away.

SATURDAY MORNING FOUND **MOHAMMED** Abu Ebara seated in the one large over-stuffed chair in the main room of his thick-walled home. It was sequestered in a private compound, one of several places that he maintained throughout the country. His narrow face was immobile in thought as he stared through a curtained window that overlooked a small garden. This would be an important day, perhaps the most important of his life.

There was no doubt that the rebellion was faltering throughout the country. The ungrateful populace of Saudi Arabia had not reacted with the storm of resentment that Ebara had both expected and promised. The people had been horribly tainted by unholy ideas and were unwilling to give up their modern comforts, automobiles, television sets, money, music, and filthy habits. They were shunning his call to exchange their lives and fortunes for his message of absolute morality and, through that, a serene life of total obedience.

Like children, they once again would have to be reminded of who they were. A stern lesson was all that was needed. Once it was properly administered, the uprising would begin anew and sweep across the land.

Therefore, he would have three men executed in the public square today. His instructions to the executioners were very clear. There would be no artistry in the simultaneous decapitations. The first sword slashes would do no more than cut deeply into shoulders and scalps, starting an orgy of butchery and torture that would be prolonged by the dull chipped blades and careful aim of the men doing the chopping. Severing the spinal cords and actually cutting off the heads probably would not happen until five full minutes of relentless butchery.

Ebara thought silently: *This is how you get votes in my world. I will rule through the oldest and surest of ways: fear and intimidation. Anyone who does not support me is my enemy and will be declared an infidel—open targets for the retribution of Allah!*

Chosen to be slain today were a university professor of archeology who believed that science could replace pure faith, a merchant who had become too wealthy to be humble, and a young man who led the Desert Leopards gang but had outlived his usefulness. The Leopards had not been aggressive enough in creating the needed urban riots and had lost many of their members while fighting the government forces. He would be replaced by an even more violent gang. There was no shortage of criminal gangs. All three of the men, even the young Leopard, were members of families with connections to the royal government.

When it was done, the pictures and the awful message would spread over the land and rekindle the fire of rebellion. It could still work. He would make it work! Ebara fancied himself as the great captain of a wonderful new movement that would combine religion, government, and military strength under his personal leadership. After all, it was he who had pushed the original idea of a coup into motion and come up with the necessary outside help.

Just as he had been wrestling with ways to begin a rebellion, the sly Russians, with oil and power on their minds, had appeared before him like a gift from Allah. The middleman was Dieter Nesch and it had taken many days of private conferences before the pieces came together.

Nesch had spelled it out carefully. A properly financed coup would replace the House of Saud and put Ebara and his religious police force in control. Ebara would subsequently request Russian troops and assistance to protect the oil production facilities. When Saudi Arabia was brought to heel, Ebara and his silent partners could move on to other oil-producing Gulf nations, picking them off like ripe fruit from a tree and spreading Ebara's religious reign while Russia clamped control on the worldwide price of energy.

The temptation had been great for an ambitious minor cleric who was not even an Islamic scholar. The banker not only promised Russian funding, but said they were in contact with a specialist who could give birth to the revolution. Once a series of attacks was launched, Ebara's men would propel the unrest throughout the country to create chaos. The man who could do this marvelous thing lived in Indonesia. His name was Juba.

The cleric sighed. Perhaps he had made a mistake there. Temptation had ensnared him again when the unexpected gift of nuclear weaponry had fallen in his grasp. With those horrible things, Ebara thought he might accelerate the timetable and reach into countries beyond just the surrounding nations. Juba, however, was proving to be uncontrollable, condescending, and rude. If Ebara could rekindle the rebellion, Juba might no longer be needed at all. There was enough money available to hire a team of devout Muslim scientists from Iran or Syria to replace him.

He turned from his reverie when there was a soft knock. His wife entered the room to tell him the driver had arrived with the car. It was time to go to the mosque to demonstrate his power. He rose with a sigh that only he could hear and ignored his two young sons, who were standing beside the door, their heads bowed in respect and trepidation, wondering if they would receive a pat on the head or a slap to the face when he passed. It was also time to deal with Juba and the banker again. But he felt good.

THE TWO REAR DOORS of a dented Ford E-150 cargo van stood open as Kyle Swanson and Jamal finished loading it. A wooden crate weighted by sandbags rested firmly just inside the sliding side door, leaving plenty of room for Swanson on the other side. A black cloth curtained off the driver's cockpit to block any outside view of what was in the rear. The van was meticulously checked, everything from tire pressure to fluid levels. Jamal lubricated the runners for the side door to help it open and close smoothly.

Then he opened the garage and got into the driver's seat. Kyle jumped in back and closed the rear doors. They did a time check—fifteen minutes until noon—then drove out, heading for the main square of Jeddah. Kyle unlocked a long, narrow gun case and removed Excalibur from its cushioned resting place.

Fifty caliber. A fiberglass stock exactly molded to fit him. A telescopic sight that was almost magic and comparable to any pilot's heads-up display

panel—computerized and extremely accurate, with an internal gyrostabi-
lizer, infrared laser, and a GPS transmitter-receiver. The scope did the math
on everything from target range to barometric pressure. It was a long-
distance, precision-firing miracle that he had helped develop for Sir Jeff,
simply the best sniper rifle in the world. If Kyle could see a target a mile
away in daylight, he could put a handcrafted bullet through it.

By necessity, this had to be a one-shot job. With Excalibur, one shot was
enough.

"A NUCLEAR MISSILE IS waiting for you." Ebara looked with disdain at the over-
bearing Juba. He longed to administer to this deformed infidel a punishment similar to that awaiting the three men in the square.

"Where?" Juba and Nesch were standing, while Ebara was seated, confidence building by the minute. He had deliberately chosen a room in the
mosque that had only one chair, and he occupied it, so the others had to
stand before him.

"It is at the army base of Tabuk, in the north, near the Jordanian frontier
and Israel." Ebara took a small sip of tea and picked up an envelope from a
side table. "The commanding general is a faithful brother who is among the
true believers to our cause. The details are written here."

Juba rubbed his chin and passed the envelope to Dieter Nesch. He assumed that Ebara knew that the mutiny at the base in the south had been
defeated. "As I expected, the coup seems to have stalled. You guaranteed a
spontaneous uprising of the citizens, Ebara. Why did that not happen?"

Ebara rose from the chair and stood to face Juba. No longer would he be
cowed and insulted. "I see now that I was wrong to bring you here," he said,
with a snort of derision. "You, Juba, have failed to deliver what you promised
for our revolution, so I am now forced to assume the overall command of
the military situation as well as the spiritual and political. Your only remaining assignment now is to go and take control of this remaining missile in
Tabuk, an assignment that I have made as easy as possible for someone of
your obviously limited capability. Then launch it immediately and lay nuclear destruction upon the infidels and our enemies. You get your choice of

targets. Tel Aviv would be good. After that, you can flee back to where you came from and hide from the world."

Nesch cleared his throat. "Be careful. Both of you. We can still make this happen, but we need to work together, not kill each other."

Ebara maintained his aggressive posture. "Banker Nesch, we have not received the services from Juba for which we have paid so dearly. I suggest that you pass that exact message, from me to your paymaster in Moscow."

Juba only smiled, the insults rolling harmlessly off of him. There was a playful glint in his eye. "Ebara, you have to be smart, not crazy, to overthrow a government. Nuclear weapons were never part of my plan, which was going fine until you reached too far above your head and meddled in things about which you know nothing. Still, we might as well play out the game. The fact is that I am here, and once I take possession of that missile, perhaps I can still rescue you from yourself. You may win this thing despite all of your bungling."

"I am done with you," Ebara declared, his voice rising. "Go now, while you still have your impertinent tongue." The cleric stalked from the room, satisfied with having placed Juba and Nesch in their proper, subservient roles. He had other, more important business waiting for him in the square.

It was noon. The crowd for the triple execution was huge. Four television cameras were present.

AS MOHAMMED ABU EBARA emerged into the sunlight and strode halfway down a small flight of stone steps to where three bound men were on their knees, a traffic problem was taking place on an overpass some distance away. A dirty van had chugged to the side of the road, steam rising from the engine, and the driver was out of the vehicle with his head beneath the hood.

Jamal muttered into a small radio transmitter, "Right on time. He's coming out."

The side door of the cargo van slid open about six inches. Kyle Swanson was squeezed into a tight sitting position, with Excalibur solid on a sandbag atop the crate beside the door. "Okay. I see him. Target acquired."

Swanson's instincts took over as he let the numbers scroll through the scope's powerful computer. The target was painted at 1,420 meters, almost a mile away. A light breeze was projected to be blowing right to left across the flight path at four-point-one miles per hour, so the bullet would move slightly to the left. The downward trajectory required an adjustment to compensate for the drop, for a bullet would otherwise tend to hit high. He agreed with Excalibur's computation and fine-tuned the scope four and a half minutes right, down two clicks in elevation. An azure stripe blinked down an edge of the scope to confirm all settings were accurate.

Ebara came to a standstill on the steps. He had memorized the words he would say to the large crowd and the condemned men, intending to send an ultimate warning that would instill fear into every corner of Saudi Arabia. He spread his arms wide to silence the bloodthirsty mob. The time had come for him to cast off any doubt and publicly emerge as leader of the glorious revolution.

KYLE SQUEEZED THE TRIGGER, slow and steady, and the big weapon barked one time, loudly, but the sound was mostly obscured by passing traffic. At the sound of the shot, Jamal let the small hood of the van slam back into place and climbed into the driver's seat without any sign of haste that might draw attention. The engine had been running the entire time.

As soon as he was done with the rhythm of the shot, Swanson reached forward and closed the sliding door. There was no time to watch what happened next, for he no longer was in control. Either the bullet did its job or it didn't. For the sniper, it was time to disengage and disappear. Jamal put the automatic transmission into gear, checked his mirrors, and the vehicle was disappearing into passing traffic as chaos erupted in the park.

THE BIG .50 CALIBER round split the air with a ripping hiss and punched a hole the size of a quarter just above the right nipple of Mohammed Abu Ebara. It spread catastrophic internal destruction around it before blowing out a hole as big as a fist from his back and ricocheting off a stone step. The cleric jerked like a puppet, and his knees buckled, toppling him face-first down the few remaining stairs. His body, with blood spurting from the wound, bounced to rest in front of the men he had picked for execution.

Dieter Nesch, standing off to one side, flinched when he heard the distinct gunshot. He watched Ebara collapse, then the crowd broke and was running wild in every direction, with people falling and being trampled. "The Americans are here," he told his partner.

Juba had not moved a muscle. His combat sense clicked into play and he instantly reversed the path of the bullet, concluding that it had come from a vehicle along the elevated highway about a mile away. It was an amazing shot, something that could be done only by a very experienced sniper. He agreed with Nesch. "Yes," he replied. As if he had been expecting this all along.

As they hurried to their car, heaving people out of the way, Nesch was puzzled. Juba suddenly seemed happy.

JEDDAH

DIETER NESCH SPED HIS black Mercedes sedan away from the plaza and dropped back to a safe and legal speed only when they reached the highway. Back at the square, the stunned crowd degenerated into a mob and broke into spontaneous demonstration for the new martyr, Mohammed Abu Ebara. The cleric's bloody corpse was picked up and passed above the frenzied crowd on a moving bed of open palms of men who wiped his blood on their faces and clothing.

"The Jews did this! Kill the Zionists!"

"Death to the king!"

"Death to the Shi'ites!"

"Death to the Americans!"

The spectators had come to the square to see death and had found much more than they had anticipated. More men were flooding into the plaza by the minute, drawn by the allure of blood and violence. After passing the body around for a while, the frenzied mob fell upon the three condemned men and hacked them to pieces.

"Death to the enemies of Allah!"

The central square of downtown Jeddah was gripped by unreasoning madness as thousands of people rioted. A traffic cop was snatched and thrown into the mob, looters broke into stores and shops, children were crushed underfoot, and in dark places, women were raped.

"Ebara! Ebara! Ebara!"

*   *   *

NESCH AND JUBA MADE the drive back to the villa in silence, each lost in his own thoughts. The German banker was mentally sifting a cascade of financial figures, adding up the potential damage and trying to forecast the next move in this deadly game in terms of risk-reward, profit, and loss.

Juba pushed the soft seat all the way back, crossed his legs and began to softly recite a nursery rhyme to himself. He had learned it while growing up as a child in Great Britain. Most people believed it was about an egg, but Juba had always been more drawn to the first verse, and the part about the master sniper with only one eye had become particularly appealing to him.

In Sixteen Hundred and Forty-Eight
When England suffered the pains of state
The Roundheads lay siege to Colchester town
Where the King's men still fought for the crown
There One-Eyed Thompson stood on the wall
A gunner of deadliest aim of all
From St. Mary's Tower his cannon he fired
Humpty Dumpty was its name
Humpty Dumpty sat on a wall . . .

NESCH DROVE THE MERCEDES into an enclosed garage and they walked into the main room of a villa. The whisky bottle, Johnnie Walker Black Label, came out and they each had a stiff jolt.

"Tell me about the shooting. You know something." Nesch needed to see behind Juba's mental veil. He poured another round.

Juba grunted. "Yes. It was a magnificent shot under very difficult conditions. The sniper knew exactly where the target was going to be and at a specific time. That required excellent intelligence, so it was not some random event. Ebara was targeted."

He took another swallow of whisky, paused to collect his thoughts, then continued. "The shot itself came from a vehicle that stopped for a moment on a busy highway overpass a mile away, again something that did not happen by chance. Then the bullet went over the crowd and hit Ebara almost the moment he stepped outside. The shooter vanished into the traffic without a trace, almost before the shot hit the target. A lot of moving parts were involved, and I agree that the Americans are the most likely ones who could have pulled it off. Low-key, effective, and spectacular."

"So?" Dieter's round eyes were almost in slits as he took off his glasses and polished them. "The world is full of snipers for hire. You can buy one off the shelf whenever you need one."

"Not for this kind of job," Juba replied. He poured another splash from the bottle. "Maybe four snipers in the world could have made that hit. It took a totally experienced specialist. Since it was probably an American show, my money would be that it was a Marine named Kyle Swanson. He sometimes does work for the CIA."

Nesch looked curiously at his friend. "Why? Do you know this man?"

Juba pointed to the blind eye covered by the black patch. "He's the one who almost killed me in Iraq. I can smell his fucking *stench* on this hit!"

The banker shrugged. "Well, my friend, it makes no difference. We have bigger problems than him."

"It makes a difference to me," said Juba. "I want to kill him."

"Fine. Then kill him. Let's finish this job first so we can get out of here."

"The job? You mean this silly rebellion? Dieter, the coup is over."

"I think so, too, but we don't want to make any rash decisions in the heat of the moment. There is too much still in play and we need to do some serious thinking when our emotions cool. So, I'm going to take a shower and a nap. Look, some spots of blood are on my suit pants. Damn. You should get some rest, too. We'll get up in a few hours, be refreshed, have a nice meal, and I will call our Russian employer. Then we will decide what to do next, if anything." The banker walked toward his bedroom.

Juba just nodded his head. He did not need to let his emotions cool because he was dead calm inside his head. He stood by the broad window, looking out at the sunlit Red Sea and thinking about the possibility of taking down Swanson.

ANOTHER MERCEDES SEDAN, A white one with heavily tinted windows, was still on the road. Jamal and Kyle had ditched the van for the luxury car and were heading southeast from Jeddah toward the holy city of Mecca and into the Hada mountains.

Their destination was the city of al-Taif, about a two-hour drive from Jeddah on a remarkable highway that lifted motorists from the seaside and desert up through a series of tunnels to the green and cool summer resort some 2,000 feet above sea level. The Mercedes hardly drew a glance, since it was a favored style among the wealthy Saudis who frequented the long highway. Jamal kept the accelerator down as they climbed.

With periodic checks by his sat phone, Kyle had finished arranging events at the huge military base outside of the small city. Everything would be in place for the arrival of the handover team. Any luck at all, and things would be done before darkness fell.

Events were moving faster and faster, and Kyle believed they were entering the critical period in which things were not going to be happening in weeks and days, but in hours. Maybe minutes. He thought: *Do the fourth nuke in Taif this afternoon, then yank out the final one tomorrow. Get it done.* He hardly gave any thought at all to shooting Ebara. That was truly in the rearview mirror and fading with every kilometer the Mercedes put them farther away from Jeddah.

Jamal worked the car through Mecca carefully. "Check it, dude. Things are stable here. They have to know about Ebara's death by now because we can't outrun the radio and TV broadcasts. I expected this place to be in an uproar."

"Maybe they haven't figured out which way to jump yet," Kyle replied, his eyes sweeping the area for danger signs. No roadblocks. No rioting. "Keep going. Sooner we get to the base, the better off we will be."

"Particularly since we're hauling around your big-ass sniper rifle."

"Gotta put it on the plane back to Kuwait, Jamal. Remove any chance of the bullet ever being matched up to an American weapon."

"I want to get on that plane, too. Doha sounds great about now."

Kyle laughed. "I need your sorry ass to stay here with me. Anyway, you're a CIA assassin now."

Jamal looked over, taking his eyes off the road for a second. Then he smiled. "Mom will be so proud."

44

RIYADH

THANK YOU FOR CALLING, Mr. President. I appreciate the information. It will make things much easier on this end. One less worry." King Abdullah was agitated but kept his voice neutral and pleasant. He listened a moment longer, then said, "Yes. We'll speak again soon. Goodbye, Mr. President."

He hung up the secure telephone but let his hand rest on it for a moment. His experience as a diplomat served him well in such situations. It was indeed good news and he would take time to be angry later on, when he was alone. He had bigger responsibilities now than spending time being furious with Gunnery Sergeant Kyle Swanson. It had to be Swanson!

This role of eternal dignity was already growing stale to Abdullah after a life of movement and excitement. Servants everywhere, anticipating his every need in this gilded cage. He was determined not to become just another isolated monarch who was distant from his people. Abdullah was playing a role that he did not particularly like. The time of the autocrat was over. The House of Saud had to change. He picked up another telephone and buzzed for his secretary. "Bring them in," he said.

The door opened and a half-dozen counselors appeared for one of his daily briefings. He motioned for them all to sit, and they did. Every command was obeyed. It felt strange. He got right to business.

"How did the unexpected removal of that dog, Ebara, impact the overall situation?" he asked his military chief of staff.

The general put on his reading glasses and scanned a briefing paper before responding. "His death caused a temporary outbreak of violence and unrest in some locations, particularly in Jeddah. It seems not to have inspired the population to general revolt. In fact, there seems to be a sense of relief spreading throughout the country as people realize that normality may be returning. The Religious Police are drawing in their horns and showing signs of caution. They are clearly worried. Meanwhile, our troops are regaining control in every region."

"The revolt is not over," observed Abdullah.

"No, Your Highness. It is not. But it is slowing dramatically. No one has stepped forward to replace Mohammed Ebara as leader of the *muttaween*."

There was a pause as the counselors waited for the king to speak. "It seems that clerics are dropping like flies around the country," he observed.

The interior minister responded. "Yes, Your Highness. There is a striking similarity between the assassination today of Mohammed Ebara and the murder of the rebel imam in Khobz. Then there was the traitorous cleric who was responsible for the revolt at the Ash Mutayr base."

Abdullah went silent, rubbing his hands slowly, an unconscious habit while he considered a new idea. *Kyle Swanson again. He just happened to be in Khobz, Ash Mutayr, and Jeddah at the time of each one. A dangerous man.*

The king gave a sharp laugh. "It is one thing to incite rebellion from the safety of a mosque and to distort Islam to cover treason. It is entirely something different to find one's self on the firing line. These men routinely sent others to their deaths, but never expected to be in danger themselves."

"We expect to turn the corner on this revolt within about forty-eight hours, Your Highness," said the interior minister. "As the rebel imams go into hiding, their followers have no leadership and guidance. When they get tired, they will go home."

"Very well. Now let me pass along some good news. I just spoke with President Tracy in Washington and he informed me that the missing nuclear device has been recovered by the Americans and is safe. He did not have the details yet. The important thing is that we now have secured three of the weapons and Prince Mishaal informed me that the fourth one will be transferred within a few hours from al-Taif. One more and that problem will be solved."

There were murmurs of approval among the counselors. They were impressed by the manner and the actions of their new king.

The interior minister studied him closely. As cousins, they had known each other since boyhood. From his years as a diplomat, Abdullah had developed an outward appearance of being suave and calm, radiating confidence and trust. The deep-set dark eyes, however, could tell a different story, a soldier's story, and often mirrored his inner feelings. Right now, the eyes were almost glowing in anger.

"It is time for us to establish a back-channel contact with the Grand Mufti and other important religious leaders," Abdullah declared with a firm voice.

"WHAT DOES HIS MAJESTY wish for me to convey?"

The king stood up and adjusted his robes, then walked to a broad desk, pulled out the center drawer and held up some notes that he had jotted during his long hours of pondering the next step. "First, I want to firmly remind them that all of us are devout in our religious beliefs. Faith is not the issue here. Then give them a little history lesson on the long and mutually beneficial relationship between the House of Saud and Muhammad ibn Abd-al-Wahhab, dating back to the year 1744. Until now, despite some difficult days, that relationship has worked. We ran the country and they ran the mosques. We allowed them a lot of power."

The king looked hard at each man in the room. "That trust was torn apart by this rebellion, in which some religious leaders have tried to overthrow the House of Saud! Even the moderate clerics stood idly by while a coup was launched, our king was assassinated, and the crown prince and other leaders, both Saudi and foreign dignitaries, were murdered. In short, they breached their sacred trust and brought the country into a civil war. You can emphasize now that these are my words: Things will never be the same between us."

The interior minister waited, with his pencil and notebook in hand, but the king stopped speaking. "This will not be well received, Your Majesty."

Again the king was firm. "I do not intend for it to be considered anything less than it is: a direct order from the king of Saudi Arabia. Tell them clearly, my cousin, that the House of Saud has survived . . . and that now it is our turn."

JEDDAH

A **DUEL OF WILLS** was underway in the villa of Dieter Nesch as the two terrorists—the money man and the killer—inched toward important decisions.

The chef had outdone himself to prepare a special meal that might cool the tempers while the demonstrations still plagued the city. The maid served a salad studded with fat *rubiyan* shrimp and a main course of grouper, sliced open and smothered in sautéed onions, tomato, garlic, hot peppers, and lemon wedges. Bowls of spices and platters of fresh bread and cheeses were at hand. The two men touched glasses of white wine in a salute and settled into the lavish meal, talking only of little things during the meal.

AFTERWARD, THEY MOVED TO the big room, which was warm and bathed in sharp orange by the midafternoon sun. Outside in the street, a small mob roamed past the villa, yelling and wildly firing AK-47s into the sky.

"I assume you have been considering what to do next." Nesch let his eyes flick briefly over to Juba. It was important to keep him satisfied. This was almost like being in a basket with a cobra. *Let him lead himself to the decision.*

Juba tasted the sharp, dark Remy Martin and welcomed its warmth. He looked out at the passing men. "Hardly more than a handful of rebels in the streets of a major city that should have been blowing apart at the seams by now," he observed.

"I agree totally," Nesch replied, settling into a chair beside a small table with a lamp, an ashtray carved from stone, and a humidor of dark Spanish cedar. "The question I now put before you is whether we can push things forward at all, perhaps on a new track entirely? I trust that tactical brain of yours, Juba. Find me an answer."

Juba sat on the low windowsill and put his drink beside him. Hands on knees, thoughts racing. "No. The few remaining rebel groups will be crushed. Too many elements changed from the original plan and the time-line has been destroyed. By now, all of my contacts will have gone to ground. I doubt if any of them would even answer my call. The pressure needed to cause the volcanic eruption of a revolution has drained away. Ebara was weak and stupid."

"Ah, Ebara? Yes. All of my sources had promised that he could deliver what he promised. We needed him in power." Nesch rubbed the flat box. "Unfortunate. How about a cigar to accompany this swish of cognac? Let me tell you first that there is a 9 mm pistol in the box."

Juba waved the offer away. "I don't smoke, and I removed the bullets."

Nesch was unperturbed. He asked, "Would you mind if I have one? They come from Costa Rica. The gun was one of my bodyguard's little toys. Didn't do him much good, did it? Did you also find the one on the top book-shelf?" Dieter removed a cigar, clipped the end, and took his time to light it.

"Yes. I did."

"Amir was unprofessional. I could only have reached that one if I stood on a stool." Nesch laughed and got a wry smile from Juba. *Good.* "So does this all come down now to, um, shall we call it, 'the nuclear option?'"

"Since Saudi Arabia is not going to turn into some radical Islamic state, that is all that is left of interest," said Juba. "Whoever has the missile holds some power. I want it."

Nesch exhaled and a cloud of fragrant smoke rolled around his chair. "Juba, I respectfully have to disagree. As a banker, I simply look at it all as numbers on a balance sheet. Our man in Moscow is going to be very nervous about the death of Ebara, and I will have to recommend that he forget about this particular enterprise. Doing this on the quiet was one thing, but Russia cannot afford to be seen as openly involved in the coup. At least, that's my opinion."

"You want to back off of everything? Give up the nuke, too?"

Nesch tapped the cigar ash into the stone receptacle. "Yes. With your approval, that would be my recommendation. I will be honest about Ebara's mistake in calling you to come here. I will also stipulate that both of us have done everything possible to carry out our assignments and, therefore, I keep my entire commission and you receive a nice bonus. Say, another million euros. How does that sound? You return home to Indonesia while I return to Germany and lay low for a while. Maybe next year, I will start shopping for another lucrative mission. Give up the nuclear missile idea, Juba. Trying to take it now would be suicide."

"Dieter, I simply don't care." Juba tilted his cognac snifter and emptied it, then placed the fragile glass on another small table.

Nesch kept a steady gaze on the battered man. "You don't care?"

"I'll take a cigar after all." It took a moment for it to respond to the lighter. "Have you asked yourself why I have not killed you today?"

"Yes. The thought crossed my mind."

"There are three reasons, perhaps chief among them was that you did not try to use that gun in the humidor. That would have forced my hand."

"What else?" The banker's throat was dry. The only noise in the room seeped in from the outside, where the rowdy demonstration was still in the street.

"Second, I still need your help."

Nesch smiled broadly and his eyes closed as relief flooded through him. "Anything. Name it."

Juba absently rubbed the patch that covered his destroyed eye. He exhaled loudly. "You probably will not understand this. I don't really care about that missile at all, but it has created an opportunity that I had worried might never come. You will recall when I told you about Kyle Swanson, the American sniper?"

"Yes. Of course."

"I know in my bones that Swanson made that shot. No evidence, but every wound in my body, the wounds he gave me when he left me for dead, is itching madly, screaming his name at me. If I can get that nuclear warhead, he will come after it. Revenge, Dieter. I have to do this. When he comes snooping after the missile, I will kill him. Your contacts, money, and influence are needed to help set this up."

"Whatever I can do, Juba, I will." Nesch had never made a more sincere promise. "You mentioned three reasons. What is the last one?"

"Dieter, I don't need to kill you. We are both already dead men. Once you make that telephone call, the Russian president will have SVR hit squads coming to eliminate both of us. My professional advice is that you get out of Saudi Arabia tonight when we finish making our new arrangements. Then run fast and run far."

AL-TAIF

JAMAL AND **K**YLE SHOWED their credentials at a bunkered entrance gate and were allowed to park inside the perimeter of the big base to await an escort. Swanson had heard of this place, but this was his first visit. He let out a low whistle. "Look at all the fuckin' Americans," he said. "How could the Saudis keep a nuke here without some homeboy from Los Angeles tripping over it?"

Jamal removed his dark aviator sunglasses. Although he had been driving away from the sun, his eyes were feeling the strain of the glare after the long drive into the mountains. "They're smarter than the average bears," he said. "A missile from here could easily protect the port and Jeddah. Lots of places for something to be stashed on a huge facility like this. If the L.A. homeboy wasn't looking for it, he probably wouldn't even see it. He wouldn't recognize what it was."

"Busy day," Swanson agreed, looking at his watch. "This should go quickly if Prince Mishaal is already on deck. The C-130 is only about a hundred miles out. Afterward, we can grab some chow."

"Look at all the fuckin' Americans," Jamal said, moving his seat back to be more comfortable.

A U.S. Army military policeman wearing an arm brassard and a shiny helmet approached, accompanied by a Saudi counterpart. They also checked the credentials. "Prince Mishaal is expecting you. Please follow our Humvee and we'll take you over to the flight line."

"Got it," said Jamal. "Lead on." When the two MPs walked away to get into their vehicle, he said to Kyle, "Look behind us."

Swanson adjusted the side mirror on the Mercedes. An armored Humvee with a soldier in the turret behind a .50 caliber machine gun had swung into position on the rear bumper. "Gunship," he said. The MP sedan moved out, with red and blue lights flashing on its roof. "Nothing like a subtle arrival."

Al-Taif was crowded. It was home to the four light infantry battalions of the Saudi National Guard Omar bin Kattab Brigade, and also hundreds of Americans who were part of an ongoing U.S. Military Training Mission. This was the base through which American senior advisors were funneled into the Saudi armed forces' command structure, which meant there was a large U.S. support staff and all the trimmings. The curiosity factor about the handover was going to be high.

Their little convoy ripped through the base without incident, and angled toward a large aircraft hangar at the end of a runway, where the large sliding doors had been opened. The nuke was already secured inside, waiting for them. Machine gun emplacements bristled at the corners of the building, snipers were up top, and patrols ranged in a far circle. The three vehicles drove inside and stopped.

Prince Colonel Mishaal bin Khalid waved from his own Humvee. Kyle got out of the Mercedes, walked over, and snapped a salute. Mishaal looked exhausted. "Good evening, Gunny."

"Hello, sir. Did you get things settled down in Ash Mutayr?"

The prince made a sardonic laugh. "Yeah. New commander is in place and everything is calm. Place needs some rebuilding."

"Yes, sir."

"So now I come up here and find that Jeddah is in turmoil." Mishaal stared at Kyle. "Trouble seems to follow you."

"I wouldn't know about any trouble, sir. Everything seemed fine when we left there a few hours ago."

"Gunny, do you remember the name of Mohammed Abu Ebara? The head of the Religious Police?"

Kyle looked lost for a few moments. "Right. I believe His Majesty, King Abdullah, may have mentioned the name to me."

The prince took Swanson by the elbow and guided him to a space where they could speak in private. "Somebody killed him today. Apparently a sniper." He arched an eyebrow.

Swanson held up both hands. "Don't look at me," he protested. "I was on the road coming up here. But is that a bad thing?"

They were interrupted by the approaching roar of a C-130 coming off the taxiway and approaching the hangar.

"No, Gunny, it was not a bad thing. The demonstrations about Ebara being a martyr are already calming down. His removal takes a lot of steam out of the coup."

"*Inshallah*, then," Kyle said. "God's will."

"*Inshallah*. His Majesty was curious about the circumstances. About your welfare."

"Is he changing my instructions?"

"No. Just being cautious and careful." The roar of the propellers dropped in volume as the plane spun about so that the ramp was in line with the hangar doors.

"Please let His Majesty know that I appreciate his concern. And that there is nothing that can connect me to the death of Ebara. You remember that gun case I brought in aboard the first C-130? Well, I am going to put that same weapon on the plane right over there. It soon will be out of the country."

"Let's get to this new job, then."

Staff Sergeant Joe Tipp was playing the major in command on this trip, and approached with the clipboard and the papers for the transfer. Mishaal held up his hand and said, "Please wait one more moment, Major." Tipp stopped, puzzled, looking at Kyle.

Swanson asked the prince, "What?"

"His Majesty is also curious about something else, Gunny Swanson. He spoke with President Tracy today and was given the good news that the nuclear missile that was taken in Khobz has been found and is safe. King Abdullah reminded me that you were in Khobz when another Muslim cleric involved in the rebellion was killed by a sniper's bullet. His Majesty is wondering about your possible involvement in that entire scenario, particularly if you had anything to do with the missing weapon."

Swanson fiddled with a pen in his shirt pocket, then glanced up at the prince. Decision time. He had to maintain the trust of both the king and the prince. If he lied about the nuke, they would find out about it sooner or later anyway, and that bond of trust would be destroyed. It was too much of a risk.

"Please tell His Majesty that I can neither confirm nor deny anything about my missions. If he wants to press the matter, I am sure that another call to President Tracy would set him at ease. It would be good to remember that Khobz was under siege and your army base there had already been attacked with an ambush. Who is to say what might have happened if that fight went the wrong way?"

Prince Mishaal turned and brushed his uniform. Dust flew off in small puffs. "I guess anything is possible, Gunny. The main thing is that the weapon was bagged safely. Now let's do this one."

While Joe Tipp and Mishaal went through the paper drill, Kyle grabbed the gun case from the trunk of the Mercedes and hustled up the ramp.

Sybelle was once again waiting at the bulkhead. "You okay? We heard about this Ebara clown going down."

"I'm good." He put down the gun case.

"Good. Because we've got a big problem," she said, holding out a clipped-together computer printout.

"How big?" Swanson asked, taking the papers and beginning to read.

"Oh, about the size of the Chinese army."

BEIJING, CHINA

THE DIMINUTIVE **G**ENERAL **Z**HU Chi sat at the end of a long table, smoke curling from the tip of his cigarette, while his staff took him through their Power Point presentation. An array of three large clocks hung on the side wall, set to the matching times in Beijing, Saudi Arabia, and Washington. It was eleven o'clock on Saturday night where he sat and the diversionary moves were to get underway at first light on Sunday. He would give the American satellites plenty to absorb and by this time tomorrow, the bandit leaders of the breakaway province of Taiwan would be frantic.

Weather forecasters predicted a sunny, warm day with gentle waters in the Taiwan Strait and the South China Sea. The tide tables were favorable. During the next forty-eight hours, the detailed planning of the Combined Staff would put in motion what would be the biggest show in the world, albeit a brief one.

Thousands of troops would march in long columns and hundreds of armored vehicles and trucks loaded with everything from gasoline and ammunition to food would crowd onto the roads, heading toward the loading points. Helicopters would mass and squadrons of fighter aircraft would be armed and in the air flying protective cover missions.

At ports all along the China coast, the complex process of loading a huge military force onto more than two hundred ships, including the commandeered merchant vessels, would begin. It would be intentionally slow and careful, so as to be seen in full. Missile sites would be activated and military radio channels would stay busy. Television crews would be allowed into selected staging areas, but no questions would be answered. The foreign reporters would draw their own conclusions.

That was the easy part. It was all a massive feint; nothing was going to happen in the Taiwan Strait or the South China Sea. Even so, the gigantic movement was excellent training, a dress rehearsal for the eventual day when such an invasion really would be undertaken.

A staff planner tapped a key to change the computer screen and another slide colored the wall screen, a light blue background with arms of gold olive branches surrounding a North Pole view of the globe—the emblem of the United Nations. On Sunday, the Chinese representative to the UN would demand a meeting of the Security Council on Monday morning to lodge a formal protest about recent behavior of Taiwan, acts that the government of China considered aggressive and warlike. Again, it was part of the deception, but the other governments of the world could not take the chance that an angry China was ready to take Taiwan by force.

"That will mark the end of Phase One," the planner announced, leaving the UN symbol lingering on the wall.

The general stubbed out the remains of his cigarette and adjusted his glasses. His eyes moved around the impassive faces of the other ranking officers at the conference table. "Very well," he said. "Issue the appropriate orders to begin Phase One."

The room erupted into activity as the other commanders and the staff members hurried off to launch the intricate process. Zhu Chi loosened his tie. He would get some sleep now and meet early in the morning with Jiang Julong, the party chairman of the Central Military Commission. They would discuss issuing final approval for the next step.

The way it presently stood, the UN delegate would not talk at all about Taiwan during the special emergency session on Monday, other than claiming the huge military moves purely an internal matter. He would say it was just a military exercise concerning national defense. That was the truth, but it would be seen as a lie, and would cause even more excitement. At the end of his address, the diplomat would shift to a different subject: the immediate need for the United Nations to place an international peacekeeping force in Saudi Arabia to secure the vital resources of that nation. The kingdom was in the throes of a rebellion and now there were rumors of nuclear weapons. The United Nations must intervene!

By then, Chinese planes would be in the air to start Phase Two.

WASHINGTON, D.C.

HALFWAY AROUND THE WORLD in a different time zone, it was only approaching noon on Saturday at the White House. President Mark Tracy picked at the tuna salad that had been served at his Oval Office desk. He would be unable to eat much of it. He had too many other things on his mind, a perfect storm of international events that still might end with a nuclear holocaust if not carefully handled. He had on tan slacks and a blue golf shirt, casual weekend clothes, as if he was awaiting a tee time. In reality, he had not played golf in weeks. Being president had a way of wrecking a social schedule.

"Let's do the Saudi thing first," he said. "This Ebara guy is dead. Where does that leave the attempt to overthrow the government?"

CIA Director Bartlett Geneen was on a small cream-colored sofa in front of the president's desk. As always, he was wearing a crisp white shirt and a dark suit and tie. He also had pushed his tuna salad aside after a few bites. He scanned a summary in his folder and said, "We think the coup attempt is in real trouble. King Abdullah is still having to deal with some hot spots, but without the incendiary presence of Mohammed Abu Ebara, the coordinated attacks we saw earlier have stopped entirely and military support is evaporating."

The President breathed a sigh. "That's what he told me in our call a little while ago. He seemed pretty confident. Plans to turn the tables and put the clerics in a box to get some modernizing social reforms going in his country. Try to curb the hate. That's a good thing."

Geneen cleared his throat before bringing up something that was out of the ordinary run of the intelligence community. "Along that line, one of our best ground agents in Saudi Arabia has been co-opted into some secret operation run by the Pentagon, working for something called Task Force Trident."

Tracy feigned innocence. "Really? Isn't that General Middleton's special ops group?"

"Yes, Mr. President."

"Did you ask the general about it?"

"I did. He said to take it up with you."

"Hmmm. Strange. I'll talk to him. Now what about the Saudi nuclear weapons? We have four of the five, right?"

Geneen was jolted by the brushoff. He was the director of the Central Intelligence Agency and recognized that he was being kept out of the loop. Then his eyes widened behind his round glasses and a little smile creased his lips. *Ebara! They nailed Ebara!* Sometimes it is best to be kept in the dark, particularly if he was ever called before Congress to explain certain things.

"Yes, sir. We have retrieved four of them, sir. One more to go."

"I let King Abdullah off the hook on the secret that we had put the one in Khobz in safekeeping. I did not give any details, which he did not really like, but rather than protesting, he kept his eye on the big picture and was relieved that it was not in terrorist hands. Abdullah was a terrific diplomat and I think I'm going to enjoy working with him as a head of state."

The president looked at the digital clock on his desk. "Generals Turner and Middleton will be here in a little while so we can talk about China. Meanwhile, Bart, I'm going to make an important executive decision without informing Congress. Screw this tuna salad: I'm ordering us a couple of Philly cheese-steak sandwiches and a pile of greasy french fries. The prospect of nuclear war makes me hungry."

THE PENTAGON

"Lieutenant Commander Freedman, you are a malcontent, a troublemaker, an irritating nerd, and an asshole. The entire intelligence community has its panties in a wad because of you." General Bradley Middleton had to brief the Joint Chiefs of Staff, and the Lizard was not making things simple.

"Yes, sir. Sorry. I'm right and they are wrong, sir." The Lizard knew Middleton was only forcing him to prove his idea, one last time.

"You got some pieces of paper, some pictures, some satellite intel, some fortune cookies, ANYTHING I can take before the Chiefs?"

"No, sir, I cannot prove a negative, that something is *not* going to happen. Think in terms of the Sherlock Holmes story about the dog that didn't bark."

"Can't do that, Lizard. The Chiefs may want a little more than Holmesian deduction. Look. All the hard intel points toward an imminent invasion of Taiwan. On that we have pictures, sat data, the works."

Freedman was determined not to wilt under the pressure. "Yes, sir. All of it, sir. It is much too accurate and easy to come by. So it is false."

Middleton glared at him. "They cannot move all that stuff into place in secret. It's right there in front of you, Liz. Plain as day and NSA traffic is showing orders are being given to start moving in a few hours."

Freedman's eyes drifted for help to the large bulk of Master Gunnery Sergeant O.O. Dawkins, who was leaning back in his chair, hands behind his head, watching the exchange. "The game, Liz," Double-Oh gently coaxed. "Show him your game."

"Game?" asked the general.

"Yes, sir. I have been running some private war game scenarios. Not the usual Red Team versus Blue Team stuff, but trying to figure out how the Chinese can beat the distance problem in getting to Saudi Arabia."

"Now tell him how you win, Liz."

"Right. Yes. I win . . . I *won* . . . by eliminating the distance as the determining factor. Squeezed the map tighter."

Middleton rolled his eyes. "Speak English, for Christ's sake."

"What the lieutenant commander is trying to say, sir, is that this invasion of Taiwan has everything out there for public viewing except long-range bombers and airborne troops. Those would be absolutely needed to carry out such an operation, and are nowhere to be found. Liz believes that about the time the loaded ships are ready to leave the China coast, a whole shitpot load of big airplanes is going to head up toward Saudi Arabia from bases in the Sudan, Yemen, Ethiopia, and Somalia."

"Is that it, Lieutenant Commander Freeman? Is that how you squeezed the map?"

"Yes, sir. That's it. I cheated."

The general clapped him on the shoulder and went out the door, into the wide, polished halls of the Pentagon to find General Hank Turner, the Chairman of the Joint Chiefs.

AL-TAIF, SAUDI ARABIA

KYLE **SWANSON CROSSED HIS** legs and puffed out his cheeks in a sigh of exasperation, and the invisible clock that had been quietly bugging him for the past few days was now clanging in his head. He tied the boot laces. *Let's go,* he thought, throwing a questioning look at Prince Colonel Mishaal bin Khalid.

Mishaal was at the front of a spacious briefing room at the huge base, where officials of both the Saudi and U.S. military forces were conducting a real-time teleconference with counterparts in Riyadh and Washington. Swanson, as only a gunnery sergeant, was not even at the big table with the senior officers. Kyle would not have been there at all if he had a choice, but the king had ordered Mishaal to lead the meeting, and since the prince was not going to let Swanson out of his sight again, he almost dragged him into the room.

He was in a straight-back chair against the wall, watchful and anxious, taking everything in. Bored. All of this talk had nothing to do with his assignment. He wanted to get up to Riyadh with the prince and lay his hands on that final nuke. Every minute spent sitting in a conference room was another minute wasted, with the mission still unresolved. They were so close, just a few hours. *Let's do it!*

Nevertheless, he had to admit that the sudden burst of intel about a possible invasion by Chinese troops merited this sort of attention by those in charge. The emergencies were not over, and in fact, were escalating. Although the rebellion was calming and the collection of the nuclear weapons was all but done, Beijing had decided to come and play in the sandbox.

The decisions to be made concerning that situation had nothing to do with him. It was high above his pay grade, which was why everyone else in the room was so tense: it was above their pay grades, too.

No one had considered the possibility that another country would try to seize the oil fields outright. The Saudis had warned the Americans not to try it, at the risk of an armed confrontation. If China came in, the Saudis would surely resist. Then the U.S. would be certain to offer help to Riyadh from the nearby U.S. fleet and aircraft. Would Beijing force the issue? Would Washington take that step? And what about this possible invasion of Taiwan? A sense of paralysis was taking hold because the series of emergencies had taken still another turn for the worse.

Kyle had read the brief, heard the experts, and knew the overall situation. The only thing he could contribute was lassoing that final nuke. Nothing he could do about China. Either the shooting would start or it wouldn't. As the voices droned on, Kyle caught the prince's eye and motioned that he would be outside. Five minutes. The big boys did not need him in the room. After all, he was only an enlisted man.

SWANSON FOUND JAMAL LEANING against their Mercedes, smoking a cigarette and drinking a soda, killing time. Kyle didn't smoke, but the cold drink looked good. "You got change for the Coke machine?" he asked.

"Nope. The machine takes a U.S. dollar."

Kyle breathed some night air to flush out the smell of the stuffy conference room. He could see a sprinkling of stars above the bright lights of the air base. The glowing red box with the familiar logo was tucked into an alcove just inside the rear door of the building to help keep it cool from the desert heat. When he pulled a dollar bill from his tattered wallet, a small white business card came out with it and fluttered to the floor, landing face-up beside his feet. He glanced down: Chinese lettering.

"I'll be damned," he said, picking it up and turning it over to read the English translation in raised lettering on the other side. Swanson bought the drink, took half of it in a single long draught, and went back outside. "Where's my sat phone, Jamal?"

"Back seat," said the CIA man, tilting his head to see Kyle better in the overhead light. Swanson got into the car and dialed in a long set of telephone numbers to make an international call.

It was a commercial telephone number that started with the prefix of eight-five-two for Hong Kong, and then the telephone number itself. There were a lot of beeps and hisses as the call was bounced from carrier to carrier until it was answered. A cryptic, sleepy voice gave no greeting other than his name, "Henry Tsang."

"Hello, Mr. Tsang. This is Kyle Swanson. We met the other day on the plane going into Khobz. Got shot at together."

There was a pause while Tsang came awake and leafed through his memory. "Mr. Swanson. Why yes? How are your fiber optic sensor security systems doing?" There was humor in the question. The game was on.

"Probably about as well as your accounting work." Kyle heard a yawn. "We need to meet."

"Why? Are you here in Shanghai? This is a very busy time for me. Tax work."

Swanson gambled. "No, I'm not in Shanghai, and neither are you. Right now I believe you are standing in your pajamas in Riyadh. In fact, my guess is that you are some type of cultural attaché at the Chinese Embassy, or have some title that hides the fact that you are a deep cover agent. Like me."

There was a snicker of laughter. "Mr. Swanson, you have a wonderful imagination. We are James Bonds? Where are you calling from?"

"The Saudi military base at al-Taif, where we have just removed the fourth of the five nuclear warheads from this country. Are you interested in some more information?"

"Yes." The voice downshifted to quiet and all business. "Tell me."

"Not over an open line. We should get together in Riyadh as soon as possible."

"Very well, Mr. Swanson. The Mediterranean Grill then, at the Marriott. I will have a table reserved in my name at nine thirty."

"Can we make it sooner? I'm only about an hour away by plane."

"I fear not." The voice firmed up. That meant Tsang was going to check with his superiors back in China before doing anything at all. "Zero-nine-thirty is the best I can do."

"All right, then," Kyle said. "See you there."

50

JEDDAH

JUBA AND **D**IETER WORKED with a sense of careful urgency while still in the villa, laying out the possibilities and honing their ideas. Two large flat-bed transport trucks, drivers, a military escort, and official documentation from the Saudi government were at the top of their list.

"Juba, what are you going to do with this thing once you get it? Is it just a decoy to lure in that Marine you want, or do you really want to set it off?" Dieter had his BlackBerry on the table beside a yellow legal pad and a leather-bound notebook filled with telephone numbers and bank accounts.

"Does a vision of a final holocaust for Israel trouble you? A destruction of the holy city of Jerusalem?"

"No. I don't care about the Jews one way or the other. I just don't want to be nearby if you detonate it."

Juba said, "I don't know for sure yet about actually employing the weapon. My main goal is to get Swanson into the kill zone. A ripe target site and a ticking nuclear bomb would solve a lot of problems."

"So it would be wise for me to stay away from Israel?"

Juba stretched and yawned before answering. "That would probably be a very good decision."

Juba worked with the German's superb computer set-up while Dieter called contacts on a secure telephone. Funds were transferred and messages were sent while the maid and the chef rushed about packing for the emergency escape. Almost all of the elements of the new plan fell rather easily into line, but there were a few stumbles along the way.

The major general in command of the huge military base at Tabuk, in northwestern Saudi Arabia where the nuclear device was resting, had been following the news closely and his courage had wavered. The coup was collapsing and he did not want to be part of the long night of retribution that was sure to follow. So far, his name had been kept out of the plot and he decided to keep it that way.

Dieter Nesch had no luck in getting him to cooperate on this final job, even after reminding the general that he had been well paid in advance and his task was not yet done. The general felt secure at his headquarters on the large but relatively isolated military base and refused to take part in any further element of the rebellion. He now had firm orders to turn the missile and the warhead over tomorrow at noon to a special collection team consisting of Prince Colonel Mishaal bin Khalid and a United States Marine by the name of Kyle Swanson. He would obey those orders.

Nesch looked at Juba and scrawled the name "Swanson" on the legal tablet. Keeping his voice steady, he replied, "I sympathize with your position, general, but a deal is a deal. Would you please hold on just a moment? Someone else wishes to speak with you."

Nesch covered the mouthpiece of the phone momentarily and whispered to Juba, "You were right! Swanson is involved in the missile pickup tomorrow." He handed over the telephone.

"My name is Juba! You know who I am." The declaration was cold, and stated with a snarl. "You have this one last opportunity to do as you are told." Then Juba calmly recited details about the general's wife and three young sons—their schools, birthdays, hobbies, friends, and other relatives— and dispassionately described how each would be killed, mentioning words like toenails, tonsils, and testicles. He advised the general that a pair of contract mercenaries were standing by near the family home and would turn off their cell phones at a specified time, beyond which Juba would be unable to stop them. He read out the proper address and also promised to personally execute the general.

"Make up your mind right now. You have something I want," he said with smooth menace. "I have personally murdered thousands of people, general. Thousands! Killing your family will not alarm me in the least."

The general agreed to carry out his agreement. He was sweating when he put the telephone down.

Similar persuasion was needed for a ranking bureaucrat in the Saudi Ministry of the Interior, who was stubborn and reluctant. When Juba was through dealing with him, that man also changed his mind and agreed to return immediately to his government office and accomplish his new task.

The work came together in a tight two-hour span. Juba, Dieter, the cook, and the maid boarded a small chartered plane that sped north from Jeddah to the town of Tabuk, which only had a population of a hundred thousand people but was the largest town in the entire desolate area. Its strategic value was that Tabuk lay less than two hundred and fifty miles from Jerusalem. Dieter shook hands with Juba as the terrorist left the plane, then made himself comfortable aboard the private jet, and accepted a drink of Scotch and ice from the maid. They would refuel in Amman, Jordan, then continue on the long journey to Switzerland and safety. He looked up another private number to call once they were on the ground and safe in Zurich. An old friend who worked for Mossad, the Israeli intelligence service, would be very interested in this new information Nesch had to sell.

SWANSON FINISHED HIS SODA, crushed the can, and flipped it into a trash barrel lined with a black plastic garbage bag. "Jamal, are you tired of hanging around here?"

"Yep." Civilian agents of the Central Intelligence Agency do not particularly like to be on American military bases. It makes them feel exposed, and Jamal had been trained to keep his cover safe by staying away from crowds of Americans, particularly soldiers.

"You have a company credit card?"

"Yep. Visa, AmEx, all of 'em. Platinum cards are almost as good as gold." They contained neither his real name nor any clue as to his true employer.

"Any objection to taking us for a ride?"

Jamal raised a questioning eyebrow. "Nope."

"Okay. Wait here a minute. Call downtown to the International and book us a couple of rooms for the night." Swanson went back into the conference room, where Mishaal was still jawing away with the command and control bunch. It the prince wasn't careful, he might get swept up in expanded military duties. Maybe that's what he wanted; to climb the ladder a few more rungs. Kyle didn't really care.

He pulled a small notebook from his combat vest and scribbled a note:

JAMAL AND I ARE TIRED & YOU MAY BE HERE A WHILE TONIGHT. CAN WE GO CRASH AT THE I'CON DOWNTOWN? MEET YOU THERE FOR BREAKFAST 0630, THEN DO THE RIYADH THING?

Mishaal kept an eye on the teleconference screens, where briefers were explaining some charts. He read the note and jotted:

FINE. BUT THIS TIME STAY PUT!

Then he underlined the sentence. Twice.

Within a few minutes, Jamal was driving the Mercedes past the lush King Fahd Park and the bright lights of the Intercontinental loomed like a halo nearby. "And just why are we doing this?"

Kyle squirmed in his seat to get more comfortable. "Well, my young CIA officer, never let the other guy set the timetable for your own operations. We will check into our rooms, so if Mishaal asks to see the register, it will confirm that we are logged in. We take a quick shower and put on fresh clothes, then slip out a side entrance. I'm betting that the prince will be too courteous to interrupt our sleep and, therefore, will not actually call our rooms. That gives us plenty of time to drive to the capital."

"Riyadh's only a two-hour drive from here," Jamal said. "We can be there by four in the morning."

"Henry Tsang expects us at 0930, but we're going to be early."

"Yep." Jamal pulled into the broad driveway of the hotel.

AN HOUR LATER, THEY joined the stream of traffic highballing along the hardball toward Riyadh. A steady column of headlights approached in the other lane, people traveling in the cool of the night hours, and a scarlet chain of taillights reached as far ahead as they could see. Everybody drove like devils were chasing them, racing toward their destination before the sun came up again. The air conditioner whirred in the enclosed Mercedes, not so much to keep out the air as to keep out clouds of diesel fumes from all of the trucks. Jamal had a stack of CDs and Kyle kept the music going. Garth Brooks was on a country-and-western mix, singing about having friends in low places. They buzzed along, taking it easy on the curving mountain roads and through the tunnels, and then hitting about 100 miles per hour where the land flattened and traffic spaced out. Dead snakes that had emerged from beneath the sand when the sun went down in search of food littered the road like sections of loose rope.

"My station chief is not happy that I'm working with you," Jamal said.

"Bosses aren't supposed to be happy. For a boss to be happy would mean he is satisfied, and that would mean he did not have enough to worry about. I think he has a few bigger fish to fry right now than bitching about the two of us working together."

"As long as we get results."

"Nobody can accuse us of not getting results, pal. They get over being mad." To Kyle, there was a big difference between following orders blindly and actually accomplishing a mission. It was a matter of control. By definition, plans were made before something happened, as if some planner could peer into a crystal ball and accurately foretell the future. A desk person trying to micromanage a fluid situation in the field would always fail because unexpected events intervened. Situational adjustments had to be made on the fly. Snipers and scouts were trained to think on their own and adapt to a reality that ranged far beyond the scope of the think tanks that originally came up with a mission. Repeated successes in operations had bred in Swanson an attitude of supreme belief in the decisions that he made himself, a deep reservoir of confidence from which he could make withdrawals as needed. He was making just such a withdrawal tonight.

Jamal kept both hands loosely on the wheel as the Mercedes shot passed a tractor-trailer, rocking slightly in the backdraft. "They say you have worked for the Agency before in some tricky situations."

"Then they talk too much."

The CIA man nodded and kept his eyes on the road. "How are we going to get to Henry Tsang?"

"Good question. Most of the people who work at embassies do not live in the buildings. Their governments lease apartments nearby and use those residences for everything from storing extra booze for diplomatic parties to providing temporary quarters for transient personnel. They might summon them all into the embassy for protection if the city were burning, but it isn't, so we won't have to break into the Chinese Embassy. The apartment building where Tsang lives probably will just have some dude at a desk in the foyer, maybe an armed guard outside."

"So how are we going to find his place? Just look up 'Henry Tsang, the Chinese Spy' in the telephone book?"

"Something like that. The Trident team back in Washington has an electronics intel guy we call the Lizard, who can find a needle in a haystack. He's already working on the problem. There aren't too many Henry Tsangs in Riyadh, and he will have left tracks somewhere if he is affiliated with the diplomatic community. Odds are pretty good that the Lizard will find him." Kyle closed his eyes and leaned back against the headrest.

Jamal watched the gray line of pavement unfolding in his lights, stark against the blackness of the sky. "Want me to give it a run through the CIA computer?"

"The Lizard will already have done that. His system sweeps everything our government has, including NSA intercepts, before he really gets down to work. Tsang has had plenty of time to contact his superiors, so he is likely to be catching some sleep before getting started tomorrow. I like to visit people before dawn."

The luminous blue digits of the clock on the dashboard caught his eye. Sunday morning. He would wait until they entered the city to contact the Lizard, who would still be at his desk although it was Saturday night in the States. The country music went away, replaced by some head-banging rock that snapped them both awake.

Traffic was increasing, so Jamal had to slow his speed as the dome of Riyadh's city lights became visible, then grew clearer as they came closer. Blinking yellow signals and orange cones marking road work were showing up on their side of the highway and cut off the left lane. Cars and trucks were squeezing over to get through the construction zone. In a couple of miles, another lane was brought to an end and finally there was only one lane left open. It was plugged solid with traffic. Jamal eased off the accelerator.

Kyle turned off the CD player. He had watched the bright warning signs, the cones and the slowing traffic, but there were no bulldozers or paving machines. Not good.

Jamal steered the Mercedes a bit to the left so he could see around the big truck right ahead of them that was blocking the view. A broad swatch of floodlights pooled the area ahead. "Military roadblock. Probably checking for rebel fighters and equipment."

Kyle automatically withdrew his laminated identification card and gave it to Jamal, who found his own ID and placed them both on the leather-covered dashboard. The line did not really stop, but inched steadily forward, more as if the drivers were gawking at an accident than the stop and go of vehicle searches.

"This line is moving too fast," he said, straightening up in his seat. "They're not checking the truck loads."

The truck ahead accelerated when the guards waved it on. It rolled between armored personnel carriers that were stationed on each side of the road. Bright lights illuminated fifty yards on each side of the checkpoint, and spotlight beams danced across their faces. A Saudi sergeant motioned for Jamal to stop. When an officer approached, Jamal pushed the button to lower the window. Another soldier appeared at the front bumper on Kyle's side and stopped, a rifle held loosely in his hands. Others approached from each side.

"Identification, please," the officer asked in perfect English.

Jamal handed over the plastic-covered cards.

The officer studied the IDs for a moment, returned them, and said, "Thank you."

Instead of moving away from the window, the captain gave a signal and other soldiers broke from a formation at the roadblock and poured into position around the car. The officer said, "Now please pull over behind that Humvee. By order of His Majesty, King Abdullah, you are both under arrest."

MOSCOW

RUSSIAN PRESIDENT ANDREI VASILIYVICH Ivanov was again at the wheel of his Ferrari F430 Spyder, easing off the accelerator as he entered Moscow after zooming in from his dacha outside Moscow. A young newspaper vendor called out from the sidewalk and the Ferrari's horn beeped a reply. The driver waved.

The Saudi plan had not worked, but no one looking at the smiling, healthy, young man could detect that anything was wrong. He was doing a big of campaigning while on the way to work. A mile later, the car stopped abruptly beside an old woman who was huddled against a wall. Her skin was drawn and wrinkled, the matted hair covered by a kerchief and the frayed clothes were wrapped tight against the biting early morning cold that said winter was coming. Ivanov hopped out and approached her. "How are you today, grandmother?" he asked with sincerity.

Her watery eyes sparkled when she recognized him. "I am good, Andrei. Thank you."

"Why are you out here alone and so early?"

Her glance toward a nearby coffee house gave her away. "I'm just taking a walk."

"A beautiful woman should never walk alone. Do you have time for me to buy you a small breakfast?" He had her by the elbow, steering her toward the restaurant, where the owner had been watching the scene and threw open his door.

"Andrei! Please come inside."

"I am afraid that I cannot this morning, unfortunately. But would you please give our grandmother a cup of warm soup and buttered bread?" He reached into his jacket pocket and peeled off a few bills to pay for the meal.

"Put away your money. It will be my pleasure." He took the frail woman's hand and led her inside, into the warmth. The fact that he did so would be noted and remembered, a small favor that would increase the restaurant's business today.

Andrei stuffed the bills into her pocket and pecked her on the forehead. "All Russian women are beautiful, just like you, my darling. I have to go to my office now. Perhaps we will meet here again some time and you can tell me a story of the old days." He hurried back to the car and was gone in an instant.

"Andrei Vasiliyvich works too hard," the restaurant owner observed. He had caught the message that Ivanov might return unannounced and that the frail woman had just become a regular recipient of morning bread and coffee. "He understands us."

"He's a good boy," she said.

A FEW MINUTES LATER, the Spyder charged through a gate in the crimson brick wall of the Kremlin, and the domes of St. Basil's glittered in the early sun. When Ivanov stopped at the curb, his usual greeting committee was already there. His chief of staff was impeccable in a business suit and his secretary was modestly dressed, which did nothing to hide her beauty. Andrei switched off the ignition and got out. Ivanov wore a black sports coat over a heavy white sweater, dark blue pants, and polished hiking boots. He was only forty-four years old, single, muscular, and healthy, and had already put in a full day of work at his home, exercised with his guard, and had received a full briefing on the domestic and international scenes while a barber trimmed his thick black hair and gave him a close shave. A manicurist buffed his nails.

"Good morning, sir," his aide said, welcoming the president of the Russian Republic. "Prime Minister Putin would like a word with you. He is in his office."

"Hah! I'll bet he would." The aides followed. "Stefan, please tell the old gentleman that I'm too busy right now."

Putin was said to be declining in strength, so the power of the state eventually would fall to the Ivanov family. Russia was going to belong to Andrei and his heirs.

The young president pushed open the door to his office and stopped short. Putin was waiting for him, seated in a chair beside the desk, running his fingers through the soft fur of that damned tiger he had adopted as a pet. The thing was no longer a little cat and it lay sprawled on the crimson carpet, purring contentedly and twitching its tail. The steady, evil eyes of both Putin and his Siberian tiger were locked on Ivanov. It did not look like anything was wrong with either of them. Fuck. Had Putin been toying with him?

Andrei recovered quickly and smiled, closing the door and moving to his desk as if nothing extraordinary was happening. There was a murmur of a growl from the tiger. "Good morning, Prime Minister," he said. "I am delighted to see you looking well. And I see that we have an extra guest today. Mashenkia is getting huge."

Putin returned the smile. Not a muscle in his face twitched and he spoke with perfect clarity. "Yes. Unfortunately, I cannot keep Sweetie at home in Novo-Ogaryovo much longer. Her front claws have been removed and we keep her calm with a low-grade hypnotic. Still, her weight and teeth make her very dangerous, so she is going to be moving to a zoo soon. Isn't she beautiful?" His hand ruffled the short hair on the face of the beast, a blend of white around the eyes and mouth, and orange with black stripes.

"How are you feeling?" Andrei sat down. "All of Russia will be pleased that you are recovering so remarkably well."

"Excellent. Long walks with Sweetie help. I do miss my judo exercises, but I seem to get a little better with each day."

"Stefan told me that you wanted to see me, and I was just dropping off my jacket before going directly to your office."

The slender face of Vladimir Putin gave away nothing. It never did. An American president once said that he could see into Putin's soul, but he was wrong. As far as Andrei could determine, the old KGB chief had no soul.

There was a brief knock, the door opened, and the secretary, Veronika Petrova, swirled into the room, her face studying the documents she carried.

She glanced up and saw Putin, then caught the look from Andrei that warned her to say nothing important. "Oh! Good morning, Mr. Prime Minister," she said. "And here is Sweetie! What a beauty!"

"Hello, Niki." Putin said. "I won't be long; then you and Andrei can get along with the business of running the country." His mouth remained a straight line. It did not require genius to determine that Andrei was enjoying the sexual favors of the tall, shapely blonde. Putin had seen the photographs. The liaison meant nothing to any of them.

"May I pet the tiger?" Niki approached to within a few feet of the cat.

"Yes. Move very slowly and speak in a loving voice. Show no fear."

Niki reached out her hand and stroked one of the strong forelegs, feeling the bristling hair. "What an amazing creature, Mr. Prime Minister." She rose and moved back slowly, then went to stand beside Andrei and handed him some papers from a leather briefcase carried over her shoulder. "Your schedule for the day, sir."

"Tell me about Saudi Arabia," Putin snapped. Andrei was momentarily off balance. Veronika took a step back, as if she might disappear into the woodwork.

Ivanov shrugged. "It did not work out, Prime Minister. The priest we had picked to replace the king was assassinated. Then our organizer, the banker Dieter Nesch, called me a while ago to say that the rebellion was over, but that Juba was pressing ahead to steal the last available nuclear warhead. He might explode it in Israel."

"What is our own exposure now, Andrei?"

"We are pulling out of it entirely. There will be no trace, no accounts or electronic data of any sort, that might indicate that we were ever involved. I have dispatched SVR teams to eliminate Nesch and Juba, who are the only links to us."

Putin stopped petting his cat. "You promised that this plan of yours would work." The question was blunt.

Andrei spread his hands on the broad surface of his desk. "It was worth the risk. The money we spent was a pittance in comparison to what we might have gained."

"Yes," Putin replied. He stood, brushed the front of his slacks, and made a clicking sound. The tiger rose in a fluid motion, a threat by its mere existence. "Andrei, my young friend, you are doing a very good job. I knew that you would excel, which was why I picked you for the position over many older and more experienced candidates."

Andrei Ivanov also stood, relieved that Putin was leaving and taking the beast with him. "Thank you, sir." The old gentleman was not going to do anything.

Putin finally broke into a smile. "Yes. I always have admired aggressive plays, as you know. The only way Russia will achieve its former glory is to take a chance now and then. What Juba does with Israel is no concern of ours. But I want you to recognize that there is another truth at our level of politics," he said.

"What might that be, Prime Minister?"

"Failure is unacceptable." Putin snapped a leash to the collar on his tiger and led it out the door. He did not want the cat to be startled.

Andrei stared at the door as it closed, feeling a wave of satisfaction. Despite the implied threat, Putin was toothless and Sweetie was nothing but a cat. Neither had claws.

Niki Petrova withdrew a small pistol from her leather case, pointed it at the back of his head and pulled the trigger twice.

RIYADH

MAJOR **HENRY TSANG ARRIVED** a little early at the Marriott, looking fresh in a charcoal gray suit with faint stripes, a white shirt, and a tasteful tie. At the reserved table, he chose the seat that would allow him to keep his back to the wall. Silverware gleamed in the bright artificial light and soft jazz music spilled through speakers hidden in the ceiling. He shook out a cigarette and lit it. Swanson would arrive in a short while but Tsang had things to arrange beforehand.

Tsang ordered a carafe of hot water and slices of lemon, promising to order breakfast when his friend arrived. After the waiter vanished through the swinging doors to the kitchen, Tsang slid a small microphone into a small arrangement of flowers and pointed it toward the chair in which Swanson would sit. Everything said at the table would be transmitted to a recording station in a blue surveillance van parked outside the hotel. The pager on his belt buzzed one time as the listeners confirmed that everything was working, picking up the sounds of the restaurant.

The waiter returned. Tsang put a slice of lemon in his cup, poured in the hot water, and settled in to wait, calmly smoking his cigarette and enjoying the drink. It was nine fifteen on Sunday morning where he sat, which made it four thirty in the afternoon back in Beijing, where things were busy and final decisions were being made and orders were being cut. This time tomorrow, his country would be at war.

Ranking people were awaiting his report of this backchannel meeting.

He was here. Where was the American?

※　※　※

KYLE SWANSON WAS STRETCHED out comfortably on a plush sofa and Jamal Muheisen was in a large leather chair, absorbed in a paperback whodunit mystery. Jamal turned the pages slowly, killing time. Swanson stared at the white ceiling. "Hell of a prison, huh?"

"Yeah," Jamal replied. "Fuckin' A-rab dungeon. You want me to call for some fresh coffee?"

"Unh-unh," grunted Swanson. "I'm coffeed out." He got up and went to the window to watch the cars and trucks go by. He could not hear the buzz of the traffic below because the huge office was soundproofed. A few military vehicles rolled past in small convoys, but the capital city was returning to normal. The morning sun was shining brightly.

The room was the spacious personal office of another Saudi prince who was senior vice president for special assignments for Saudi Aramco, the petroleum giant that controlled the vast oil fields of the nation. The place was immaculate, with several bright hand-knotted carpets, tall bookshelves, chairs, tables, and a few sofas. A large desk dominated the area before a set of windows, and every paper on it was squared neatly with all of the others. Framed pictures of members of the royal family and foreign dignitaries hung on the dark walls. A full bathroom, including a shower, was just through a doorway.

"Fuck this," Swanson said as he returned to the sofa and plopped down. The two soldiers at the door watched, but remained silent. The security team was changed every thirty minutes, and another pair of guards was just outside.

Swanson knew any hope of surprising his Chinese contact was blown at the time of their arrest. Now the entire meeting was at risk. All methods of communicating with the outside world had been removed from them and, although the borrowed office had every creature comfort, even a game console, there were no telephones, no TV sets, and no device that would let him call for help. They were trapped in an air-conditioned cave of riches.

Big chunks of time were falling away like an iceberg calving in the summertime. A nuclear warhead was still out there to be collected, but it was fading in importance with the anticipation that the Chinese were about to attack. *Stay calm. Wait it out. Be ready.*

*   *   *

THE MAIN DOOR OPENED at nine seventeen, according to Kyle's watch. The guards snapped to attention but never took their eyes from the prisoners. Prince Colonel Mishaal bin Khalid walked in, grim and unsmiling, and went straight to the desk. He flung his black beret down in exasperation, then sat in the chair and stared at Kyle. "You lied to me."

Swanson returned the glare. "Don't expect an apology."

"You were under my orders," the prince retorted in a frosty tone. "I gave the two of you permission to go to the hotel and you tried to play me for a fool. When I had my aide check up on you, he found that you were gone."

"I was never under your orders, colonel. We are working together. There's a big difference. Instead of finishing our mission of getting all of the nukes, you became wrapped up in that conference with the talking heads on television screens and I was left sitting there with my thumb up my ass while a war may be brewing. Why the hell should I wait around when there was work to be done?"

"*How dare you speak to me like that!*" Mishaal was on his feet and his voice thundered. The guards became more alert. "Your job was to help me collect the nuclear weapons and we have done so, except for the one in Tabuk. We will go and retrieve it right now, and then you both will be expelled from the country. I've already discussed this with His Majesty and he approves. We appreciate your help, Gunny, but your job is almost done. You are too much of a loose cannon."

Kyle shook his head in dismay. "Of course I'm a loose cannon, Colonel. I do what needs to be done, even when things escalate out of control, even in an entirely different situation. I am a scout-sniper and the rule for any commander is to not tell a sniper how to do a job."

Mishaal sat back down. "You have no idea what has been going on. Our military is in the midst of cleaning up the mess from the coup attempt and have zero time to get reorganized. Those conferences that you so disdain involve the highest level of national security and how we will respond to this possible Chinese aggression. We are talking all-out war here, Gunny Swanson."

"Don't count your nuclear chickens before they are hatched, Colonel."

Mishaal looked at his watch. "Then let's go get it, Gunnery Sergeant. I have a plane waiting. And then I can kick your impertinent ass out of the country and get to work on the other major threats facing us. I don't need your ego eating up my time."

"Fine by me," Kyle snapped. "But aren't you even going to ask me why we left early to get to Riyadh if the only thing I wanted to do was pick up the last nuke? As you say, that now seems like a routine job, and anyway it is several hundred miles away in Tabuk."

The colonel grabbed his beret. "I really do not care, Gunny. And I had roadblocks set up there, too. Now move out."

"I know who one of the Chinese point men on the ground is, Prince Mishaal." Kyle took the edge off of his voice. "I had set up a meeting for this morning and was trying to get into Riyadh and trap him beforehand and throw him off balance. I hoped to persuade him to tell his people to back off of the military action by confirming that both the Saudis and the Americans would oppose them."

The prince stopped in mid-stride. "Why didn't you tell me this?"

Kyle stuck his hands in the pockets of his jeans and looked the prince in the eyes. Ignored the question. "The contact is a special forces type named Henry Tsang, a guy that I met down in Khobz. He probably has a straight pipeline into the Chinese central command, and I thought he would trust another special operator because we are cut from the same cloth. I considered it best not to have your fingerprints, or the official imprint of either of our governments on this meet. I was going to tell you everything, when it was done."

Mishaal dropped the beret again and sat back down. He spun the chair away from the Marine and the CIA agent and looked out of the windows, his thoughts moving fast, grabbing for passing details. He turned around again. "Can you still make a meet?"

"He's waiting for me at the Marriott Hotel right now."

"Very well. But I want in on this, too, Swanson. This is my country and we're running out of time."

54

RIYADH

THE RESTAURANT WAS ALMOST empty when Kyle and Mishaal walked in. They saw the Chinese man seated alone in a rear booth and made their way over to him. At the entrance to the room, an attendant turned around a "Closed" sign. Privacy was needed.

"Mr. Tsang. Thank you for meeting me. I apologize for being late." Kyle slid into one side of the U-shaped booth. "This is my partner, Prince Colonel Mishaal bin Khalid."

Henry Tsang hardly batted an eye. Every word was being recorded and he was perfectly safe. He would let things develop at a slow pace. "My pleasure. Please sit down, Colonel. Would you gentlemen like some coffee? Breakfast?"

Mishaal took a place on the other side of the booth. "Thank you for meeting with us."

Tsang smiled and took a sip of tea. "This was supposed to be a private meeting, Mr. Swanson. No insult is intended, but it is most regrettable that I was not made aware that the prince colonel would be with you."

"It was a last-minute development. I thought that he might be of help if you have some questions."

Tsang folded his hands on the table. "Questions? About what? Frankly, I do not even know why I am here. Except for our brief encounter in Khobz a few days ago, I don't even know you."

Swanson grinned. "People down there say you got in the middle of that fight and did very well. Pretty good for an accountant."

Tsang did not change his expression. "It was fight or be slaughtered. There was no real choice. Now, why are we meeting here today? What can I do for you gentlemen?"

Mishaal was in no mood for polite verbal fencing. "You can tell your masters back in Beijing that we know about their plans to attack the oil fields and that we are ready to stop them!"

Still, Henry Tsang betrayed no emotion. "I am totally at a loss, sir. I know nothing about any such plans, and I am just a low-level functionary at the embassy, not the ambassador. Perhaps you should contact him."

"Bullshit, Henry. A few days ago you were an accountant, now you're working for the embassy. You're a spook. I'm a spook. Mishaal is part of the House of Saud. Talk to us. What the hell do you guys think you can accomplish with an invasion?"

Tsang looked at him in silence. "I repeat, I know nothing about any invasion, Mr. Swanson. Please, if you have such concerns, contact the ambassador immediately."

Kyle shushed Mishaal when the Saudi was about to speak. Instead, he said, "Henry, let's just speak in hypotheticals. Just for shits and giggles. Three friends at breakfast considering the geopolitical picture."

There was a bit of hushed silence. Henry Tsang reached into the flower arrangement, pulled out the small microphone and dropped it into the cup of tea to kill the signal. If ever challenged, the recording of the conversation thus far would show he had done nor said anything improper. Now it was time to get down to business. "That might be an interesting exercise. Please continue."

PRINCE MISHAAL RUBBED HIS hands flat and hard over his eyes in frustration. He felt about ready to explode. "You are wasting time, Mr. Tsang. So, hypothetically, if Chinese aircraft enter Saudi airspace without permission, they will be shot down."

"Also hypothetically, the United States will likely join the fight on the side of our Saudi allies. That final decision will come from Washington, but for this conversation, you can consider it to be a certainty."

Henry Tsang let his mask drop a bit and looked steadily at Mishaal. "One thing that is absolutely not in question is that Saudi Arabia is gripped in a rebellion against the monarchy. That uprising is still underway as we speak. In turn, it has rendered your government to be unstable. News reports say that your own pilots assassinated your king. I can understand why the leaders of other nations would be worried about protecting the vast Saudi oil production capability during such a crisis."

Kyle Swanson started to respond, but Tsang had more to say. "Please. Let me finish. In addition to the threat to the oil production, there are reports that Saudi Arabia also has nuclear weapons. That is another valid point that the United Nations would consider in determining whether some international intervention is required. In short, Prince Mishaal, your country appears to be in great difficulty and in need of help."

"Not your kind of help," Mishaal gruffly said.

Swanson fished in his vest pocket. "They already have help. Ours." He laid an empty .50 caliber cartridge on the table and gave it a little spin with his finger. "Say, back to the hypothesis, that at the time I fired this shot recently, the leader of the rebellion, Mohammed Ebara, died unexpectly. As I said, Mishaal is my partner. In other words, our countries are in this together. You guys try to come in, you'll get clobbered. Your people won't even get near the drop zones."

Tsang picked up the bullet and smelled it. Some cordite still lingered, the signature of a recent shot. "I would have to believe that any country planning to establish protective custody of the oil fields would have taken such contingencies into consideration. In other words, you don't scare us."

Mishaal pushed back against the tufted cushion and composed himself. "I tell you the truth now. We have cracked this rebellion. The removal of Ebara took away the leadership and our government is reasserting control in every city and region. King Abdullah is firmly on the throne and the Religious Police have been muzzled. In other words, Mister Tsang, without a doubt, it is over except for the mopping up. We intend to prove that is so in the United Nations on Monday. Without the rebellion, the oil interests are safe. There is no reason for a Chinese . . . I mean, international . . . intervention in our internal affairs."

Henry Tsang nodded his head and gave a smile which meant nothing. He looked at Swanson. "No reason? Even if you are correct, the Saudis still have nuclear devices of military application. There is established UN precedent for a foreign power to intervene in order to remove the threat of weapons of mass destruction. An international threat, I might add."

Swanson smiled right back. "And that, finally, Major Tsang, is why I wanted this meeting. Yes, we know who you are and that is beside the point. With authorization of King Abdullah, the prince and I have been busy removing those weapons for the past few days. The Saudis had a total of five. We have removed and secured four of them, so that threat already has been greatly diminished."

"That leaves one still out there. One is still one too many." Tsang wondered how they found out about his rank and real position. No time to worry about that right now. "I cannot see how anything has really changed."

Kyle responded, "We are on the way out to pick up the final one right now, Major. I invite you to accompany us to confirm the removal with your own eyes and report that back to your superiors. It is at the King Abdul Aziz Military City at Tabuk, near the Jordanian frontier."

Tsang knew of the huge base, the center of the Northwest Area Command. It was home to infantry and armor brigades of the Royal Saudi Land Forces, the airborne and armor schools, and an air base. "It's almost seven hundred miles away," he said. Tsang rolled his white napkin into a ball and tossed it on the table. "Then why are we still sitting here? Gentlemen, shall we go?"

"My plane is waiting," Mishaal responded, and slid out of the booth. There was a commotion at the door, where his aide was listening to a staff officer as they approached. Captain Omar al-Muallami shot out his hand and grabbed a fistful of the briefer's sleeve and dragged him off to the side, at the same time motioning for Mishaal to follow. Al-Muallami took them into a small cloak room beside the reception desk and closed the door behind them.

While Swanson and Tsang looked blankly at each other, Jamal drifted over to join them. "He's with me. CIA," Kyle explained. Tsang said nothing. All eyes were on the door.

It opened and Mishaal stormed out. His fists were clenched and his face was flushed with color. "It's gone," he growled. "The damned nuke has disappeared!"

TABUK, SAUDI ARABIA

E**VEN WITH THE PILOTS** pushing the throttles through the firewall, it took Mishaal's executive jet several anxious hours to fly from Riyadh to Tabuk, hours that seemed to stretch into eternity when an urgent message was received en route. Intelligence services were reporting that the Israelis were scrambling their forces and getting into high gear after receiving a cryptic and brief advisory that a nuclear weapon had been captured by terrorists in Saudi Arabia. The unidentified source was considered highly credible, and the target was to be Jerusalem, the ancient and historic city that was revered by Jews, Christians, and Arabs alike.

Henry Tsang had grabbed his war bag from the trunk of the diplomatic vehicle that had taken him to the Marriott and was now out of his suit and into jeans and a blue T-shirt that emphasized his muscular upper body. He did not have much to say during the flight, but missed nothing that was going on. The passing hours would be pushing China closer to launching the invasion. If Jerusalem went up in a mushroom cloud, the international community would probably applaud the Chinese for moving so decisively to stem the possibility of other nuclear attacks elsewhere in the region. Beijing and Washington might even work together instead of fighting. It was most confusing, Tsang thought.

Mishaal was glowering silently out of the window while fielding messages on the situation. The King Abdul Aziz Military City was totally locked down, and would stay that way until he got there. The commanding general had committed suicide. Mishaal was embarrassed and infuriated. If he had not attended those long conference meetings, this missile would already have been packed safely away. He had personally spoken with King Abdullah about the dire situation and the monarch was clearly worried. If that missile—a Saudi weapon that had been kept secret until only a few days ago—struck Jerusalem, there would be no stopping the Jews. Others would pile into the fight until the House of Saud was gone and perhaps the whole country with it.

Kyle Swanson ran the mental tapes over and over in his head, staring straight ahead at the empty seat in front of him. He was thinking about it this way; it makes absolutely no fuckin' sense.

A SMALL CONVOY LED by the commanding general had arrived at the main gate just after dawn, a flag of Saudi Arabia fluttering on a small pole attached to one fender of his luxury sedan and his two-star flag of rank on the other. Although his authority was unquestioned, the sedan intentionally stopped to allow the sentries to verify his identification both by sight and credentials. When the guards snapped to attention, the sedan rolled through, followed by an armored Humvee and two giant M920 8×6 tractor trucks, each hauling a M870A1 lowboy semitrailer that was more than twenty-five feet in length.

The vehicles were driven straight to the interior compound in which the nuclear missile system was secured, and the general told the colonel in charge that there had been a change in the orders. He had received a fax from the Interior Ministry that called for the immediate pickup of the weapon, and cancellation of the original schedule set for later in the day. Faced with the major general's personal presence and the official government document, the colonel and his troops complied.

The two long lowboys had been parked side by side, with their huge engines rumbling at idle, and the armored personnel carriers—one containing the warhead and the other with the missile—were positioned on specific load spots on each flat deck, where they were locked down with chains and load binders.

The transfer papers were signed, the convoy left in the glow of the morning light, the colonel disbanded the guard unit, and the commanding general went back to his office, stuck a pistol to his head and blew his brains out.

A smooth and flawless operation, Kyle decided.

That was the mechanical side. What had him puzzled was why a sealed envelope with his name on it was among the paperwork given to the colonel.

THEIR PLANE MADE A smooth landing at the King Faisal Air Base within the military city and taxied to a stop near a group of senior officers standing stiffly before a line of sedans. Prince Mishaal was the first person off the plane and his grim face gave them no solace. He was in a rage, and their nervousness was made complete as his aide went down the line making a list of their names.

Kyle went down the stairs into the heat lifting from the tarmac, determined to keep Mishaal in check. It would do no good at this point to have him just fire a bunch of officers because he was angry. "Get that envelope," he said from just behind the prince's shoulder.

Mishaal barked an order and a full colonel stepped forward and handed him the sealed manila envelope. A rather elegant looping handwriting had written the name of the addressee.

"Now take us to the office of the commanding general," Mishaal ordered. "Is the body still there?"

"Yes, sir. No one has touched anything. We were awaiting your arrival."

Kyle and Mishaal got into the rear seat of the second sedan, with Henry Tsang given the passenger side in the front. As the line of cars blasted away from the flight line, Swanson ran a finger beneath the sealed flap and tore it open. An eight-by-ten piece of common writing paper, folded one time, was inside.

I am waiting at the end of the world. Juba.

"Shit!" snarled Kyle. He passed the brief note to Mishaal, who read it and gave it to Tsang.

"What does it mean?"

"It means we are facing down a total madman, a terrorist who is responsible for thousands of deaths, someone I thought was already dead."

Henry Tsang spoke up. "Juba. The terrorist from the biochem attacks in London and San Francisco a few years back? He's behind this?"

"Maybe not the entire plot, but he probably was the one pulling the triggers to order the specific attacks." Kyle looked out the window as the sedan screamed toward the headquarters building. "I can't believe he lived through that mess in Iraq. Not only did I shoot him, but we dropped a bomb on his head at the same time. Unbelievable."

"So this message is a challenge to you? He wants some kind of duel to exact revenge?"

"It looks that way. Like I said, he is crazy and has apparently become fixated on killing me. Don't expect logic from someone who is insane."

The car slowed and curved into a broad parking area before a large whitewashed building that was three stories high. Guards were at the doors.

"And he wants to meet you at the end of the world," said Mishaal as he opened the door to the office of the commanding general.

56

TABUK

THE SMELL OF DEATH blocked them at the door, an overpowering combination of a body already decaying in a small space. The general was slouched back in his chair behind his desk and the cushion behind his head was saturated with dark blood. A torrent of blood also had swept from the large exit wound onto his uniform. A dark circular bruise the size of a gun barrel surrounded the single entry wound and specks of unburned gunpowder stippled the skin. The pistol was still gripped in his right hand.

"It looks like he considered what he was doing, maybe hesitating at the last minute," said Kyle. "He finally just jammed the pistol hard against his temple and pulled the trigger."

"The filthy animal had nothing to live for. He had dishonored himself and his family and got caught on the wrong side of the coup." Mishaal's eyes rested on the dead man. "I never liked him. Now let's get back to work." The prince spat on the corpse and led the group back outside. Investigators took their place.

A colonel escorted them to a fresh office in a nearby building and then briefed them on how the general had led the unauthorized raid to take the nuclear weapon. The colonel handed Mishaal a piece of paper, an official fax of authorization from the Department of the Interior in Riyadh, in proper form, on letterhead and signed by a deputy minister. "After we spoke with you this morning, I tried to contact the man who signed that authorization. He apparently is nowhere to be found."

Mishaal passed the paper to his aide and said, "Call Riyadh and give them my orders to find him. Colonel, please speak in English for our guests."

Kyle cleared his throat and the prince nodded that he could address the colonel. "About how many men did the general have along with him this morning when they took the device?"

"Just the driver in each truck, somebody else was with him in the command car, and four men in the Humvee escort. The general said they were to rendezvous with a special unit that was unaffiliated with the base. I thought about questioning that, since we have thousands of men on the base here, but he was my commanding officer and had the transfer document."

"So in total, less than ten men were in the raiding party. Nine, now that the general whacked himself."

"Yes," said the colonel.

"Who was the other guy in the command car?"

"An American who had CIA credentials." The colonel checked another list. "The name was Jeremy M. Osmand."

Kyle turned to Mishaal. "Damn. Juba is a Brit. His real name is Jeremy Mark Osmand. What arrogance! He really wants to be sure that I get his message."

Mishaal instructed the colonel to throw as many planes and helicopters in the air as possible to expand the search already underway between the base and the border, then dismissed him. Kyle, Mishaal, Henry Tsang, and Jamal were alone in the office. "You have been very quiet, Major Tsang," the prince said.

"The situation is troubling. When we were back at the hotel, for a moment, I thought you might really have something that my country would find of great interest. Now, with the general dead and the nuclear weapon missing, I have grave doubts." The Chinese intelligence officer spread open his palms in frustration.

"Jamal? What do you think?" asked Kyle.

"I'm also uncertain, just like the major. This revenge thing Juba has going with you is not the same for a decent terrorist as dropping a nuke on Israel. No offense, Kyle, but you're a pretty small fish in comparison."

Swanson rose from his chair and went to a white greaseboard hanging on a wall. "I assure all of you that this lunatic's obsession is not returned by me. He should have learned the last time we met that there is no honor involved; I just want him dead. We literally blew apart the house in which he was hiding, and he was buried under the debris. Plus, I'm certain that I hit him with a .50 caliber bullet just before the bomb struck. Somehow he lived through it. I'll do the same thing again, and use every weapon available to us. This is no duel. It's just his fantasy."

Mishaal stood and stretched. The tension was locking up his muscles. "Still, he is very dangerous. He has the weapon. We must get it back."

"Maybe it is not quite as urgent as we first thought. Juba coming out and identifying himself actually is a help. Hell, I didn't even know he was in the game until now. Under his terms, we have a time cushion before he even tries to set off the nuke because he wants me within range."

"But Kyle, he can punch the button at any time," Jamal said. "Let me play psychiatrist for a minute with this nutcase. Maybe he just wants you to be close enough to watch him do the launch, to show you that you failed to stop him. Then, once the missile is away, he can try to settle accounts between the two of you."

Swanson picked up the black grease pen and uncapped it. "That's where he has a real problem. I don't think he can do it."

"Why?" Mishaal rested against the edge of the desk. "Look at everything he has done, or caused, so far. The man is diabolical."

Kyle wrote a big number "9" on the board. "That's how many men he has with him. It's not enough. Think about it, guys. This is no fire and forget weapon. Nukes are sophisticated. They need special crews for taking them from a warehouse, crane operators, crews for convoys, command and control personnel, vehicle operators, communicators and escorts. Every man involved is highly trained, and those who work with the weapon itself must be trained and certified. Codes are kept in steel boxes with combination locks. This thing is in two separate parts, in two separate APCs. I don't think he has the manpower or the know-how to even string the cables between the missile carrier and the command track, much less actually be able to mount the warhead. Juba's brilliant, but he doesn't know everything and he cannot do it alone. I do not think that bird is going to fly anywhere."

They all jerked around suddenly when there was a loud pounding on the door and Captain Omar al-Muallami charged inside and shouted, "We have found it!"

THE ENTIRE HIGHWAY SOUTH from Tabuk was instantly commandeered and police and troops cleared it of all civilian traffic to make way for the trucks and armored vehicles swarming out of King Abdul Aziz Military City toward the reported location of the missile, some fifty miles away. Thick clouds of sand were pulled behind the moving vehicles and fighter aircraft took over the skies. A pair of large command helicopters flew above the storm in a tight side-by-side formation. Prince Mishaal, along with his aide and a few senior officers were in the lead bird. Kyle Swanson, Henry Tsang, and Jamal were aboard the flanking chopper, which had been constructed to ferry generals around, not to wrestle its way into combat zones.

They sailed along through the copper-tinted sky, wrapped in comfort. Soft blue cushioned seats faced forward like easy chairs bolted to the metal deck. Side doors closed out the passing wind, while internal soundproofing reduced the rotor noise to a whine. Strong air-conditioning filtered out the dirt and kept the passengers cool. Kyle thought that it would have been an enjoyable flight if nuclear Armageddon wasn't brewing at the other end of the trip.

The two command helicopters slowed and settled into a lazy circle at about a thousand feet when they neared the scene, the pilots wary of possible shoulder-launched missiles from the terrorists who were assumed to be somewhere below. Kyle looked out and down. No question. They had arrived; there it was.

Juba's lethal little convoy had left the main road at a small unmarked crossroad and driven down into a hidden valley of sand and rock, where hundreds of old vehicles had been dumped over the years to rust away beneath the blistering desert sun. The rare rains that would transform the dry wadi into a raging river would also rearrange the hundreds of metal carcasses in haphazard fashion, burying some, stacking others against one another, and resurrecting steel skeletons that had been buried in earlier floods. A few abandoned huts were scattered along the high sides of the valley, and their empty windows and doors yawned open and dark.

Swanson looked at it all with the practiced eyes of a sniper. Juba had chosen the place well. Over the years, this changing landscape had created plenty of places in which to hide.

The missile was clearly visible in the vast junk field, thrusting up out of its armored carrier and locked into its proper firing position of a 60-degree angle, pointed north, toward Israel. A conical shape was on the top, and the ominous missile looked ready to fly.

The second APC, which had carried the nuclear warhead, was abandoned about fifty meters away, and its strong crane hung over the side. The chain hoist had made it possible for the thieves to lift the heavy payload from its carrying crate and mount it atop the blunt end of the missile.

Even before they had taken off from the military city, Prince Mashaal had ordered the wadi blocked off in all directions and surrounded. From the air, Kyle saw a developing scene that was taking the shape of a huge donut as a ring of steel, mobile firepower, and soldiers closed in. Scout helicopters drew no antiaircraft fire when they swooped low across the zone, so the two command helicopters dashed in and landed on the far side of the highway even as military traffic continued to grind past.

Kyle returned his radio headset back on its rest, unbuckled his seatbelt, and pushed the door back. The sudden blast of heat and rotor downwash came as a shock when he stepped from the protective cocoon, and he shielded his eyes and jogged forward to escape the thick dirt cloud. When he was clear, he looked up and realized that, standing at ground level, he could not even see the wadi that descended on the far side of the highway.

The rest of the command group was also dismounting, but were standing around like spectators at a soccer match, in awe of the might of the military machinery that was parading all around. Henry Tsang stepped next to him and Kyle said, "Somebody is probably going to have to get killed before they realize this is no exercise."

"I see tanks and soldiers, but I don't hear any shooting," the Chinese commando agreed. He carried an AK-47 in his right hand. "I do not like it when things go so easily."

"Juba is drawing us in closer," Swanson replied. "He wants to see some targets of value."

"He really just wants you, Gunny," said Jamal, slapping a fresh clip of ammunition into an M-16.

"Well, that's fine," Kyle said with a smooth calmness. "I'm here to kill that missile. I can deal with Juba when the job is done. He used to be a sharp and shrewd fighter, but now he's just a crazy son of a bitch. Not really much of a threat."

CAPTAIN AL-MUALLAMI HAD BEEN the first man out of Prince Mishaal's helicopter. The efficient aide had quickly ducked through the rotor downwash, found a break in the passing traffic, and trotted off to find a good overview position. The wadi opened before him as the side road breached the canyon wall and headed down to the floor of the valley, but that only provided a limited view. Prince Mishaal would need a better vantage point from which to direct this battle, and Captain al-Muallami spotted a slight incline that led to a higher, irregular ridge. He sprinted to the crest.

Behind him, the rest of the command group was moving across the road, following him. From the top, he was able to see the missile and the arid acres of debris. He removed his sunglasses and brought a pair of binos to his eyes, swept the area, and decided that this position would do. He raised his hand to signal the command group.

The sudden slam of a heavy rifle barked from somewhere in the junk yard, and a heartbeat later, Captain al-Muallami was staggered as a big bullet punctured his throat. His eyes flared wide in surprise as he grabbed at his neck, then he toppled to his knees and fell sideways.

PRINCE COLONEL MISHAAL WATCHED in disbelief as his aide fell, mortally wounded. Al-Muallami, always so sure of himself and seemingly indestructible, now lay dead only thirty yards away, his life erased in a blink. When Mishaal broke into a run to reach the fallen captain, Kyle Swanson reacted immediately, took two steps forward and drove into a hard tackle that knocked the prince sprawling. Kyle immediately rolled free but kept a strong hand on Mishaal's arm as a deafening staccato of return gunfire erupted from the gathered troops to answer that deadly single round. The soldiers had not seen the source, so they did not have a target. After the initial volley, all shooting stopped and silence covered the wadi.

"Stay down, Mishaal," Kyle ordered. "Juba is doing exactly what a good sniper is supposed to do: take out key officers first. Captain al-Muallami had the look of being important and walked into the open, so he became a natural target. If you go over there, he will pick you off, too."

Another shot lashed out and the sergeant wearing the heavy backpack radio for the command team caught a bullet in his chest and fell backward, pulled down by the weight of his communications gear. The long aerial on his radio had pinpointed him for death. Juba was throwing the entire attack off balance. A thousand eyes scanned the battlefield. *Where is he?*

When an armored personnel carrier roared off the road and lurched to a stop to provide a shield of protection for the command team, Swanson released Prince Mishaal and helped him up. "Sorry about the tackle, sir. Juba would love to clip you, and we can't afford that. Keep control of the situation from here and tighten the net so he can't escape," Swanson quietly told the prince. "Please stay under cover. I'll be back in a minute."

JAMAL AND HENRY TSANG had worked their way up the backside of the ridge where Captain al-Muallami had been killed, and found an observation point behind a rusted Volkswagen bug that was resting upside down on its curved roof. They could see through the blown-out windows. Kyle wiggled in beside them. The interior of the skeletal automobile was shaded. A scattering of rocks and a few bushes provided concealment while they surveyed the area. A tremendous amount of noise covered the place as helicopters took off, big vehicles growled about, men shouted, and gunfire chattered. "Spotted anything?" he asked.

"No shooter," Tsang answered and rolled onto his side. He smoothed some dirt with his palm and poked a finger down to make a hole, then drew a straight line. "This is the missile and this is the road. No more than 200 meters. Can't-miss range for a decent sniper."

Kyle agreed with the judgment of the Chinese operator. "That can work both ways. He could see those two targets that he took down, so there has to be a sightline from this ridge to his hide, with nothing in between that would block a clear shot." He let his eyes roam the area. *Where would I hide?*

"We don't care about him," Tsang said with a sharp tone. "We are here for that nuclear weapon and to prevent a real war. The deaths of a few soldiers mean nothing."

Kyle was getting edgy himself. "But Juba's the one who will launch the damned thing! We spot him and we can end this."

"It doesn't matter. I say we have the Saudis go charging in there immediately and take it down. Deal with the sniper and anything else later."

"Major, he may be using the missile as bait, but he would sure as hell launch it the moment he sees an attack start."

Tsang and Kyle reached the same conclusion at the same time and the Chinese commando officer said, "If he has control of the weapon, then why isn't it already in the air?"

Jamal edged in closer. "Simple answer, guys. Like Kyle said before. He hasn't fired it because he can't."

Kyle said, "Because it's his best leverage. As long as it is there, Juba still has a chance that I will be exposed for that one second he needs to get me. And as soon as the missile flies, the Saudis will roll this place up like a rug . . . he dies and I'm still alive."

"No, no, no, no!" Jamal replied, shaking his head. "I mean it literally: I don't think he can make the shoot."

The surprise explosion just behind them was like a shout of doom, a warning they heard too late.

A ROADSIDE BOMB DETONATED by a cell phone signal went off with volcanic force, the violent explosion destroying a Humvee that was on the highway. The unarmored vehicle flipped end-over-end in a bloom of flame, and the driver and three soldiers inside were killed instantly.

The tsunami of shrapnel scythed through a nearby squad of soldiers walking nearby, causing more injuries, then the blast force reached into the position where Kyle, Jamal, and Henry Tsang already were on the ground. It picked them up and slammed them back to earth with bone-jarring suddenness. Needles of shrapnel pinged and clanged against the upside down Volkswagen, which teetered from the pressure and started a slow topple down the ridge like a large pebble. They were showered with a hurricane of dirt that caked their faces and left all three of them momentarily dazed and blinded.

Swanson was on his back, stunned and gasping for air, with brilliant colors swirling in his mind as he lay semiconscious, aware only of the desire to fight back, the need to be a warrior, not a victim. The brush with death had forced him into a zone of comfort and familiar feeling in which everything but survival became secondary, and new strength was pumping through his body with each heartbeat. The world was a slow-motion, black-and-white movie that he was watching alone, in the private theater of the mind. The zone: his private roosting place when fighting loomed, an exclusive and wonderful place. Usually, Swanson would wrap himself in that comfortable cocoon just before he squeezed the trigger. His sight and hearing grew sharper and his senses of smell and touch began to return. As his thoughts reassembled, he wanted to grab a long rifle and finish this private fight. He had gotten the better of Juba in previous encounters and he could do it again! Just the two of them! *I'll blow his ass away!*

Kyle staggered to his knees, starting to stand, but Henry Tsang grabbed his arm and pulled him down hard and, as he fell, a bullet sizzled through the airspace where his head had just been, and the sound of the shot followed.

Ambush! Juba had planned the ambush in advance, picking the wrecked VW as the logical observation position on the high ground. The bomb was hidden specifically to hit it, but at the last moment, the Humvee arrived and soaked up most of the devastating blast.

Jamal was muttering a string of Arab curses and holding his blood-spattered leg. Henry Tsang was shaking Kyle and yelling into his face, and Swanson slowly swam back to the surface of consciousness. He blinked his eyes, knowing that the automatic killer instinct in him had almost been his undoing. He hauled himself back under control and felt pain jabbing in his side, where his vest, shirt, and skin had been ripped in a six-inch gash by a piece of sharp flying metal. His leather belt had been sliced neatly apart as if by a razor. A Saudi soldier arrived beside him and poured water into his eyes and the cool wave cascaded over his face and into his mouth. He swilled it around and spat onto the ground. The medic began to clean the wound.

"Damn!" he said, collecting his thoughts. Juba had come close, but he had not won. Kyle steeled himself now from moving quickly, determined to make this a different kind of fight. His enemy had almost made him step into the trap, but there would be no personal gunfight in this godforsaken valley today. *I once bombed him, and now he has bombed me, and we both lived through it. I played right into his hands.*

Swanson looked over to where another medic was working on Jamal, whose face was contorted in pain. The leg was bent at an impossible angle and was bleeding hard. "How about you, Major?" he asked Tsang. "You okay?"

"Yes. A couple of scrapes. This was a boobytrap," he declared with a sweep of his hand. "This Juba is a tricky one." The Chinese commando was bleeding from his nose, a result of the concussion, but wiped the crimson stream away with disdain.

Swanson sat still while a pressure bandage was applied. Speaking in Arabic, he told the medic to concentrate on the more seriously wounded men. "Jamal, you look like hell," Kyle said in English.

A syringe of painkillers had taken hold of Jamal, and the CIA agent managed a weak smile, then his eyelids fluttered and he passed out. Medics tore at his clothes to get to the multiple wounds. He was out of the game.

Kyle pushed his right hand firmly against his abdomen to hold the bandage in place, and wormed backward down the slope. "Come on, Major Tsang. Stay low, but let's get back over to the prince and finish this off."

Kyle hobbled along with his left arm across Tsang's shoulder until they reached the safety of the armored personnel carrier where Mishaal had organized a makeshift staff. Two more APCs had moved into flanking positions to provide even more protection. Swanson leaned against one and drank some more water.

"Can you still function with that wound?" Mishaal asked. He was all business as the situation seemed to be deteriorating.

"Jamal is down. The major and I are good to go. This is just a flesh wound. It looks worse than it is." He kept his hand on the bandage but refused to let any clue of discomfort reach his face. *Christ, that stings!*

Mishaal was studying him carefully and Kyle quickly changed the subject. "We need some confirmation," he said. "Can you call the commander of the unit that had operational control of the weapon?"

A young captain at the edge of the command group raised his hand. He was anxious, expecting the worst, feeling disgraced that his missile had been taken from under his nose and had created such a dilemma. He believed he faced certain demotion and perhaps even a court-martial.

The American who was with Prince Colonel Mishaal spoke. "Do you speak English, Captain? We need your expertise."

The officer replied in English that he had carefully examined the scene before them through his binos. He started to apologize again, but Mishaal cut him off. "You did nothing improper, Captain," Mishaal said. "Give us your best advice." The captain did not smile, but a sense of relief flooded him.

Kyle continued, "There are no cables visible between the missile launcher and the command and control track. They might have been buried, but there is no linear sign of disturbed dirt between the APCs. So is there any other way to fire that bird by an electronic signal, just by pushing a button?"

The captain was at rigid attention. He knew his job and his reply was unambiguous. "No, sir. A full mission cannot be carried out unless the launch platform is mated exactly to the package in the C-and-C vehicle. The weapon was never meant to be simple enough for a common soldier to operate. The cables are needed to update the targeting data and feed auxiliary off-site electrical power to the missile before launch. It is a somewhat archaic system, but provides a good redundancy. Electronic signals can easily be jammed."

Kyle came to the main point. "What about the warhead? Is it still operable?"

The captain's face brightened. "Sir, in my opinion, the warhead may not even be properly connected and aligned. Assembling the entire system requires precise steps and special tools. Certified technicians, not infantrymen under battle stress, are needed to arm and fire it."

"So that warhead is just sitting up there?"

"That is very possible, sir. It fits into place easily enough and can be held in place by a few clamps and bolts. But again, special connections between the warhead and the missile must be made before it is fully seated. Only then can it accept the targeting data, which is another intentionally complicated procedure."

"So they were able to steal it, but ran out of time for the assembly?" Mishaal said, putting his hands on his hips. "It is just an empty threat?"

"No, sir. Not that. It is still a nuclear device."

Mishaal made a decision and turned to Kyle. "I'm going to call in an air strike and incinerate the thing."

The captain shook his head, gulping as he faced down the prince colonel. The calm he had felt moments before vanished. "Sir, to do so would risk cracking the warhead shielding. The bomb would not explode, but the core might be exposed. Radiation would spread on the wind."

THE NEW COMMUNICATOR MINDING Prince Mishaal's radio network called to him. "Sir! Someone has come up on the command net, an English voice identifying himself as Juba. He demands to speak to Gunnery Sergeant Swanson."

"Ignore him. He is trying to find out if I was killed in the explosions," Kyle said. *Let him stew.*

Mishaal spoke: "Major Tsang? Are you satisfied with the inert status of the nuclear warhead?"

The Chinese operator had studied the missile carefully and weighed his delicate situation. "I agree with the circumstantial evidence. Before I can contact my superiors, however, I still need a closer look."

"We're going to give you one," Kyle said. He looked over to where an M60A3 tank was lumbering into position beside their cluster of APCs. With laser sighting and a digital ballistic computer on its upgraded fire control system, the tank's 105 mm main gun was extremely accurate. Swanson pointed to it and said, "Prince Mishaal, please have that tank lay a high-explosive round exactly at the base of the missile launcher. That should wreck the launch vehicle and collapse the entire structure. Cut it down like a tree and the missile problem is solved."

"Sir!" the communicator interrupted. "Juba is on the radio again, demanding to talk to Swanson. He is shouting!" The radio operator was nervous. Kyle shook his head. No. *Don't give him what he wants.*

Mishaal summoned the tank commander to join them and personally issued the crisp orders so there would be no misunderstanding. "Fire when ready," he said, and the commander returned to his huge tracked vehicle.

The gunner sighted a ruby laser carefully on the slim target while everyone held their breaths. When the big cannon roared, the recoil jarred the sixty-ton tank backward on its treads and the concussion slammed the dirt directly beneath the barrel, raising a torrent of dust. The high-velocity round covered the approximately two hundred yards in a mere instant and crashed into the thin-skinned launch vehicle with a shattering impact.

The entire APC bucked into the air and crashed back down to a hard landing as pieces flew off of it. The tower of the missile was disjointed from the launcher and fell over on its side. The warhead spun away like a toy top.

Kyle watched it with satisfaction, still holding his side. The bleeding was not slowing but he would not give in to the pull of pain. *There's my answer, Juba. Long-range precision fire, just like you wanted.*

"Good job," he told Mishaal. "The rest of the fight is yours. Juba only has a few men racked up in those shells and huts. It's open season out there now, so use everything you've got to pound the hell out of them. And really hammer that little hut next to the command track. That's where I think Juba is hiding."

"Why there?"

"The first shot he fired did not come through a silenced rifle. Remember how loud it sounded? Still, there was a muffled echo, which indicated that it came from an enclosed space. Not much around here fits that description. Then the same thing happened on the second shot that took down your radio guy. Finally, there was the shot that just missed me. All of the angles are good from there. The darkness inside that single window prevents us from seeing inside. He's in there in a static position, perhaps in a dug-in and protected position with overhead shelter. He can't move to a new hide with all of your troops around. My advice is to just run right over him."

WITH A FEW INSTRUCTIONS to his staff, Mishaal quickly got the attack rolling. And for ten minutes, heavy gunfire shook the field. Violent explosions of big shells blew apart junk cars, ferocious machine-gun fire chewed into everything standing, and grenades added to the chaos. When the ground fire paused, two helicopter gunships lanced in on runs with rockets and machine guns. Only after the barrage was done did the Saudi government ground troops move in to clear the few buildings.

There was some feeble resistance, then things went quiet and Mishaal ordered a cease fire.

The radio buzzed. A squad had entered the heavily damaged hut believed to be Juba's hideaway and called Mishaal to report a badly wounded white man was found beneath the floorboards.

"Got him," the prince told Kyle.

Swanson responded, "Good. Glad that's done." He took a deep breath and slumped into a sitting position. "Major, Juba was the brain behind the uprising and he's through. All five missiles are now accounted for. I'll stay here and get patched up while you two go over and confirm the warhead is no longer a threat. Then the major can pass the word to his people."

Major Tsang and Prince Mishaal boarded an APC and it trundled away toward the ruined missile launcher. As soon as it left, Kyle was on his feet again, biting his lip in pain but trotting to the hut.

Juba lay in the shadows, absolutely mauled and bleeding profusely. Two Saudi soldiers and a medic had already strung up an IV tube. Kyle was startled by the man's condition, not only the bleeding, fresh wounds but by the hideous old scars and twisted features. Juba stared up with his only good eye. "Swanson," he croaked.

"Hello, you son of a bitch," Kyle growled. "You're hard to kill." He wasted no time on sympathy. "No painkiller!" he snapped at the medic. "Not yet."

Kyle ordered the soldiers out of the hut. They hesitated for a moment, then backed away to rejoin their unit because they did not worry about the care of a foreign prisoner. There was a lot of junk yet to search for terrorist hiding places.

Kyle knelt beside Juba and yanked an IV tube out of the man's arm. "Your death is overdue, Jeremy. You are not getting another chance."

As he bent over, Swanson felt a stab of pain from his wound, more potent than before. He had to hurry while he still had strength. He grabbed the moaning Juba by both arms and dragged him out of the hut and into the sunshine. The man weighed almost nothing and blood gurgled from a half-dozen new, gaping wounds.

A rusting old Mercedes sedan rested on its wheel rims nearby, with its big trunk yawning open like an empty mouth. Summoning his strength, Swanson picked Juba up and stuffed him into the car. He slammed the trunk lid down hard and the lock snapped shut.

As he turned away, he could hear Juba screaming, somehow finding enough strength to scream and claw and kick in the hot and suffocating darkness. It sounded like he was saying, "Don't leave me!"

To his right, Kyle could make out the figures of Mishaal and Major Tsang over at the destroyed launch vehicle. They were shaking hands beside the immobile warhead. Almost over.

The M60A3 tank was still beside the command team when Kyle limped up beside it. He shouted in Arabic to the commander who was in the turret. "See that old yellow Mercedes sedan over by that hut? Put a high-explosive round right in the rear of the car, in the trunk. Just one shot." The Saudis may have seen what he had done, but Kyle didn't care.

He moved away while the tank gunner bore-sighted his big weapon and the red laser painted the target.

Kyle slumped into a sitting position on the ground nearby, his eyes locked on the Mercedes. The pain was surging deep into him. *Something's wrong down there. Hold on for just another minute.* Even as he covered his ears, Kyle Swanson could still hear faint screams coming from the man trapped in the dark, tight trunk of the old car.

"No loose ends," he whispered, and the big 105 mm cannon thundered.

EPILOGUE

P *LINK!* **THE YOUNG SURGEON** working with long forceps picked another sliver of steel, a small fragment no bigger than a pencil point, from the left thigh of Kyle Swanson and dropped it into an aluminum pan. With a local anesthetic deadening the area, Swanson felt only a slight pull. "That's seven," the doctor said. "The X-rays show three more small pieces lodged down a little deeper but they will be harder to reach. Since they are not bothering anything right now, we'll leave them alone and just watch them closely." After patching the leg wounds with a fresh sterile bandage, the doctor rolled Kyle over, tugged down the hospital gown, and removed the gauze on the abdomen.

"That smarts," Swanson growled. Sometimes it hurt just to breathe.

"Two broken ribs will do that," the doctor replied. "Not much we can do but let them heal for a couple of months. The wound itself is coming along well. You have an almost perfectly shaped "C" carved in your abs, Gunny, from whatever punched you there. It hit hard, then bounced off the ribcage as if it hit a helmet, so it didn't get into your vital plumbing. My stitching is perfect and the infection is almost gone." He smeared some new ointment onto the dark incision and covered it up. Purple and yellow and blue bruises.

Kyle blinked when the doctor shone the light into his eyes. The headache was still there, a persistent dull throb that was better today than yesterday, aggravated by intermittent nausea. "The concussion will cause no permanent damage. It was a good knock on the head and should have put you out cold on the spot."

"I still can't remember everything that happened after the explosion," Swanson responded in a soft, weak voice. "Just bits and pieces, like pages of photographs."

"You sustained a mild traumatic brain injury, Gunny. Not fatal and not permanent, but a hell of a shock to your system. With enough time and some therapy, it will all come back to you eventually. You walked through a tornado and got little hurts in lots of places, but nothing permanent. Lucky guy. Take the pills and rest. I'll see you at dinner."

A husky male medical orderly rearranged the patient and the bedclothes. "Would you like to go outside for a while? See if we can find some sunshine?"

"Yeah. That would be good," Kyle said, struggling against the strong pain pill in order to stay awake. He wanted to see the others. The orderly helped him into a wheelchair and pushed it easily across the deck.

THE ORDERLY EASED THE rolling chair into place beside a small table and locked the wheels. "Thanks, John," Kyle said. The big man nodded and went back below deck. Swanson fished a pair of sunglasses from a pocket on the chair and put them on.

"What's the verdict?" asked Sir Jeff Cornwell, who was sprawled on a mat as a physical therapist massaged his legs.

"I'm better off than you, old man. My brain is fried."

"Mine, too." Cornwell gritted his teeth when the therapist lifted his left foot straight up until it could go no higher. "Lucky that we have beautiful women, good cigars, and whisky on board." The Englishman laughed. The pallor of the stay in the hospital was gone, having evaporated with the daily doses of sun.

They were aboard Jeff's big yacht, the *Vagabond*, riding easily in gentle swells about two hundred miles east of Jamaica. The normal small dispensary had been upgraded on an emergency basis to a first-class medical suite. The long vessel could both serve to bring Sir Jeff back to health and simultaneously keep him in a safe and unknown location.

Kyle and Jamal both had received first aid treatment on the battlefield in

Saudi Arabia, then were transported to a Saudi military hospital for a day until U.S. authorities could arrange new lodgings. Since both men were undercover operators, they were spirited out of the country, Jamal going back to the States while Kyle was transferred to a British base and then onward to the *Vagabond*. He didn't remember much of the trip because of the heavy sedation.

He *wanted* to remember. He knew that Juba was dead, but did not recall exactly how. And the missile, and Henry and the Chinese invasion. His memory circuits were sparking like a piece of silver in a microwave oven. The whole episode was there, but it just did not make sense. He closed his eyes. Tired.

Lady Pat was nearby, reading from a weekly newsmagazine. A story about how the Saudi royal family had crushed the militant uprising and apparently intended to use the victory to springboard into some overdue reforms in politics and human rights. She cleared her throat and resumed reading aloud, now assuming the serious voice of a television news reader. "In Washington, the president and the Pentagon strongly denied reports that American troops were involved in any way with the military effort to defeat the rebellion and secure the nuclear weapons. All U.S. troops and training personnel were confined to their bases throughout the brief conflict. American civilians stayed in their homes, said a Pentagon spokesman. This was a magnificent achievement by the Saudi military forces loyal to their government. They neither needed nor requested our help."'

She turned some pages. "Toward the back of the magazine is a brief article on China conducting a massive military exercise that was carried out in full view of the press. A spokesman in Beijing said the exercise was normal and successful and all troops had returned to their bases."

Swanson sighed, drifting off. A hand found his and gently squeezed, and Kyle felt a warm kiss on his cheek. Delara. "Sleep for a while," she whispered. "You're home."